MORE CHURCH FOLK

Also by Michele Andrea Bowen

CHURCH FOLK
SECOND SUNDAY
HOLY GHOST CORNER
UP AT THE COLLEGE

MORE CHURCH FOLK

Michele Andrea Bowen

GRAND CENTRAL
PUBLISHING

NEW YORK   BOSTON

Copyright © 2010 by Michele Andrea Bowen

Grand Central Publishing
Hachette Book Group
237 Park Avenue
New York, NY 10017

www.HachetteBookGroup.com

Printed in the United States of America

First Edition: July 2010
10 9 8 7 6 5 4 3 2

Grand Central Publishing is a division of Hachette Book Group, Inc.
The Grand Central Publishing name and logo is a trademark of Hachette Book Group, Inc.

Library of Congress Cataloging-in-Publication Data
Bowen, Michele Andrea.
   More church folk / Michele Andrea Bowen.
      p. cm.
   ISBN 978-0-446-57776-2
   1. African American churches—Fiction.   2. Church membership—Fiction.   I. Title.
   PS3552.O8645M67 2010
   813'.54—dc22
                                                          2009042989

This book is dedicated to my uncle James and my aunt Bessie,
aka Bishop James D. Nelson, Sr., and Mother Bessie Nelson,
Greater Bethlehem Temple Apostolic Church
in Baltimore, Maryland

Acknowledgments

More Church Folk...Hallelujah!!!! I cannot believe I am writing the acknowledgments to this book. It's been a long time coming. And you know I have to send some shout-outs for this book.

First, to my Grand Central Publishing family: Karen Thomas, my editor, thank you for letting me be me in this book. And I am so glad that you said this is the book you wanted me to write. Latoya Smith, you are always so sweet and helpful and you laugh at my jokes. Tanisha Christie and Nick Small, you two always have my back. Linda Duggins, you've been there for me since *Church Folk*. Mr. Don Puckey. You have been blessing me with awesome covers for close to a decade. And to my copy editor, S. B. Kleinman, and the other folk who help me out at GCP.

To my agent, Pamela Harty of the Knight Literary Agency. You are the best, and I am blessed to have you as my agent.

My own church folk at St. Joseph's AME Church in Durham, North Carolina. It's true: St. Joseph's really is a friendly church. Love to you all, and mad love to my pastor and first lady, Rev. Philip R. Cousin, Jr., and First Lady Angela McMillan Cousin. You all always have my back.

To Ava and Ken Brownlee. It's now a tradition. You guys have to be in the acknowledgments.

My family: My girls—Laura and Janina. My mom, Minnie Bowen. My grandmother, DaDa. My aunt Brenda and uncle Twayne and their crew in KC, MO. My aunt Laura in the STL. My cousins—the B'More crew—Jonathan and Jason, I remember the first solo performances (God is good). And my cousins in STL, Memphis, Chicago, ATL, and down in Charleston, MS (Essie Lane Simmons's hometown).

My readers—THANK YOU FROM MY HEART—LOVE Y'ALL!!!!

Thank You, Lord!!!! If I had 10,000 tongues, I couldn't thank You enough. For You are good and worthy to be praised.

"You thrill me, Lord, with all that You have done for me! I sing for joy because of what You have done."

Psalm 92:4 (NLT)

Michele Andrea Bowen
October 6, 2009

An Abridged History of the Gospel United Church

The Gospel United Church was established in 1817 at the Meeting Plantation in Chapel Hill, North Carolina, by Z. T. Meeting, a slave and ordained minister, with the help of a former slave, Hezekiah Meeting. Z. T. was a master carpenter who designed and built most of the buildings on the Meeting Plantation, as well as several houses for the friends of his owner, the Reverend Cornelius Meeting, an economist who specialized in agricultural commerce at the University of North Carolina at Chapel Hill.

Cornelius Meeting, who owned hundreds of acres of land in Orange County, North Carolina, along with several hundred slaves, was an ordained minister in the United Gospel Congregations of America. He was also one of the area's top scholars on slavery, and had won accolades for a pamphlet he wrote and published, "Protecting the South's Commodities: Teaching Slaves the Bible to Protect Your Properties and Investments."

Rev. Meeting discovered that when he told his slaves what he wanted them to know in the Bible, carefully editing out the most liberating qualities of the Gospel of Jesus Christ, they found it more difficult to oppose chattel slavery, for fear of going against the Word of God and risking going to Hell when they died.

Despite Rev. Meeting's popularity, caused by fellow slaveholders' excitement over this economic plan, his successes within the actual slave community were quite modest. Cornelius was discovering that his theory worked only if the slaves were converted, and then fed enough propaganda to steer them far enough away from the truth of the Word to accept this false doctrine being perpetrated by Master Cornelius. Plus, they had to be watched and carefully supervised during church meetings, to avoid one of those super-reverent, in-the-fields-praying slaves receiving a revelation from the Holy Ghost that ran contrary to the propaganda Cornelius was working over-time to get them to accept.

So Rev. Meeting enlisted the help of Z. T., his most devoutly Christian and industrious servant on the plantation. Cornelius pro-vided Z. T. with high-quality lumber supplies to build a new cabin, some extra yard space for a garden, a few fat hens, and a new set of clothes, before he told Z. T. that he would be responsible for increas-ing the number of born-again slaves on the plantation, as well as supervising their conversion process. This strategy proved effective and clever until a year later when Z. T., who didn't believe anything Cornelius told him, finished teaching himself to read in secret, and then read the Bible for himself.

Z. T. Meeting was a quiet, private, and extremely observant man. He accepted the call to serve as the slaves' pastor with the dedication and enthusiasm his master had hoped for. He then set out to give the men, women, and children whose uncompensated labor made the Meeting Plantation a premier agricultural enterprise, the true Word of God, and not some false-prophet-spewed craziness that would put him second in line for a first-class train ticket to Hell. Z. T. surmised that Cornelius would be first in line, since he was white, wealthy, and a slaveholder, and the tickets would be distrib-uted below the Mason-Dixon Line.

While in the process of completing a second thorough reading of the Bible, Z. T. Meeting learned about the African Methodist Epis-copal Church from a newly purchased slave who had lived outside of Baltimore, not too far from the Pennsylvania border. He was told that the AME Church was run by a colored man, Bishop Richard Allen. The slave also told Z. T. that he was in a position quite simi-lar to the one Bishop Allen had been in when he started the AME

Church. Z. T. had been bestowed full ordination by a bishop in the United Gospel Congregations of America, and if he followed in Bishop Allen's footsteps, he could start his own denomination and serve as the first bishop.

The new slave understood that Z. T. had been ordained by a bishop who was in the apostolic line of succession that began with the Apostle Peter, and was therefore able to establish a new denomination. As soon as Z. T. processed this groundbreaking information, he immediately went to his owner and told Cornelius that the best way to convert the slaves was to allow them to have their own "slave church." Once Cornelius Meeting's eyes finished lighting up at the thought of the accolades he hoped to receive from proving his theory correct, he agreed to contact the bishop presiding over his district, and arranged for Z. T. to be consecrated as the first official bishop of the newly established Gospel United Church.

With the onset of their new denomination, the slaves on the Meeting Plantation increased their productivity by twenty-five percent, they seemed happier, and the need for floggings dropped by eighteen percent. Cornelius Meeting was in Heaven. And frankly, so were his servants, especially after Z. T. located Cornelius's slave brother, Hezekiah, who was the mirror image of his white sibling.

The slave, Hezekiah, had been banished, along with his mother, to the West Indies when he was twelve years old by Cornelius's mother, who feared for her own son's life with a slave boy running around looking just like him. She knew of the slave revolts that were kept secret. And she also understood just how easy it would be for the slave child to change places with her precious Cornelius, if the bondmen on her plantation ever took a notion to engage in an uprising. So she sent the boy and his mother away to the West Indies, making allowances for Hezekiah to run her family's holdings there, as long as they promised never to return to North Carolina. Hezekiah's mother, fearing for her own son's life, agreed to this arrangement, while her son merely nodded, knowing that he was going back to North Carolina to settle some wrongs the first chance he got.

Hezekiah's chance came when he connected with freedmen in the fast-growing AME Church. Determined to learn more about this religion of freedmen, Hezekiah began to make secret runs to the United States to meet with the leaders of this great church. But meeting and praying and talking with folks in Philadelphia just wasn't enough. Soon Hezekiah was going farther and farther south with each trip, until he found himself at one of the secret meetings for aspiring AMEs in a remote location in Orange County, North Carolina.

Z. T. and Hezekiah Meeting met at that secret meeting on African Methodism. The very first time Z. T. laid eyes on Hezekiah, he was awed (and inspired) by the man's carbon-copy resemblance to Cornelius. The two men became fast friends, prayer partners, and co-conspirators in a plot to adopt the tenets of African Methodism into Z. T.'s new denomination for the sons and daughters of Africa—freedmen and bondmen alike—in the Old North State. They also decided that it was high time to set some wrongs right on the Meeting Plantation.

So they planned what would be the smoothest, cleverest, and most clandestine slave revolt in North Carolina. They sneaked Hezekiah onto the plantation, stole Cornelius's clothes, and waited for the most opportune moment to introduce Cornelius to his own brother, right before they drugged him and put him on the first ship "back home to the West Indies."

Cornelius slept the entire trip in a very comfortable cabin. The crew was told that he was a well-respected businessman, who was also quite ill and determined to get back home. The crew was also informed that it was imperative that Brother Hezekiah be given his vials of medicine in his wine, to make sure he was able to sleep peacefully most of the way "home."

Cornelius was kept in a drugged state until they arrived, and several members of the crew delivered him to his "home" and "family." Hezekiah's mother recognized her son's nemesis on sight, and immediately set out to make him as comfortable as possible. She knew that a comfortable bed, a pretty room with a view of the ocean, wine from the cold cellar in a crystal goblet, and fresh tropical fruit would be important when he woke up a colored man.

As soon as Cornelius opened his eyes, felt the warm and fragrant tropical breeze bathing his face, and stared into the intent gaze of a woman he had not seen since he was twelve years old, he gasped for air, groped his chest, and died. Hezekiah's mother said a quick prayer, shed huge crocodile tears, and then told everyone it was imperative that she journey back to the States to check on her nephew, Cornelius, now that her "beloved son" was dead.

Bethany Meeting left the West Indies with much fanfare and amid many tears from those who worked for her. Never had any of her people ever met a "white landowner" with such compassion for, and understanding and acceptance of, slaves and colored people. She would be sorely missed by the two "whites" she left in charge of her lands.

Many years ago Bethany Meeting had left Chapel Hill, North Carolina, a frightened slave woman, desperate to protect the life of her only child. She returned a wealthy white plantation mistress in whose presence her only nephew, "Rev. Cornelius Meeting," delighted. At that point, the Meeting Plantation became the official birthplace of the Gospel United Church and one of the most clandestine and active stops on the Underground Railroad, as well as a secret military training post for slaves preparing to run away and work for the Union Army during the Civil War.

"Cornelius Meeting" retired from his position at the University of North Carolina in Chapel Hill so that he could devote all his energy to building his plantation into a top-rate agricultural enterprise. He then withdrew from public life to do the work of the Lord on his own property. This strategy proved wise and prudent in the years to come because the Meeting Plantation was one of the few to survive the economic collapse that ensued at the close of the Civil War. Eventually the "owners" of the Meeting Plantation sold their vast holdings to the state of North Carolina for millions of dollars, made sound investments, got richer, and then relocated to Durham County to establish what would eventually become Evangeline T. Marshall University.

Bishop Z. T. Meeting, Jr., became the first president of the church-based university, and then set out to build up his father's church. He established a ministerial training school that was originally set up at the historic Fayetteville Street Gospel United Church, located several miles north of Evangeline T. Marshall University in Durham County. After several classes of ministers received full ordination, the aging Bishop Meeting moved the training school to the university and founded the Evangeline T. Marshall School of Divinity.

Bishop Meeting commissioned this new crop of Gospel United Church ministers to set up churches outside of North Carolina. Soon the Gospel United Church became what Durham County's *The Colored Gazette Newspaper* coined the fastest-growing colored denomination in America. With the growth came a need to consolidate the clusters of churches in the states, and then regions, each with a minister appointed to preside over the new districts by Bishop Meeting.

As the denomination continued to grow, so did the need for more districts. This denomination grew so fast that it wasn't long before the Gospel United Church had representation in every state, parts of the Caribbean, and four countries on the continent of Africa. This is the church that Rev. Theophilus Simmons and his best friend, Rev. Eddie Tate, would find themselves governing as the church entered the twilight years of the twentieth century, looking forward to what the new millennium would bring decades later.

Episcopal Districts—Gospel United Church

The Gospel United Church is a historically black denomination established in Chapel Hill, North Carolina, in 1817. It has Episcopal districts covering all fifty states, the Caribbean, and four countries on the continent of Africa. The denomination is broken down into eighteen districts and two Episcopal offices. There are twenty-one bishops. Eighteen bishops administer the Episcopal districts, two are assigned to the Episcopal office positions, and one is elected by the body of delegates from across the denomination to serve as the Chief Administrative Officer, or Senior Bishop, over all bishops and the entire Gospel United Church.

Chief Administrative Officer/Senior Bishop, Percy Jennings*

District One
Virginia, North Carolina, South Carolina, Georgia
Presiding Bishop, Will Dawson*

District Two
District of Columbia, Maryland, Delaware, New Jersey
Presiding Bishop, Zeebedee L. Carson, III**

District Three
Pennsylvania, New York, Connecticut, Massachusetts
Presiding Bishop, Silas Jones***

District Four
Rhode Island, Vermont, New Hampshire, Maine
Presiding Bishop, Josiah Samuels***

District Five
Alabama, Florida, Mississippi, Tennessee
Presiding Bishop, Matthew James Robertson*

District Six
Kentucky, West Virginia, Ohio, Indiana
Presiding Bishop, Richard D. Lewis*

District Seven
Louisiana, Texas, Oklahoma, Arkansas
Presiding Bishop, Jimmy Thekston***

District Eight
Kansas, Missouri, Illinois, Nebraska
Presiding Bishop, Murcheson James*

District Nine
Michigan, Wisconsin, Minnesota, Iowa
Presiding Bishop, Jerome H. Falls**

District Ten
California, Nevada, Oregon, Washington
Presiding Bishop, Willie Williams***

District Eleven
Utah, Colorado, Arizona, New Mexico
Presiding Bishop, Alexander G. Anderson**

District Twelve
Montana, North Dakota, South Dakota, Wyoming, Idaho
Presiding Bishop, Conrad Brown***

District Thirteen
Hawaii, Alaska, Puerto Rico, Dominican Republic
Presiding Bishop, Buddy Marshall**

District Fourteen
West Indies, Virgin Islands, Bahamas
Presiding Bishop, Thomas Lyle Jefferson**

District Fifteen
Nigeria
Presiding Bishop, Ottah Babatunde***

District Sixteen
Ghana
Presiding Bishop, Bobo Abeeku**

District Seventeen
Mozambique
Presiding Bishop, Rucker Lee Hemphill***

District Eighteen
Swaziland
Presiding Bishop, Otis Ray Caruthers, Jr.***

Bishop assigned to the Office of Urban Affairs, Mann Phillips*

Bishop assigned to the Office of Community Concerns for Districts with Small Black Populations, Yadkin Peters**

---

* Bishops who are upright, trustworthy, and live by the Word of God
** Bishops who are questionable or double-minded, and follow the lead of the crooked bishops because of their personal wants, fears, and greed
*** Bishops who have lost their way and keep a mess going in the denomination

MORE
CHURCH
FOLK

"When the godly are in authority, the people rejoice. But when the wicked are in power, they groan."

Proverbs 29:2

ONE

The Reverend Theophilus Henry Simmons, Sr., was sent to serve as the Senior Pastor of Freedom Temple Gospel United Church in St. Louis, Missouri, at the conclusion of one of the denomination's most corrupt and volatile Triennial General Conferences. Only one other conference had made it to the "Crazy Triennial Conference Hall of Fame," and most of the folk responsible for that meeting had gone on to their just rewards. But back in 1963, good, stalwart, saved, and sanctified church folk feared that the Devil had managed to get such a firm foothold in the church, God was going to strike each and every one of them dead just for being listed on the church roll.

At that conference folks were shocked and dismayed to discover that some of their top leaders had the unmitigated gall to run a brothel right in the midst of the conference, as if it were the first in a chain of franchised ho' houses—and in a funeral home of all places. Whoever heard of a bunch of black people—no, back then, Negroes—wanting to party at a place where dead people were in "escrow" en route to their final destination? Black people didn't make a habit of hanging out in funeral homes. And anybody foolish enough to differ from this norm was clearly either crazy or corrupt and without a lick of sense.

There were a lot of mad church folk who were ready to throw down on those preachers with "memberships" at the ho' house. When that "blue book" hit the conference floor, with the names of the members, folks bombarded the conference floor platform in Virginia Union's gymnasium and found out who was wrong and who was right. That information led to some much-needed changes in the Gospel United Church—changes that led to Rev. Murcheson James's being elected to an Episcopal seat and to Theophilus's appointment to Freedom Temple.

Twenty-two years later Freedom Temple had grown from a respectable congregation of five hundred members to one of the major players in St. Louis's black church community, boasting three thousand dedicated and tithing members under the leadership of their senior pastor, Rev. Theophilus Simmons, Sr. Shortly after Theophilus took over the helm, the church bought up all the property within a ten-block radius. It rebuilt the church building into an impressive structure with a beautiful state-of-the-art sanctuary and a suite for the pastor that included a full bath, library, kitchenette, and conference room. There was a small bookstore and two more libraries—one for the youth and another one for the adults.

The First Lady's mother, Lee Allie Lane Hawkins, had worked alongside her husband, Pompey, to design the new church kitchen and cafeteria, which was large enough to host the Annual Conference and most wedding receptions. There were also a nursery, teen room with video games, gymnasium, first-aid room, and several good-sized education rooms. In addition, there was a large conference room where big meetings and workshops could be held.

The actual grounds of the church had been landscaped by Dannilynn Meeting, a well-respected architect out of Evangeline T. Marshall University in Durham, North Carolina. Dannilynn was the granddaughter of the premier black architect in the country, Daniel Meeting, who had been responsible for designing many buildings on Eva T. Marshall University's campus.

There were flower gardens to walk through, sitting areas, a playground that was so enjoyable that many of the teens and adults loved to share in the fun with the younger children, and the best basketball court in the area. And that was a good thing, because Freedom Temple Gospel United Church had the best teen basketball teams for boys and girls in the St. Louis metropolitan area.

Freedom Temple was a happening place. And if you listened to any of the members talk, you found out that it was a great church to attend, with a wonderful pastor and First Lady. The women admired Essie Simmons's style, they shopped at her boutique, and they all came to her whenever they needed a one-of-a-kind designer outfit—be it a handcrafted wedding gown, debutante gown, or honeymoon wardrobe for a bride's trousseau. Essie received so many requests for her designs that she had to hire a second designer, two seamstresses, and a tailor to keep up with the volume of requests.

As far as Theophilus and Essie were concerned, it was an even better church to pastor than it was to attend. They loved Freedom Temple and felt blessed that the good Lord had seen fit to let them serve in the capacity of Senior Pastor and First Lady. Their members were warm and loving people. They were also people who loved the Lord, were hungry for His Word, and were determined that they would not stay baby Christians once they turned their lives over to Christ. The folks at Freedom Temple kept their pastor on his toes. Since taking over the pastorship at Freedom Temple, Theophilus had found himself needing to study Greek, Hebrew, Latin, and Arabic just so he would be able to continue to inspire and educate his members about the Word and the goodness of the Lord.

Today was the third Sunday, and Theophilus had been at church since six a.m. Every third Sunday he met with his ministerial staff so they could pray together, cover each other in prayer, and encourage one another in their walks with the Lord. Preaching was hard work. Pastoring was harder. Folks just didn't know—they didn't even have a clue of what it took to be a good pastor and a great preacher.

Rev. Simmons was both—and that was saying something. Some ministers could preach Lazarus out of the grave. And some could pastor a whole city to the pearly gates of Heaven. But to be able to do both? Man, oh man! Now that took some doing.

Theophilus knew that he was both, just as the young brother sitting next to him—Rev. Obadiah Quincey, from Durham, North Carolina—was well on his way to becoming. Obadiah was a graduate of the School of Divinity at Evangeline T. Marshall University, and he had been selected by Theophilus to do his requisite two-year apprenticeship under him at Freedom Temple. Obadiah was sharp and well-read, and had a great sense of humor. He had done well here. About the only problem Theophilus could discern was that the young man, his wife Lena, and their family were all homesick for Durham.

Theophilus was so sleepy this morning he could barely keep his eyes open while the announcements were being read by Mrs. Tommie Ann Jenkins, who at eighty-three was one of the meanest members of the church. He couldn't stand the way that old woman abused the status of her age. Mrs. Tommie Ann was definitely blessed to have lived this long, and to be as healthy and robust as she was. But she was (and according to some of the other older members had always been) the worst announcement person in the history of announcement people at Freedom Temple.

Once, when he felt guilty about wanting to throw Mrs. Tommie Ann up a tree and leave her there, one of his ninetysomethings told him, "Pastor, don't feel bad about that old heifer. She has always been like that—ain't nothing changed about Tommie Ann in all of the years that I have known her. She was mean and stupid at twenty-five, she was a dumb cow at forty, she made folks want to slap her at sixty-six, and now she's lived to be old enough to make somebody in this church give her a personal invite to go and visit the Lord and never come back.

"I am just amazed that Tommie Ann has lived this long and not been cut or shot by some woman who was mad at her for sleeping with her husband. So don't you feel bad about that, Pastor. 'Cause that thang is a piece of work. And now she's just old enough to get away with being crazy."

A bunch of folk, mainly his senior members, had begged the pastor to retire Mrs. Tommie Ann from this position. But God had not given him the go-ahead. When Theophilus first took the matter to the Lord in prayer, God touched his heart with these words: *"Wait. Just wait and let her fire herself."*

Theophilus couldn't even begin to imagine how someone who was so prideful and thought so highly of this particular church job would find a way to fire herself. He would have thought that a person like Mrs. Tommie Ann would be very good at finding a way to keep such a position. But the Word said that God's ways were not our ways, and His thoughts not our thoughts. So, given that biblical truth, Theophilus was obedient and trusted that if God said wait, and he waited, one day Mrs. Tommie Ann would up and fire herself. He just hoped that day would be sooner rather than later.

The only other thing that stopped the church from rebelling against Mrs. Tommie Ann's reading the announcements every third Sunday was that she'd been at Freedom Temple so long, she knew way too much about just about everybody at the church. As one of the members of the Senior Usher Board said, "Don't nam-nobody wanna mess with that evil-tailed heifer and make her mad enough to start giving the morning announcements on who been creepin', who been stealin', who been drinkin', and who sittin' at home from church 'cause they been fired and don't have no money to put gas in they car."

The young people in the congregation—including the three Simmons offspring—secretly hoped Mrs. Tommie Ann would continue to do the third Sunday announcements because she was some of the best entertainment they could expect to have during the morning service. It was wonderful to attend a church that was so on point, and did so much right. But it could be kind of boring if nothing crazy, outlandish, or just blatantly ridiculous happened at your church. You needed these incidents to happen so you could go to school on Monday morning and compare notes with teens attending other churches in the city.

Freedom Temple teens frequently bemoaned that they didn't have enough crazy church folk in their congregation to talk about with their friends at school. But this morning things were getting ready to take a turn for the worse. And as far as the young people in the church were concerned, it wouldn't get any better than this.

Mrs. Tommie Ann had steered her walker up to the smaller podium in the pulpit to the left of where the pastor sat. She started off the announcements with the week's list of birthdays and anniversaries. Then she went into a lengthy discussion about the members using up too much toilet tissue in the restrooms.

That woman held out her hand and waited for the rumored

newest old man in her life to place a roll of toilet paper in it. She held it up and said, "Freedom Temple, this is how we can stop using so much tissue in those bathrooms downstairs. As head of the Tissue, Paper Towel, Napkin, and Toilet Paper Ministry in this church, it is my duty to instruct you properly about the use of such in the church."

"By whose authority?" Rev. Quincey leaned over and whispered to his boss very carefully. He did not want to have to deal with Mrs. Tommie Ann if she happened to overhear what he said and threw a hissy fit on him.

Theophilus whispered, "I don't know because this is the first time I've ever heard of the Tissue, Paper Towel, Napkin, and Toilet Paper Ministry."

"Rev.," Obadiah whispered, "she's about to do the demonstration."

Mrs. Tommie Ann rolled off three sheets of toilet paper, folded them, and patted the side of her hip as if it were her bottom, to show how this was supposed to be done by the members of the church.

Essie was sitting in the designated First Lady spot, right down from the pulpit. She willed herself away from making eye contact with her husband. She was having a hard enough time keeping it together sitting next to her mother and stepdad. They were passing notes, poking at each other, and trying not to laugh under their breaths.

By now the teens were riveted to their seats. They could not believe that old woman had a roll of toilet paper and was showing them how to save on it by using her hip as her pretend butt.

Mrs. Tommie Ann patted her hip again before giving the usher the toilet paper roll, along with the sheets of tissue she'd used for the demonstration.

"That mean old lady knows good and well that she needs more than a few sheets of toilet paper for her big butt," Linda Simmons, the middle Simmons child, whispered, praying that her mama and grandmother weren't looking up at the balcony, watching her every move with those old Charleston, Mississippi, hawk eyes. They could get on your nerves—saw everything. And then, if that wasn't bad enough, they always had a comment—*always*.

"Mama's staring at us," Linda's older sister Sharon whispered.

By now folks were assuming that Mrs. Tommie Ann Jenkins had gotten enough attention with that toilet paper lecture to go somewhere and sit down. But as Essie always told her husband, "When did the Devil ever become satisfied enough to just go somewhere and sit down?"

Mrs. Tommie Ann was not happy with the way her own church members were sitting there looking bored and passing notes, obviously too spoiled and selfish to take note of what she'd tried to tell them. That is what she hated about spoiled and selfish people—they were always so caught up in themselves and what they wanted to say and do. Never mind the other person. It was always all about them.

Her eyes scanned the balcony, where most of the teens and young adults liked to sit. She knew why they were up there instead of on the main floor. They loved that perch—it gave them a perfect view of everything going on in church on a Sunday morning. And on top of that, it afforded them the opportunity to whisper, snicker, and pass notes about what was going on during service.

She stared at them for a second, eyes narrowing into slits when they landed on that little red hussy Linda Simmons. Mrs. Tommie Ann couldn't stand that little girl. It wasn't that Linda had ever done anything to the lady. Mrs. Tommie Ann didn't like Linda because she knew Linda saw straight through her and never tried to act as if she didn't.

"She is staring at you, Linda," T. J., or Theophilus, Jr., said to his sister.

"I see her," Linda retorted, and stared back at that mean woman without flinching.

That Linda is just like her mama, Mrs. Tommie Ann thought, as she picked up the announcement bulletin.

"I don't know why Theophilus has so much trouble with his announcement people," Essie's mother leaned over and whispered to her husband, Pompey Hawkins, who nodded, remembering some past announcement people at Theophilus's old church, Greater Hope in Memphis. As good a pastor as Theophilus was, he always managed to have one fool on his team of folk giving the Sunday-morning announcements.

Mrs. Tommie Ann fumbled with the bulletin for a moment. She looked as if something else was bothering her. She put the bulletin on the podium and pushed the false teeth at the top of her mouth up and down for a few seconds with her bottom lip. She looked as if she were trying to scratch her top gums with the bottom of her mouth. When that didn't work, Mrs. Tommie Ann sucked the teeth up loudly and wiggled her mouth around in a feeble attempt to make the proper adjustments to her teeth. And when that attempt failed, she reached down to the pocketbook anchored on her walker and got something out.

Mrs. Tommie Ann hung the pocketbook back on the walker, took her top teeth out of her mouth, put some extra Poligrip on them, put them back in, sucked them into place, slipped the tube of Poligrip in her pocketbook, and said, "Christian friends, before I finish with the announcements, you all need to get your registration straight for the upcoming Triennial General Conference in Durham, North Carolina, before they run out of hotel rooms and the prices go up. I keep telling the pastor that he needs to do something about this since he is such a big shot in the Gospel United Church. But the pastor is so hardheaded and thinks he knows everything."

Theophilus couldn't even get upset with the old lady for talking that junk because he was still trying to keep it together from the Toilet Paper Ministry's demonstration and her teeth. Mrs. Tommie Ann had done some crazy stuff while giving the announcements during his tenure as pastor, but she had never fixed her teeth in front of the entire congregation. It reminded him of the time an old man's teeth shot out of his mouth at an Annual Conference in Memphis, Tennessee, back in the early 1960s. That old man had been talking crazy, too—just like Mrs. Tommie Ann. And his teeth had landed right on the altar, looking as if they were trying to grin at somebody from outside his mouth. That teeth mess had been funny then, and it was still funny now.

The kids, and especially Theophilus and Essie's three children—Sharon, Linda, and T. J.—were sitting up in the balcony about to lose it, trying not to laugh at that crazy old lady. Their dad knew they had worked hard to keep it together when Mrs. Tommie Ann did the toilet paper thing. But the teeth sent them right over the edge.

The entire balcony row of young people was now ducking down under the pews, trying hard not to laugh too loud. Linda, who was the spitting image of her mother, got up and tried to sneak out of the sanctuary without her dad seeing her. But she didn't escape the pastor's scrutiny, especially since she was standing in the vestibule laughing loud enough to be heard back in church.

The parents all looked up to the balcony and tried to give their children that age-old stare that said, "I'm gone come up there and beat your behind if you don't sit up and act like you got some dag-gone sense." But it didn't work because every time they looked at those children they fell out with laughter themselves.

Essie leaned over and whispered to Precious Powers, who was now a member and good friend, "What possessed that old woman to do that up in that pulpit like that? It ain't like she is senile. She crazy but all of her gray matter is intact. And look, that thang has the nerve to get mad."

Actually, Mrs. Tommie Ann was past mad this morning—she was furious. She picked up that big orange-and-yellow pocketbook hanging off her walker and said, "I cannot believe those bad-tailed children of yours is up there laughing in the Lord's house like that. Now, Pastor," she said to Theophilus, "I've been reading the announcements for over sixty years, and nobody ever laughed at me like those children are doing right now. And that lil' red gal of yours owes me an apology."

Theophilus took a deep breath to get a grip on his anger. He looked over at Essie, who was on her way over to the pulpit, and shook his head. This was something that he had to handle as the pastor, even though that old heifer had pushed every single parent button he had in him. He walked up to the large podium in front of the pastor's chair, grabbed each side, tilted his head a bit, and stared at Mrs. Tommie Ann for a few seconds. The church was so quiet you could hear folks holding their breaths in anticipation of what the pastor was going to say to that mean old lady.

Most folk in this congregation had been waiting for the day when the pastor told the crazy Jenkins woman to take her walker-toting-orangey-reddish-brown-dyed-and-thickly-drawn-on-eyebrows self somewhere and sit the heck down! Today Mrs. Tommie Ann had finally gone far enough to make the pastor check her, and check her good. It was enough to make some of the saints get up and start running all over the church, praising God for this mighty miracle in their lives.

Freedom Temple folk loved themselves some Rev. Simmons. Theophilus was a good pastor—superb preacher, astute business-man, exceptional clerical leader, patient and compassionate. It was his compassion for souls like Mrs. Tommie Ann that had stopped him from zooming down on her the first time she showed the rim of her britches to everybody. But this morning folks knew that she had gone as far as to "tear her draws" with the pastor.

You didn't mess with Rev. Simmons—especially over some pure-tee foolishness. You didn't take it upon yourself to roll up on the First Lady. And you definitely didn't get crazy enough to take pot-shots at the Simmons children. If there was one thing their big, fine, chocolate pastor hated, it was "church mess"—particularly when that mess was directed at a member of the church family, or a member of his own family. At some point the pastor would eat you up alive if you didn't stop while the going was good.

"Sister Jenkins," Theophilus said sternly, opting to forego calling Mrs. Tommie Ann by her pet church name—Mrs. Tommie Ann.

"Yes," she answered, matching his stare, as if to say, "I ain't *scared* of you."

"I just want to take this moment to thank you for your sixty-some-odd years of service to this great church as a long-standing member of the Announcement Ministry. And since this is your last Sunday working in this capacity, I would like for the entire congre-gation to stand and applaud you for such dedicated and constant service. Freedom Temple has never and *never, ever* will experience the way you have handled the relaying of information to this great church each and every third Sunday of the month.

"Thank you, Sister Jenkins, and God bless you as you take a seat and witness the service of the next person who will assume this responsibility. Come on, Church. Stand up and give Sister Jenkins the send-off she deserves."

Everybody in church stood up and gave Mrs. Tommie Ann Jenkins a round of applause. She had been mean and hateful to so many of her fellow members, and they were ecstatic to see her go. A couple of folks she'd been especially mean to, because she thought her family was better than theirs, started giving out whistles and were cheering. People at Freedom Temple were sick and tired of being sick and tired of this woman.

Mrs. Tommie Ann was outdone. She had been holding this post for decades. She'd been getting away with doing other people in the congregation bad. And frankly, she hadn't ever thought all of that would come to an end.

Oh, she had known the pastor wanted to get rid of her, and she had prepared to fight him down to the ground to keep her position of power in this church. But she wasn't prepared for this. It was hard to cut the fool when folks were up clapping and cheering over you.

Essie caught her husband's eye and winked. She had to hand it to her man, he was good. Few folk, including Essie herself, would have thought of handling that woman as he had. She winked again, and blushed when he winked back. Essie knew that wink, and the promise behind it. She picked up her church bulletin and tried to fan away the heated flush that was spreading across her face.

Theophilus grinned that mannish grin, completely unaware of the churchwomen who suddenly felt an urge to fan themselves with their church bulletins. He walked over to Mrs. Tommie Ann and gave her a big hug and a kiss, trying not to laugh when she rolled her eyes at him. Then he said, "I would like my financial officer on the Steward Board to make sure you have a parting gift of five hundred dollars at the close of today's service."

He turned back toward Obadiah and said, "I want you to oversee this, Rev. Quincey. Make sure that Mrs. Jenkins receives this gift before she leaves this church."

Obadiah nodded, fighting the urge to blurt out, "Why me, Pastor? Why me?"

Mrs. Tommie Ann Jenkins was the last church member he wanted to be bothered with this morning. Folks just didn't know that preaching was not easy—not by a long shot.

Mrs. Tommie Ann wanted to cuss out the pastor but was stopped dead in her tracks by that unexpected gift of five hundred dollars. Instead she thanked the pastor, got a good grip on her walker, and with the help of one of the ushers standing nearby, came down from the pulpit and sat down.

Theophilus started smiling. It was so good to know the Lord, to be able to hear His voice, and to have sense enough to do what He told you to do. Mrs. Tommie Ann had done exactly what God said she would do—fired herself. All he had had to do was wait on the Lord and be of good cheer. And lawd knows he was of good cheer right now!

TWO

Bishop Murcheson James, Bishop Percy Jennings, Uncle Booker, and Mr. Pompey were sitting in Pompey and Lee Allie Hawkins's kitchen eating and playing a friendly game of poker. Murcheson put his hand on the table and smiled as he collected a fistful of dollar bills. Uncle Booker threw his cards on the table and said, "I can't believe you, Murcheson. You always win and you always want to play for money. And you a bishop. What's up with that?"

"I beat you, just like I have always beaten you since we were young bloods down in Charleston, Mississippi," Murcheson told him, laughing.

"That sho' is right, Booker," Pompey said. "You a doggone good poker player. But you ain't never been able to beat Murcheson. I don't know why you keep trying, giving that negro all of your money like that."

"Why you have to go there like that, Pompey?" Booker chided. "Always got to tell the history and then rub it in."

Pompey ignored Uncle Booker. They had all been friends for a long time. Murcheson and Pompey were used to Booker getting all bent out of shape when he got beat.

"Obviously, your hand wasn't good enough, Booker," his sister, Lee Allie, said between chuckles.

Booker was one of the best poker players in St. Louis, East St. Louis, and their hometown of Charleston, Mississippi. But he could not beat his boyhood friend Murcheson James. In fact, there were fewer than a handful of people who could beat Murcheson at a game of poker. The only thing that stopped the bishop from running game on folk was his relationship with the Lord. Murcheson had given up gambling when he got saved.

Pompey, who was quiet and watchful by nature, got himself another bowl of his wife's famous chili. He was in the food business and could cook like nobody's business. But when Pompey Hawkins came home from working in one of his three restaurants located on the north side of the city, the Central West End section of St. Louis, and the suburb of University City, all he wanted to do was eat some of his baby's good home cooking.

"Didn't you tell me that Theophilus and Obadiah Quincey were coming over this evening?" Percy Jennings, the senior presiding bishop for the entire Gospel United Church, asked as he started shuffling a fresh deck of cards. He had flown up from Atlanta, and Murcheson had driven up from Charleston, Mississippi, to meet about some pressing concerns over some serious rumblings of problems that were beginning to surface in a troubling way in the denomination.

"Not this evening," Murcheson told him. "I just wanted to play cards with some old heads this evening, so we could talk in peace. Percy, you and I have just found out that there is some trouble brewing. We need to talk this out together before we go and get those youngbloods, who still smelling themselves, up in here trying to give us their opinion on the matter. Heck, I don't even have a clue about my own opinion on the matter, and I sho' don't want to hear from any of them right now."

Percy nodded. Murcheson had a point. They didn't know what they were dealing with, or who exactly was behind it and why. Bringing in those two at this stage would just run his pressure up. Theophilus would try to tell them what to do. Obadiah would want names and some background information so he could chart out which mind game he was going to run on them. And then Theophilus would go and hook up with his boy, Rev. Eddie Tate, who would want to come down from Chicago with his assistant pastor, Denzelle Flowers, so they could get some mess started.

If those four didn't like a good church fight, Percy didn't know who did. And this was especially true of Eddie Tate. Sometimes Percy believed Eddie loved fighting church battles more than he did preaching. And if there was one thing Eddie Tate loved to do, it was preach.

"Y'all missed it at church yesterday," Mr. Pompey said, right before he blew on his spoonful of chili.

"Missed what?" Uncle Booker asked.

"You know Theophilus fired Mrs. Tommie Ann Jenkins."

"That old lady who wears those tight, low-cut dresses and has to use a walker?" Uncle Booker asked.

"Yeah, that's her," Pompey continued, and then busted out laughing. "You know she took her false teeth out of her mouth, put some Poligrip on them, and then put them back in her mouth while giving the announcements."

"She did what, Pompey?" Percy asked, shaking his head.

Just when he thought he'd heard it all concerning some of the outrageous stuff black folk could do during Sunday morning service, somebody came along and took church-pew craziness to a new level.

"You heard me," Pompey said. "That old woman got crazy and showed her natural behind."

Murcheson James was cracking up. He said, "You have to be talking about that old woman in the tight 'I'm-gone-sleep-with-your-man' outfits."

"That girl kinda long in the tooth to be trying to creep with another woman's man on that walker," Uncle Booker said.

"What long teeth?" Lee Allie asked in between blows on her spoon, which was dripping with a heaping scoop of chili. She had been eavesdropping but missed a few "bars" of the conversation when she was putting some food away.

Murcheson was tickled at Lee Allie trying to be so slick. He said, "What is it with our denomination and teeth? There is always some kind of teeth malfunction happening at a service at one of our churches."

"You know," Percy was saying, "I'm still stuck at old girl wearing club clothes on a walker. I'd pay some good money to see all of that."

"I don't know about that, Bishop," Uncle Booker was saying. "I've seen it. All of those years stuffed up in a tight black leather skirt, some high-heeled boots, and a tight red turtleneck sweater is just about enough to make a brother kind of envious of Ray Charles or Stevie Wonder."

"You wrong, Booker," Percy told him. "You know you wrong. Ray and Stevie haven't done anything to you."

"Bishop, Ray and Stevie wouldn't be mad at me for understanding why they wouldn't want to have to look at that."

Pompey scraped the bottom of his bowl of chili. He said, "You know something. I can't help but wonder what would make someone her age act like that."

"Living your entire life without ever making Jesus the Lord of your life," Murcheson stated solemnly. "That lady probably got distraught enough at one point in her life to break down and say the Sinner's Prayer. And even though she *technically* qualified for salvation, she never went farther than getting saved. She continued to live her life so immersed in matters of the flesh, there were times that she had to remind her own self that she was supposed to be saved. I bet she rarely read her Bible, thought going to Bible study was boring and a waste of time, and only prayed when she was desperate and out of options.

"You know," Murcheson continued, "this is the very thing the Apostle Paul was talking about over and over and over again in his letters. He knew that people would act like this lady, and live their lives muddled in defeat and foolishness."

"Amen," Percy said. "And it is one of the reasons we have so many problems in our church. Folks, including some preachers, will get saved because they are scared of going to Hell. But they are not scared enough to make Jesus Lord of their lives. As soon as they get what they mistakenly think of as a 'get-out-of-Hell-free card,' they go right back to raising hell. They live their lives in defeat, and never get even a whiff of the victory and joy due a child of the King."

"That's why I called this meeting," Percy went on. "Three of our four districts in Africa are being practically demolished by some so-called 'baby Christians.' I keep getting bad reports that Mozambique, Nigeria, and Swaziland are in trouble. Their Connectional Conference budgets are shot to..."

Percy paused. Lee Allie was staring straight at him. She said, "You watch your mouth, Bishop."

"Okay," Percy said. "You know something, I don't even know if I can even dare to qualify what the districts have been forced to operate off of a budget. It's a mess. Pastors are not receiving their salaries on time or even at all. They move the pastors around too much. And don't let a pastor be good enough to draw a loyal and tithing group of members to the church. A pastor who does that over there won't be at his church very long. And that is especially true for the Eighteenth District in Swaziland.

"It's gotten so bad in Nigeria that the indigenous pastors have been begging to be moved to districts outside of Africa. Mozambique has good pastors but they are always given the worst assignments. They are sent either to the most conflict-ridden spots in urban areas, or so way out in the boonies you need a guide, a compass, and some kind of military night gear to find the so-called churches. On the other hand, the meanest and corrupt preachers have been given most of the better churches. And very little of the money sent to Mozambique from my office gets past the Seventeenth District's administrative office."

"Who are their bishops?" Uncle Booker asked. He had been about to call his wife, Rose, who had stayed in Charleston to work with the decorator on the interior of their newly built hotel. But the call could wait—this conversation was getting good.

"Bishop Rucker Lee Hemphill is over Mozambique, Bishop O. Ray Caruthers, Jr., has Swaziland, and Bishop Ottah Babatunde runs the Nigerian district like he heads the Gestapo," was Percy's answer.

"I met Bishop Babatunde at a Triennial Conference about six years ago," Uncle Booker said. "I've never met a negro as mean as that preacher. If Bishop Babatunde wasn't a preacher, he would probably be hooked up with one of those scary regimes on the continent. I don't know how he flew low enough to get under the radar with the Gospel United Church."

"Yeah, that Ottah Babatunde is a piece of work," Percy said, shaking his head in disgust. He had fought approving Ottah's candidacy for an Episcopal seat tooth and nail because he knew that man was foul, dangerous, and not in the least bit interested in spreading the Gospel of Jesus Christ on Nigerian soil.

"Rucker Lee Hemphill ain't nothing but a straight-up crook," Pompey interjected. "I knew him back in the day. He was always looking for a hook or angle to get some money that didn't belong to him. And we don't need to say a word about the son of Bishop Otis Ray Caruthers, Sr. The saying that the apple doesn't fall far from the tree ain't never been truer when you look at Junior."

"And that is precisely why we need to get across the Atlantic Ocean and find out what is going on over there," Murcheson told them. "Look, Percy, you are the senior bishop, and I'll be taking over your spot at the Triennial Conference. We can't go to Durham to elect new bishops and not know what the heck we are up against."

"Don't we have some allies in Africa who are willing to give up the goods on what's really going on?" Uncle Booker asked. He had never had an inkling to go into the ministry. But he did have a calling to serve as an armor-bearer for his two favorite bishops and good friends. He was glad he had listened to Theophilus and gotten his passport just a few months ago.

"Bishop Bobo Abeeku in Ghana has been a pretty decent ally so far," Percy said with a heavy sigh.

"So what's wrong with him, Percy?" Pompey asked. That heavy sigh of resignation concerned him. He could tell that while this Bishop Abeeku was their best choice, he was definitely not their first choice.

"He has a sneaky streak in him that can jump out and bite you on the butt when you least expect it."

"So he's an undercover crook."

"Booker, aren't most crooks, especially the good ones, undercover?" Murcheson answered.

"Yep, because they have to be," Booker replied. "Abeeku sounds like the brother who'll keep one foot tapping lightly on the right side of the law, just so he can slip off and do wrong when he needs something he can't get right. Y'all following me?"

"Umm…hmm," Pompey said, because he knew exactly what Booker was talking about. "Bishop Abeeku is the brother who will sell weed just long enough to pay off some bills or earn enough money for a down payment on a house or car. And then will have the gall to turn state's evidence on his supplier, sneak and get all of the weed, and then set up somebody dumb enough to do his bidding long enough to get arrested after he's made the money he needs for a permanent trip to the Caribbean."

"That is Bishop Abeeku in a nutshell," Percy said. "But he does have information and I know that he'll share it in exchange for a favor."

"And what would that favor be this time?" Murcheson queried, remembering that the last favor was helping Bobo get his son a scholarship to Evangeline T. Marshall University. That had taken some doing because the Abeeku boy had horrible grades and abysmal test scores, even though he had spent years at an excellent, high-priced English boarding school.

"Plane tickets for him, his wife, and his three presiding elders to the Triennial Conference," Percy answered.

Murcheson shrugged and nodded. It wasn't cheap but it was definitely doable, and certainly a heck of a lot easier than getting that son of his into an American university. And if he knew anything about Abeeku, Abeeku would produce the goods. Murcheson just hoped he wouldn't try and pull something extra over on them once he got to the conference. Murcheson was just a tad bit uneasy about Abeeku's being their sole resource for getting the goods on what was happening on the other side of the Atlantic.

THREE

Bishop Rucker Lee Hemphill sat up in his prized handmade leopard-skin-and-leather Queen Anne chair to sip on the cognac he had recently received from France. He swished the liquor around in the glass, inhaled the exquisite aroma, and then took a long sip.

"Umph," he said, "that is almost as good as sex."

Bishop O. Ray Caruthers, Jr., who Rucker thought looked so much like his father it was like looking at a ghost, said, "Negro, are you serious?"

Rucker sipped some more and said, "Nahhhh...ain't nothing that good—especially if you are lucky enough to get a hold of one of those good and freaky girls from back home."

He closed his eyes and inhaled the memory. It was during a moment like this that he really missed the States.

"You are a wise man," Bishop Ottah Babatunde said with a chuckle, and took a sip of his own drink. As much as he hated having to meet on Bishop Hemphill's territory, he did appreciate the luxurious amenities. No one could ever accuse Rucker of not appreciating the finer things in life. He only wished that Rucker could import one of those freaky American women for his pleasure. Now that would be the perfect way to end this meeting.

Rucker and Ray exchanged quick glances that didn't escape Ottah's scrutiny.

"You Americans are so entertaining with your animated exchanges," Ottah said, with a hearty chuckle that did not hide the deadly glint in his eyes.

Ottah had tried his best to have this meeting in Nigeria. But they had refused because they were scared of that crazy Nigerian. There was no way they were going to go to Ottah Babatunde's house, say something to make that big, black negro with royal family members mad, and then have to pray that he didn't get mad enough to prevent them from going home. But they were not going to tell him that. They just hoped that Ottah couldn't completely sniff them out.

"Sometimes," Ottah began slyly, "I wonder why the two of you never plan these meetings at my house. The accommodations are certainly fit for a king."

"Bishop," Ray responded smoothly, "I know you live in a palace that has everything I could ever want in it. But...uhhh...I ain't exactly comfortable with some of your countrymen, who may stop me to give me a speeding ticket for driving the speed limit, and then expect a huge helping of some American cash to pay him for my own troubles. A brother gotta watch his budget, you know."

Rucker snickered. Ray Caruthers had a budget to watch all right. It was so big he could have paid off half the members of the police force in Ottah's entire Episcopal district—which was huge, when one considered the size of Nigeria.

Ottah conceded. He knew that Americans, even the corrupt ones, were very protective of their individual rights and didn't appreciate anybody toying with them, or being what they thought was unnecessarily unjust. His way of doing things got on a lot of Americans' nerves.

"I hear you, Bishops. Some things in the Old World can set the teeth of you African children in the New World on edge. I've been to your neck of the woods many times, and can empathize with how you feel about how we do things."

Both Rucker and Ray smiled in relief. They needed Ottah, and he needed them. But they did not want to make that crazy black man mad. Ottah was not the one to mess with.

"So," Ottah was saying. "We need to make some extra money. I haven't paid my pastors in six months, and they are quite angry. A few have even been telling all of my business to some of your bishops over in the States."

"Which ones?" Ray asked. Not all of the stateside bishops were right. But there were enough to cause problems.

"Bishops Jennings and James."

"I hate those negroes," Ray said and slammed his fist on Rucker's very expensive imported Italian table.

"Watch yourself, man," Rucker admonished, upset that some of Ray's cognac had spilled on the table. He looked at one of the servants, who scurried over to clean up the mess.

"Sorry, man," Ray said, genuinely apologetic. He pushed back so the young man could get all the liquor off the table as quickly as he could. Ray took the fresh drink another servant was holding out to him.

"You know," Ray said, and slurped up his drink, "my daddy hated those negroes until the day he died."

"So, they are troublesome like a mosquito?" Ottah inquired. He had very little experience with Murcheson James and Percy Jennings, and was under the mistaken assumption that they were more irritating than anything else.

"You really don't have a clue about who you are dealing with, do you, Ottah?" Rucker asked him.

Ottah shook his head, wondering how bad these two Americans could be.

"Those two have a lot of clout and power and they can take a brother down in a heartbeat," Rucker told him. "You need to do something with those blabbing preachers of yours. They have just created problems for plans we have yet to make. Because mark my words, Percy and Murcheson are not going to ignore what those preachers have told them. I'd bet some good money they are sitting down planning what to do right now."

Ray nodded in agreement. A preacher couldn't do anything without those two getting up in folks' business. They were worse than the FBI.

Ottah frowned and made a mental note to have the churches of those preachers burned down to the ground when he got back home. He had no idea how much damage they had done when they called the powers that be in the denomination back in the States.

"What we need," Ray was saying, "is a way to get more folks in power who are on our side back in the States. I looked at the roster of bishops for all of the districts, and we are outnumbered. We need something that will help us buy one of the two Episcopal seats that will be open in June. And we'll need some folks, preferably presiding elders in a few choice districts, in our back pocket."

"Boy, if you don't sound like your daddy," Rucker said, and reached out his hand for some skin.

"Yeah," Ray said. "But the only problem with Dad was that he wasn't slick enough. Dad didn't pick enterprises that could be run in the shadows. His stuff always had to have some kind of venture folks could actually go to."

"Like that ho' house in the funeral home back in 1963!" Rucker said and slapped the side of his chair. "I was there, Ray. You ain't never seen nothing that good in your life. And the women. Ooooo... eeee...ooooo...laaawwwwdddd if they didn't have some women there who could lay it down, pick it back up, and toss it high, only to come back down and land right on you!"

Ray started laughing. His daddy had been something else back in the day. Ottah looked at both of them, hoping they would let him in on this good secret.

"Aww, sorry man," Rucker said. He'd forgotten that only recently had the Gospel United Church voted to put indigenous folk in the administrative seats in the African districts. Back then Ottah wouldn't have been a bishop, and he certainly wouldn't have been invited to run with the big boys in the denomination, if he had been lucky enough to be one of the few indigenous African preachers to participate in the Triennial General Conference. Back then the bishops, presiding elders, and prominent preachers had not treated the Africans right.

"Ray's dad was on the same page that we are right now. He got together with some of the very people we'll be working with, and opened up a brothel for the preachers at the 1963 Triennial General Conference in Richmond, Virginia—which is less than three hours north of Durham, this year's conference site. That place was the baddest meeting place for preachers that I've ever been to. They made a lot of money and were collecting dirt on folks left and right. That is, until Percy Jennings, Murcheson James, and their boys, Theophilus Simmons and Eddie Tate, got involved. It was all over then."

"But didn't two women help bust that up?" Ray asked.

"Yeah, the late great Bishop Harrell's grandbaby, Saphronia Anne McComb James, and her friend Precious Powers. Both of them were going with Ernest Brown's son, Marcel. He made those heifers mad, and they helped to engineer a plan that took everybody clean out."

"But they are women," Ottah said, frowning. "What business did they have being there, and then destroying something a man had built up?"

"Uhhh...Ottah," Ray said carefully, "they are some sisters from Mississippi and Detroit, and their man messed over them and they were not having it. *That* was their business."

"If they had been my women, I would have disciplined them and put that insubordinate behavior to a stop."

"African, please," Rucker said. "They wouldn't have been your women because in their minds you don't know how to treat women like them."

"I heard that," Ray said, cracking up. Sometimes Ottah could be so full of himself. He honestly believed that African royalty mess carried weight with black people from Mississippi and Detroit.

"But they were the kind of women you took your pleasure with and dismissed—right?"

Ray's mouth hung wide open. He could not believe this African was talking about their fellow Americans like that. It was time they got Ottah straight. He'd gone too far. Ray said, "Look, *DR.* Saphronia Anne McComb James is a well respected First Lady of a big Gospel United Church in Atlanta, and a distinguished professor at Morehouse Medical School. She ain't exactly the kind of sister you talk about like that. Marcel Brown was her fiancé, he cheated on her, made her mad, and she got his butt back big time. End of discussion. That girl didn't even sleep around—not even with the good Rev. Brown."

"And the other woman," Ottah said with a smirk. "What is her alleged pedigree?"

"Precious Powers is a good and decent woman. She made a mistake and believed that Marcel was in love with her. She is married to a good man and has part ownership in a fancy women's boutique with Rev. Theophilus Simmons's wife, Essie. You mess with that girl, and you will get your butt kicked. You hear what I'm saying?" Rucker told Ottah with a stern expression on his face.

He was greedy and a crook, but he wasn't letting this man down the women in his country. He got tired of folks from other countries thinking that sisters in America were all loose and hos. For sure there were some freaky hos across the water, like Ernest Brown's newest woman, Nadine Quarles. But they did not represent most of the sisters. Most black women were sweet, hardworking, and decent folk who deserved better than the kind of mess the Ottah Babatundes of the world were always trying to dish out when they crossed the Atlantic.

"Okay, I stand corrected," Ottah spat out. He was of noble birth, and detested being chastised by these commoners over women of all things. He went on. "But in my country."

"Brother, when we go to make this money and buy that Episcopal seat, you'll be in *our country*. And don't you ever forget that," Ray said, and then got up to go to the bathroom. He was pissed off and would have called off the whole deal if he hadn't been so crooked and greedy.

Chief, Rucker Hemphill's head of security at the district's compound, hurried down the hall to sneeze without being heard by the men in that room. He had slipped the two servants a few American bills to let him sit near the door of the room where the meeting was taking place, so he could figure out what those three crooks were up to. Chief had been listening in on Rucker's plots and schemes to get his hands on a lot of money for weeks.

Unlike the bishop, Chief really did know of a way they could make money. Chief had figured out that he couldn't pull this off without Bishop Hemphill. He wished he could, but knew that wasn't going to happen. And he had watched Rucker carefully to make sure that he was the kind of man who would be interested in his business proposal. Only thing, he would have to wait until the other two bishops left before approaching Bishop Hemphill with his idea. Chief was not going to put his cards on the table while those other two were around.

Chief didn't like Bishop Caruthers because he looked like the kind of man who would sleep with your woman behind your back if he thought he could get away with it. Chief couldn't stand Bishop Ottah Babatunde because the man was evil and stuck on himself. As far as Chief was concerned, Babatunde forgot that folks outside of Nigeria didn't care who he or his people were—and they were not scared of him, either. Mozambique had some folks just as mean and dangerous as Bishop Babatunde. And they would take you out, toss your body in some secret ravine, and then go home to eat and catch a nap.

Chief figured, correctly, that those other two bishops were not leaving anytime soon when two good-looking women walked into the study carrying trays loaded down with more food and liquor. Just hours ago the food, liquor, and cigars had been carried in by the male servants. He slipped the menservants a few more bills and left the compound.

When the time was right, Chief knew that Bishop Hemphill would be very interested in what he had to say—especially after a "field trip" to his great-great-uncle Lee Lee's watermelon farm. Uncle Lee Lee was ninety-five years old, and didn't look a day over seventy. He, with the help of his thirty-two children, ran one of the best watermelon farms this side of Mozambique—raising the highest quality of that fruit—red, yellow, orange, and the rare black watermelon.

But that wasn't all Uncle Lee Lee raised. That old man had come up with something that would wake the dead. Or, to be more exact, what he had would give rise to what some men had believed to be lifeless, limp, and practically dead to the vitality they had known many moons ago.

FOUR

As soon as Chief was comfortable that the other two bishops were far enough out of town that they wouldn't turn around and come back to the compound, he invited Bishop Hemphill out to Uncle Lee Lee's farm. Chief hoped he was playing the right hand. This was the first time he had taken a chance on bringing an American out to the farm.

Americans, black and white, were some nosy and inquisitive people. And he'd never met people who were so comfortable about being open with their thoughts and feelings. And black Americans? They were a trip—nothing like them on the planet. Chief always found it comical to watch Bishops Hemphill and Caruthers make all those faces at each other whenever Bishop Babatunde got on their nerves with his royal-descendent talk.

Rucker didn't jump at the chance to take a field trip out to Chief's great-great-uncle's farm when Chief first approached him about this. He was not a farm boy by nature, and couldn't even fathom what was so important that he needed to stop what he was doing to ride out to the middle of nowhere. He was knee-deep in going over the budget reports of his pastors. And this was taking more time than usual because they had started getting good at hiding money from him. He knew they didn't like it when he raised their connectional dues, and believed that if they reported less revenue they wouldn't have to pay him more money that never came back to make things better in their churches.

Plus, Rucker was skeptical about taking a day off to go to this farm because he couldn't figure out how a visit to a farm was going to help his situation. He needed a lot of money, not some fresh fruits and vegetables from some old African man's farm. But Chief wouldn't let up on him, and kept promising that what he wanted to show him would make his life a whole lot better. Rucker knew that Chief always put his money where his mouth was, and decided that maybe a mini-vacation to the edge of nowhere was what he needed.

Chief had been driving the big and rugged Toyota Land Cruiser on dirt roads for over an hour. Rucker could count the houses he'd seen in that hour on his hand. They made a sharp right turn onto what Rucker could only surmise was a grass road, about three feet after seeing a beat-up wooden sign with STAMINA AND LONG LIFE written on it in green paint. If Chief hadn't known where he was going they would have missed the turn completely. Rucker didn't think the term "out in the boondocks" could even apply to wherever they were.

"Why is the sign written in English, Chief?"

"To ward off the neighbors—makes them think some rich white Europeans involved in something out here, and it keeps them away, and out of our business."

"But why would it keep them away?" Rucker asked. He knew that if that sign had been posted somewhere in the States some inquisitive white folk would have investigated it and found out what was up. Where did folk think the concepts for all those horror movies, where some nosy folks started investigating stuff that was better left alone, came from?

Chief slowed down the Land Cruiser, which was coasting through some of the most beautiful countryside Rucker had ever seen.

"Would you, a black man from America, venture off down a grass road that supposedly led to some white folks bold enough to live out here by themselves?"

"Hell, naw," Rucker exclaimed.

"And neither will the folks who live nearby."

Rucker looked around and noticed that there was absolutely nothing nearby, with the exception of the animals in the area. He said, "What do you all consider to be 'nearby'?"

Chief started laughing and said, "You Americans are so funny. Bishop, *nearby* is anybody near enough to get by here without us knowing about it. If you haven't noticed, we have a lot of land. There are enough people within walking distance to wander on our land."

Again, Rucker looked around. "Walking distance" took on a whole new meaning out in the African countryside.

After driving for about twenty minutes, they came to a dirt road that led to a very modest farm nestled in the midst of acres and acres of land covered with acres and acres of watermelons.

"You see those green watermelons?"

Rucker nodded.

"That's the cheap fruit. We put those closest to the entrance, so that people can't get to our treasures."

Chief drove on some more, and the green watermelons gradually gave way to yellow watermelons, and then orange watermelons, and then, when they entered the actual family compound, rich black watermelons. Rucker noticed that all the workers had guns and machetes hooked to their sides.

"Those are my cousins," Chief told him. "This is a family-run business. But we never know when somebody might get back here and try to find out what is going on. Our family has great wealth but we don't like to advertise."

Rucker raised an eyebrow. There were several very plain wooden homes, some Jeeps, and a few old cars, horses and buggies, and Chief's relatives all over the place. If this was wealth, he was afraid to find out what poor looked like.

Chief started laughing. "Bishop, you are a hoot, and so American."

He stopped the car in front of the largest house, which had an old shed way off and out back that was so rickety it looked as if it would topple right over if one of those children running around the farm leaned on it too hard during a vigorous game of hide-and-go-seek.

"Do you think that a poor family could own all of this land and raise this crop, and look as healthy and robust as we do?"

Rucker shook his head. One thing that he had always noticed about Chief was how handsome and robust and healthy he always looked. Chief always had plenty of money—American money. He dressed well, and had an air of authority about him that made people stop and take notice when he entered a room. Rucker had never known Chief to have trouble getting folks to do what he told them to do. He was not arrogant or mean, just a man who knew who he was and felt real good about it. Maybe that is why Ottah Babatunde couldn't stand Chief. Ottah wanted everybody to kiss his feet and Chief would just as soon tell Ottah to kiss his butt.

They got out of the car amid all of Chief's folks running to the car to greet him as if he were a celebrity. It had never occurred to Rucker that Chief was connected to anybody—especially anybody running around all excited to see him. Obviously he was, and it was an impressive display of affection for a man who was cool, even for an African. But as impressive as all that jumping up and down was, it was not nearly as impressive as Uncle Lee Lee strolling up to the Land Cruiser with that fine woman hanging on his arm.

"Are you sure your great-great-uncle is in his nineties?"

"Yes. Uncle Lee Lee is as old as dirt, and that is pretty old when you think about how old Africa is."

Rucker tried not to stare at that woman, who was a lot younger than her old man. He said, "So, how old are you, Chief?"

"Fifty-five," was the answer that came from a man who didn't look a day over thirty-five.

"Is that beautiful woman one of your uncle's grandchildren?" Rucker asked hopefully, knowing full well from the way she was all up on Uncle Lee Lee that she wasn't. He wanted to know how that old man was able to pull all of that fine in his direction.

"She's his wife," Chief told him in a stern voice. He knew that the bishop loved women, especially the ones who looked like Uncle Lee Lee's wife. "They just got married not too long ago. She is thirty-four, and expecting a new baby in about six months."

"And the father? Did he leave her or something like that?" Rucker asked sincerely.

"My uncle is the father, Bishop. And does he look like he is interested in leaving that woman anytime soon?"

All Rucker could do was shake his head, while Chief went and got his bags out of the back of the Land Cruiser.

"So many questions that we will answer, Bishop. I didn't bring you here just for a friendly outing."

Rucker took in a deep breath and practically smelled money. There was something about these watermelons other than their being good fruit. He wondered if it had anything to do with how good these folks looked, and the fact that Uncle Lee Lee had fathered a child with that fine woman at his age. Rucker wondered if that baby would enter the world looking like an old man. The old folks used to always say that a baby would look real old if the daddy was an old man with a young woman.

He couldn't help but think about the great Old Testament patriarch Abraham. He could never quite picture how Abraham got that baby. And now he had a better idea, even though he knew that Abraham's situation had been purer and not tampered with as he suspected of this situation.

"Bishop," Chief said, after Rucker and Uncle Lee Lee, who was extremely quiet, had exchanged quick introductions, "you go down that hall, and you'll find your room on the left. It's the one with the purple-and-ruby silk spread on the bed. Get some rest and we'll come and get you for dinner."

Rucker was surprised to see his bags already in the room, which was very rich and opulent. The outside of the house was plain and unassuming. But the inside was another story. Everything on the inside was luxurious, beautiful, and plush. These folks had stuff only the very rich could afford, and be able to have brought way out here, wherever "way out here" was.

He took off his shoes and sat down on the side of the bed. He was exhausted and fought sleep as he tried to take in every detail of his room. The high four-poster bed was super-comfortable, with plenty of pillows and an extra gold silk throw on top of the spread. There was a gold satin chair, a mahogany antique writing desk, and heavy gold silk draperies at the window. Rucker took off his socks and slid his feet across the exquisite gold-purple-and-ruby area rug. These were definitely not poor folk, Rucker thought as he loosed the top button of his shirt, lay back on the bed, and fell into a deep sleep.

Two hours later Rucker was awakened by the soft touch of a woman he would later learn was Uncle Lee Lee's new sister-in-law. She was as beautiful and lush as her sister, only this woman was far more interested in the American bishop than her sister, who had stood next to Uncle Lee Lee with her nose turned up in the air the entire time they were standing outside.

"Beeship," she whispered sweetly, enjoying the way this cute American man with a trim physique, light brown skin, wavy hair with shots of silver running through it, and winning smile responded to her feather-light fingertips. "It's time for you to get up and freshen up for dinner. There is a bowl of soapy water on the pedestal over there."

She pointed to the fancy wooden pedestal and the hand-painted porcelain bowl of water with some of the most fragrant soap in it.

"That is the best-smelling soap, baby," Rucker said, hoping this woman didn't have a husband. His own wife spent as little time as possible in Mozambique, leaving him with plenty of time to explore the real landscape of Africa.

"It is nice, isn't it," she answered with a smile. "I made it just for you."

"Uhhh... baby girl, where is the bathroom?"

She pointed down the hall to one of three full bathrooms in the house. Chief was right, these folks were loaded. A full bath out here in the middle of nowhere took some doing, and some money.

Dinner was good, the liquor was homemade and strong, and the conversation and company were delightful. Rucker hadn't had this much fun since he went to his last family reunion in Grenada, Mississippi. Everybody was talking and cracking jokes, and eating and drinking all of that good food and fine liquor. Everybody, that is, but Uncle Lee Lee. Rucker noticed that although he smiled at the jokes and family anecdotes, he barely spoke the entire evening.

It wasn't until the women started clearing off that table that Uncle Lee Lee said more than three words to Rucker. He beckoned for Rucker to follow him outside and said, "Let's walk around the farm to help our food settle, Bishop."

Rucker nodded and followed the old man outside, hoping this old man wouldn't want to walk too far. But he knew the wish was in vain. Uncle Lee Lee was still getting folks pregnant. He probably could walk twenty-five miles one way without even busting a sweat.

It was a beautiful evening. The stars were twinkling in the silky navy blue sky, and the moon was full, providing a natural light for the two of them, and adding to the illumination of the huge flashlights they were carrying. They walked through a few of Uncle Lee Lee's prized sections for his watermelons, and he gave Rucker all kinds of interesting tidbits on each kind of this fruit.

Uncle Lee Lee stopped walking and bent down to pick a ripe and fragrant black watermelon off the vine. He dropped it on the ground so that it would break open, then stooped down and scooped up a piece. He snapped it in half and gave Rucker a piece of it.

Rucker bit a piece out of the rind and closed his eyes, that watermelon was so good. He'd never ever tasted anything like it—and that was saying something, since they'd had the most delicious watermelon salad he'd ever tasted at dinner. Plus, that homemade wine was also made from watermelons, and Rucker had gotten tipsy from drinking so much of it. Folks bragged on palm wine. But this stuff was something else.

"You know, Bishop," Uncle Lee Lee began in that perfect English one learns in a British preparatory school, "I am ninety-five years old, and when my woman calls me 'big daddy' she means every word spoken out of her mouth. And the reason my wife doesn't pay attention to younger men like yourself, is because one, she is a decent and honorable woman. And two, she knows that there isn't anyone walking around who can give her what she needs like me."

Rucker smiled. He was embarrassed. He never heard a man this age talk like this. Oh, he had always suspected that men in their eighties and nineties still talked like that. They just didn't talk like that around a younger man like him.

Uncle Lee Lee chuckled. "Son, you are just like my oldest boy.

He is seventy-four years old and always gets so embarrassed when I say things like that."

Rucker was searching his mind to figure out who Uncle Lee Lee's oldest son was. The oldest person at the table had been a man who looked to be close to sixty. He said, "Uncle Lee Lee, I hope I don't sound rude but which one was your son?"

"The young man sitting to your left."

Rucker couldn't believe it. That "close to sixty-year-old" was the "young man" Uncle Lee Lee was talking about. Amazing.

They walked around some more, and then made their way to that rickety old shed way off from the main house. The shed was well lighted with motion sensors. It was so old and decrepit it looked as if it were going to disintegrate into dust. Rucker wondered if that shed was as old as Uncle Lee Lee, then surmised that it was probably older.

Uncle Lee Lee stepped up inside the shed and invited Rucker to follow him in. But Rucker Hemphill was a city boy. He was from the South, but had always lived in a town or city. He had never liked the country, and was squeamish about crusty old buildings. The bishop did not want to go into that raggedy shed. So he held his place on the porch, hoping that he wasn't looking at Uncle Lee Lee as if he were crazy for asking him to come into that place.

That building was so unsteady it moved from side to side when Uncle Lee Lee went inside. But Uncle Lee Lee gave no heed to Rucker's fears. He came back outside and snatched him by the arm and dragged him up to the door. Rucker was shocked at the old man's strength. But still, he would not go into that building. So Uncle Lee Lee went behind him and pushed Rucker inside with such force, he sailed right across the narrow and dusty room.

Uncle Lee Lee waited for Rucker to get up and dust off that fancy suit he had no business wearing to a farm out in a rural section of Mozambique. He then went over to a wooden chest. Rucker stood back and away from the chest because it was covered with four huge spiders. Uncle Lee Lee dusted those spiders off as if they were butterflies or some other pleasant insect. One flew off the chest and landed on Rucker's shoulder.

"Ahhhhhhh," Rucker screamed in such a high pitch he sounded like a woman. He was terrified, and almost peed on himself when that huge and hairy spider resting on his shoulder began to walk up toward his neck.

Uncle Lee Lee got closer to Rucker and popped the spider off him and onto the floor.

"Aren't you going to kill it?"

"No, I like them. They don't bother anyone and they keep everybody who doesn't need to be in my shed out."

"How many spiders do you think are in this building?"

"Oh, I don't know, ten or fifteen perhaps," Uncle Lee Lee answered him matter-of-factly. He didn't see what the big fuss was about. They were just spiders.

"Are they all this big, Uncle Lee Lee?"

All Uncle Lee Lee did was nod and say, "Quit whining and acting like an American sissy boy. They are just spiders. Now come over here so I can show you something."

He pulled out a huge pickle jar filled with some greenish-gray powder. He opened the jar and handed it to Rucker, who started gagging. That was some stanky stuff—smelled like toe jams mixed with smelly underarm juice and butt. Rucker handed the jar back to Uncle Lee Lee, his eyes watering the stuff was so stinky. He jumped when that big brown-and-gray spider started crawling up his pants leg.

"Stomp your foot on the floor," Uncle Lee Lee told him, and then got impatient when Rucker stomped like a girl, and came and knocked the spider off. He flipped open his pocket knife and sliced up some of the powder. He poured it into his hand and told Rucker to hold out his own hand, so that he could give him some.

Rucker held out his hand gingerly, as if Uncle Lee Lee were putting a big clod of poop in it.

"Boy, hold out your hand," Uncle Lee Lee commanded, and then poured some of that stuff into the palm of Rucker's hand.

"Now, lick it up like this," he said, and showed Rucker how to lick up the powder. Uncle Lee Lee looked as if he were licking up the powder kids loved in those candy straws.

Rucker sniffed at the powder in the palm of his hand and gagged.

He squinted his eyes tight to help quell his nausea. When he was better he closed his eyes tight, like a kid taking some very nasty-tasting medicine, and willed himself to put that stuff in his mouth, gagging and coughing and sputtering the whole time.

"Swallow it right now, Bishop," Uncle Lee Lee ordered and then put the jar back. He picked up one of those spiders and placed it on the rack with the jars of that nasty stuff.

Rucker forced the stuff down. Uncle Lee Lee walked out of the shed with a gagging Rucker hot on his heels. He locked it and watched Rucker carefully, waiting on the powder to work.

The first thing that Rucker felt was rumbling and cramping in his lower abdomen. He started sweating when he looked around and all he saw were grass, bushes, watermelons, wildflowers indigenous to the area, and trees.

Uncle Lee Lee assured him that this side effect would pass quickly if he would just quit being so theatrical and calm down. Several minutes later Rucker was feeling better—much, much better. In fact, he had not felt this good physically in a very long time. He felt limber, he felt more energetic, and he felt a good twenty years younger.

Rucker wanted to run back to the house but had to slow down and wait on Uncle Lee Lee. By the time they reached Uncle Lee Lee's house, his wife's sister was sitting on the porch waiting on them.

She smiled and said, "Beeeshiiipp" in the sexiest voice, took Rucker's hand, and led him across the way to her home. He was glad it was dark, because while they were walking, his body reacted with such force and potency, Rucker would have scared somebody—unless of course that person was this delectable African violet pulling him through the front door of her house, murmuring, "Oh my... Beeeessshhhiiiippp."

Rucker spent a hot and passionate night with Uncle Lee Lee's sister-in-law. Much to his delight he didn't get tired, and his body reacted as many times as he wanted it to. It was amazing, and all as a result of taking what was less than a teaspoon of that horrid powder. Rucker couldn't believe it.

The next morning he walked out of the sister-in-law's house over to Uncle Lee Lee's house with some serious swagger in his every step. Chief was sitting on the porch waiting for him.

"Liked that, huh, Bishop?" he asked Rucker, who just smiled and said, "Like it? Chief, man, I love that stuff."

"I have been taking that powder since I was in my teen years. It has kept me young and robust. You want that, don't you?"

"Umm…hmm," Rucker replied. "You can't imagine what I could do with a bunch of that stuff back in the States."

"Oh, I can imagine," Chief told him. "That's why I brought you out here, and my uncle let you try the potion. You need a money-maker that you can sell at this upcoming Triennial Conference. And you need something that doesn't require a lot of work to sell. You are a living witness to the power of this potion. You know it will sell, and you know word of mouth will be all that you'll need to convince your people that you have something worth trying."

"That's true," Rucker answered. "But what's in it for you?"

"Bishop, as you can see, we have a lot. We like to live well. But we have trouble getting the kinds of luxury goods we like without hav-ing to pay ridiculous amounts of money for it. I know that you have fine European shoes, suits, shirts, and silk ties. And you are able to get your hands on the finest liquor, highest-quality cigars, and the best caviar—not to mention your cars and what you have in your beautiful home. That's what we want without having to pay what you Americans would call an arm and a leg for it.

"Now, all you'll have to do is order the goods at the best prices and we'll make sure the money is always there when it's time to pay. I'll pay you for your trouble, and come and get our goods when the shipments come in. Plus, we'll give you a supply of the potion to sell at the conference in the United States."

Rucker knew this was the kind of business deal he'd been look-ing for. That watermelon-powder stuff was the equivalent of every luxury item Chief had just listed. He had never spent an evening with a woman like the one he had just had. He should have leaped for joy over this but didn't.

Rucker Hemphill was selfish and always wanted to be the one with more goods and privileges than other people. He relished the fact that he was one of the few people around able to get his hands on the stuff Chief's family wanted at a better price. It made him the man around here, and he could use that stuff to barter for power and control when necessary. Rucker was not about to diminish his influence and standing in his district by making it possible for Chief and Uncle Lee Lee to get their hands on luxury goods without going through him.

Uncle Lee Lee had told Chief that this was his concern when he first laid eyes on the bishop. Rucker Hemphill wanted to be the one who was running things and determining who got what and when. But that wasn't going to be the case this time.

"So, do you think we have a deal, Bishop?" Chief asked.

"Is there anything else you will want, Chief?"

"We'll want you to handle the shipping fees yourself."

Rucker was so glad that he was tired and not up to sparring with anyone. It saved him from blurting out, "Have you lost your doggone mind, Chief?" Instead he said, "Why would I want to do that?"

"To earn all of that money you'll earn with my uncle's powder," Chief answered him evenly. "You'll have so much that the shipping and handling fees won't even make a dent in your budget."

Rucker shook his head. He hadn't stopped to think about the kind of money he'd make. They were headed to the Triennial Conference in a few months. There was always a lot of money to earn in a setting like that. Church folk came to conferences with money to spend. And there would be plenty of brothers lining up to get a taste of what he and his cronies would be offering.

He stuck out his hand to Chief and said, "We have a deal."

Chief shook Rucker's hand solemnly. He wished he could say that he was disappointed in this greedy and corrupt American preacher but he wasn't. Chief knew that Rucker wouldn't play the game right because he was too stupid, greedy, and selfish to do so. Plus, Rucker was a crook. Chief was shady and slick but he wasn't a crook. What Rucker didn't know was that Chief and Uncle Lee Lee knew he wasn't getting those goods in honestly, and some of that stuff had not even been ordered—it was stolen.

Rucker went into the house to make a pit stop before they hit the road. Chief's brothers got busy putting the bishop's things in the Land Cruiser, checking the tires, and gassing it up, to give Chief some time to give Uncle Lee Lee the skinny on their pending business deal before they left.

"It's just as I thought, Nephew," Uncle Lee Lee said. "He is acting like he's paying top dollar for that stuff, and then has to dig way down deep in his pockets for shipping and handling. Rucker Hemphill needs this deal but he is greedy and will not do right by us if we are not careful."

"But it was okay to shake on it, right?"

Uncle Lee Lee nodded.

"So that means we are going to supply the bishop with the powder, right?"

"Yes, that is exactly what we are going to do—but with a twist."

Chief grinned. He loved it when folk—especially Americans and Europeans—tried to pull one over on his uncle because he was an old African, giving him cause to do business with them "but with a twist." It was all of those "but with a twists" that had made them as rich as they were.

"And the twist is?" Chief asked, laughing, watching the door for the bishop.

"We'll give him just enough of the powder to get started, and give us time to make the right connections with his suppliers. Then they will be on their own. Plus, I know that once the bishop gets back on his native soil, he and his clerical associates will find someone to make this stuff, so that they will not have to pay us."

Chief looked at him expectantly for the twist.

"And that will work out just fine until that stuff they make starts doing them in. Because the one thing I did not include with the potion was this."

Uncle Lee Lee dug down in his pants pocket and showed Chief that bottle of liquid that made all the difference in the world concerning how that powder affected you. Uncle Lee Lee had learned the hard way just what that stuff could do to your body if you didn't make it right, didn't take it right, and didn't have what was in that old bottle. His own mother, who knew a lot about natural medicines, had made this for him to counteract the negative effects of the potion.

The liquid was simple and made from the safest and most common herbs available in most countries. But you would know that it was essential to the safe use of the powder only if somebody told you, and then showed you how to make it. The powder that gave Rucker so much pleasure was potentially lethal without this simple, pleasant-tasting, and cheap homemade liquid.

"My people perish for lack of knowledge," Chief said with a soft chuckle that ended when Rucker walked out on the porch. Now he knew what had taken so long. The bishop had changed into his purple clerical shirt and a pair of conservative black slacks. Clearly he wanted the people they might happen to pass, once they got into more populated territory, to know that he was an important minister.

Chief thought that this black American was a piece of work—even for a spoiled American, this joker was something else. The ancestors who survived that horrific passage to the New World must have been some of the toughest Africans on the continent. How else could you explain these sons of Africa, who crossed back over the ocean to be the piece of work that the ones like Bishop Rucker Hemphill were?

FIVE

That particular dose of the watermelon powder stayed in Rucker's system for two weeks. During that time, it felt as if he had taken some kind of miracle drug—almost as if he'd found the fountain of youth. Rucker noticed that his energy level and physical prowess were at a peak. Plus, he slept better, his appetite was better, and he found himself wanting to exercise. He also felt a need to do some manual labor—something he'd never wanted to do. If his memory served him right, Rucker felt as he had in his early twenties. If there was ever such a thing as a youth potion, the bishop was beginning to think he had stumbled upon it.

But that state of euphoria came to an end. The vitality Rucker experienced from the potion came crashing down when the last remnant of it was out of his system. And what a crash it was. Just days ago Rucker had been vital, energetic, and full of longevity. His prowess had been at an all-time high, and he'd had more to work with. The bishop's "honeys on the side" could not hide their delight over this new and improved, greatly enhanced, and extra-endowed Rucker Hemphill.

Now Rucker felt like a shriveled-up old man. Even worse, he noticed that he also looked like one when he caught a glimpse of himself after coming out of the shower. And that was very disturbing since he hated cold water, and always took hot showers no matter how high the temperature outside. He looked like a little boy running around in a pair of Underoos.

The potion had stayed in Rucker's system so long that he hadn't expected to experience any side effects. He certainly hadn't expected anything to change back to the way things were before he took the stuff. Not only did the effects of that potion not last, it had set off the worst withdrawal symptoms he'd ever experienced. Not even the high-quality cocaine he snorted every now and then affected him like this—which posed a problem. How could Rucker hope to sell something that promised so much at first and then spiraled all the way down into a bottomless pit?

Rucker felt like a plop of poop. And nothing he did was able to make him feel better. Chief had noticed the change in the bishop, and knew immediately what the problem was. Uncle Lee Lee's potion made you feel like somebody with an incurable disease when it was finally out of your system. The letdown had an opposite effect on your body. Instead of feeling young, virile, and robust, you felt old, sick, and frail.

The last thing Chief wanted to happen was for the bishop to feel so bad he decided to just chuck their whole arrangement and continue on with business as usual. Chief really wanted to see this deal go through with Bishop Hemphill. His family craved luxury items the way some people craved drugs. Plus, there were a lot of folk who would pay him good money to get their hands on things the bishop possessed, like state-of-the-art stereo equipment, home-office IBM computers, blue jeans and blue jean suits, Michael Jackson cassette tapes, pantyhose, perfume and cologne, Avon, Hostess Twinkies and Cupcakes, televisions, boom boxes, and on and on and on.

And the way the bishop was able to get his hands on all of this was so close to looking legal, it would be so so easy to take it to the next level. Because Chief had figured out a way to open a high-end "store" for a select clientele, with "select clientele" prices. "A piece of cake," as the Americans would say. The only thing left to be done was for the bishop to let his suppliers know that Chief was the inside man.

But Chief had to be able to get on the inside to be the inside man. And so far, the only way Chief had found to gain access to this profitable and well-run black market business was to get Bishop

Hemphill a decent supply of Watermelon Powder 21, or WP21, as he'd heard the bishop refer to the potion before he got sick.

That name had gotten stuck in Chief's head when the bishop said, "Man, that Watermelon Powder 21 is some bad-tailed stuff. Who would have ever thought that something as simple as a powder made out of watermelon and who-knows-what would make you feel like you twenty-one all over again?"

Even though Chief told the bishop that he had taken this stuff since he was in his teens, he hardly ever messed with it now that he was a mature man. "WP21" tasted like something out of the crack of your behind—nasty. Plus, he could "do the do" with his wife and his women, to everybody's satisfaction, without the potion—*thank you*. But Chief knew that the sooner he got the bishop some more of that powder, the sooner he'd be up and running his new "import" business.

So Chief hurried out to Uncle Lee Lee's farm and persuaded him to toss up another, bigger batch of the potion—enough to last the bishop awhile, with some left over for his cronies to try out. Chief knew that as soon as Ray Caruthers and Ottah Babatunde took some of that stuff, those three would be high-tailing it across the Atlantic to set up shop with the only other people as corrupt, crazy, crooked, and covetous as they were—Bishop Larsen Giles, Rev. Ernest Brown, Ernest's son Rev. Marcel Brown, Rev. Sonny Washington, and Cleotis Clayton, who was their most direct connection to the streets.

Chief had met them all on one of their trips to Africa in search of something to take back to the US for personal gain. He didn't like any of them, with the exception of Cleotis Clayton. Despite the man's criminal record, he was the only honest black man in that bunch.

What a horrible testimony to a man like Chief. He had read the Bible from cover to cover, and he knew that every word in the Word was the living truth. But Chief was unable to let go of all that he believed he was gaining in the world just for a life with Christ. The thought of salvation soothed Chief's soul when he felt empty and had panic attacks in the middle of the night. But it didn't take long for him to relinquish that urge for the Lord. As soon as he thought about the men who had been sent to build up the Gospel United Church in Africa, he took a swig of that strong watermelon wine, woke up his wife, and then went back to sleep, mind completely clear of those concerns.

Chief thought that the edicts of Paul in the New Testament Book of Titus were never truer than when applied to these men. They were the very people Paul was writing about. These men needed to walk right and strive to be worthy of their calling—which was the exact opposite of just about anything Rucker Hemphill and his "boys" could ever conceive of doing.

Sometimes Chief wished that the bishops and preachers he'd heard Bishop Hemphill bad-mouthing would make their way across the ocean so that he could meet them in person. He had figured out that Hemphill, Caruthers, and Babatunde disliked Murcheson James, Percy Jennings, Theophilus Simmons, and Eddie Tate because they were honest preachers and true men of God. It was clear that Rucker, Ray, and Ottah couldn't stand to be around those men because wrong hated to be exposed by right.

Chief truly hoped that he could meet one of them, or someone like them, before it was time to take his last breath on this Earth. He had so many questions about Jesus and salvation, and nowhere to go and get ministered to. Plus, the last place Chief wanted to be, the day he woke up dead, was on the wrong side of eternity—way south of Heaven. And he knew that men like Rucker Hemphill would never be able to show him how to steer his way north.

Rucker was relieved when Chief showed up with a new batch of the potion. As soon as he managed to get that nasty stuff down he felt like new money in an old money account. Rucker discovered that he felt at his best if he took WP21 every five days. He always made sure he took the exact amount given to him by Uncle Lee Lee. If he took too much the crash was so severe it made him feel as if he needed to be in an intensive care unit. If he took too little he was sluggish, couldn't sleep, and suffered from joint aches like someone with severe arthritis.

Once Rucker believed that he had the use of the potion under control, he got excited all over again about all the money he planned to earn at the 1986 Triennial General Conference in Durham, North Carolina. He tried to tell Ray and Ottah about the potion by phone, but found that he couldn't describe with any accuracy just what WP21 was, and all that it could do. It was at that point that the ever-observant and efficient Chief stepped in and said, "Bishop, you cannot possibly explain to any man the beauty of this elixir. You should invite your Episcopal brethren to the compound and let them experience this miracle for themselves. You know, there is nothing like word of mouth to advertise the true merit of a product—even in America, where I'm told advertising reigns king."

Chief was right. Bishops Caruthers, Jr., and Babatunde had to experience this for themselves. Rucker would need their support in Durham when it came time to buy himself a new district stateside, purchase an Episcopal seat for a man of their choosing, and buy a few presiding elder spots, along with one or two pastorships at choice churches. That would take money, work, and some skillful dirty politics. Ray and Ottah required an incentive, and taking WP21 out for a test drive would be all the incentive those two would need.

So Rucker invited Bishops Babatunde and Caruthers to his compound—he even paid their way to Mozambique, and made sure they traveled first class all the way. Then Chief, along with his cronies on staff at the Episcopal compound, threw the three bishops a WP21 party. They had plenty of food, plenty of liquor, plenty of privacy, plenty of WP21, and, of course, plenty of women.

As soon as the women showed up looking fine, smelling good, and smiling from ear to ear, Chief rubbed his hands together and went and put on one of Bishop Hemphill's favorite songs. Rucker Hemphill loved himself some Howlin' Wolf. As soon as the bishop heard the song "Tail Dragger" blasting from the boom box, he got to grinning and singing:

"I'm a tail dragger. I wipe out my track.../When I get what I want/ I don't come sneakin' back."

Chief liked that song, too. Nobody could say it like Howlin' Wolf sang it in a song. And that song said it all. Chief was a tail dragger, too. He was dragging his tail, wiping out his tracks, getting what he wanted, and not sneaking back.

When Ray and Ottah got ahold of some WP21, nothing else had to be said. They were now customers with testimonials, and couldn't wait to take it to the Triennial Conference. They had never had anything like WP21. And they knew that if they had never had this stuff, the folk across the ocean had never had any of it, either.

By now Rucker was so excited about this stuff, he started singing another Howlin' Wolf song, "Do the Do." Babatunde wasn't going to even try to find the right song for the potion. As far as he was concerned, those two Americans wouldn't have been able to handle the Nigerian lyrics he was thinking about translated into English.

Ray Caruthers didn't have a song because he didn't like WP21 and vowed never to take it again. Oh, he'd enjoyed the benefits of WP21 during the party—but he didn't like it. For starters, Ray didn't trust the Africans or their "elixir," as Chief called it. Secondly, the changes he witnessed when he looked down and saw all of that increase scared him. And as soon as Ray felt the initial effects of the drug, he knew there would be trouble when that stuff was out of his system. And he was right—the aftereffects were as bad as the results of using the powder were good.

Ray's dad, Bishop Otis Caruthers, Sr., had died in the most disgraceful manner because of an addiction that led him to take substances just like this. If there was one thing the elder Caruthers's death had taught his son, it was that some things were best left alone. He might have inherited his father's greed and penchant for delving into things preachers needed to stay away from, but he had also gotten a good dose of his mother's cautious approach to anything that promised to do *too* much for you. Things like that always came with a higher price than Ray Caruthers was willing to pay.

The three bishops all agreed that WP21 would prove to be a big success at the conference. While they could make a lot of money with the "import" business, the potion was better, cheaper, and easier to manage. Getting luxury items and selling them at high prices wasn't an easy venture. Plus, they had to form partnerships with the wrong kind of people to make it all work and turn a profit—thieves and smugglers, who would do whatever they had to do to get the job done.

Even Ottah Babatunde, who believed it was his due to have the best of the best at bargain-basement prices, was uncomfortable dealing with the men who provided them with their luxury items. Ottah was a crook, but he valued being a preacher, and relished the prestige and level of respectability that came with being a bishop in the Gospel United Church. And more and more he realized that the power brokers in the denomination would not put up with behavior that was too risqué and questionable for a man of the cloth. Those men were straight shooters. They would shut Ottah down, take his district, and revoke his preacher's license.

Folks mistakenly believed that Bishop Babatunde was crazy. Ottah had trained under Ray's dad, Bishop Otis Caruthers, Sr., who really had been crazy. But Ottah Babatunde was not crazy. He was just the meanest black man on either side of the Atlantic Ocean. Rucker and Ray hoped that Ottah would watch himself when he was at the conference. He got away with running a reign of terror on the preachers in his district. But he would feel a foot up his royal behind if he tried to pull that stuff on some brothers in the States.

When it was clear that everybody was on the same page, they began to make plans. They had to get the potion into the States, and then be able to market and sell it, while at the same time avoiding the close scrutiny of the power brokers in their denomination. They knew that Bishops James and Jennings were like some bloodhounds, and they would sniff out some mess as soon as a whiff of it hit the air. Unfortunately, they didn't know that their nemeses had already gotten a whiff, and were gearing up to find out just what that smell was.

Rucker's district was always under close scrutiny. Percy Jennings was never satisfied with Bishop Hemphill's reports. It was clear from Rucker's finely tailored Italians suits, ties, and shoes that he was dropping some serious cash somewhere. Percy wore some very expensive clothes, but he didn't have anything in his closet to rival what Rucker was wearing whenever he was in the States. The shoes alone were a month's salary—and that was for somebody with one of those "good jobs."

Both Percy and Murcheson knew that Rucker didn't have

anything legal on the side that could bring in that kind of cash. The bishops and preachers in the denomination who were wealthy on their own were usually high-ranking professors or college presidents at prestigious institutions, they owned businesses, some were lawyers, a few were doctors, they were wise investors, or they had wives who had made a mark in their own right. Theophilus Simmons and Eddie Tate were perfect examples. Their churches had huge budgets, and their wives were pulling in some serious cash with their investments and enterprises.

Johnnie Tate had a business degree, was a financial consultant, and had a high-powered job at one of the big Chicago-area banks. And Essie Simmons had just expanded from having a boutique to hiring designers, and was in the process of building a small factory to produce a line of clothes and hats. Rucker's wife, on the other hand, stayed at home, was in every wealthy black women's organization there was, and lived like the wife of a millionaire. She was in the Links, Inc., a regional officer with her sorority, the AKAs, and the only black woman to be invited to join her city's Junior League.

It was no secret that the Hemphills had money, and lots of it. The question that was being asked was where was all of the money coming from? And how did they get enough of it to support a lavish home on either side of the Atlantic? Because everybody in the denomination knew that Mrs. Hemphill didn't like Mozambique. She'd taken one trip over there, walked into the compound, turned up her nose, booked a flight, and come home. And she said that she was never going back—not ever.

So folks also knew that the bishop was going to try to come home as soon as he could. And this meant that he would do whatever he had to do, to get reassigned to the States. That was not good—not good at all.

The Gospel United Church was very concerned with what its overseas bishops were up to—and with good reason. The stakes were high going into this next Triennial General Conference. Rucker was going to get back to the States, and he didn't care how he did it. Ray Caruthers didn't care about staying in Swaziland for another term but he was always greedy for more money. And Bishop Ottah

Babatunde was going to want to get the Americans out of his business, since he couldn't understand how a bunch of foreign commoners believed they had a right to intrude in on what was happening on Nigerian soil.

Twice Babatunde had asked for full control of the Nigerian district. And twice Percy had told him that he could control whatever he wanted to control, as long as it was not connected to the Gospel United Church. When Babatunde jumped up in Percy's face, Bishop Jennings had reached inside his suit coat and said, "Ottah, you have a God-given right to be head of whatever you want to be head of. And if you want to be the 'Head Despot In Charge' over the church activities in your native land—you go right ahead and do it. Because, bro-man, you can start your own church any daggone day that you choose. But if you are planning on doing anything in *my* church, you gone do it *my* way."

Bishop Babatunde was incensed at that meeting. He spat on the floor and said, "I am African royalty. And if you were in my territory, you'd be subject to me."

At that point Percy Jennings, who was a slightly built, light-skinned brother in that five-eight-to-five-nine range, walked over to Ottah and got up in that big African's face. He said, "Negro, if I were in your country, I'd still mop this floor up with your raunchy behind. But since you in my country, I suggest you take your funky royal tail out of this meeting, and hightail it back home before something real bad happens to you."

The other bishops had been quiet the entire time. One or two had exchanged words with Ottah on occasion. A few were getting some kickbacks from him. But none of them had ever jumped up in his face like Percy just did. That day Percy Jennings scored some serious points with his colleagues, and even his enemies had a new level of respect for their senior presiding bishop.

As much as they were being watched by their own church folk, the Seventeenth, Eighteenth, and Nineteenth Districts were also being watched by one other group of folk. The FBI had been trailing a dope-and-smuggling ring that was headquartered in the Northeast, with two satellite command centers somewhere on the Eastern

Seaboard. They knew the goods were being acquired from Europe. But the trail always went cold when they followed it over there.

Just recently, one of the few brothers assigned to this case began to wonder if that trail would pick up in a warmer spot like Africa. It was the perfect detour, and in a place where the white agents couldn't easily infiltrate. Plus, Agent Gregory Williams had also discerned that the African trail was leading them to territories with a visible black American presence through the Gospel United Church—Swaziland, Nigeria, and, most importantly, Mozambique.

It had taken Greg Williams weeks to connect the dots on this. But he started getting some disconcerting news from one of his informants—a disgruntled preacher who was struggling to hold on to his church in the Seventeenth Episcopal District in the Gospel United Church. Agent Williams knew that this district was run by Bishop Rucker Hemphill, who had all kinds of luxury items, including some high-powered guns a preacher shouldn't have in his possession.

From what the preacher told him, Hemphill had plenty of money, despite the fact that he was assigned to a district with limited resources. The Seventeenth District's headquarters looked like something out of a James Bond movie, where the evil Dr. Somebody-or-Another resided at the expense of the native residents. Plus, the preacher kept talking about some kind of watermelon-based herbal powder that did some mighty interesting things to a brother. At first glance it just appeared to be some home-remedy type of exotic aphrodisiac. But on closer look this potion, if made with some man-made ingredients, had the potential to become a lucrative street drug.

Something was not right. The denomination knew it, and the feds knew it, too. They both needed a person who was not a potential threat to Bishop Hemphill, to go over and check things out. Not that the bishop would tell this brother anything. But if it were the right brother, he wouldn't have to. The two organizations ended up selecting the same person to do this job—Field Agent/Rev. Denzelle Flowers, a unique combination of professional skills and training if there ever was one.

Denzelle Flowers was one of those ultra-cool and super-smart brothers. He had finished his bachelor's degree in religion and earned a master's of divinity from Evangeline T. Marshall University in four years, while also serving as a star player on the school's basketball team. He had finished his ordination training in record time, and was now doing his apprenticeship in Chicago under Rev. Eddie Tate.

Rev. Flowers was recruited into the FBI by Agent Gregory Williams while he was still an undergraduate student at Eva T. He graduated in the top two percent of his FBI class, and had been given special permission to serve as both a preacher and an agent. It had taken some fancy, Michael-Jackson-quality footwork for Greg Williams to convince the higher-ups that they would do well to have Denzelle well placed in the community. And what better placement could he have than as a preacher, with his finger on the pulse point of what was happening. Right now Agent Williams, who was also Denzelle's supervisor, thought it wise to work with Rev. Flowers's church and send the brother to get the inside scoop on what was happening in Mozambique.

Gregory knew the senior bishop in Denzelle's denomination was not happy with the bishops in the motherland. And Bishop Jennings was more than happy to have one of his preachers go over there for the church and the FBI. Talk about a blessing in disguise—a brother with a clerical collar at his neck, and a standard-issue FBI gun anchored on his hip.

As far as Percy was concerned, it didn't hurt that Denzelle was ordained to enforce the law. And for Gregory, it sure did help to have an agent who was ordained to call on the name of the Lord— especially since that agent was sent to scope out some crazy-acting preachers.

The day Chief and Uncle Lee Lee decided to bring Rucker out for another visit to the farm, Percy Jennings was putting Denzelle on a plane to Mozambique, with the blessings of Agent Williams. On that day, Rucker Hemphill received a call that made his day about a trip to the farm to discuss the business. And five minutes after hanging up the phone he received another call that made his blood run cold in his veins.

Rucker almost peed in his pants when he heard Percy Jennings's voice on the telephone. Percy never called Mozambique for anything other than to run a check on Rucker. And this time he was calling to tell the bishop that he was sending someone to check up on what was happening in the Seventeenth District. Chief had already told him in that first phone call that an FBI agent was scheduled to come their way. Rucker hoped that the preacher and the agent didn't cross paths. The last thing he needed was to be checked up on by one of the senior bishop's cronies, and a federal agent, too. Little did he know that his worst nightmare, Rev. Agent Denzelle Flowers, was about to step off a plane.

SIX

Rucker Hemphill was no longer anxious about Bishop Jennings's sending Rev. Flowers to his district. Now, he didn't appreciate having a junior-level preacher, who wasn't even a full-fledged pastor of his own church, being sent to check up on him. But it could have been worse. Instead of suffering through an official fact-finding visit from a rookie preacher, he could have been on the receiving end of a question-and-answer session with the FBI agent.

Rucker was so happy that he didn't have to deal with the feds, he thought about going to get the good Rev. Flowers from the airport himself. But he quickly tossed that notion back to wherever it came from, and sent Chief instead. He wasn't in a mood to be bothered with the young preacher, and would savor the time he had left before he arrived at the compound.

While Chief was on his way to the airport, Rucker had come up with all kinds of schemes to get rid of Denzelle Flowers. He settled on a rogue version of the kill-'em-with-kindness strategy. Rucker figured that rolling out the red carpet would make the good Rev. Flowers feel so comfortable and at home he would pay little attention to what was going on around him. If Rucker could accomplish that, he would go a step further and slip the good reverend enough bills to discourage him from wanting to talk to Percy Jennings about his trip to Africa.

Denzelle wanted to come to visit Bishop Rucker Hemphill in

Mozambique about as much as Rucker wanted him standing around the compound's storage room the day the luxury delivery man came to town. Denzelle had fussed and carried on about being ordered to take this trip so much, he received a formal reprimand twice—once from Percy and once from Greg Williams. Truth was, Mozambique was not on Denzelle's must-see list of places to go. The arsenal of immunization shots and malaria pills alone was enough to make a brother want to stay at home.

Just thinking about that long plane ride over all of that water almost caused poor Denzelle to clean out his desk, turn in his robe and collar, then turn in his badge (he wasn't going to turn in that gun) and tell his bishop and his boss to forget it. And he came real close to blurting that out the day Bishop Jennings put the first-class plane ticket in his hand and said, "You *are* going to Mozambique, son."

"Sir," Denzelle said, desperately hoping that something he said would discourage the bishop from wasting good denominational money sending him on this trip. "Do you honestly think that Bishop Rucker Lee Hemphill is going to let *me*, a rookie preacher, in on what's going on just because I'm there?"

"What I think," Percy answered, "is that Rucker will do everything he knows how to do to make your stay there so good, you will not want to see anything, hear anything, or tell me a thing when you get back.

"But you didn't earn those high scores at Langley, become a sharpshooter, and carry around two Bibles—one loaded with the Word of God, and another with the inside carved out to hold extra clips for that piece strapped up under your arm—to be duped by a poot-butt like Rucker Hemphill."

Denzelle chuckled at the bishop's description of Rucker Hemphill. But he still wondered why his senior bishop believed he was the one to send to the Seventeenth Episcopal District. Did Bishop Jennings honestly believe he could hop on a plane to Mozambique and then boom, the information would run free and rampant as soon as he got through customs?

Percy wasn't paying that young buck any mind. He'd been in this business a long time. And the one thing he'd learned over the years was that unrighteous preachers always did something to tell on themselves. They couldn't help it—something about trying to get over on the Lord always jammed them up. Some of these preachers couldn't get over on each other. What made them think they could pull one over on the Creator of the entire universe?

He knew the Lord. And Percy knew the Lord had laid it on his heart to send Denzelle to Mozambique, even though he also knew Denzelle dreaded taking that long flight over to Africa. Percy knew Denzelle had law-enforcement eyes and instinct reinforced by Holy Ghost–inspired direction. Percy knew the God he served was able and never failed. And Percy knew that if God called him to send Denzelle Flowers over there, God would give the young brother every piece of information he needed and then some.

Galatians 6:7–9 came searing into Percy's heart and mind, causing him to stop for a second to digest what the Lord had seen fit to bless him with. He said, "Denzelle, *Do not be deceived: God cannot be mocked. A man reaps what he sows. The one who sows to please his sinful nature, from that nature will reap destruction; the one who sows to please the Spirit, from the Spirit will reap eternal life. Let us not become weary in doing good, for at the proper time we will reap a harvest if we do not give up.*"

Denzelle wasn't sure if what the bishop had just said fit with what they were talking about concerning Bishop Hemphill. He didn't know how to respond, and nodded as if he and Bishop Jennings were seeing eye-to-eye on the subject.

Percy just looked at that rookie preacher and chuckled. That boy really thought he could slide by an old-school church player like himself. He said, "Boy, you don't have a clue about where I'm coming from. Do you?"

"No sir, Bishop," Denzelle answered contritely.

"Son, you and I love the Lord. We fear Him, we honor Him, and we respect Him. And with the help of the precious Holy Ghost, we do our best to obey the Lord. Son, we know that God knows our very thoughts and the exact timbre and tone of the beat of our hearts. We know that He knows the subtlest of nuances in the deepest depths of our hearts. He can catch a tear before it even rises high enough to trail down our cheeks. And we know that you cannot get over on the Lord. And if you are dumb enough to try, especially if you are a preacher, you are making a mockery of Him. So know that God will not be mocked and you will reap what you sow.

"Are you following me now, Denzelle?"

"Yes, sir," Denzelle answered, still not sold that he was the one with the skills to get the goods on an old coyote like Rucker Hemphill.

"Son, you have the Lord, a gun, a badge, a collar, a Bible, a thumbs-up from the Federal Bureau of Investigation, and an official letter from the highest-ranking bishop in the Gospel United Church. Honestly, Denzelle, what else do you think you'll need to do what you have to do over there? Rucker is just an asthma breath short of being a crook. He is slick and he is greedy. But what he is not, and will never be, is wise enough to hide the truth from someone who can cut through some bull with a plastic church knife like yourself."

Denzelle cracked up, gave his bishop some skin, took that first-class ticket, called his boss, Gregory Williams, to make sure these plans corresponded with those of the Bureau, and got ready to leave for Mozambique.

The flight over the ocean was as long, tedious, nerve-racking, and tiring as Denzelle had feared it would be. He was miserable, ready to go back home, and just plain ornery when he reached his final destination. When he had to go through customs they started giving him a hard time.

At one point during the ordeal, Denzelle stood in the middle of the floor and said, "Father, give me strength," for all to hear.

When he pulled out his Bible and a white handkerchief, and started reading Scriptures in his preacher voice, they rushed him through before Denzelle got so upset he started preaching and then decided to take up a collection.

He had just collected his bags and gone through them to make sure everything was just as it should be when a well-dressed African man walked up to him.

"You are Rev. Flowers, are you not?" Chief asked him politely.

"How did you figure out I was me?" Denzelle questioned. He wondered how this man, who looked as if he could have been a bouncer at the roughest club on Chicago's South Side, worked for the Seventeenth. He didn't look like a dedicated churchgoing man. And he certainly didn't look like anybody's preacher or presiding elder, either.

Chief said, "Wait here a minute, Reverend," and picked up Denzelle's luggage. He nodded at Denzelle to follow him to the car, then stopped and looked Denzelle up and down, taking in his black leather blazer, expensive American jeans, long-sleeved gray T-shirt, and high-priced athletic shoes. Chief especially liked the shoes because they looked like something an NBA star, or rap stars like Run D.M.C., would wear. Then he said, "Rev. Flowers, do you see anybody standing in this place dressed like you—an all-American black man in those fancy NBA shoes?"

Denzelle looked around and had to admit that he was pretty visible in the crowd. He had BORN IN THE USA stamped all over him.

"Come on, Reverend, I need to get you to the compound. You have to be tired after such a long flight."

Denzelle nodded wearily and reached down to pick up one of his bags. Chief waved him away.

"Let me get this."

He followed Chief to the Land Cruiser and hopped in on the passenger side. Denzelle was so tired. He didn't think he'd make this ride to wherever they were going on his first trip to Mozambique without falling into a deep sleep. And that wasn't an option, since he didn't know Chief, didn't know where he was, other than in Mozambique, and certainly didn't know where the heck he was going. For all Denzelle knew, the headquarters for the Seventeenth District could be in Zimbabwe, Zambia, Botswana, the Congo, Sierra Leone, or anyplace in Africa.

Chief dug around in a cooler, pulled out a cool bottle of Coca-Cola, and popped off the top with a pocket knife.

"Here, Reverend, take a few swigs off of this. It'll keep you awake until we get to the Gospel United Church district house. I also have some imported Evian water in the cooler."

Denzelle took the bottle and drained it in less than a minute.

"Thanks, man," he said.

"Chief."

"Huh?"

"Chief. That's what everybody calls me."

Denzelle wanted to ask Chief what his real name was so bad, but changed his mind when he happened to catch a glimpse of the man's biceps. They looked like something on Mr. T on *The A-Team*.

"Okay, thanks, Chief. In fact, thank you for picking me up. I didn't know what to expect when I got off of that plane."

"I bet you didn't," Chief told him and turned out of the parking area.

Denzelle knew he was safe with Chief. It wasn't because Chief looked all that safe. He was safe because he wasn't someone Chief would want to bother—which made him curious, since he knew that Chief was one of Bishop Hemphill's top employees.

He stared at the road and took in all the sights. Africa was something to see. There was no place like it on Earth. Denzelle took in the scenery for as long as he could. His eyes were so heavy and he was so tired. Before he knew it, Denzelle was sound asleep.

Chief thought the young preacher was pretty good folk, even if he was over here to get the scoop on what the bishop was up to. He could tell that this preacher was not going to let the bishop roll up in that conference in the United States with some mess that would harm folks in that church they were so enamored of.

He laughed softly, so as not to wake Rev. Flowers. The bishop had good reason to be nervous about this man coming to his home. Rev. Flowers was a federal agent—a very good federal agent, capable of taking the bishop out with one swipe.

The young preacher's holdup getting through customs didn't just happen. Chief paid the customs officers a handful of Benjamins to get as much information on Rev. Flowers as quickly as possible. Chief knew that Bishop Hemphill didn't even suspect that this man was the FBI agent he was so worried about. He just thought he was coming to spy on him for their head bishop—and he was. But this Denzelle Flowers was also coming to put a case together for some far more dangerous folk than a bishop capable of moving you to another district, or casting you out to the never-never land of being "on location."

For bishops, being located was worse than being a cop forced on leave by Internal Affairs. A located bishop's hands were tied. He didn't have a district, he was stripped of power, and he couldn't earn money. A bishop had to have a district or special Episcopal assignment to get paid. And about the only thing a located bishop could do in the Gospel United Church was put on a fancy purple clerical shirt and run around trying to look important.

Chief laughed some more. He was going to enjoy watching this play out. And he wished he could go over to America to witness the finale. This fact-finding trip was only the beginning.

The car stopped and Denzelle popped up, hand resting on the inside of his jacket, body poised for an altercation. If Chief hadn't known he was FBI before, he sure knew it now. Chief couldn't help but wonder what it must feel like to walk around with a double calling. He was about to ask the young preacher this question, but changed his mind when he remembered how fast Rev. Flowers was able to locate a gun practically in his sleep.

Denzelle was happy when Chief turned down a street and drove to an impressive stone wall that went around what had to be several acres of land. He was exhausted, hungry, and anxious to get to his room, take a warm shower, and then go to bed.

Chief pulled up to the gate and waited until two men came and swung it open. He drove into the compound, which didn't look like any of the other houses on this street. This place was incredible. Denzelle hopped out of the Land Cruiser as soon as Chief turned the engine off, and stood in the courtyard turning around in a circle, taking it all in, when it occurred to him that folks were watching him curiously.

But he couldn't help himself because the courtyard was

lovely—storybook-quality lovely. This landscape put the terrain of an English country manor to shame. Brick archways took you from the main house to a series of lovely shaded spots all over the carefully tended grounds. While the outside of the house practically yelled "English aristocracy," the house on the other hand was on the order of a fancy Italian villa in the Tuscan hills. Denzelle couldn't help but wonder what the heck the inside of the house looked like—a French chateau?

He wondered how much all of this cost. It couldn't be anywhere close to cheap, or even budget chic, with these three overpriced European styles clashing with every blink of the eye. Denzelle had seen the before pictures of the Seventeenth District's bishop's quarters. They hadn't looked anything like this. In fact, if his eyes served him right, Denzelle didn't think this house was on the same plot of land, or even in the same neighborhood.

Three of the fifteen staff members came out to greet their American guest. The cook, a woman close to Denzelle's age, was standing there eyeballing him as if he were something good to eat. He rested his hands below his belt buckle, hoping to steer her eyes in another direction. It only made her look harder. The heat from that woman's eyes was so intense, poor Denzelle feared he had contracted some kind of sunburn disease. The woman saw him blushing and mumbled, "Little American boy," loud enough for him to hear.

He almost forgot himself and grabbed at his American goods, thinking, *You let this "little American* boy" *get a hold of your behind, and you'll be mumbling all right . . . you'll be mumbling my name.*

"I do believe, Reverend," Chief said, "That you have made quite the impression on that cook. If I were you, I'd lock my door tonight."

Denzelle raised an eyebrow. He was about to blurt out, "I ain't no punk, bro," but changed his mind when it occurred to him that this Chief person would probably miss the best part of his retort.

"So where's Bishop Hemphill?" Denzelle asked, glad that the cook had gone inside with the rest of the staff.

"Inside waiting for you."

"Well, okay," was all Denzelle said. He couldn't get over being treated like this. But then, he shouldn't have been surprised. This wasn't exactly a goodwill trip. Why would the bishop want to come out to greet somebody who had been sent to find out as much dirt on him as possible?

They walked inside the most opulent house Denzelle had ever been in. It was a treat to the eyes but highly inappropriate. He had seen some beautiful countryside on the way in, but he had also seen a lot of poverty. And if his memory served him right, this was one of the districts Bishop Jennings had targeted to receive additional money to fund economic development, along with health and human services projects.

But judging from this setup, about the only thing being funded and developed was Bishop Hemphill's bank account. Denzelle now understood why the bishop lived in a compound surrounded by a stone wall with razor-sharp barbed wire at the top, and armed security guards walking around with Uzis hanging on thick straps from their shoulders. This place looked like something owned by the Mafia instead of the church. Don Corleone could have taken a few notes from Rucker Hemphill about luxury, safety, and security.

There was no way that Bishop Hemphill could live like this *and* serve the community. And what about all the preachers who worked for the Seventeenth Episcopal District? Were they getting paid? And if so, how much? Denzelle knew of preachers in some of the wealthiest districts back in the States who were not getting paid right. So it was hard to imagine that Rucker Hemphill was doing right by preachers who couldn't even afford to call the folks back home to file a complaint against the bishop and how he was handling church business.

One of the servants took Denzelle's bags, while another one led him and Chief to the library, which looked like something out of an old Sherlock Holmes movie. There was mahogany paneling all around the room, floor-to-ceiling windows with gold brocade drapes framing them, and a Persian carpet that looked as if it could have taken you on a magic carpet ride for real, it was so expensive. A massive mahogany desk and burgundy leather chair sat in front of one of the four huge windows in the room. There was a gold brocade love seat, charcoal-colored velvet chairs placed around the room, and two black-gold-and-charcoal-colored tapestries covering two walls in the huge room.

All the oil paintings were encased in gold-leaf frames. It was clear that they had been *acquired*. The cop part of Denzelle knew in his gut that not one of those pictures had been purchased properly. All the items were museum-quality pieces—and not for the "museum" started by your cousin Bootsy who used to be in the black power movement in his neighborhood back in the day.

Fresh flowers in crystal vases were placed on the gold-and-glass end tables near the chairs, and the gold-and-glass coffee tables in front of the sofas. But the best feature in the entire room was the built-in bookshelves that lined an entire wall, with those fast-rolling ladders that reached up near the twenty-foot ceilings. Denzelle wished he were alone, so that he could get on one of those ladders and roll halfway around the room.

"Pretty fancy, huh?" Chief asked solemnly.

"Yeah it is. But is the rest of the house like this?"

Chief nodded. Bishop Hemphill had never been one to half-step where his comfort was concerned.

They both sat down on one of the couches. Denzelle hoped Rucker Hemphill, who he suspected was making him wait on purpose, would hurry up and come. He was tired and suffering from jet lag, and wanted to take a shower and get in bed.

Chief hoped the bishop would hurry up and come, too. He was tired, and not in the mood for any of the bishop's antics. Chief looked at his Rolex and searched for an excuse to get up out of here.

Five minutes later Rucker Hemphill walked into the library wearing a black-gold-and-charcoal silk brocade smoking jacket over charcoal silk pajama pants, and charcoal Moroccan slippers. Denzelle thought Rucker looked as if he'd sneaked into the Playboy Mansion and stolen one of Hugh Hefner's outfits. Hugh Hefner looked odd and eccentric in his getups. Rucker Hemphill, on the other hand, just looked crazy.

Rucker adjusted the gold ascot he was wearing, and went and

sat behind his desk. He didn't make one effort to acknowledge his guests, and proceeded to shuffle through a pile of papers.

Chief had seen the bishop do some ridiculous stuff but this was a bit much, even for him. He stood up and said, "Bishop, I need to go and check on your latest shipment. I'll be back in the morning."

He turned to Denzelle and extended his hand.

"Rev. Flowers, it has been a pleasure meeting you. I hope you enjoy your stay in Mozambique. And be ready by eleven in the morning. I'm taking you and Bishop Hemphill to my great-great-uncle's farm."

Denzelle grasped Chief's hand and said, "Looking forward to going with you tomorrow."

Rucker straightened out the stack of papers, moving the stack from the right side of the desk to the left side. He pushed his chair back, stood, and came from around the desk. He had to work hard not to bust out into a huge grin. He had been hoping for another trip to the farm for weeks, and couldn't wait to get out there and see that woman.

Chief knew exactly what to say to be able to leave. He watched Denzelle take in the bishop's reaction as if he were one of those IBM home computers having information put in it to form a database. That preacher was good—dangerous, but good. Chief was happy that he and Denzelle didn't have a reason to face off. He was starting to like the young American, and didn't want to have to kill him.

Rucker walked over to Denzelle, shook his hand, and welcomed him to the Seventeenth Episcopal District. This behavior was a 180-degree turnaround from the cold and imperious posture the bishop had taken just minutes ago. But once that greeting was done with, Rucker tried to come up with every excuse imaginable to send the good reverend up to his suite, so that he could have some time to talk to Chief, who he knew was ready to leave, about tomorrow.

Denzelle didn't miss a thing. And if he did nothing else while he was there, he'd be ready to go to this farm when Chief came a-calling. He knew in his heart that a lot of what he needed to know was out at that great-great-uncle's farm. Denzelle had met Bishop

Hemphill on only a few occasions when he traveled back home to the States. He had found the bishop to be pompous and particular. He didn't even think the man was capable of smiling, and here the negro was grinning from ear to ear. Denzelle absolutely couldn't wait to get "his self" out to that farm.

SEVEN

Denzelle was beginning to wonder if they were ever going get to this farm. It was so far out, he was certain they were on their way to the original middle of nowhere. Denzelle had almost left his pistol back at the compound. He was glad that he had not done that, and was strapped. A brother didn't need to be out traveling like this without some backup. Being a federal agent came in handy when traveling. He could flash a badge and official papers and get his gear through just about any airport security system. Denzelle didn't travel anywhere without his stuff. And sitting in this car driving all over Africa made him happy to have what was on each of his ankles.

He couldn't wait to get to this place to find out what had the bishop so excited about coming. He knew all about the so-called import business Bishop Hemphill was running. Hemphill told folks that it was to raise money. But Denzelle knew it was one of the cool and safe spots for a smuggling ring based in America and Europe. There was no way the business ventures Bishop Hemphill had described in his Episcopal reports to the denomination could support his lifestyle.

The one thing that concerned Denzelle was whom Rucker Hemphill was working with. Smuggling was a very dangerous business, run by some pretty scary folk. And if the bishop was not careful he could find himself swimming in some deep, shark-infested water with a bucket of somebody's blood thrown all over him.

Denzelle's boss, Greg Williams, had given him an extensive

overview of the gun smuggling that had a direct link to Chief, and to some extent to Bishop Ottah Babatunde in Nigeria. Denzelle didn't think that Bishop Hemphill was the sharpest knife in the drawer, and figured he probably didn't know all the ins and outs of this business.

This smuggling ring was proving to be far more lucrative than anything the FBI had previously thought it to be. And if the bishop, who was kind of stupid and full of it, was making the kind of money displayed in his lavish home, he had to be getting closer and closer to dealing with some people he would do well to leave alone.

Denzelle was struggling to stay awake. He was tired and the breeze coming through the windows wasn't helping any. He closed his eyes, his head went back, and then his neck jerked, bringing Denzelle out of the nap that had slipped up on him. He sat up straight and forced himself to snap out of that slumber, brain clicking, as he began to process some information.

He knew that Bishop Hemphill was about as interested in being a smuggler as he was in taking it upon himself to clean that house he lived in. True, the bishop relished all the goods he had acquired. But he was a cash man—the kind of brother who didn't feel right unless he had his hand wrapped around a thick wad of hundred-dollar bills. The bishop wasn't trying to find a place in the ranks of the smuggling trade. What he really wanted was something that would put hard, cold cash (lots of it) in his hand to use to purchase some things that couldn't be displayed in a house.

Chief turned onto the grassy road leading to the main section of the farm. Denzelle hadn't missed Chief's watch or the quality of his shoes and the cut of his clothes. He had also noticed how self-assured and comfortable the man was around wealth and power. Now he understood, looking at all of this land. This farm was not the property of a poor agrarian African family. These people were rich and they had been rich for a very long time.

They pulled up to the main house, which Denzelle suspected held a lot of surprises on the inside. He smiled and thought about how many black people back home were always careful not to display too much of their actual wealth. It was always better to let people think that you didn't have anywhere near what you actually possessed.

Denzelle glanced over at the bishop and knew that he was not in the know about who this family really was. Shame—because these were some people a sensible bishop would want to come to the church, get saved, and become some powerful allies to the Seventeenth District. The operative word, however, was *sensible*. Judging from that outfit Bishop Hemphill had been sporting yesterday, he didn't appear to have a reasonable supply of sensibility.

Chief hopped out of the Land Cruiser and went to embrace Uncle Lee Lee. It had been over a week since he'd been out here, and he was eager to be back home. While he liked being in an urban area, the folks working for the Americans' Seventeenth Episcopal District got on his nerves. Plus, Chief missed his wife, who was standing there with open arms. He ran to those arms, savoring the love and security he felt. His mistresses offered good comfort. But none of them could hold a candle to his wife.

Chief held his wife close, and then remembered his home training. He let her go, reluctantly, to introduce Rev. Flowers to his great-great-uncle—the patriarch of their family. He was about to present the bishop to Uncle Lee Lee. But Rucker had hopped out of the Land Cruiser, too, and run across the road to where his uncle's wife's sister lived, before Chief could open his mouth. He started to send one of his nephews to get the bishop, but changed his mind when Uncle Lee Lee's sister-in-law ran out of her house and into Rucker's arms.

Chief cracked a crooked grin and shrugged when Rev. Flowers stared at him with raised eyebrows. Clearly, there were things on this farm that Rucker Hemphill lusted after. One was that fine-looking woman across the street. The other was big enough to get him out here in the boonies. That second reason had to be a doozy to get Bishop Hemphill out in the country. Rucker Hemphill didn't look like the kind of black man who liked being in the country—on either side of the Atlantic Ocean.

Uncle Lee Lee liked Denzelle the moment he shook the young preacher's hand. At first he wished that he had been the one sent to run the Seventeenth Episcopal District, then quickly reneged on that notion when it dawned on him that Rev. Flowers was smart, shrewd, and an honest man. He liked that but didn't want to have to do business with him around. Plus, the preacher had too many ways like a cop for his comfort.

Denzelle liked Uncle Lee Lee, too. This was a smart man, with his feet planted firmly on all of this good, rich African soil. And when Uncle Lee Lee told him his age, Denzelle had to take a second look at this old man, with that fine and lush-looking woman hanging on his arm. Ninety-five years old and pimping like a big dog in his prime. What in the world was this old man up to? And more importantly, what did it have to do with Rucker Hemphill? He caught Chief watching him and quickly reined in his curiosity. Denzelle liked Chief but didn't want to ever have to get into an altercation with the man, and then have to kill him.

After a delicious lunch and a good nap, Denzelle woke up to discover that Bishop Hemphill, Chief, and Uncle Lee Lee were sequestered in a back room talking about something he definitely wanted to hear. He eased down the hall and tried to find a safe place to eavesdrop but changed his mind when he noticed that two of those very friendly relatives he'd eaten lunch with earlier were close by with guns in shoulder holsters.

"Umph," Denzelle muttered to himself, "these people have their own militia."

"Is there anything we can do for you, preacher?" one of the men asked. He had a very thick accent, which caught Denzelle by surprise. He had gotten used to listening to Chief's and Uncle Lee Lee's impeccable English.

"I was looking for somebody to hang out with," Denzelle answered, thinking that was such a lame explanation, and then relaxed when he realized they weren't sure what he was talking about. Both men were now looking at him as if he had one of those little tiny boogers hanging on the tip of his nose.

"I mean, I was wondering if anyone was up for showing me around, a game of cards, or just sitting on that nice porch and talking. I'm bored silly."

"No one available for that, preacher. But you are our guest, and welcome to walk around the land at your leisure. This is a lovely farm and you can entertain yourself with nature."

Denzelle sighed and nodded. He'd learned a long time ago about trying to argue with some Africans who had already made their point. He said, "Thanks, man," went back to his room, and sat down. Maybe he needed to read his Bible.

"Naaahhh," Denzelle mumbled, and surveyed his surroundings. No TV. No radio. He lay back on the bed with his hands behind his head, staring at the ceiling. That got old quick. He sat up. Maybe a stroll around this farm would be just what the doctor ordered.

Denzelle picked up his shades and headed out to explore the farm before one of those brothers decided that he didn't need to be cooped up in that room, and took him on a walk around the farm at gunpoint. Denzelle had been pissed off when they told him to go for a walk and then started laughing at him. But now he looked upward and thanked the good Lord for this blessing in disguise.

He didn't need to be with anyone right now. He knew in his gut that what he needed to know was out there on this land. He walked around, enjoying the sights. This really was some beautiful land.

Denzelle walked quite a distance before deciding to head back to the main house. He would use his compass to help him find his way back, using a slightly different route. He felt a nudge from the Lord, urging him to go south, which was down and away from the main enclave of family and their houses. There was something in this section of the farm, which was confirmed by the rows and rows and rows of every kind of watermelon imaginable. He had never seen this many watermelons in his life.

It didn't take Denzelle long to roll up on that old raggedy shed. It was in sharp contrast to the other buildings, which though simple and unassuming, were very well kept. This thing looked as if it would crumble to the ground if you ran your palm across the side. The Lord nudged at him a second time, and Denzelle knew that he wasn't supposed to be anywhere near this shed.

He looked around and made sure that no one was nearby before stepping onto the porch. He stood there for a moment debating whether or not he should go inside. He knew it was okay when the nudge in his spirit was so strong Denzelle felt as if a hand had shoved him up on that rickety porch and to the front door.

Denzelle reached out toward the doorknob and then suddenly drew back in fear. What if the door was locked, and then the floor gave way under the weight of his muscular frame? That would be very embarrassing and could get him shot, or his butt kicked. He breathed in and out, looking up, and whispered, "Can a preacher get some help down here?"

Suddenly his heart was flooded with the words from 2 Timothy 1:7.

For God has not given us a spirit of fear, but of power and of love and of a sound mind.

Denzelle felt relief pour all over him and he closed his eyes, whispering, "Thank You, Lord." He tested the floorboards and discovered that the building was a whole lot sturdier than it looked—a revelation that made him more determined to go inside and investigate. There was something in here.

He saw those huge spiders as soon as he walked in. It was a pretty good deterrent but Denzelle wasn't scared of spiders like most people. Plus, he was well educated on the various species, and had studied up on the bugs and spiders in Mozambique before getting on that plane. Nonetheless, he still didn't want one of those bad boys hopping all over him.

Most of the spiders were over near a shelf with some grubby-looking pickle jars filled to the brim with nasty-looking grayish-brown powder. He opened the top of one of the jars.

"Good laaawwwd," he exclaimed, and then remembered to lower his voice. "Whew...eeeee...that is some funky stuff. Smells like butt, toe jams, and stanky underarms."

Denzelle pulled out a handkerchief and wiped at his eyes. He'd never smelled anything like that that wasn't in the toilet waiting to be flushed away. He swallowed hard and braced himself. He took in a deep breath, dipped a fingertip into the jar, and put the tiniest amount possible on the tip of his tongue. Denzelle gagged and put his hand over his mouth to make sure it didn't come back up and out onto the floor. It tasted three times worse than it smelled.

But on the bright side, he knew it wasn't poison. People didn't leave lethal poisons out for the simple reason that if they had the poison, they intended to use it and/or sell it for profit. And if they were planning on doing either of those two activities, they wouldn't want that stuff lying around so that the law or some enemies could find it.

His stomach was queasy and he felt as if he might have a huge bout of diarrhea. But in less than a minute he started feeling better. And in roughly three minutes Denzelle Flowers was feeling like a million bucks. He was glad this stuff wasn't poison because he sure would have been a dead man, it worked so fast.

Denzelle's achy shoulders and his legs, tired from the guns weighing down his ankles, felt better. The mild headache, which had been bothering him all day, was gone. And even though he was still tired, he noticed that he was feeling unusually energetic. In fact, he felt he could run around this farm several times without giving a thought to stopping.

As nasty as this stuff tasted, Denzelle couldn't help but wonder why Uncle Lee Lee was hiding it. He wished he could run out and talk to Uncle Lee Lee himself, and ask him about this stuff, and then find out what it would take for the man to go the legitimate route and patent it. He thought about the potential benefits for fellow FBI agents who were working long hours under very dangerous conditions, and soldiers in combat situations. He could make a killing if this old man would work with him.

Denzelle was excited and decided that he was going to find a way to broach the subject with Uncle Lee Lee. He put the top back on the jar and walked to the door, peeping out the broken window to make sure that no one was close enough to see him coming out of the shed. When all was clear, he eased the door of the rickety shed open, then stopped dead in his tracks when he noticed himself poking the door with such potency it sounded as if he were knocking on it with his fist.

Denzelle looked down past his waist, eyes stopping right above his thighs, and almost screamed. He'd never seen anything like it—not on his body. He hadn't even known there was that much to him. And it would have been an impressive sight, if a fine and sexy sister from his home state of North Carolina had been standing there to ooohh and ahhh over this remarkable scenery. But that was not the case, and here he was standing in this predicament without anyone to appreciate the view. Sometimes life was not fair.

Right now, however, he needed his body and his mind to be at one—not going in completely opposite directions. So Denzelle tried to distract his own body by thinking about every ugly girl who had tried to get next to him. It didn't work, though. He was in such a rigid state that thoughts of the ugly girls made things worse—they were, after all, girls. And in the dark, they could become cute for a second or two.

The situation wasn't getting better. And it threatened to get worse when he heard people outside the shed, and it was clear that they were looking for him. He slipped all the way back inside and eased away from the windows, hoping that one of those big spiders wouldn't get on him.

Someone walked up on the porch, looked around, and then walked off. Denzelle let out a deep breath. He began to pray that his body would be restored to the state it had been in before he walked his big bad self up in this messed-up shed and tasted the powder from Hell. He heard them calling his name, and was relieved to know that Chief sounded worried. That was good. They would be more likely to believe him when he gave them the sob and woeful "I got lost" tale.

That boy let those people look for him for another twenty minutes, until he was sure that his body had receded to a more normal and comfortable state. He sneaked back out of the shed and wandered around, following their voices. Then, he decided it was time they found him. They all looked relieved when Denzelle appeared, looking like he was so happy to see them. Chief was glad the young preacher had not found that shed, and couldn't believe he had been dumb enough to go off alone in a place he knew nothing about.

Chief patted Denzelle on the shoulder and said, "You Americans are so impetuous—always running off to explore something new. You better be more thoughtful before you go off like that next time, preacher. Remember, the last time some Africans walked off like that, they were shipped across the water to become Americans."

"Sorry, Chief," Denzelle said, hoping he looked contrite and relieved to be found. He was glad to be around a bunch of men because they would be less likely to look at the part of his body capable of displaying the last remnant of the effects of that powder. Well, he certainly hoped they wouldn't want to look at him like that.

When they got back to the house, he would have been home free if they had not gone past Uncle Lee Lee's wife's sister. She sneaked a look at the young pastor and winked when she knew no one was paying attention to her. She liked the bishop but he was an older man. The powder worked wonders for him. And she could only imagine what remarkable things it would do for a man Rev. Flowers's age.

While the rest of the evening was pleasant enough, Denzelle was more than ready to go back to Bishop Hemphill's compound, and even more ready to get to the airport so he could put his feet on American soil.

Despite finding the miracle potion, Denzelle hadn't found anything that could be used to snatch Rucker Hemphill out of this spot and sanction him to the never-never land of being a located bishop. Because he knew that is exactly what Bishop Jennings was planning to do—and that he wanted to get this unpleasant task over with before the Triennial General Conference began.

Now, the FBI? They were after something completely different. Denzelle's boss, Greg Williams, had started getting more disturbing reports that one of the smuggling cartel's command centers in North Carolina was looking to become the hot spot for drug trafficking. And Greg was beginning to get concerned that somebody in the Gospel United Church's group of Africa-based bishops would in some way aid and abet this endeavor.

Even though Denzelle had seen a lot, he hadn't seen enough for Agent Williams to get a warrant to search the alleged supply centers in North Carolina. But what he had seen made him suspicious that Bishop Hemphill was going to get Chief's family to fix him up with enough of that nasty powder to take to the Triennial General Conference in Durham. And since Denzelle was a praying man, he knew when the Lord was trying to tell him something.

Chief had them up and out early the next morning. He knew the bishop was anxious to get back to the compound because an extra shipment was due in by late evening. He glanced back at Denzelle, who was trying to get comfortable in the backseat of the Land Cruiser. The more he thought about it, the less he believed that Denzelle had gotten lost. He just hoped that the preacher had not gone to their new storage building and found all of that stuff from the shipment that had just come in. He liked the young preacher, and would definitely have had to kill him—which would have made him sad.

Denzelle, who didn't want to be bothered with Bishop Hemphill, stretched out across the backseat and closed his eyes. Rucker pulled out a cigar and trimmed the end. He loved a good cigar on a long ride. Chief put on an Anita Baker cassette tape. He loved the way that woman sang. She had a voice that made him think of the sky, late on a starry night. And listening to Anita Baker would make the trip back to the compound seem shorter, and definitely more pleasant. He'd been waiting on this tape, and was happy to find out it had come in with the last shipment.

Denzelle was a guest of Bishop Hemphill for a week. He was ready to go back home but couldn't leave until he could get a good flight out and hopefully get more information than he'd accumulated so far. On day six Chief came by and went off with the bishop to the library. This time there were no relatives with guns guarding anything, and Denzelle was determined to find out what the deal was with the bishop and this family.

He knew that wherever it was, Chief and the bishop were going to discuss it in that library. At first, Denzelle tried walking back and forth in front of the closed library door. But that got old quick when a servant kept asking him if he needed anything. He thought about sitting down in a chair near the door, then changed his mind. That would be more conspicuous than pacing at the door.

There had to be a way to get this information without drawing attention to himself. There was. Denzelle went outside and found a seat on one of Rucker Hemphill's fancy stone benches near an open window. He couldn't believe his good fortune. It was a library window. Denzelle couldn't have had it better than this, if he had gone and opened the window himself. He could hear everything.

Denzelle had been right, too. That potion-powder stuff was the key. Chief wanted full control over the smuggling when Hemphill went back to the States for good. It was clear that Chief wasn't interested in anything crossing the Atlantic. All Chief wanted from the bishop was full control over the import business. And the bishop was ready to give up his import business in exchange for getting as much of that powder stuff as he could when he left for Durham en route to the Triennial Conference. It was the plan to bring loads of the powder into the States that concerned Denzelle, as he would quickly discover that something was terribly wrong with this "miracle" drug.

It was during what Denzelle had planned on being the next-to-last evening at Bishop Hemphill's home that he discovered something very disturbing about the potion-powder. He had been feeling energetic and rested but now Denzelle was so exhausted he was concerned that he was coming down with a nasty virus. In fact, the last time he had felt this bad was when he had the flu and was flat on his back for two weeks. The last place he wanted to be sick was this far from home. Denzelle's head hurt, he had a fever, every muscle in his body ached, and he was so sleepy his eyelids hurt when he tried to open them.

He dragged down to the kitchen and found Rucker there scooping some powder out of a scuzzy-looking glass jar that was in stark contrast to the otherwise immaculate area.

"Bishop, you wouldn't have any Tylenol, would you?"

Rucker poured some whiskey into the glass with the powder in it. Denzelle sniffed the air. It smelled just as bad as Uncle Lee Lee's shed when he took the lid off that old pickle jar.

"This is some funky stuff," Rucker told him. "But it will get rid of everything that ails you, preacher."

Denzelle raised his hand and said, "Bishop, I just need some Tylenol, that's all."

"Tylenol? You want that weak stuff?"

Rucker took a long swig of the whiskey and ground his teeth together. His eyes started to water when he forced the rest of the whiskey down.

"Whew...nasty. But if you want to feel better, you need some of this stuff."

The last thing Denzelle wanted was some of *that* stuff. He'd rather go back to his room and suffer through the flu cold turkey. Cold turkey—of course. How could he have missed that? He didn't have the flu. He had a terrible case of withdrawal. And judging from the way the bishop was sweating and heaving as if he was trying not to hurl, he was, too.

That had to be some potent stuff, if that little dab on his tongue had caused all this suffering. The powder may have worked for Uncle Lee Lee, who he suspected had some kind of antidote that counteracted the highly addictive qualities of the powder. But this drug was not something to mess with on its own. And you certainly couldn't be dumb enough to think that you could get away with using it on a regular basis.

This powder was highly addictive, and it would be like a dangerous weapon if placed in the wrong hands, like the ones holding on to the old pickle jar on the table. Denzelle hoped that stuff would start working fast. Because Bishop Hemphill gave him the impression that he was a hurl away from throwing up all over his fancy Italian marble floor.

What was it about crooked folk? They always had to have the best, the top of the line, or the rarest of the rare. It was ridiculous and evil. Here they were standing on marble, and the bishop's neighbors lived in houses with worn-out, or, better yet, dirt floors. It was downright shameful.

It wasn't surprising that the membership rolls for the Seventeenth District had been dropping steadily ever since Rucker Hemphill became the presiding bishop. Who would want to join a church where the bishop lived in a huge mansion with a bunch of fancy stuff, while you had to do the best you could with your little bitty shanty. Plus, just how much church work could Bishop Hemphill do, now that he had a monkey on his back?

Denzelle was convicted down to the bone when he remembered his thoughts about figuring out how to sell that powder in the States. He closed his eyes and whispered, "Lord, forgive me. I did not know what I was doing."

"Are you okay, Rev. Flowers?" Bishop Hemphill asked him in the nicest voice Denzelle had heard coming out of his mouth since he had first gotten there.

"Not really, Bishop. I still feel like crap. And I have yet to find a Tylenol tablet. Can you help me out here?"

Rucker fixed himself another glass of that stuff. Only this time it was mostly liquor. He said, "You sure you don't want any of this stuff? I guarantee that you'll feel a whole better."

"Naw . . . that's okay, Bishop. I don't like the way that stuff smells. It would be like drinking an eight-ounce glass of butt-juice."

"Man up, son. Everything can't taste like fruit punch."

"But it doesn't have to taste like something that fell off the garbage truck," Denzelle told him.

Rucker frowned. He hated being reminded that the stuff was horrible. The only way he could take it was to mix it into some whiskey.

It occurred to Denzelle that the bishop had taken a lot of the potion. He hoped that the liquor would slow down Rucker Hemphill's body's reaction to that stuff. No brother needed to see something like that—especially at such a close visual range. Heck, you tried not to shoot folks when they were too close to you because it could be one nasty mess. And you definitely didn't want to get a zoom-lens view of that stuff on another man's body. That was enough to make a brother feel that he needed to put some Novocain on his eyeballs to numb them from the pain of having to see all of that.

All of a sudden the maid, who Denzelle had discerned was the eyes and ears of the bishop, rushed into the kitchen. She pretended to load up the dishwasher, which Denzelle found a bit unusual. The folks in houses surrounding Rucker Hemphill's didn't seem to have the kind of plumbing that was dishwasher-friendly.

The maid brushed by the bishop, gave him a sultry smile, and then looked at Denzelle as if to say, "You're dismissed."

He couldn't believe this heifer, with her head all wrapped up with that fancy piece of material. There was no way she was going to get away with that bama mess, and he didn't care if he was in Africa. He said, "Bishop, I had hoped to be able to say hello to Mrs. Hemphill before I headed back to the States."

"Well, son, that won't be possible. The missus decided not to stop by here, and went on to Paris to shop. She will be back in the States in a week or two to show off her new Parisian clothes."

"Hate that I missed her," Denzelle said. "But maybe I'll run into her when I get back home."

The maid rolled her eyes at him, and Denzelle resisted an urge to stick out his tongue at that mean woman and say, "Na...na... nanana."

"I hope that spoiled American woman never comes here," the maid grumbled under her breath.

Rucker heard the maid and said, "Girl, you better watch your mouth talking about my baby like that."

The maid, who had honestly believed the bishop preferred her over his own wife, said, "Your baby? Bishop, you cannot be serious."

Bishop Hemphill's eyes narrowed. He said, "Mrs. Hemphill is my baby, and she'll be that until the day she dies. Now, do you have a problem with that? Or do I have to send out for someone else?"

It was that "do I have to send out for someone else" that did it. The woman blinked back tears before she mumbled an apology, and then followed Rucker Hemphill out of the kitchen.

Denzelle didn't like this powder. And he especially didn't like it that Uncle Lee Lee had left out the most important ingredient—the one that made the drug a welcome supplement rather than a lethal substance. And he knew something was missing because that old man's male relatives took that stuff.

He had seen the men putting teaspoonfuls of the powder into their tea like it was sugar. He had wondered if the sugar was going bad because there was a point when the room smelled like the crack of somebody's butt. Those men had sipped a lot of that stuff, and remained okay and in control of their bodies the entire evening. They worked the version of the potion they took. It didn't work them.

Not one of those men showed any immediate "reactions." He also noticed that they didn't get nauseated right after taking it. Rucker Hemphill had needed some whiskey to get his dose down—but those folks had only tea, if that.

He went back to his room feeling horrible, and decided to just go cold turkey and suffer it out. Cold turkey was a hard way to go. But it was one of the most effective methods of purging your system of a drug.

There was a soft knock on the door right before another maid, who was a very sweet and anointed woman, walked in carrying a tray with a pot of tea, some broth, and saltines on it.

"Rev. Flowers," she said, "I made this especially for you. Eat what you can of the broth, and then drink this tea every two hours. It will make you feel better."

Denzelle wasn't so sure about taking another thing on Mozambique soil. He stared at the teapot as if it had some kind of toxic waste in it. The maid started laughing.

"You Americans are so funny and so suspicious of your African brothers and sisters. This tea is made from ginger root, some peppermint, honey, and just a tiny bit of chamomile to help you rest better through the night. And I also blessed it in the name of Jesus, so that it will aid in a speedy recovery.

"I know all about WP21, Rev. Flowers. It is a vicious and wicked drug. I also know about the powder that Chief's great-great-uncle makes only for his family. It is better, but not that much better. They do experience some mild withdrawal symptoms if they decide to stop taking it. But I've never known anybody to get addicted to it like it is heroin or something like that, until I saw its effect on the bishop.

"Rev. Flowers, do not let them get that stuff in the United States, and especially around our beloved church members. I do not like the bishop but I do keep him lifted in prayer for his sake, Mrs. Hemphill's sake, and this district. He is a bad leader and the Seventeenth District deserves better than someone like him. I don't know why our church will not pull from the cream of the crop right here on African soil to lead our district."

Denzelle blinked back hot tears. This woman had spoken the truth—a hard truth that all the preachers in the Gospel United Church needed to hear and take heed of. How had they gone so low that he was over here in Africa suffering from the aftereffects of a drug some preachers were trying to take to the US, and use to get rich and powerful in the denomination?

Rucker Hemphill and his cronies wouldn't even have to go outside the denomination to make money from WP21. All they needed was a loyal and hooked following to make this work. And the best place to get all that established was at a major gathering of church folk like the Triennial General Conference. They could put on some good-looking sheep outfits and blend in with the folks who were there for all the right reasons, to do as much wrong as they could. Denzelle's older brother, Yarborough, always told him that the Devil liked to go to church because that's where he could do the most damage. He already had the folks at the club and in the streets.

It was no secret that some preachers came to these conferences to do stuff they had no business doing. They could prance around in their preacher suits, mop their faces with some handkerchiefs, talk shop, and network, all the while scoping out women and opportunities to get into something better than a conference session. And unfortunately there were plenty of women who were willing and able to go the whole nine yards. It was a perfect setting to capitalize on WP21.

On the surface this thing appeared kind of Mickey Mouse, for a bunch of old players past their prime. But in reality it was a very dangerous game, and nothing good would come from it. Denzelle's heart was heavy. He loved his church and could not abide anyone doing anything that threatened its well-being. He got down on his knees and began to pray.

"Lord," he whispered, "Help me to help my church in the name of Jesus. Let no weapon formed against the Gospel United Church prosper. I cancel out this assignment of the enemy against this church in the name of Jesus, amen."

He wiped his eyes and stayed there on his knees until he felt the power of God touching him in his heart. He didn't have a clue how all of this would work out, or even play out for that matter. But he did know that no matter what happened, how it looked, or even what it seemed like, God was running this show. Now all the good Rev. Agent Flowers had to do was keep his heart in tune with Heaven, and his eyes focused on Jesus.

Denzelle drank a cup of that tea. It did work wonders. He climbed into bed and rested better than he had since getting off that plane. As soon as his feet touched American soil he was going to his mentor, Rev. Eddie Tate, his best friend, Rev. Obadiah Quincey, and his supervisor, Agent Gregory Williams. Together, with God's help and guidance, they were going to stop this mess right when it started.

As far as Denzelle was concerned, Ottah Babatunde, Ray Caruthers, and Rucker Hemphill were not coming back to America to pawn off some jacked-up male super-drug on more church folk. They were not using that potion to make a quick and easy buck, and to collect enough dirt on some dumb and reckless preachers to buy votes, presiding elder spots, Episcopal seats, and an Episcopal district or two. This kind of scheming hadn't worked back in the 1960s when Ray's dad had tried to do the very same thing, and it wasn't going to work twenty-three years after the good preachers in the denomination had shut those crooks in clerical collars down. He thought about the singer Ann Peebles, and started humming, "I'm gone tear your playhouse down."

Denzelle Flowers and his colleagues had their work cut out for them both on the natural and on the spiritual level. Bishops Jennings

and James were right. The only way to defeat and destroy the stronghold he saw the enemy building around the church was to put as many
right-minded folk in Episcopal seats as they could. They needed more
good bishops to effectively counteract the mayhem caused by the bad
ones, and ignored by the double-minded ones who also wanted the
extra money, access to the available and willing women, and choice
church assignments, all without getting their hands dirty—even
though they were incapable of keeping them clean.

Both Bishop Murcheson James and Bishop Percy Jennings had
been riding Denzelle's boss, Rev. Eddie Tate, to run for bishop at
the Triennial Conference. Two Episcopal seats were up for grabs,
and Eddie was a formidable opponent who would blow holes in the
enemy camp. Denzelle only wished his friend, Obadiah's mentor,
Rev. Theophilus Simmons, would run, too, instead of volunteering
to serve as Eddie's campaign manager. He didn't know why Theophilus Simmons, who had been groomed and tapped as one of the
next Episcopal leaders, had decided not to run for bishop.

Denzelle walked out of the terminal to board the plane. He was
happy to be leaving Mozambique, and couldn't wait for the plane to
take off and fly him home. This had been one of the worst trips he'd
had to take in a long time. He was about to whisper, "Thank You,
God, for taking me back home," when he turned around to see the
maid who had given him that tea when he was so sick. She and her
husband and children were waving at him with huge smiles lighting
up their faces.

This trip had been to a church district, and Denzelle had not
met one truly "churched" person since he first set foot on Mozambique soil. And he certainly hadn't met anybody who struck him as
being saved and filled with the Holy Ghost. That is, not until this
moment. How had he missed this in this lady? She'd been nothing
but kind, and had made it clear that she prayed for people—even
her enemies. Denzelle realized that he had been so wrapped up in
himself and his issues that he had failed to see the blessing God had
put right at his feet in the form of this anointed lady. To think that
she thought enough of him to come with her family to see him off
touched his heart deeply.

Denzelle smiled and waved. His heart was full and flooding with the joy of the Lord. In the midst of all of the darkness he'd seen over the past week, light was piercing through. His heart brimmed over with love for his new friends. Denzelle waved back one more time and boarded the plane.

EIGHT

Denzelle's plane landed at Dulles Airport. He rented a car and drove down to Quantico to meet with Greg Williams. Throughout the entire interview, Greg sat there looking at Denzelle as if he had an extra head sprouting out of his shoulder.

When Denzelle gave his boss the skinny on how WP21 worked, Greg almost fell out of his chair, he was laughing so hard. He slapped the desk, wiped at his eyes, and said, "My man, my man. Agent Flowers, I swear I thought I'd heard it all. Preachers?"

"Actually, it was a bishop," Denzelle told him, trying his best to keep a straight "agent" face. He'd been upset the entire flight back. And now, after hearing himself talk about that stuff, he had to admit that it was some funny mess.

"I still can't believe that some preachers, who don't know anything about dealing and the streets, have come up with a cockamamy scheme like this," Denzelle continued. "And they are just dumb, greedy, and crazy enough to think that they can pull it off when they get stateside."

"I know," Greg said, finally sobering up when he thought about the potential harm WP21 could do if it were turned loose on folks as a street drug. It was funny to hear how WP21 worked. But that stuff was highly addictive and lethal. And it would become something akin to chemical warfare against American citizens, if some brilliant souls decided that they could make even more money if they used cheaper and synthetic materials to make larger batches of the stuff. They were already up to their armpits with the crack cocaine epidemic—a drug that had morphed just as this WP21 had the potential to do.

"So what do you suggest we do, sir?" Denzelle asked. "Because our one advantage is that we have the rare opportunity to stop this before it starts."

Greg's first choice was to be waiting for the bishops when their feet touched American soil, dangling a Bible in one hand and handcuffs in the other. But that would be jumping ahead of the game. While he could get a few wayward souls, he risked missing the chance to catch the "big dawgs" and annihilate the entire operation. Greg knew that the best thing he could do was give them some rope, wait, and watch. He said, "Agent Flowers, we are going to let them get the stuff the best way they can. I suspect they will have to use more than one strategy because they do not know what the heck they are doing. And that's a good thing. Because it will lead us straight to the people who will be going crazy to get in on this operation. Folks like the Dinkle brothers in western North Carolina, who have connections with the Southern-based drug cartel leaders who have been slipping by us for years."

"But sir, what about the innocent people who will take that drug?"

"What about them?" Greg asked Denzelle coldly. "I hope that some of the preachers in your denomination, and most of those church folk, have sense enough to bypass something like this."

"But..."

Greg raised his hands. He'd heard enough.

"Agent Flowers, you are a preacher. How about you getting on your knees and asking the Lord to protect those folks while we do our jobs? Isn't God big and strong enough to do that?"

Denzelle nodded. God was all that and more.

"I had hoped that would be your answer," Greg said. "You know I'm not much on church because I just don't see why I need to be there if I am a decent person. And to be honest, I want to see if God can do all that you've been telling me He can do at this conference."

"Sir, we shouldn't put the Lord to a foolish test."

"Denzelle, I'm not putting the Lord to a test, I'm asking Him to put the rubber to the road and let me see Him work. That's all—I just want to witness this mysterious move of God, the hand of God, in my work."

Denzelle didn't know what to say. Gregory Williams was one of those smart brothers who loved to preach on some weak form of humanism. And now he wanted to know if God was as big and real and powerful as church people told him He was. He said, "Sir, the Lord just laid this on my heart. He said to tell you that you will see Him work. And it will be in the land of the living."

Greg frowned as he tried to grapple with what Denzelle had just said. Working with an agent who was also an ordained preacher was an experience like no other. You never knew when the brother would be a preacher, a cop, or a little bit of both.

"Sir, I'll call you as soon as I have a chance to meet with my church people," Denzelle told him and left. He had another plane to catch to St. Louis, so that he could talk to his field officers on the church side of this sting. Only these superiors didn't wear bullet-proof vests, they were clothed in the full armor of God.

But that debriefing would have to wait. As soon as Denzelle got off the plane at Lambert Airport, he saw Obadiah was waiting for him at baggage claim looking upset. He said, "Everything all right, Obie, man? You look like somebody just died."

"Somebody did just die," Obadiah told him, with tears in his eyes.

Denzelle searched the carousel for his bags. None had showed up yet.

"Bishop..."

Obadiah shook his head.

"No, none of our own people. It's Mr. David Green."

Denzelle looked puzzled. He could not place Mr. David Green, even though he knew he should have been able to if Obadiah was at the airport waiting for him and upset.

"Old Daddy," Obadiah told him.

"Old Daddy, Old Daddy?" Denzelle asked in disbelief. "The president of the Mellow Slick Cougar's Club, Old Daddy?" he asked a second time, trying to digest what he'd just been told.

Obadiah nodded and wiped at his eye. He loved Old Daddy. He had learned a lot talking to him. And even though Old Daddy was over a hundred years old, he was still a top-notch player and full of vitality and life. Obadiah wondered if this is what the "back in the Bible day folk" felt when people like Jacob, Joseph, Moses, Joshua, and David died.

Old Daddy, or David Green, was the ultimate North St. Louis player. At a hundred plus he was still spry and fashionably dressed in the latest men's apparel. There was never a day when David Green wasn't dressed in a suit—three-piece, leisure, two-piece ensembles in peach, mint, purple, turquoise, yellow, and the definitive player color, red. He had a pair of gators to match every suit, and enough hats to start a millinery shop.

He had been healthy and active, and a hard worker in the men's ministry program at his church home, Gethsemane Missionary Baptist Church, where Rev. George Wilson, Rev. Theophilus Simmons's good friend, was the senior pastor. And with the exception of cataract surgery four years ago, Old Daddy rarely had so much as a cold. But one day he started running a fever, passed out, and never regained consciousness.

Old Daddy's wife, Warlene Green, was so distraught she had to be hospitalized. And her best friend, Queenie Roper, had to take charge of her young son, Isaac David Green, or "Lil' Old Daddy," as he was so affectionately known at church. It always shocked people to learn first of all that Warlene, who was well into her fifties, had given birth to a healthy baby boy, and two that the baby's daddy was really Old Daddy. There was no hanky-panky going on behind Old Daddy's back. Because as Warlene proudly told any woman up in her business, or any man trying to hit on her, Old Daddy took care of home *real good*.

Plenty of times folks still questioned Old Daddy's ability to pull that off—not to mention how Warlene squeezed back the effects of the change just long enough to get that baby. But the older Lil' Old Daddy became, looking more and more like his dad, the more folks shut up and left that matter alone.

Even though the folks at Gethsemane Missionary Baptist Church loved them dearly, they still sneaked and called Old Daddy and Warlene "Abraham and Sarah" behind their backs. And those two didn't help matters when they announced that the baby's real name was Isaac. And if that was not enough, Isaac was old-acting. Plus, they dressed him like a little man in suits, baby gators, and little hats just like his daddy. That baby looked old, even though he was technically only six. One of Gethsemane's older members, Louise Williams Loomis, would look at little Isaac and say, "Didn't they know that two old people didn't need to have a baby because the baby would come out looking like he old."

Denzelle's bags finally popped up on the luggage carousel. He grabbed one, while Obadiah hurried to get the other one.

"What is in this bag, D?" Obadiah asked, massaging his shoulder because it was so heavy.

"Heat," Denzelle answered him evenly.

"They let you do that, man?"

Denzelle didn't answer. He just reached inside his denim jacket and flashed his badge.

"That thing definitely has its privileges," Obadiah said, and hurried them out of the terminal.

"You parked in the wrong place, Obie?"

"No, but we have to get going. The funeral is in an hour."

"Whose funeral?" Denzelle asked.

"Old Daddy's."

"But, Obie, I thought you said he just died."

"Denzelle, he didn't just die. He died five days ago. And the funeral is today."

They made it to the church just minutes before the family finished lining up to march in. They hurried to a seat with the other pastors. Denzelle wished he had had time to change clothes. Everybody had on a collar and robe, and Denzelle was dressed in a black denim suit and a purple-black-and-mint-green silk shirt. He felt very underdressed, even though several women in the congregation smiled when this deep caramel brother walked down the aisle with that high, round behind wearing the daylights out of those black jeans.

Denzelle felt better when he caught a glance from a sister with some DDs. He flashed her that winning smile that made his large, round eyes light up. Rev. Flowers was good-looking, he could wear some clothes, and he had something about him that the ladies couldn't resist.

Based on the way the Green family was standing and holding on to each other while they waited for the funeral director to tell them who went where, and when they were to start down the aisle in the processional, Denzelle and Obadiah knew this was going to be a long and emotionally charged funeral. It also felt a bit like old home week for the two young pastors, with so many folks from North Carolina standing outside with the family.

Folks had forgotten that David Green (aka Old Daddy) had come to St. Louis from Durham County, North Carolina, and was part of an extensive family of Greens back in Durham. Joseph Green and Lamont Green's father were David's nephews. Cousin Buddy Green was Old Daddy's great-grandson. Cousin Buddy was different, slower, bigger, taller, and more special than the rest of his kinfolk. And the fact that he was at the funeral wearing a Carolina Blue football helmet didn't help to make him appear any less different from the other Greens.

"This is going to be one long and sad funeral," Obadiah whispered.

Denzelle nodded and said, "I was just thinking the exact same thing. Check that out."

Obadiah's eyes followed Denzelle's gaze all the way over to where Old Daddy's son, Lil' Old Daddy, was standing with his mother, Warlene, and her best friend, Queenie.

"Denzelle, man, why did that woman have to dress the baby like that?"

"Like what?"

"Like that," Obadiah whispered too loudly, drawing attention from his wife, Lena, who cut her eyes at him. She knew they were over there talking about that baby in his little funeral suit. He tried to sneak and point, but lowered his fingers when he saw Gethsemane's First Lady, Mrs. Sheba Wilson, raising an eyebrow at him. He lowered his finger and was about to mouth a "Sorry, Miss Sheba," but stopped when he saw her trying not to laugh.

Denzelle raised up in his seat just enough to see Lil' Old Daddy without drawing too much attention to himself. He didn't know what it was with black folk and funerals. They couldn't just put the deceased to rest. They had to put on a major production. And today's ceremony qualified for a Tony Award nomination.

That baby was wearing a little bitty Old Daddy suit. It was a lime-green pinstriped suit with a long coat that came to the knees, with a white shirt and black tie. The baby even had on a pair of black gators trimmed with lime-green piping, and was holding a little black fedora with a lime-green band in his hands, as if he were sixty-five years old.

Denzelle closed his eyes to try not to laugh. The funeral had just started, and he honestly didn't know how he was going to get through it in one piece. A church laugh that had no business coming out was the worst thing in the world. It was like having a bad case of gas in a room full of other people—maybe worse.

Lil' Old Daddy patted his mother's hand. Warlene smiled down at her son, and then took her walker and positioned it for walking down the aisle.

"I didn't know that Miss Warlene was on a walker, Obadiah. Has she been sick or something?"

"She doesn't need a walker, man. I think the funeral home people got it for her so she wouldn't fall out during the processional."

Warlene pushed the walker forward several inches. She leaned down on the walker and said, "Laaaawwwwdddd, my man gone. He dead as a doorknob, laaawwwddd. Help me, Jesus. Jeeeeezzzzaaaaaaazzzzzz!!!!!"

The senior pastor, Rev. George Wilson, sat up in the pulpit wondering how he was going to get through this funeral without, first, slapping some black people, and, two, laughing his head off. It wasn't that he didn't care about Old Daddy's family—to the contrary. He loved them a lot. But if they weren't some overly dramatic folks, he didn't know who was. Plus, he had told Warlene, when he counseled her and Mr. Green before they married, that her husband was way up in years. He advised her to enjoy the time the Lord had given them together because it could be much shorter than she wanted it to be.

Warlene had gotten mad at her pastor for telling her that. That day she hopped up and said, "Why you got to spread the ugly talk over me and my man. I just cancel those words out, Rev. Wilson. I cancel those words out. You trying to kill Old Daddy and make me a lonely widow before my time."

George stared at Warlene in amazement for a minute. He wondered if the words "your man is almost older than a *century*" meant anything to her. He was at a loss as to how to tell the girl that a man Old Daddy's age more than likely had only a good ten to fifteen years left. But God was good, and tempered that desire to tell Warlene that to her face.

George discovered in that moment that with the right person, there really was a lot to be said for wisdom and age. Old Daddy, who hated to see his fiancée so upset over the inevitable, had patted Warlene's knee and said, "Baby, you know I don't have a heap of time ahead of me. That's why we are back in church and living right, just so I can hear the Lord say, 'Well done, thou good and faithful servant' when I meet Him face-to-face in glory. But before it's time for me to tug at the pearly gates, I want to enjoy these last good days with a good woman. Now, you get your little young self together and apologize to Rev. Wilson. 'Cause he's only trying to do right by you, Warlene."

Warlene teared up at just the mere thought of Old Daddy dying and said, "I'm sorry, Rev. Wilson. I know you doing what the Lord leads you to do. And if every pastor did that, we'd have a whole lotta more saved, sanctified, and Holy Ghost–filled people in our churches."

Now here he was, sitting up in this pulpit getting ready to watch the "Black People's Funeral Show." George wished he could have sat with his wife, their children, and their friends. A brother could use some backup and somebody to pass notes to during moments like this.

Warlene had a few near misses for falling out. It was a good thing that she had that walker—or else it would have taken them half an hour to get in, rather than the fifteen minutes they took to take their assigned seats. When everybody was seated the funeral home folk rolled Old Daddy's casket down the aisle.

It was a magnificent casket. George Wilson had seen many a casket in his day, but he'd never seen one like this.

First, the casket was painted a sparkling lime-green. Even the metal casket rack was lime-green. Then it was trimmed in gold. But as if that weren't enough, the casket had pictures of Old Daddy painted on both sides. Instead of flowers on the top, they had anchored one of Old Daddy's black silk top hats, with a lime-green brocade band around the crown.

Denzelle poked Obadiah. He said, "Man, what..."

They both stopped when Lena leaned forward to give them a look.

The men's chorus, The King's Men, was the choir of choice. They walked in behind the casket, humming "At the Cross," while Gethsemane's premier soloist and newest gospel recording star, Sister Hershey Jones, sang the solo. It was Old Daddy's favorite song and Hershey was putting a serious hurting on the number when she sang:

"Alas! And did my Savior bleed,/And did my Sovereign die?/ Would He devote that sacred head for sinners such as I?/At the cross, at the cross where I first saw the light,/And the burden of my heart rolled away,/It was there by faith I received my sight,/And now I am happy all the day."

The King's Men went and took their place in the choir loft. In honor of the memory of Old Daddy they were wearing lime-green suits with black trimming on the lapels, the buttonholes, the pockets, and the cuffs, with black shirts, and black gators trimmed with the same lime piping as on Lil' Old Daddy's shoes. The members of The King's Men had special-ordered those outfits through Old Daddy's favorite store, Londell's Men Shop.

When everybody was in place Hershey sang the last verse of the song and went and sat down while The King's Men remained standing. The the organist lit that Hammond organ up, and the pianist, bass guitarist, lead guitar, and drummer followed suit. They jumped the beat up from the slower gospel rendition given by Hershey Jones to a funky blues beat that had folks up on their feet clapping and swaying to The King's Men good singing. The music and men's chorus were sounding so good that some people almost forgot they were at a funeral. But they were quickly reminded where they were when the pallbearers placed the casket at the front of the church, right below the pulpit area.

The funeral director took a deep breath and prayed before she and her assistants removed the top hat and proceeded to open that casket. She had begged Mrs. Green to leave the casket closed until it was time to view the body. But all Warlene said was, "What y'all trying to do, make it so that Old Daddy can't be a part of his own funeral?"

The funeral director had simply raised her hands in concession to the request and said, "We will abide by your wishes, Mrs. Green."

But the funeral director knew it was a mistake. She knew it the moment her assistant recommended that they rent Warlene Green a walker from the medical supply store near Barnes Hospital because the woman kept falling out when they were trying to make the funeral arrangements.

While the director had hoped for the best, she knew Warlene would not be able to stand looking at her deceased husband throughout the entire service. As soon as Old Daddy's remains were in full view, Warlene stood up with the support of the walker and made her way to the casket while The King's Men were putting the finishing touches on their song. She stared at her man's body, all decked out in his favorite outfit—a lime-green three-piece suit with matching lime-green shirt, tie, and hat. A few folks had inquired about the hat. But all Warlene had said was, "Has you negroes ever seen my Old Daddy walking around with his head uncovered? Do y'all think I'll be so ghetto that I'll send my man to meet Jesus bareheaded?"

Nobody said a word because nobody had ever seen Old Daddy without a hat, and they were not about to try and see something like that now.

At first, Warlene just looked at Old Daddy with tears streaming down her cheeks. She had *loved* that man. He may have been old, but he was the best man she'd ever had in her life. And Warlene Green had had her share of men—but none of those jokers could hold a dim candle to Old Daddy.

She shook her head and started shaking and sobbing. Sheba took a deep breath and hoped for the best in vain. When it looked as if things were getting ready to get kind of wild, she leaned over and whispered to her friend, Essie Simmons, "Girl, you better fasten your seat belt."

Sheba Wilson had barely gotten those words out of her mouth when Warlene tossed the walker aside and started hollering, "Take me with you, Old Daddy," right before she climbed up in that casket and tried to close the top over both herself and the deceased.

Her best friend, Queenie, hopped up and tried to pry the girl out. The baby, Lil' Old Daddy, started running around the church hollering and crying.

"Lawd, help my mama cuz my daddy done and got he-self dead."

The baby was running so fast the adults couldn't catch him, so they looked up into the balcony and made a silent appeal to the young folk. Theophilus's and Essie's oldest daughter, Sharon, ran track in college. She hurried downstairs and sprinted until she caught up with and got a good grip on Lil' Old Daddy. With the help of her two siblings, Linda and T. J., Sharon managed to get him over to one of the older church mothers, Miss Mozelle, who took a comb out of her purse and spanked Lil' Old Daddy's behind.

"Isaac David Green, you hush now, and calm youself down,"

Miss Mozelle admonished. "Your daddy has gone to be with the Lord, and he can't hear his registration instructions right for your little antics."

Lil' Old Daddy sniffled, wiped his eyes, and then sat back on Miss Mozelle's lap. It wasn't long before he had put his thumb in his mouth and slipped into sleep. That baby was exhausted. Lil' Old Daddy was so grown, folks sometimes forgot that the baby was only six years old.

Denzelle and Obadiah were laughing so hard they had to duck down under the pew, as they had as children when they didn't want to get in trouble. This was some wild mess, and from the looks of things it was about to go up another notch, if that was possible.

The entire deacon board was now at the casket, trying to get Warlene out of it without tipping it over and spilling the body on the floor. They grabbed her arms and ankles and struggled hard to get her out. But that proved to be very difficult because Warlene was a big girl. And when they started getting tired another church mother, Louise Williams Loomis, came over to that casket and whispered, "If you don't get your big red behind out of the casket, I'm gonna give you something to really holler about."

Warlene calmed down, and the men were able to lift her out of the casket and put her back in her seat. Bert Green, who was a member of another Green family in the congregation, reached down and picked up the walker. He folded it and placed it next to Warlene's pew.

She was getting wound up to holler some more when her eyes landed on her estranged sister, Osceola, sitting in a pew with her new husband from North Carolina, Harvey Knowles. Warlene hadn't seen Osceola since Osceola left St. Louis in 1976 after trying to pretend she was white. And here she was again, sitting up with that mean-looking white man as if she were still white. But before Warlene could open her mouth to tell her sister to take her black, impersonating-a-white-woman self out of the church, one of the North Carolina Greens recognized Harvey Knowles and put the finale on the floor show.

Sheba Wilson leaned over and whispered to Essie Simmons, "That is a mean white man. Look at him—he is sitting there like he is wishing for the days when being a paddy roller was an honorable profession."

Essie peered over at Harvey Knowles and shook her head. Sheba was right. That was one mean white man.

The North Carolina Green knew that he was at a funeral, and was supposed to act right on behalf of the Green family from Durham. But he couldn't—not with that man sitting up in here like that. He stood up and shouted out, "Warlene, why is that man, Harvey Knowles, at your husband's funeral? Don't you know who and what he is?"

Harvey Knowles stood up. He was very well dressed in a conservative black pinstriped suit, crisp white shirt, and what a lot of black folks called "the white boy tie"—a pale yellow silk tie with brick-red stripes in it. Harvey was getting a bit nervous. He didn't know why his new wife, Becky, had insisted on coming all the way out to St. Louis, Missouri, just to attend some old—no, really, really old—black man's funeral.

The only reason he'd conceded after that big fight they had was that there was a homeowners' association in St. Louis's west county area needing help with collecting its dues. That was worth coming out here for. Harvey Knowles had made a fortune stealing homes from people who got behind on their homeowners' association dues, and he swooped down on them and foreclosed on the homes for less than what a White Castle hamburger cost, before they had a chance to figure out what had happened to them.

Harvey was a bully who did not back down easily. He did not appreciate this black man calling him out and embarrassing him. He was going to put him in his place the way any self-respecting white man corrected an ignorant black man who had gotten out of line. It didn't occur to the man that he was in a black church full of black people. He said, "Now, you see here, buddy. You keep talking like that and something bad is going to happen to you."

"Oh...I'll see here all right," the North Carolina cousin said.

"Church, this is the same man who tried to steal my mama's house from her for $132.11. And you know what he told her when she tried to get him to work with her? This trash told my mother that something bad was going to happen to her."

The church was quiet. They wanted to hear this. The funeral could wait. That white boy had some nerve coming up in their church, and then telling a member of Old Daddy's family that something bad was going to happen to him. That was horrible. And he didn't just say it one time, that Harvey had had the nerve to say that mess to the man's mama, too.

"My mama lives in Gregson Hills in Durham, North Carolina. She got laid off at the tobacco factory for six months, and got behind on her homeowners' association dues while she was off work."

"I can't stand that mess," somebody shouted out. "Those homeowners' associations can be a ripoff!!! Whoever heard of paying people to live on the street where your own house is? That man is a thief and he steals black people's houses."

"AMEN!!!" came from around the church.

"Yeah," someone else proclaimed. "What did the homeowners' association think they were going to do after they stole the house—throw a mortgage party and pay the bank for it?"

"THE DEVIL IS A LIAR!" one of the church members, Bertha Green Vicks, shouted out.

"Amen," Rev. Wilson said. He had heard about this man when he talked with his friends in the Triangle area of North Carolina. He couldn't believe that he had set foot in his church.

"Then, Church, he tried to foreclose on her $68,000 home for $132.11. And he at my cousin's funeral? NO!!! NO!!! NO!!!"

The North Carolina cousin ran over to where Osceola/Becky and Harvey Knowles were. He then commenced to beating the slop out of that man until the church was satisfied that Knowles had been dealt a proper hand for his misdeeds. When he started calling for mercy and Jesus, the deacons pulled the cousin up off of him.

Harvey Knowles let the deacons help him get up. He wiped the blood off the corner of his mouth, ran his fingers through his tangled gray hair, pointed at the North Carolina Green and said, "You are going to be one sorry ni—"

One of the deacons, Melvin Vicks, Jr., who was also Bertha's husband, punched Knowles in the head. He said, "Do you and the black woman who got you fooled into thinking she's white want to get out of this church in one piece? Didn't you drive up here in a silver Mercedes?"

Harvey Knowles nodded carefully, while he studied his wife. She looked a whole lot like that black woman who had tried to crawl up in the casket with her dead husband. When he didn't answer fast enough, Melvin, Jr., said, "I'll tell you what. We are going to escort you and this thang here out of our church. And if you agree to leave these good people alone, like you should have done in the first place, we'll walk you and this woman to your car and make sure you get out of here in one piece."

"And what if I don't?" Harvey snapped, still thinking he could do something.

Melvin, Jr., held up a walkie-talkie. He said, "This connects me to the security guards outside watching the cars and making sure nobody tries to mess with the cars on the lot. The head of one of St. Louis's most notorious car-theft rings has two baby mamas living just four blocks away. Now, I saw a little thug eyeing your car, and I had told my main man outside to watch it. But there is no law against me telling him he can take a break when you walk out of this church door. So what's it gone be?"

Harvey Knowles conceded. When his wife kept standing there, he snapped, "Becky, if you wanna stay up in here with these ni—people, you will do it at your own risk."

Osceola/Becky hurried behind her new husband. She looked back at her sister, envying the kind of love she knew Warlene had shared with David Green. Her eyes filled with tears as she made her way out of the church and away from her folks. Pretending to be white for Harvey was beginning to wear on Osceola's last nerve. That man wasn't worth all this pain and suffering, with his mean, conniving, and thieving self.

The folks in the church were glad for the funeral services to resume. They had known this was going to be the funeral of the year when they first learned that Old Daddy had died. Nothing, however, had prepared them for this. But then again, Old Daddy never did anything without drama and flair. Why expect his home-going celebration to be any different?

NINE

The next day Denzelle and Obadiah met with Bishops Murcheson James and Percy Jennings, along with Theophilus Simmons and Eddie Tate, at Freedom Temple. Denzelle was so tired he could hardly see straight. He'd spent all of yesterday at a funeral and was still suffering from jet lag. He was sitting up in Rev. Simmons's conference room, in a comfortable chair, asleep.

He woke up to a hard nudge from Obadiah.

"You're snoring, man."

Denzelle sat up and wiped the drool off his mouth with a handkerchief. Rev. Simmons handed him a cup of coffee.

"Son, tell us what is going on across the water," Percy said. He'd been anxious to get Denzelle's report ever since Denzelle had called him from Virginia.

Denzelle took a deep breath. This was the first time that his job as a minister and his dedication to fighting "the bad guys" as an FBI agent had bumped heads. He had always thought that all of this would fit together quite nicely...well, except for the times when he had to shoot some folks. But it didn't. He had been given the task of bringing down what had the makings of a burgeoning drug cartel. And if Denzelle was successful he was going to find, bust, and arrest preachers in his own church. He didn't like what was going on with Bishop Hemphill. But it hurt that he might have to arrest Rucker, along with several others, and send them straight to jail.

"Look, Bishops Hemphill, Caruthers, and Babatunde have worked it out so that they could hook up with this family business run by an old man named Uncle Lee Lee out of rural Mozambique. Hemphill is the main person in the deal."

"And not Ottah?" Eddie Tate asked. "I'd always thought that he was the head crook across the water. At least that is the impression given by Bishop Abeeku the last time I was in Ghana."

"Rev. Tate," Denzelle began, "Bishop Abeeku has some other issues. He and Bishop Babatunde can't stand each other and are always finding a way to get one another. Abeeku wants to fully discredit Babatunde (which isn't hard to do), so that he can be the 'Head African in Charge' on the continent. He's not a crook like Babatunde, but he still bears watching.

"As for your question about who is running things, it's Hemphill. The other two are just along for the ride. I was surprised, too. Because the bishop never gave me the impression that he was a businessman. He's too lazy, too greedy, and too eager for a quick return on the little bit of work he plans on putting out. But lazy, greedy, or not, Rucker is planning on greasing his palms, lining his pocket, padding his accounts, and filling every empty suitcase he can lay hands on with cash."

"What about this WP21?" Murcheson James asked.

Denzelle and Obadiah exchanged looks as if to say, "Dang, they are good."

"Bishop," Denzelle said, "WP21 is made on this farm that is a half a day's drive from the Seventeenth District's compound."

"Com-what?" Theophilus asked.

"Compound, Bishop," Denzelle answered, smiling inside as he felt God's hand on his heart, causing him to speak in faith, that substance of things hoped for with regard to Theophilus becoming a bishop. Denzelle didn't know how it was going to happen. He didn't know how God was going to do it. He just knew what he knew. Theophilus Simmons was going to become one of the other bishops at this conference.

"What does Rucker need with a compound?"

"Well, they don't need a compound, Rev. Simmons," Denzelle told him. "But they have one. It's huge and luxurious, and it definitely does not sit well with the other folks living nearby."

"So, WP21—what is so special about it?" Bishop James asked again.

Denzelle wasn't quite sure how to tell Bishop James about the drug. He looked over at Obadiah for some help. But all Obadiah did was start laughing.

Denzelle couldn't believe Obadiah would clown him like that. He said, "Bishop, I really don't know how to put this delicately, but WP21 does things to people, well, more like men, after they take the drug."

"What kind of things?" Eddie asked. He was very curious about something that had the big and bad Denzelle Flowers so uncomfortable he was practically blushing.

"Special things," was all Denzelle said.

"Spell it out, son," Murcheson said. "What is *so special* about this stuff?"

"Bishop, it makes a man feel and act real special—so special that he can keep on acting special like that for a couple of days."

Theophilus and Eddie started laughing. They slapped palms and said, "Now that's special, mighty special indeed."

"Is it a synthetic drug?" Percy Jennings queried.

"All-natural as far as I could tell."

"What do you mean, 'as far as I could tell,' Rev. Special Agent Flowers?" Eddie Tate asked, now cracking up. He knew Denzelle had tried some of that stuff because he knew Denzelle.

By now Obadiah was hollering with laughter.

"It works better than anything you can imagine," Denzelle answered in his best FBI voice. "It is made from some kind of combination of ground-up watermelon powders—from several different kinds of watermelon. It's strong and potent, and I think there is some other ingredient in it.

"But as great as this stuff is, it has some awful side effects. You crash horribly, and you feel like you have the worst case of the flu when the stuff starts to clear your system. But the curious thing is that I noticed that the family who makes this stuff, along with the Africans in the community they did business with, didn't seem to experience any side effects. And they didn't take it all the time, either. But for folks like me, the effects were pretty bad, it is highly addictive, and you started craving it real fast. Bishop Hemphill was taking it every day when I left."

"So," Theophilus said, "what you are telling us is that one of our bishops is an aspiring drug dealer, who has opted to use his own product like the greedy knucklehead that Rucker Hemphill is. And the meanest bishop in the denomination, Ottah Babatunde, is in cahoots with him and the son of the late Otis Caruthers."

"Yep . . . pretty much, Rev. Simmons," Denzelle answered.

Theophilus sighed and rubbed his temples. He had thought it was bad back in 1963 with the funeral home brothel. But this stuff was something. He said, "The denomination can't survive this if it busts loose at the Triennial Conference. This kind of scandal could take us out."

"For though we walk in the flesh, we do not war according to the flesh. For the weapons of our warfare are not carnal but mighty in God for pulling down strongholds, casting down arguments and every high thing that exalts itself against the knowledge of God, bringing every thought into captivity to the obedience of Christ, and being ready to punish all disobedience when your obedience is fulfilled," Percy spoke evenly.

The room was quiet for a moment as they all meditated on 2 Corinthians 10:3–6.

"Percy, man," Murcheson said, "when you put it that way, it's pretty clear to me that this isn't simply another scandal just waiting to take a big bite out of the church. Looks like we are facing some serious spiritual warfare disguised as a scandal, and waiting to annihilate the souls of those who serve and worship in this church. And what better way for the enemy to attack the church than to try and infiltrate it from the top down with something that is seemingly harmless and 'natural' like this WP21?"

Murcheson rocked back in his chair for a few seconds, quiet and thoughtful about what God wanted him to say next. He sat up straight and said, "Preachers, I want you to stand up and pray with me because we are getting ready to go to war."

They all stood, formed a small circle, and grasped each other's hands with their heads bowed as Bishop James led them in this prayer.

"Father, we thank You for revelation knowledge. We humbly submit ourselves to doing Your will, and we ask that You show us how You want us to proceed in this battle. Lord, put a lamplight to our feet, to guide us. Father, keep us safe beneath the shadow of Your wings. And Lord, be with us as we put on the full armor of God: the helmet of salvation, the breastplate of righteousness, gird our loins with truth, shod our feet with the preparation of the Gospel of peace, we hold up the shield of faith, and we wield the sword of the spirit, which is Your Word. Lord, we bless Your Holy Name, and we thank You for all that You do, have done, and will do for us. We claim the victory over this, for we are more than conquerors. In Jesus' name, amen."

"Amen," was all the rest of them said.

"Now," Murcheson said, still on fire on the inside from the anointing from Heaven that had come down on him when he was praying, "the first order of the day is this. We need our own candidate running in this race for bishop. There are now three seats up for grabs, and we are going to get one. I know that our adversaries will come up with one person—just don't know who he is right now. And there is one seat that could go either way. But that third seat belongs to us."

"Bishop," Obadiah asked, "why not go after two seats instead of one?"

"That is a very good question, son. And while I would love to do that, we have to be prudent. First, the conference is less than a year away. Most of the candidates have been planning this at least two years in advance. Secondly, this will take a powerful campaign team, and money—a lot of money."

"How much?" Denzelle asked. He knew folks spent a lot of money running for bishop, but he had never thought about how much it would take to run a good, strong, and clean campaign by the right folk.

"About eighty-five grand," Percy told them matter-of-factly.

"Eighty-five thousand dollars, Bishop?" Obadiah asked, hardly believing what he was hearing. "Why?"

"Well, first off, Obadiah, eighty-five grand is considered to be a very small budget. Most folk, even the more conservative spenders, will shell out close to $150,000."

"That's a whole lot of money, Bishop."

"I agree, Obadiah. But the money is needed for advertisement, gifts to help out struggling churches, gifts to the bishops and presiding elders, helping out the campaign team, and a bunch of stuff."

"Like the golf carts that boy who is over the Twelfth District, Bishop Conrad Brown, had all over the place when he ran for bishop. That wasn't cheap," Murcheson said.

"Neither were the limos he sent to the airport to pick up all of the bishops and bring them to the hotels," Percy added, thankful that he had run his campaign during a time when all of that was unnecessary.

"So who are you considering sponsoring at this late date?" Eddie asked.

"You," Murcheson told him evenly. "I thought we made that clear to you when we first gave you this news."

"I don't want to run for bishop. I'm happy where I am."

"Well, Pastor, you are running. God put your name on my heart, and if you don't like His choice, then I suggest you go in your prayer closet and take up this matter with the Lord."

Eddie didn't say another word. Murcheson did not tell you that God had laid something on his heart unless God had laid something on his heart. He looked up and mumbled, "Why me?" And then he got very repentant when he felt a stirring in his heart right before he heard the words *"Why not you?"* whispered to him.

Eddie smiled to himself. The Lord was something else. Folks just didn't know how incredible God was. Plus, He was funny and didn't always give you a word in the way you would think He would. But that was because He was God and didn't have to adhere to any rules or protocol that Eddie thought necessary or of any importance.

Theophilus was grinning from ear to ear because he was happy that the Lord had not placed his name on Bishop James's heart. Like

Eddie, he was very happy being a pastor and had no aspirations to walk around in a purple clerical shirt. Black was just fine.

"What you grinning about?" Percy asked. "'Cause I know you don't think you are completely off the hook. You do know that you are responsible for running this campaign, Theophilus?"

That grin was wiped clean off Theophilus's face. He couldn't even begin to imagine what he'd have to go through running that campaign for this Triennial Conference, and especially when he considered what was brewing in the shadows.

"Percy," Theophilus asked. "What are we up against with this campaign? I mean other than Bishop Hemphill and his group trying to make some money, who else is in the game that you know I will not want to deal with?"

"First, know that if Hemphill is coming to make money, then Ottah and Ray are coming with him, too," Percy told him.

Theophilus rolled his eyes upward as if to say, "Father, give me strength." Ray was sneaky and good at working behind the scenes and keeping some kind of mess going. But Ottah Babatunde? Ottah was just plain crazy, and Theophilus hoped he didn't have to snatch the brother by his regal Nigerian garment and commence to beating the tar out of him.

"And Theophilus," Percy continued. "You have to remember that some of all that money they plan on making will be used to purchase one of those three Episcopal seats."

"They can actually do that?" Obadiah asked, shaking his head because he already knew the answer to this question.

"Of course they can," Percy told him matter-of-factly. "Do you honestly think that Bishop Thomas Lyle Jefferson over in the Caribbean actually *won* his Episcopal seat three years ago? Man, Tom strolled up into one of those backroom conference meetings with a greasy cardboard box full of hundred-dollar bills. He had to have at least thirty grand on him. And then he strolled out, en route to the preacher robes booth, and placed his order for a sharp purple silk brocade robe like he had already been consecrated as a bishop."

"And," Murcheson put in, "since this is the case, you can bet some of *their* money that you will be back up against the likes of

Marcel Brown, Sonny Washington, Marcel's daddy, and Bishop Larsen Giles."

Eddie just closed his eyes. Those negroes made you understand why Peter would lose it and pull out a sword, and then get to cutting the fool as he had in the Garden of Gethsemane.

"Who or what else do we have to be concerned about?" Theophilus asked. If he had to run this campaign, he might as well know everything up front.

"We need to watch what is going on in Bishop Jimmy Thekston's district," Percy told him. "The most dangerous candidates are coming out of his district. I know that the Ernest Brown/Larsen Giles camp will support Thekston even though there is no love lost between those two factions.

"One of the candidates coming out of the Seventh District is Thekston's newest woman, whose name escapes me right now. He has been pushing her hard in the Seventh and telling everybody that she is a maverick and trailblazer. But she has never pastored a church, or served as an assistant or associate pastor for that matter. Baby is fine. But I haven't seen anything in her to justify granting her a preaching license, let alone running for bishop."

"So, Bishop," Obadiah said, "is this just Thekston playing with the girl because she is his main squeeze for the moment?" And he knew it was only for the moment because Bishop Jimmy Thekston was mean and couldn't keep a woman long.

"Not quite, Obadiah. The girl is power-hungry, that's for sure. But uuuhh...I think Thekston is using her to create some divisions between the men and women delegates. He doesn't think she is bishop material but he knows that the women will flock to her. And he hopes that they will weaken the vote for the few good candidates running in this election. That way his real candidates will have a better chance of getting through."

"So what's in it for the woman?" Obadiah continued.

"Exposure and an excuse to be in close company with Bishop Thekston, and travel with him," Denzelle said.

"Good call, preacher," Murcheson said.

"You know we cannot let the Seventh District gain momentum

at the conference," Theophilus began. "I hate to malign an entire Episcopal district but there is just too much going on in the Seventh for my comfort."

"Yeah," Eddie added. "Remember the preacher Bishop Thekston put in the hospital?"

"Why and how did he do that?" Obadiah asked. He had heard about Bishop Thekston fighting preachers, but he didn't know the dude was hospitalizing folk.

Percy opened his mouth to answer that question but stopped when Murcheson said, "I got this one."

"Son," he said, "Jimmy assigned one of his better preachers to a small and dying church outside the Houston area. When the man went to the church there were twelve members, all seventy and older. The building was practically a shack, and they could barely pay the church's utility bills.

"The new pastor, who was a high school science teacher and friends with his school's wood shop teacher, got the building in shape. He put the original members to work, and sent them out into the community to invite folks to come to Sunday service and then eat dinner with them at the church. Several of the members were excellent cooks, and soon the church's membership rolls had quadrupled.

"It wasn't long before they bought a new building and the church grew some more. They were scheduled to celebrate going to the new building right after the Seventh District's Annual Conference. But Thekston, who wanted to give this church to one of his cronies, reassigned the pastor. That man went to the bishop and told him it was wrong to move him at this point and he was staying with his church."

Murcheson paused for a second to shake his head. He was telling this story, and it was just as wild to him now, as the first time he'd heard it. He said, "When the man confronted that fool, Jimmy jumped up in his face, knocked him to the floor, and stomped on the man's shoulder. The pastor's members got so mad at the bishop they pushed him down and told him that he'd better not ever touch their pastor again. And they told him that he if tried to move the pastor they were coming back to kick his butt.

"And that is just *one* of the stories coming out of the Seventh Episcopal District. There are many more, and most don't have that same kind of 'happy ending.'"

"So where do we start?" Eddie asked. As much as he didn't want to run for bishop, he knew in his heart of hearts that he had been called for such a time as this.

TEN

Bishop Larsen Giles hung up the telephone, shaking his head in disgust. His day had started out pretty good. But it began going downhill when he was told that Jimmy Thekston's woman had just quit him because he refused to leave his wife for her. Then, when Thekston refused to give her a senior pastor church appointment, the girl got mad and called the wife. When Jimmy slapped her for calling his house she withdrew her candidacy for bishop, throwing a big monkey wrench into their plans. She knew why the bishop was sponsoring her, and as dumb as she was, she also knew that this would hurt their plans to split the female vote.

Now, if that was not enough bad news, he'd just been told that Rev. Eddie Tate had thrown his hat in the race for bishop, and Theophilus Simmons was his campaign manager. Eddie was a formidable opponent on his own. But to have Theophilus at his side, running stuff? Could it get any worse?

Larsen sighed heavily, and then buzzed for his wife Jackie to come to his office at the back of the house. When she walked into the room full of attitude, he surmised that it could get a whole lot worse. Sometimes he wished he'd never married Jackie. The girl was still fine after all of these years. But she had the nastiest attitude in the state of Michigan. And snooty as all get out—which he found curious for a woman who had been earning her money twirling tassels around on her butt when he first met her.

"Here is your bologna sandwich," she said, sighing and rolling her eyes as if he had asked her to process the bologna on the sandwich from scratch, and with her bare hands.

"Why do you always have to eat a bologna sandwich, Larsen?" she snapped at him. "You are a wealthy bishop in the Gospel United Church. You should be setting an example and eating something with some class. How about a pastrami sandwich?"

"Jackie, who is in this room to watch me eat my lunch? And if they were here, do you think that I would care?"

"I care," she snapped.

"Why?"

Jackie blew air out of her mouth and snapped her neck. Sometimes she couldn't stand her husband.

"Get out of my office," he told her, making a mental note to leave that evil woman right here in Detroit when he left for the Triennial Conference in a few months.

Jackie walked out and slammed the door as hard as she could. He could hear her calling him every name but "child of God" on the other side of the door. He closed his eyes and shook his head. The worst thing a man could do was live his life in such a poor and raunchy manner that the only woman he could lay claim to was one like his wife.

Larsen picked up half of his sandwich and then threw it back down on the plate. That girl had fingerprints pressed down in the white bread. He flicked off a piece of chipped-off orange nail polish. He was so mad he picked up the plate and threw it against the door. He buzzed his wife and said, "You get your tail back in my office and clean up my mess."

Jackie didn't do anything but say yes, and then went to get a broom and some wet paper towels. She'd heard the crash and knew better than to cross Larsen. Last time she did that he took her favorite pair of diamond earrings and flushed them down the toilet.

Two weeks later Larsen scheduled a business meeting with Ernest Brown, his son Marcel, and Sonny Washington at Detroit's only private gentlemen's club for upscale black men. The membership roll had the names of some of the wealthiest, most influential elite black men in the Detroit metropolitan area. It was an exclusive organization and near to impossible to become a member of without the proper sponsorship. And the proper sponsorship was not forthcoming to any upscale brother. Money and clout, alone, wouldn't do it. A brother getting the key to this club passed the scrutiny of the old heads running the show. And the old heads didn't let anybody in who didn't share their views of the world.

Both Larsen Giles and Ernest Brown were longtime members of this club, and it didn't even have a proper name. It was just known as "the Club," and few people even knew of its location—which was somewhere on the outskirts of one of Detroit's elite all-black neighborhoods. It was one of those "black establishment" organizations that gave credence to the idea that well-heeled black folk existed, and they were plentiful enough to allow for excessive exclusivity. It was a shame that "the Club" had made it on the list of such establishments.

The Club's building was a huge mansion with plenty of meeting and conference rooms. But Larsen, who had the most expensive membership package, had booked them a suite for this meeting. He felt that they would get down to business, and then bring in some entertainment for some much needed R & R once the official meeting was over.

It had been a rough two weeks that had worked his last nerves and left him frazzled. Larsen had gone through three of his "I need to call somebody" women, along with three bottles of his best liquor. Right now Larsen's nerves were so bad that he was contemplating rolling a joint out of the stash he had smuggled in on his last trip to visit Bishop Lyles in the Virgin Islands.

Larsen put the bag away when Ernest Brown called to tell him that Marcel and Sonny Washington had just gotten back from Africa. He hoped they had some good news to share, so that he wouldn't have to smoke up all his good dope.

Sonny and Marcel, though much younger, were Larsen Giles's partners in crime from back in the day. They ho'ed together, drank together, snorted some high-quality coke together on rare occasions, and shared tips on how to get your hands on church funds without getting caught. They had made a lot of money in Richmond back in

1963, and they were all anxious to find a business venture with the same potential as the Richmond brothel. Only this time their plans were going to succeed. Because they were determined that Theophilus Simmons and his boys were not shutting down a daggone thang *this* time.

Whenever Marcel and Sonny went to Africa they always visited Mozambique, Swaziland, and Ghana. They rarely went to Nigeria because Sonny Washington couldn't stand Ottah Babatunde, and was always threatening to "kick King Negro's tail." This time they also opted out of going to Ghana because Sonny didn't want to do the preacher circuit. Bishop Abeeku got on his nerves when he had them scurrying across the Ghanaian countryside, going from church to church. Sonny and Marcel were not trying to go to church while they were in Africa. Neither did they want to meet with all of those preachers and church folk, pretending they were really enjoying those all-night services and prayer meetings.

Those two preferred the amenities offered by Bishop Caruthers, and especially Bishop Hemphill. None of the African districts could offer what was available to them in the Seventeenth Episcopal District. The accommodations were superb, there was good food, and of course the women—oh, the women. And if that was not good enough, this time they had been treated to some products from Uncle Lee Lee's farm. They came back to the States believers. As Sonny would say, "There's gold in them there melons."

They brought back samples of WP21 for Bishop Giles and Marcel's father. It had been easy to slip this small amount past customs. And they needed this meeting to discuss how they were going to get enough of the potion into the States, to Durham, North Carolina, and into the hands of their customers.

Plus, they had some serious questions that needed to be answered before they embarked upon this venture. How could they best market WP21? How would they advertise something like this in a quiet and discreet manner? And what would be the criteria for identifying and approaching their potential customers?

Bishop Giles poured himself some of the watermelon wine Sonny Washington had shipped back to the States. He sipped some, then quickly reached for a glass of ice water and gulped it down in the midst of choking with the tears streaming down his cheeks. Sonny, who had hoped to score some points with the bishop by giving him this gift of the wine, got worried. He sighed and exhaled when Larsen slapped the table and said, "Boy, that's what I call liquor. It's good and powerful like some good tail. You know, a woman who knows what she is doing can make your eyes water like that, too."

The bishop took another sip, and banged on the table some more.

"Whew! I haven't had anything this good since my daddy made his last batch of moonshine down in Batesville, Mississippi."

"Batesville, Mississippi, Bishop," Marcel asked. "Where is Batesville, Mississippi?"

"It's right off of Highway 55, about thirty minutes north of Charleston, Mississippi, where your favorite bishop, Murcheson James, is from, along with Theophilus Simmons's wife, Essie, and your old fiancée, Saphronia James," Cleotis Clayton answered as he walked into the suite looking like a million dollars.

"Maybe that's why I've never wanted to know where it is or go there," Marcel mumbled to himself, thinking that it had been a while since he and Cleotis had crossed paths. In fact, the last time they had been face-to-face had been on their very first trip to Africa. It didn't seem as if it had been that long. But they hadn't laid eyes on one another in years.

Marcel frowned. He thought about how Cleotis had stood back and watched his then-fiancée, Saphronia Anne McComb, jump on him and bang his head on a hard wooden floor because she was so angry over his cheating on her. Marcel would never understand women. They got so bent out of shape when they found out you were sleeping with someone other than themselves. That was so stupid. Women needed to understand that some of them were wives, and some were the women men slept with on the side when they were bored with their wives.

Cleotis had filled out, and was buffed up as if he was eating right, sleeping well, and staying out of trouble. It was obvious that he had made good use of the correctional institution's athletic train-ing program when he was in prison. He used to look like a black, semi-churchgoing Shaggy from the *Scooby-Doo* cartoon series. Now he looked like one of the brothers the other prisoners made it their business to defer to whenever he came on the scene.

Marcel had always thought that Cleotis was ugly, especially with that conked Jackie Wilson hairstyle he used to wear. But stand-ing before them wearing an expensive rust-colored silk leisure suit, rust alligator shoes, a slender gold chain hanging around his neck, and the freshly done fade haircut, Cleotis almost looked like a man capable of pulling some fine women his way. And that was a very good thing because this business venture, like most of their failed ventures, required an arsenal of fine women.

Cleotis Clayton had just returned from Nigeria. Bishop Giles had sent him over there when Marcel and Sonny threw temper tan-trums about going, complaining that they couldn't stomach "King Negro." Cleotis couldn't stand King Negro either. But if there was one thing prison had taught him, it was to lay his personal likes and dislikes aside when there was important business at hand.

Cleotis poured himself some of that irresistible watermelon wine. He downed his wine, barely blinking, and glanced down at his watch. As if on cue, his new help came walking through the door, grinning and running his mouth like he was the brains behind this huge undertaking.

Rico Sneed of Durham, North Carolina, could not believe his good fortune. He had been doing what he called "dirty work" jobs for several years. Rico earned good money on the side designing computer programs for folk who knew little if anything about com-puters, and needed everything they didn't want others to know about put in order and formatted on a personal computer.

It was rare for Rico to come face-to-face with the people he worked for. Usually it was just a go-between who brought the com-puter to him and then picked it up when he was done. And now he'd come up in the world because tonight he was dealing directly with the most notorious preachers with something to hide. Rico could hardly contain himself, and tried to think of something to say that would make him stand out from Cleotis Clayton.

Cleotis kept right on talking as if Rico weren't even there. He needed Rico, and hated that he did. But they had to have someone from Durham working for them. Not only did Rico have the expertise to develop a sophisticated computer system for the business, he also knew where they should be located, whom to hire to help them out, and how best to proceed when they got to Durham, North Carolina. The only problem with Rico, other than his being a jive-time punk, was that he was an opportunist and the biggest phony Cleotis had ever met.

But all in all, this new business was a go. They had a location, people to help them run it, and a growing customer base. Rico had painstakingly gone through every district's roster of preachers, pastors, assistant and associate pastors, and lay members with some kind of administrative responsibilities in their respective districts. He had put all this information on a file for the computer, so that they could identify and categorize potential customers. Plus, he had copied all of the information onto floppy disks so that they could carry the business around in a briefcase or coat pocket.

This was essential to the business. Everyone in this room knew that an attempt to sell WP21 to the wrong person could spell disaster at this conference. But they would make a whole lot of money if they were successful in identifying the right folks, and approached them with finesse and discretion. They would also be able to lay the groundwork for a business enterprise they could continue to run and use to make even more money once the conference was over. This business could make millionaires out of the key players at this meeting.

Rico Sneed had set up the system so well that the business was like a very efficient portable office. He could take this business anywhere and set up shop wherever he had access to a computer. But as well as that worked, it wasn't good enough. Without his own personal computer Rico didn't have anything other than the floppy disks for designing, storing, cataloging and updating all this important information.

The business needed a permanent home in the hard drive of a top-of-the-line personal computer system.

Rico had been pestering Cleotis to invest in an IBM home computer. Right now he had to sneak and use the computer at his job after hours. If he'd had a home computer he could have done even more with the database because he would have more time to work out all the kinks in the system he was creating.

There was so much they could do with this technology. But it was an uphill battle trying to explain all of this to the men in this suite. They didn't want to understand how investing five grand in computer equipment half of them didn't know how to use would make a difference in setting up and running this business. It also didn't help Rico's case that he was expecting them to give him the equipment once the conference was over. That was a whole lot to ask of this group of men, who spent most of their waking hours scheming on how to get, not give up, something for free.

Bishop Giles examined his copy of the detailed report Rico had put together, copied, and bound for each member of the "committee." Larsen was impressed with what the young dude had done, even if he didn't like Rico. The negro grinned too much, and he was always trying to act like more than he was. Plus, Larsen had never cared much for men who invested too much of their spare time and extra money in movies that could not be shown at a reputable theater.

The bishop had noticed that Rico Sneed spent too much of his time and money in that very vice. And even though the young man was college-educated, gave the outward appearance of being clean-cut, didn't drink heavily, wasn't too partial to marijuana, and shunned cocaine, he was grimy—way too grimy for his comfort.

Larsen had learned the hard way from the late and very infamous Bishop Otis Caruthers, Sr., that it didn't bode well for a man to get caught up in the activity of watching films you couldn't watch with other folk. He'd watched his friend go from being corrupt to the point of outright perversion before he died of a massive heart attack and stroke.

It had hurt Larsen something terrible to watch Otis disintegrate like that, and there wasn't a thing he'd known to do to help him. If

Larsen had been a praying man he would have been on his knees petitioning the Lord to tear down those strongholds in Otis's life. But he didn't have a personal relationship with the Lord like that. Larsen Giles knew all about the Lord. But he didn't know the Lord, and certainly didn't spend any time trying to make His acquaintance, either. The best he had to work with was what someone else had told him about the Lord. Sadly, after decades in the ministry, Larsen Giles didn't have a clue concerning how to pray a decent prayer of intercession for the man he loved like a brother when he needed it most.

When everyone had finished reading over Rico Sneed's report, carefully reviewing all the numbers, Sonny Washington grinned and said, "We are going to make a killing on this stuff." He sniffed at the air. "Smell that, Rico?"

Rico Sneed eyed Rev. Washington curiously and asked, "Smell what, sir?"

"Money, boy. What you just gave us smells just like money."

Marcel sniffed the air right before he took a long swig of his vodka.

"Heck yeah...smells like money all over the place to me."

While Sonny and Marcel were grinning and drinking and sniffing "money" in the air, Ernest and Larsen were waiting on Cleotis to tell them how they were going to pull this off. It was one thing to get a fancy report from the so-called computer expert. It was another thing for Cleotis to outline what this was going to look like and cost in real life.

"We will have to use several different ways to get WP21 to the conference," Cleotis told them as he put a résumé on fancy gray linen paper down on the table before them.

"What's this?" Larsen asked as he picked it up. Odd—he'd never seen credentials like this on a formal résumé.

"What does it look like?" Cleotis shot back. He'd worked with these preachers over many years, and had yet to develop a fondness for them.

"A résumé for a crook," was all Larsen said as he handed the résumé to Ernest Brown.

Ernest read it over quickly and asked, "Is this his real name?"

"It's a résumé, Ernest," Cleotis answered, laughing. "Of course it's his real name."

"So what you're telling me is that this man's name is Big Dotsy Hamilton," Ernest said.

Cleotis laughed some more. He and Dotsy Hamilton had just recently met via a contact from his days in jail. Cleotis liked the brother a lot. Dotsy was straight up, did what he said he would do, and would not try and double-cross a brother when the deal went down. He'd forgotten that his boy had put "Big" in front of his proper name.

"His real name is Dotsy Hamilton. He has good connections with the kind of folk we'll need to help us get WP21 into the conference, and enough of it to help us turn a good profit. Dotsy has said we will not be able to get the drug—"

"It's not a drug," Sonny corrected him. "It's a supplement."

"How about a 'potion,' 'love potion,'" Marcel added. He didn't think of WP21 as a drug. Because the first thing he thought about when he got his hands on the stuff was that it worked just like a magic potion.

"I agree with my man here," Rico stated. "This stuff will go over better with your buyers if folks see it as a potion."

Cleotis threw his hands up in the air.

"Okay," he exclaimed in exasperation, "it's a potion—a *PO-TION*. We'll call that daggone drug a potion. Now, will that make you negroes happy?"

These preachers were such butt-holes. And they always thought they knew stuff, even though they didn't. All of them were sheltered from some of the hardcore realities of everyday life.

They thought they were bad with some gangsta leans. But Cleotis was the only one who had been to prison, he had friends who were lifers, he'd shot several folks, people had been afraid of him in prison, and he'd killed a man who attacked him while in prison, just to make a point. Cleotis Clayton was one of the few who came out of prison a better man, he had plenty of money, he had managed to get a passport, he looked good and felt good, and he had a good woman in his corner back in Memphis. Now, if there was one thing he knew, it was the difference between a "supplement," a "potion," and a drug. "Rev. Washington, WP21 is a drug," Cleotis said. "Now, you and pretty boy over here"—Cleotis pointed at Marcel—"You all may have taken the stuff and it supplemented you so well, it made you feel like you had just swallowed a magic potion. But make no mistake, this is a drug. And all of you better treat it that way if you are smart and don't want to end up as a casualty of your own product."

Sonny stopped grinning. He did remember having some problems when the powder—no drug—started leaving his system. It had scared the daylights out of him when he got back home and a week passed before he was able to perform for his wife. And Sonny's wife, Glodean Benson Washington, was not the kind of woman you left hanging after leaving her alone while on a big trip to Africa. When he called Rucker Hemphill about the problem, all the bishop had told him was to take some more. Fortunately for Sonny, he didn't have enough WP21 to take without risking falling short when he brought a sample to this meeting in Detroit. It was no wonder Rucker was taking the stuff the way he did.

"Okay, Cleotis, it's a drug," Sonny conceded. "But if we want to make money in Durham, we better get used to calling our drug a potion that can work magic."

"It's made from natural products," Marcel countered. He liked this stuff, and was having a hard time accepting that it was a drug.

"Natural, like mescaline or real pure marijuana?" Rico asked, never taking his eyes from the *Players* magazine he was so enamored of.

"Yeah, nig…negro," Cleotis snapped, "natural just like that. Now, if you don't mind…"

Rico put the magazine down. Gazing at that magazine made him feel bold. He glared at Cleotis and said, "You need to watch your mouth with me."

Cleotis didn't open his mouth. He walked over to where Rico was sitting and flipped him and his chair over onto the floor. He'd learned hard and fast in prison that you didn't waste time talking when a man was jumping bad on you. It was important to put that man in his place as quickly as possible.

Rico flailed around for a few seconds and then tried to get up. But Sonny, who had seen the way Cleotis was looking at the young brother, went over to him, put a firm hand on his shoulder, and said, "You need to calm down and stay here a moment, if you know what's good for you."

Rico's nose flared open and he blew air out of his mouth. Rev. Washington needed to shut up and get out of his face. Because what he needed to do was hop up and deal with this jailbird. Rico made a move to get up, but found himself being held firmly in place by Sonny Washington. It had never occurred to Rico that Rev. Washington was that strong.

"I said to calm down. Now do as I've told you, Rico, before you get hurt."

Rico struggled for a few seconds, and then gave it up when Sonny slapped him upside the head.

"It's natural," Marcel was saying again. It was clear that he didn't think Cleotis knew what he was talking about. "What harm can a natural powder made out of watermelons do to you, to me, or to anybody? Huh, Cleotis?"

Cleotis didn't even deign to honor that stupid question with a comment. Marcel had eyes. He'd seen Rucker Hemphill. The man looked bad—like somebody who had been sucking on a crack pipe. Not everybody was affected to that degree by WP21. But one person messed up like that was enough for him.

They were going to the Triennial General Conference to convince some brothers that using this stuff was the way to paradise— and that the supplement would make them better, not worse. Now, whether or not that was completely true was not an issue for Cleotis. What concerned him, however, was whether this stuff was as addictive as it appeared to be.

WP21 could enhance a man's performance and make his woman go gaga when he unveiled the goods. But if you took too much of that stuff, and then couldn't replenish your system with more, that so-called "magic potion" would backfire on you in the most terrible way. The goods would not only diminish in your sight, they would lose their ability to operate at maximum capacity.

"Man, what part of *natural* do you not get, Cleotis?" Marcel demanded. He wanted an answer, and was tired of waiting for this no-good ex-con to answer him.

Cleotis still refused to answer Marcel Brown. But he did say this to the other three men: "You all are sitting up in this fancy-tailed club, in a fancy-tailed suite that few of the very people you've been called to serve can even afford. You might bear a license to wear a purple or a black clerical shirt. But if you go through with this enterprise, you are drug dealers pure and simple. And natural or not, WP21 is a drug—a good drug as far as the street value is concerned, but a drug nonetheless. And with any street drug—"

"Wait just one daggone minute," Marcel said, jumping up in Cleotis's face.

At first Cleotis flinched and got ready to floor this negro just as he had the other one. But his instinct told him to wait and hear what the fool had to say.

"You are talking to a bishop, a senior-level pastor, and two upstanding preachers in the Gospel United Church, like we are some common criminals like you . . ."

Cleotis thought back to when they had gotten involved with the late Bishop Otis Caruthers with that funeral home brothel fiasco in Richmond, Virginia. He had been leery of working with them then, and he was even more leery of getting tangled up with these crooked fools now. He said, "You think that collar you wear will protect you from Hell, Marcel? You think that wearing a black robe trimmed in red with a cross emblazoned across it will make you right and above the law? Well think again, preacher."

Marcel bristled and raised his hand. Even his daddy thought he had gone too far this time. But Ernest was not about to intervene. If Cleotis mopped the floor with that foolish boy, so be it. Ernest was tired, his bank account was too low, and he was ready to retire with some financial security. He was also fed up with always having to bail that boy out—wasting his money on all the foolishness Marcel had been involved in over the years.

Cleotis backed away from Marcel. He was not going to waste time and energy on this man. Marcel was lazy, dumb, and greedy—a very bad combination. He turned toward Bishop Giles and said, "I have a team of folk in Durham who will help me figure out how to get enough WP21 into the Triennial Conference to make it worth your putting your careers and personal freedom in jeopardy. If this works, we will make a whole lot of money. We just have to do this right, keep it out of the wrong hands, and keep control over our product. My team and I will work out the logistics and get back to you as soon as we can."

He started for the door. Cleotis had reached his saturation point with these fools and couldn't wait to get back home to Memphis, after he made a quick stopover in Durham, North Carolina. Hanging out with Dotsy Hamilton and Dotsy's boy, Grady Grey, would be a welcome respite from dealing with these crazy preachers.

Rico Sneed hopped up and followed Cleotis out of the suite at a careful distance. He could have stayed longer but was anxious to get to another destination. Cleotis knew exactly where Rico was going. And if he had cared an iota for this negro, he would have tried to stop him from going to watch that filth.

Cleotis knew from Rico's nervousness and secretiveness about where he was going that he had made an appointment to watch a movie in private. He also knew that Rico had to meet his contact at a precise time, or the deal was off. Cleotis couldn't believe that a man with as much education as Rico Sneed, and his talent for computers, was setting himself up for complete disaster with this kind of addiction. He had witnessed the destruction of Otis Caruthers, and would never forget those telltale signs of this horrific obsession.

One day Rico Sneed was going to wish he had taken the time to crack open a Bible rather than working overtime to live a lie and feigning respectability. One day he was going to cry out in desperation, and feel nothing but the cold, dark emptiness that came from cloaking yourself in secret degradation. One day Rico was going to be surrounded by people he wouldn't even think worthy of a passing nod on the street, and be glad they were there simply because there was no one else.

The day would come when he wouldn't be able to sleep because the images he'd poured in his mind all these years wouldn't let go. It was a vile existence. And as much as Cleotis could not stand Rico Sneed, he didn't wish this problem on him.

In the meantime they were stuck with Rico because he was the only person Cleotis knew with that level of computer skills who would work with them. There were other computer-trained black folk out there. Some were women who would slap the black off of them over this. And the rest were honest men who would shun using their skills for this kind of endeavor. But it was going to be hard to spend the months leading up to the Triennial Conference with so much contact with Rico Sneed.

As soon as Cleotis and Rico were gone Bishop Giles pulled out a quarter, looked at Marcel and Sonny, and asked them to choose heads or tails. Marcel, who always liked to be first, called out heads, leaving a silent Sonny with tails. Bishop Giles flipped the coin up in the air, caught it, and then slapped it on his wrist. He stared intently at Sonny Washington and said, "You have four months to run for bishop."

He then turned toward Marcel and said, "And you have four days to get his campaign up and running."

"Bishop," Sonny said, "I don't want to be a bishop. I'm happy with my church in North Carolina."

"How could you possibly be happy living out in the middle of nowhere?" Larsen asked him.

"Yeah," Ernest said, laughing, "who in their right mind would want to live out in Bouquet Farina, North Carolina?"

"It's Fuquay-Varina," Sonny said tightly. "And it's a nice place to live, thank you."

What he wanted to say was that he couldn't understand why anybody in his right mind would want to live up here in Detroit. At least he had land and trees and flowers and a very comfortable lifestyle at a modest cost. He wouldn't want to live up here with all of this cold, all of this traffic, and folks all up on each other for more money than he was trying to make with WP21. He didn't know why folks in big Northern cities like Detroit always felt that people living in small communities in states like North Carolina were missing something.

Glodean kept telling him to quit trying to get Larsen Giles down to their estate on the outskirts of the community. She said, "Baby, you do realize that our home is a whole lot bigger and nicer than Bishop Giles's house? You invite him to our home, and you are going to open the floodgates of Hell on yourself. Don't do it, Sonny. There are lots of things I wish you wouldn't do. But this is one thing you better not do, if you know what's good for you."

At first he hadn't wanted to give credence to what Glodean was telling him. But after eating a fancy, chef-catered lunch at Larsen Giles's brand-new twenty-eight-hundred-square-foot home situated on one and a half acres of land, he thought it best to keep him away from his own six-thousand-square-foot spread, nestled on twelve acres of beautifully landscaped property.

Larsen fingered the coin. He secretly wondered if Marcel and Sonny would really be able to pull off a successful campaign for bishop in so little time. They weren't all that bright, and had to face off against Theophilus Simmons and Eddie Tate, who could take those two down in their sleep. But on the bright side, Marcel and Sonny didn't ever fight fair. They would give those two goody-goodies a run for their money.

ELEVEN

With only three months to go before the Triennial Conference, Eddie Tate's church, Mount Zion Gospel United Church in Chicago, Illinois, was hosting the Eighth Episcopal District's Triennial Conference planning meeting. Several candidates had invited themselves to the meeting to announce their eleventh-hour candidacies for an Episcopal seat at the opening service. It was a long service with all those preachers stepping forward to give mini-sermons to convince folks that they were "the one" to become one of the two next bishops in the denomination.

Some of the candidates were mild surprises. A few were expected, like the two preachers out of the Ninth District who always announced their candidacies at this stage in the game. They never got any further than galvanizing a small team of workers, who helped them to raise enough money to pay off bills, have extra money in their pockets, and live large until they ran for bishop again three years later.

As soon as those two preachers showed up at the planning meeting and asked for permission to speak at a service, Theophilus told Eddie, "Those two negroes have the best fund-raising program I've ever seen—folks giving them money for days on end to do who knows what. I bet they take cash and all of the checks are written out directly to them."

All Eddie could do was laugh and pity the fools who greased their palms every three years, and then had the nerve to wonder why they never won an election for an Episcopal seat. A run for bishop could have so many twists and turns. And unfortunately it could be fertile ground for unscrupulous preachers to run some serious cons on church people.

Now here was Sonny Washington, sitting on the first pew of Eddie's church, waiting for an opportunity to announce that he, too, was running for bishop. Who knew that Sonny Washington would have bitten the bullet and decided to run, *and* that Marcel Brown would take a second-row seat and become his campaign manager?

Eddie's first inclination was to tell Sonny, "Heck no. You can't tell folks you are running for bishop at my own church." But he tempered himself and gave him some time in the pulpit, when he discovered that his crew was not the only group of people who weren't going to be happy when Sonny made this announcement.

Sonny did a smooth pimp-daddy walk up to the pulpit podium. He shook Eddie's hand and smiled out at the congregation. His wife, Glodean Benson, blew him a kiss. She was looking good in a pink silk two-piece suit with a peplum jacket, pink patent leather sling-back pumps, and two-carat pink diamond studs in her ears. Glodean had cut her beautiful hair to a shoulder-length bob, and looked better than she had when she made that infamous walk down the aisle in Memphis twenty-something years ago.

Eddie's wife, Johnnie, who couldn't stand Glodean Benson, eyed that sharp suit for a moment, and then leaned over and whispered to Essie, "Does that hussy have some kind of secret stuff she takes to stay so young? Makes you wonder if there is a picture locked up in a special room of her house, getting older and uglier by the minute."

Essie nodded. She'd never been able to make sense out of Glodean Benson Washington. The woman was absolutely beautiful. And Johnnie was right—she didn't seem to age. Glodean was also very smart and a good businesswoman. But was she crazy. She was married to Sonny Washington, and she helped him do a lot of dirt whenever making more money and acquiring more power and visibility were concerned.

Sonny mumbled, "It's on, baby" into the microphone, and then reached into the breast pocket of his hot pink three-piece suit with white chalk stripes in it, and pulled out a speech. His white shirt glistened against his rich brown complexion, and the suit, which was actually quite sharp, was set off by his hot pink, pale pink and black diamond-print silk tie, and pink gators with black trimming all around the shoe.

"Yeah...yeah...amen," Sonny said in his raspy voice that sounded as if he were the MC at one of those South Side Chicago clubs where the music was good, the liquor was good, the rib tips could make you hurt yourself, and the women were better.

"I was just telling my baby, here"—he pointed down to Glodean, who blew him another kiss—"I was saying this morning, Mother."

He stopped and gave Glodean a long and sensuous stare before continuing.

"You know, Eighth District, that *Mother* is the term we use for the wife of an esteemed member of the episcopacy. So if my baby is 'Mother' you know what I must be."

"Bishop," Glodean called out as if on cue.

Essie and Johnnie rolled their eyes at each other. It took considerable restraint for Essie to resist acting on her urge to stick her forefinger in her mouth and act as if she were about to throw up.

"Kind of makes you wish for back in the day when you stuck that pinked-out heifer in her butt with a hat pin," Johnnie said, and then reached up and pulled a long ruby-and-diamond hat pin out of the red silk hat with silk tulle layered around it that she was wearing. She put it in Essie's hand.

"Here girl, it's on the house."

Essie started laughing.

"Johnnie, girl, you are just as crazy."

Sonny Washington got comfortable in Eddie Tate's pulpit. Never in a million years would he have ever thought he'd be standing in this spot. After the fiasco of 1963, Sonny was glad that he was still a licensed minister. Then, if that wasn't enough, he was given a church in his home state of North Carolina, which Glodean had helped him build into the largest church in the area.

And now here he was, getting ready to tell all of these negroes that he was the next bishop in Eddie Tate's own church, and Bishop Murcheson James's own district. At that moment Sonny felt it couldn't get much better than that.

He cleared his throat and said, "Solid," when he saw his "ace boon coon" Marcel Brown giving him the black power sign. He raised his fist in solidarity with his ace. And when several of the folk from the Ninth Episcopal District—aka Marcel's District—raised up some black power fists, too, Sonny said, "Ummm...umgowah...Sonny Washington's got that soul power."

His supporters stood up and started chanting this slogan, which had a smooth R & B rhythm. They started swaying from side to side as if they were at the club, chanting:

"Ummm...umgowah...Sonny Washington's got that soul powah... Ummm...umgowah...Sonny Washington's got that soul powah!"

Theophilus glanced over at Eddie sitting on the other side of the pulpit podium and just shook his head. This was going to be a long campaign. He was glad that they had only twelve weeks left to go.

When the chanting started to die down, Sonny stopped dancing from side to side and said, "Church, I don't have much to say to you today, at this great planning meeting of the great Eighth Episcopal District. But...oooohhhhh, laaaawwwwddd. Umph, Jesus."

He stopped, looked up, pointed to the ceiling, said, "You the Man," and then switched gears and started dancing as if he were shouting. When the organist got up and started playing the shouting music, Sonny started jumping up and down, and then ran out of the pulpit, did two laps around the sanctuary, and came back to the podium. He jumped up and down a few more seconds, and when the music stopped he started punching the air and moving his feet in a weak imitation of Muhammad Ali. He said, "I can't stand the Devil, and I'm gone punch him out, Church."

He hit at the air some more.

"So how can he stand there and not punch himself out?" Eddie whispered to Murcheson James.

"Don't know, since he is one of the biggest devils around. Sonny probably mails a Hallmark card to Hell every Father's Day," Bishop James answered and then reached out his palm for some skin from both Eddie and Theophilus.

"So, Church," Sonny was saying. "I am going to put the Devil in his place by running for bishop at the Triennial General Conference in Durham, North Carolina. I ask you for your support. My wife, Glodean, will be at the back of the church with pledge cards. We take cash, checks, and credit cards because my baby bought me one of those credit-card machines for my birthday. Didn't you, baby?"

Glodean stood up holding the "birthday present" high above her head. She said, "Yes, I did, Big Daddy."

Some folks stood and clapped, to let Eddie and Theophilus know that they supported Sonny Washington and were going to do their best to give the two of them pure-tee hell. Then a good number of folks sat there with their arms folded to let Sonny and Marcel know that they were going to have a fight on their hands. And then there was the surprise of the day when Bishop Willie Williams, who both Eddie and Theophilus assumed was in the Sonny Washington camp, got up and walked out, looking pissed and signaling for his entire constituency to follow suit.

Bishop Williams had come to this meeting with the Eighth District to find out what his adversaries were up to, and to try to promote the pastor in the Tenth District he was hoping would fill an Episcopal seat. Just six months ago Sonny Washington and all of the folks in the Ninth District had pledged their support to whomever Willie Williams picked to run out of the Tenth. Now those two-timing, talking-out-of-the-sides-of-their-mouths preachers were about to pee on themselves over Sonny Washington's running for bishop.

Bishop Williams stormed out of the church before he lost complete control, found Sonny, and beat the daylights out of him.

"Bishop," one of the newest pastors in the Tenth District called out.

"What!" Willie snapped. "What in the hell do you want?"

"Nothing," the man said.

"No, don't tell me *nothing*, preacher. You started this, now finish it."

When Bishop Williams had first called and invited this pastor to go to Chicago with him, he had been excited and full of pride. In fact, he had started thinking that he was better than the other preachers in their district because Bishop Williams had selected him over some others to be a part of his personal entourage. He had even started picking and choosing which preachers he would speak to, based on whom he saw Bishop Williams speaking to. Now he wished that he had remained in LA, living large and enjoying all the amenities of pastoring a wealthy West Coast church instead of wasting his time being forced to play flunky to Willie Williams, and having to deal with his moods and outbursts.

"Bishop," the preacher said carefully, "you think we need to pull the plug on our candidate and put all of our energy into Rev. Washington's campaign?"

Willie Williams could hardly believe what he was hearing. He got so mad the folks standing around him thought he was going to have a stroke. Willie grabbed that preacher by his collar and started punching the man all upside his head. The other preachers in his entourage rushed over and struggled to pull the bishop up off the brother.

"If," he said in between blows, "I...put...anything...behind... Sonny...Washington...I won't know..."

"Bishop, Bishop," the men said. "Please stop, Bishop. You can't beat him like this in Eddie Tate's church."

Willie Williams was breathing hard and sweating, now more angry because he was messing up his new suit. He backed up off the preacher and took a moment to collect himself. Just as he started calming down, he heard Eddie Tate's voice coming through the sound system.

"And, after much prayer and fasting and seeking the Lord's guidance," Eddie was saying, "I know the Lord has called me to make a bid for an Episcopal seat in Durham. I need your help, Church. I need it bad. We cannot continue to put the wrong people in these Episcopal seats. You keep electing the wrong kind of men for bishops in our denomination, and they will make Paul's New Testament church in Corinth, the same one he is writing to in Corinthians, look like a nursery school for the children of the saints."

Bishop Williams had thought he'd heard the worst when Sonny Washington said he was running for bishop. But now Eddie Tate was in the race. He felt nauseated. If enough men like Eddie Tate got elected, it would mess up everything. It was bad enough battling with Percy Jennings and Murcheson James all the time. But with Eddie serving on the Board of Bishops he wouldn't be able to get away with anything. There would be no more kickbacks from pastors of big churches in his district, no more under-the-table bonus checks from his district, no more all-expenses paid trips anywhere in the world courtesy of churches with pastors who wanted a favor, and on and on. It would be the end of life as he knew it, and he couldn't let that happen.

Willie Williams reached over and put an arm around the shoulders of the preacher whose butt he had just kicked. He dusted off the man's suit, gave him a friendly slap on the cheek, and said, "Pastor, you raised a good point. We need to throw all that we have behind Rev. Sonny Washington. Because if there is one thing we can't let happen, is to let that big red Eddie Tate become a bishop in the Gospel United Church."

The preacher finished wiping his bloodied nose with the fancy breast-pocket handkerchief he'd spent too much money on because it looked so good with his new suit. He was full of mixed emotions. He didn't know whether to jump for joy that the bishop had praised him in front of the other preachers, or to cuss the bishop out for giving him that public beat-down.

He smiled at his bishop and then grimaced when the cut on his swollen lip stung. He grabbed Willie Williams's outstretched hand and said, "Bishop, it is a pleasure to be back on the team."

Another pastor in the group made a silent commitment to the Lord to cast his delegate vote for Rev. Eddie Tate. He was tired of this kind of mess in his church. And he hoped with all of his heart that the presence of a man like Eddie Tate would help the other decent bishops put a stop to the kind of mess that he'd just witnessed.

The Eighth District was considered one of the most peaceful, prosperous, and well-run districts in the denomination, thanks to the anointed administrative skills of Bishop Murcheson James. Bishop James had gotten rid of all the incompetent and problem pastors during his first tenure as bishop of this district. And he worked hard to make sure that each man or woman coming into the ministry via the Eighth Episcopal District was saved and determined to make Jesus Lord of his or her life, that each strove to live in the manner Paul outlined in 1 Timothy 3, got a BA degree, got trained by the Board of Ministerial Studies in the denomination, and then got a divinity degree from an accredited master's degree program.

These requirements had caused a big stink when Bishop James first proposed and then implemented them. And to be sure, some of the "bad eggs" among the Eighth District's preachers ran to other districts. But once things were in place the district flourished, the membership rolls were increasing in all the churches, tithes were up, and they were beginning to witness a mighty move of the Lord among the church folk.

But when God's people are doing the right thing en masse, it is inevitable that the Devil will get mad and busy, working overtime to start some mess. So it came as no surprise that the *last* folks the Eighth District wanted at their pre–Triennial Conference planning meeting would make it their business to be there. However, as Percy Jennings was known to say, "God has a wonderful sense of humor." And the Lord certainly got a good and hearty laugh at the expense of these ne'er-do-wells.

Most of the troublemakers were trifling and not prone to reading any booklets or newsletters with information about any changes that might affect them. And what they didn't know was that whatever district planning meeting a pastor chose to announce his candidacy for bishop, that pastor would have to give a finance report to that district. It had taken some maneuvering to get this policy passed by the Board of Bishops. But Percy Jennings, the senior bishop, pulled off this coup when he called for a vote during a time when he knew his opponents would be getting into trouble in Bishop Thomas Lyle Jefferson's Fourteenth District, when they went to the Bahamas for some alleged R & R.

Eddie and Theophilus were cracking up with laughter at Sonny and Marcel when the latter two discovered that they would have to give the Eighth District a report on Sonny Washington's campaign activities. And to add insult to injury, the report would have to be approved by both Bishop James and Bishop Jennings. Plus, Sonny would have to give them information about the "fund-raising" efforts that had gone on at the back of the church during that service the night before.

Knowing that Sonny's report was going to take some time, Eddie volunteered to come before the committee, which consisted of Bishops James and Jennings, three pastors, and three presiding elders out of District Eight. Since Eddie had just announced his intent to run, his presentation was short and complete with a written report that outlined expenses and any funds that had been collected and spent to date.

Most of Eddie's campaign funds came from fund-raising activities that took place outside of normal church functions. Any money raised and donated by the church had been voted on and cleared by his church's Steward Board, collected by the stewards, and then given to Eddie via a check. This check had not been written to Eddie but to the campaign fund account Theophilus asked his own Steward Board to set up and monitor. It was a smart plan, with checks and balances, and a record of money collected and money spent.

So far Eddie had raised $75,000 in the three months since he had committed to running for bishop. Twenty-five thousand dollars had come from the Steward Board's fund-raisers, $15,000 had come from private donations, and $35,000 had come from a big raffle for a brand-new Chevy Monte Carlo that had been donated to the campaign by Eddie's wife Johnnie's brother, who owned a car dealership on the South Side of Chicago.

Sonny came to the podium trying to look cool, but started sweating in his pink "Easter suit" and tugging at his shirt collar when Percy Jennings started flipping through Sonny's hastily prepared ten-page report that told them absolutely nothing. It was obvious to even the most untrained ministerial eye that this report had been written to be convoluted, boring, and so hard to follow that whoever was reading it would throw up his hands, throw the report across the room, and move on to the next candidate.

But Percy Jennings, who had worked for the IRS many years ago, had a remarkable amount of patience with matters such as these. He said, "Rev. Washington, my mind should be on this report, but it keeps wandering to a song by the King of Soul, James Brown. Every time you open your mouth I want to start singing, 'Talkin' loud and sayin' nothin'.' 'Cause that is exactly what you have been doing the whole time you've been before this committee."

Percy glanced around at the men seated at the conference table with him.

"Am I right on this, preachers?"

"You 'bout to take it to the bridge," Murcheson said, laughing because he was definitely enjoying this. He gave Sonny a hard stare and said, "Now, Rev. Washington, I notice you, like Rev. Tate, were able to raise some funds before officially announcing that you were running for bishop. And based on the report on this table, you've raised $37,000 so far—that is, if we don't include the unknown amount you collected last night.

"Aside from you being $39,678.89 in the hole, I am confused about a few things you put down. I am thinking that you will want to deduct the $8,200 worth of tailor-made suits off of your taxes as a business expense—which I do understand. But what confuses me is why these items are necessary to your campaign. I've been watching you for a long time, and I've never known you to be poorly dressed and looking like you needed some new clothes to run for bishop. You want to enlighten an old country preacher like myself on these matters?"

Sonny shifted from foot to foot, suddenly wishing he had not worn this brand-new and obviously very expensive suit. He was looking good and as if he had a bunch of money, which he did. Just last night at least ten women had put hundred-dollar bills in his hands for the campaign. One woman waited until Glodean went to the ladies' room. She slid over to Sonny and said, "Bishop, watching you shout like you did when the choir was singing last night really did something special to me. And if I were a delegate, you'd have my vote. But since I ain't, I'll make sure you get my money. And if there is anything else I can do for you, Bishop—and I mean *anything*—you let me know."

She slipped one of her hotel room keys into Sonny's hand, wrapped in five one-hundred dollar bills, and then hurried off when she saw Glodean.

"Now," Percy continued. "Rev. Washington, help me understand why you felt it necessary to spend $1,800 on your hair. I know that you are still wearing a Jheri curl. But since the back of your collar isn't greasy and dripping with curl activator, I don't see where your money is going with regard to your hair."

While Sonny searched for a plausible answer a woman with gold-frosted hair stood up to reveal a big round behind trapped in some very tight skinny-leg jeans. She said, "Pastor needed to spend that money because he has a campaign travel team. I'm his hairdresser. He has to pay me to keep his hair cut and trimmed, touch up that perm, get rid of the gray, and make sure that he has all of the right hair-care products while on the road. And Pastor has to pay for my travel expenses, along with my salary. You know running for bishop is like trying to be a congressman or senator. You need a whole team."

"Is that so, Miss…"

"Heidi Johnson, Bishop Jennings. Miss Heidi Johnson."

Murcheson tried not to laugh but couldn't keep it in. If that sister looked like a "Heidi," he looked as if he and President Ronald Reagan were first cousins.

Heidi was barely five feet tall. She was shapely but thick. She was brown and had a head full of gold-frosted weave. And the girl had a booty hanging off the back of her that seemed more suited for somebody named "Lil' Pooh."

"And," Heidi continued, "Pastor got some pretty clothes, and he needs somebody like my cousin, Tarleetha, to handle his wardrobe—taking suits to the cleaners, alterations, laundry, and so forth."

"Wow," was all Percy could say, as he prepared to go in for the kill where Sonny Washington and this suspect budget were concerned. But before he could open his mouth there was a warm stirring in his heart that gave him cause to pause long enough to know that the Lord didn't want him to venture down that road just yet. So he retreated, content to let the Lord fight this battle. Percy knew that if God told him to wait, there was a whole lot worth waiting for.

Eddie Tate's members and supporters were sitting in the sanctuary wondering when it had become fashionable for dumb folk to run for bishop. Rev. Tate was a big and bodacious man. He was also very smart and knew the denomination's discipline and bylaws the way he knew his Social Security number. Plus, Eddie knew black church people, along with the nuances of how church policy was implemented in the Gospel United Church from state to state and in the Caribbean and Africa.

Most of the folks in the First, Fifth, Sixth, and Eighth Episcopal Districts knew that Rev. Eddie Tate was the best candidate for bishop and that he could be counted on to bring about some much-needed change in the denomination. Business as usual just wasn't working anymore. And there were too many bishops who were not right or were too comfortable with riding the fence between right and wrong.

Until now Theophilus had not been all that committed to running Eddie's campaign. And Eddie hadn't been enthusiastic about running for bishop, despite the fact that increasing numbers of pastors from around the country were coming forth and endorsing him, and the delegates were openly pledging their votes. But after sitting here and watching a preaching pimp like Sonny Washington try to run a Boston on the entire church, Eddie and Theophilus decided that it was high time they got girded up in the Lord, and charged up about this run for bishop.

TWELVE

It was less than three weeks before the Triennial General Conference. The hustle was on at Evangeline T. Marshall University, the place where this event would take place. All the nearby hotel rooms were sold out, even the ones on the Wake Forest, North Carolina, side of Raleigh. With the shortage of rooms, some folks were forced to find rooms as far away as Henderson, North Carolina, and Greensboro. To help give relief to conference attendees, the denomination decided to go old-school and contract with folks in the area to open up their homes.

In the 1960s Rev. Theophilus Simmons had won kudos for designing a wonderful home hosting program. It was only in the last six years that the church had allowed this program to fall by the wayside. But now they were short and Theophilus appointed Obadiah Quincey, a Durham native, to oversee this project. And Obadiah didn't let them down. The young preacher used his considerable connections in Durham County, along with his computer skills, to create a program and manual that could be used across the entire denomination. It was this demonstration of administrative skills that put Obadiah in the running to get a church in Chapel Hill, so that he and Lena could finally come back home.

While everyone was preparing for the trip to Durham, Cleotis Clayton was already there, working with Big Dotsy Hamilton to make all the necessary connections with Durham's most respectable criminal element. Cleotis didn't have patience for anyone trying to perpetrate a reputation. He needed people who would walk the walk

...d not just talk bad. He also wanted folks with a steady and available supply of capital for their enterprises. It was never a good idea to work with broke crooks. He had tried that back in the sixties and ended up doing a short stint in prison as a result.

Despite his criminal record, Cleotis had managed to remain a licensed mortician. One of the ways he and Dotsy had initially come up with to get WP21 into North Carolina was to create a way for bodies to come into the state for Eva T.'s budding medical examiners' studies program. But they couldn't come up with a plausible reason for shipping bodies in from Africa without sending out red flags to the authorities in every government agency monitoring shipping the deceased to the United States.

Cleotis needed another way to get WP21 in fast. The only person on Earth who could help him was Chief over in Mozambique. So he called the brother, wired him a chunk of American money, and hoped that Chief's plan to send the stuff over in a bunch of traditional outfits one of the preachers working for Chief's family planned on selling at the conference would work. Chief made good on his promise and got the supply to Cleotis in record time. But it wasn't enough. Plus, after the second shipment arrived the airport authorities started getting curious and began nosing around their stuff.

They had enough to get started, but not nearly enough of the WP21 to make this plan work once the conference was off and running. Cleotis, following Big Dotsy's advice, took some of the powder in the second shipment to try to figure out how they could make this stuff on their own. And since they still needed more to come in from Africa, he was able to route a few more shipments through Europe and Canada, and then down to the US.

This time the powder came in with some mail-order items from a Canadian "company" run by one of Big Dotsy's old contacts. This plan had actually worked out just fine with regard to getting past the authorities. But all of that making-the-trail-grow-cold activity cost too much money. There were just too many people to pay off to make getting WP21 into the country this way work. At some point they would start losing money, and end up in the hole. The last thing

Cleotis and Big Dotsy wanted was to be in debt to some men who reminded them of some criminals in a Charles Bronson movie.

So Cleotis and Dotsy found themselves struggling with figuring out how to make the drug on their own. Cleotis had a basic knowledge of what the stuff was made of. He didn't know how many watermelons were used, how many different kinds were blended to make the powder, if there was anything else that went into the powder, or if something else was used to minimize the aftereffects of the drug.

The last time Cleotis was in Mozambique, he had noticed that Chief, Uncle Lee Lee, and their male kinfolk didn't appear to experience the same withdrawal symptoms that he and his people had experienced. And judging from the way they walked—as if they all had a special kind of weight causing them to stroll with exceptional swagger—they didn't seem to be suffering from any of the more severe side effects, either. And he knew that they had been taking that drug regularly for many years.

They had to be taking something else with WP21. Or they had altered the formula. Or they were doing both. And it was this missing piece that made WP21 work at the optimal level. But since Cleotis didn't have a clue what the missing link was (especially since Chief had been curt and dismissive when he asked these questions), he and Big Dotsy would to do the best they could.

Cleotis and Dotsy had yet to piece that formula together, and now the Triennial Conference was only ten days away. The hotels were filled to the brim, which meant that more and more potential customers, with plenty of money to spend, were landing at the Raleigh-Durham Airport every day. They had to do better, and do it fast.

By the time the conference was four days away, the campaign booths had sprung up all over the Evangeline T. Marshall University campus. Eddie Tate's people had come in before him, and they were running the booth and campaigning hard for the first wave of uncommitted delegates who had come in early for some preliminary meetings.

Eddie's wife, Johnnie, had flown out to Durham a week earlier.

Prior to marrying Eddie, Johnnie had worked in food service along-side Theophilus's big sister, Thayline. The two had been friends for years, and Thayline, who was a fabulous cook, had a recipe for homemade Neapolitan ice cream that was to die for. She and John-nie got in touch with the Eva T. Marshall food service manager and were able to convince her to help them produce the ice cream, prom-ising to tithe 15 percent of the sales back to the Home Economics Department at the university.

The ice cream was a hit. Folks came by Eddie's booth for sam-ples, and then left with gallons in hand, grinning because the ice cream was so good. Johnnie and Thayline were making a whole lot of money with this campaign fund-raiser. They were drawing folks to the booth. And the Tate for Bishop campaign committee was able to reach the people when Thayline's husband, Willis, did his presentation on Rev. Eddie Tate while they were waiting on their ice cream orders to be filled.

But their booth was not the only popular one with people lined up waiting to get some goodies and then some information on the candidate. It appeared as if Marcel Brown had the magic touch with a lot of the male delegates. But they couldn't figure out why since they never saw anything other than campaign paraphernalia being distributed. Plus, there was no music (Eddie's booth was jamming all of the hottest gospel tunes), and Marcel didn't even seem to be saying all that much to get folks excited about Sonny Washington. But they were doing something. And it was enough to make the Eddie Tate campaign committee concerned, especially when Cle-otis Clayton seemed to be ever-present at the Washington booth throughout the day.

There just didn't seem to be a legitimate reason for Cleotis to be in Durham, and at a campaign booth for someone running for bishop of all places. He was still a longstanding member of Greater Hope Gospel United Church in Memphis—which was the congre-gation Theophilus had pastored before he was assigned to Freedom Temple in St. Louis. But he had not demonstrated that he had expe-rienced such a change of heart that the next natural thing for him to do was work a campaign booth for a church-based election. And

Sonny Washington's being married to Cleotis's first cousin, Glo-dean, wasn't a good enough reason for him to be there either.

Cleotis was here for a reason—and it sure wasn't anything reasonable about church and the Lord. Johnnie made a mental note to find out as much as she could about what was really going on over at the Washington campaign booth. Because the last time Cleotis Clayton had teamed up with the likes of Marcel Brown and Sonny Washington, their entire denomination had been a heartbeat away from being torn to shreds.

THIRTEEN

Cleotis was tired and frustrated. They were running into trouble, snags, and setbacks at every turn. Every time he felt he had made two steps of progress, something popped up, and he ended up taking four steps back past the first two steps. Frustrating. Nerve-racking.

If the frustration of this week was not enough, Cleotis now had to deal with the competition coming from Eddie Tate's booth. The Tate campaign was packing church folk up in that booth with ice cream—*ice cream*. How in the world could ice cream compete with what was at their booth?

But Cleotis knew why. He'd sneaked and tried that ice cream. It was so good it would make you want to hop up and slap somebody. Plus, many of the delegates liked Rev. Tate and the folks on his campaign team. Unfortunately, a lot of folk had issues with Sonny Washington and Marcel Brown. And they preferred socializing at another campaign booth—unless, of course, they had enough of something good to counteract that.

This was going to be a long week. At least Cleotis hadn't had to be worried with all of these preachers in a cramped-up campaign booth when they were in Richmond back in '63. Heck, on some days he hadn't had to be bothered with anybody. He could get lost in one of the rooms with the bodies in the funeral home, and be confident that nobody was going to follow him there.

But that was not the case this time. Cleotis hoped that they would get this operation right. Because right now he felt he was coming close to wasting his time. And after time in prison, time was very precious to Cleotis Clayton.

Every single time he got tangled up with Bishop Larsen Giles, Ernest Brown, Marcel Brown, and Sonny Washington, something funky went down. And Cleotis had said as much to his cousin, Glodean, when she complained that he was not supportive enough of her husband's campaign.

Glodean was right, too. Cleotis wasn't supportive enough because that would require something akin to caring about Sonny, this campaign, and Sonny's being a bishop. And since Cleotis didn't care about any of that, he wasn't supportive enough of his cousin's husband's cause.

Glodean and Cleotis had fought like cats and dogs since they were little bitty things. And they still fought with each other many decades later. Glodean thought Cleotis was a spoiled ne'er-do-well. Cleotis thought his cousin was bratty and had an overinflated opinion of herself. Both were right in their assessments of each other.

Cleotis flushed the toilet and washed his hands. He had ignored the phone the first two times it rang off the hook. He had only been back in his hotel room for ten minutes. But it occurred to him that it might be something he needed to attend to—especially since the person wouldn't stop calling him. It could be Big Dotsy with some good news about making more WP21. He snatched the phone up, and then rolled his eyes the moment Glodean's voice came through the receiver.

He sighed heavily and said, "Yes, Glodean. What do you want from me now?"

"I would think that my own first cousin would be running around the campus practically shouting over the possibility of one of our family members becoming a bishop."

"That negro you lay up with, who used to beat your behind until you got some sense and started controlling the purse strings, ain't one of my relatives. I've told you that before, and I'm telling you again."

"Jealous, just jealous," Glodean snapped. She didn't know why she had called Cleotis. He was her cousin, and even though she loved him, she also couldn't stand him. Why did this jailbird *always* have to be right?

Cleotis used to be right when they were little. Cleotis had been right when he told her that he was getting as much money up front as he could because the Richmond ho' house was doomed to fail. And Cleotis was right now, when he told her husband and his boys that getting the WP21 business up and running wouldn't be as simple and easy as they wanted to think it would be.

"You are working my nerves, Cleotis."

"Then hang up the phone. You called me, remember? And by the way, quit calling Mother and telling on me because you don't like the way I handle things."

Glodean acted as if she hadn't heard that and said, "Sonny is not happy with the way the money is coming in with that potion stuff. So you need to get on it and do whatever it is that you do when you are doing your criminal activities. Understand?"

Cleotis hung up the telephone, and didn't answer it when Glodean called back. He wasn't going to hurt his cousin's feelings (as much as the girl got on his nerves) by telling her why they were having so much trouble with the supply of WP21. If Sonny's people would quit dipping into the stuff to use it with some of those loose "conference women," it's possible that they would have more of it to sell while they struggled to duplicate the formula.

Sonny and his crew were really making this harder than it had to be. Plus, as if dealing with them weren't bad enough, he now had to have more contact with that Rico Sneed. Cleotis hated that he needed Rico as much as he did. He wished that he had not been so lazy and taken that computer class offered in prison. That class had had everything he would have needed for this business, and he could have done this all on his own. But for now he was stuck with Rico, who was working on a computerized program that would tell them who really needed WP21, who just wanted the drug, and what amount was safe for each client. WP21 was nothing to mess with. It had to be measured out according to age, height, weight, and a rough estimate of the client's health and physical prowess.

Cleotis had tested this drug on himself, Big Dotsy, Big Dotsy's ace Grady Grey, and a few of their other business associates. After they had all "worked" the drug off during a visit to the Sock It to Me Club out in Warren County, North Carolina, they figured out how best to package and sell this moneymaker. They learned about the necessity of giving doses of the drug based on the potential client's height, weight, and physical health from Big Dotsy.

Big Dotsy, whose personal philosophy was to live large and with great gusto, ignored Cleotis's warning about how to use WP21. Naturally, since he was Big Dotsy, he took too much. Dotsy mistakenly assumed that his weight and thick muscular build would offset any problems that would befall a brother with a slighter build.

Unfortunately, Dotsy hadn't accounted for his height. Dotsy was short, and as Cleotis said, the drug didn't have too far to go, causing him extreme discomfort when his body refused to return to a more relaxed state.

At first they were having a good time out in the country at the Sock It to Me Club. If you were going to give WP21 a test run, this was definitely the ideal location. This club specialized in providing everything that a man was not supposed to have. And prior to Dotsy's mishap, they were looking into making the club one of their main clients in the area. But before they could get that far, Dotsy experienced complications from the drug and found that he couldn't leave the premises when they were ready to go.

"Dotsy, man, let's go," Cleotis hollered to that back section of the club where all of the stuff you didn't want people to know you were doing was happening.

"Cleotis, man, I...I...I'm in trouble. You and Grady got to come back here to help a brother out."

Big Dotsy was sounding so pitiful Cleotis got scared, and went and found Grady Grey. They hurried to the back with the safeties off their pistols, only to find Dotsy standing facing the wall, his back toward them.

"Man, you all right?" Grady asked, trying to conceal the worry creeping into his voice. Dotsy wasn't even standing right.

"I can't leave, Grady," Dotsy answered. It was clear he was fighting back tears. "This stuff got me messed up."

"What stuff?" Grady demanded.

"WP21. It's messed me up, man."

Cleotis started getting nervous. He knew how WP21 could mess a brother up, and had hoped he wouldn't have to share that information with Grady and Big Dotsy. Brothers on the streets were suspicious of something that made you grow way beyond capacity, then caused you to shrivel up real small as if you were walking around in Antarctica dressed in some lightweight plaid Bermuda shorts. Something like that made brothers think that this so-called miracle potion was in reality a part of a conspiracy of "the Man" to take out brothers in the hood, and reduce the black population by lowering fertility rates.

Cleotis was hoping that Dotsy would not turn around. But that is exactly what Dotsy did.

"Ohhh...laaawwwwd," Grady yelled out and then put his hands over his eyes. "Man...that's...that's...not natural, even for a smooth operator like yourself."

"I know," Big Dotsy said, sniffling up snot that was running down his nose and into his mouth. "This is horrible."

"I told you to be careful taking that stuff, man," Cleotis admonished, now very worried and trying with all his might to keep his eyes off Big Dotsy. But that effort proved to be quite futile. It was not a sight for sore eyes. It was an eyesore.

"Can you walk out the club, man?" he asked Dotsy, knowing good and well what the answer would be.

"Naw, Cleotis, man. I'm having trouble walking right. And I can barely sit down."

Dotsy started toward the door. His whole body was so stiff, it made him take his steps like the Mummy all dressed up in a smooth orange playah's suit.

"That's messed up, man," Grady told him. "You cannot walk out of this place like that. Why don't I get behind you, and then Cleotis, you get in front. Maybe we can walk him out without things being too obvious."

"Grady," Cleotis said, "if you think that I am going to walk out of here in front of Dotsy, you on something you ain't been telling us about."

Grady glanced over at Dotsy. Cleotis was right. They couldn't walk out like that. He said, "Why don't we go and get the club's bouncer, Twilight? I know he'll walk out in front of Dotsy."

"That is because Twilight is flaming gay!" Dotsy yelled, and then got so upset he passed out. But he came to immediately, and in excruciating pain because Dotsy had had the misfortune to fall flat on his face. Actually he hadn't really fallen all that flat but he was on his face—sort of.

"We can't take our boy out of this room like that," Grady said. "We can't leave him here alone for the night to let the drug get out of his system, either."

As much as he didn't want to see his "boy" like that, Grady was concerned about a bunch of things. He said, "Dotsy, man, can you pee?"

"Grady, man," Dotsy said. "Does it look like I can pee? I mean, if you were jacked up like me, would you be able to pee?"

Grady shook his head.

Cleotis said, "Looks like we're here for the night," and went to get them some food and liquor. He made a secret promise that once he left the Sock It to Me Club in Warren, North Carolina, he would never ever return.

They made Dotsy as comfortable as they could before making themselves comfortable. A few bottles of the house's best liquor later, they were feeling better. And after checking the door and their pistols, they settled in for the night. By early morning Dotsy was limber enough to leave. They went and got Twilight, who eased them out of a side door and then helped them get Dotsy, who was now sick as if he had a terrible case of the flu, into Grady's car. Twilight, who was big and tough, as well as trustworthy, promised to get Dotsy's prized silver-and-black Cadillac Seville back to his house before the club opened back up.

Watching the effects of WP21 on a cat like Dotsy Hamilton made Cleotis and Grady wonder if they needed to leave selling this stuff alone. Dotsy was a man who could drink a fifth of the strongest liquor like a can of Pepsi-Cola. Grady had seen him smoke four fat joints of his best weed—the stuff Grady grew in his backyard—and barely get a case of the munchies. If WP21 messed up a dude like Dotsy Hamilton, that was some scary, scary mess.

But they did learn this much from Dotsy's ordeal—that WP21 worked. This drug was no joke. It worked fast and was definitely long-lasting—maybe too long-lasting if last night was a gauge of the drug's effectiveness. But the jones that came down on you when WP21 was leaving your system was like nothing any of these three men had experienced. It made them all wonder how that old man over in Africa had survived this drug for so many years with the kind of monkey on his back that could eat you up alive.

Spending the night at that raunchy Sock It to Me Club made Cleotis give some serious thought to joining the church and turning his life over to the Lord. That thing had scared him pretty bad, and it made him very nervous about what could happen if the greediest and raunchiest of their customers took too much WP21. For starters, all those negroes he was working for in the denomination were at risk for hospitalization, stroke, and a heart attack if they kept going at this stuff as they had been doing over the past weeks. As both Grady and Dotsy had noted when they met with those preachers, Bishop Rucker Hemphill was already a goner.

What had started off as a sure moneymaker was now becoming a sure-shot mess. It was also getting out of hand—which made criminals like Cleotis Clayton, Dotsy Hamilton, and Grady Grey nervous. They knew from experience that anything that could make money like that would draw in the wrong folk and pique the interest of the folks with the badges. Cleotis hoped that they could get into the conference, make their money, and get out in one piece.

He wasn't going back to prison for these preachers. They weren't worth that kind of disruption to his carefully rebuilt life. Cleotis had taken the fall for these preachers back in 1963. But he wasn't going down like that again. Ray's dad, Bishop Otis Caruthers, had paid him a nice chunk of change for going down like that. But he wasn't traveling down that road a second time. If Cleotis got caught with this, he was telling on everybody.

Cleotis didn't understand preachers like Sonny Washington, Marcel Brown, Ernest Brown, and Larsen Giles. On those rare occasions when he felt a need to talk to the Lord, he always asked Him why those men had been allowed to enter the ministry. Cleotis had never witnessed them bearing fruits of righteousness. He'd seen good fruit coming from Theophilus Simmons when he pastored Greater Hope in Memphis. And even when Cleotis himself wasn't doing right, at least he was honest about being on the wrong side of the law. He had never tried to pretend that he was a godly man when he knew he wasn't.

Cleotis had read the Bible—Genesis to Revelation—three times while he was in prison. Every time he finished reading Chapter 22 in the Book of Revelation he was amazed to discover that nothing in the Word supported the works of these preachers, or the other ministers in the Gospel United Church who were like them. And for those on the fence, the Lord was quite specific in Revelation 3:15–16, when He said, *"I know your deeds, that you are neither cold nor hot. I wish you were either one or the other! So, because you are lukewarm—neither hot nor cold—I am about to spit you out of my mouth."*

The New King James Version read, *"I will vomit you out of My mouth."* Cleotis thought those words said it best. Whenever someone "vomited," the substance was so repulsive the person *could not* keep it in—it had to be forcefully discharged from the system.

Those were powerful words. And Cleotis Clayton knew God meant every single word spoken in the Scriptures. So, if he, a man of the world, knew this, why didn't those so-called men of God know it, too? Just thinking about it made Cleotis break out into a cold sweat. Sometimes he wanted to fall prostrate before God's throne—but couldn't. He wasn't ready to give up the world. And men like the preachers he dealt with were making it real easy for him to cling to his carnal ways.

FOURTEEN

Marcel Brown picked up a large baggie filled to the brim with WP21. He wrinkled his nose. This potion was some funky stuff. He pulled a pale blue silk handkerchief out of the breast pocket of his gray suit jacket and dabbed at his eyes.

He had been using this stuff regularly, and then suddenly lost his taste for it. For some reason neither he nor Sonny had had the same withdrawal symptoms as the others. Marcel thought that it may have been because they took the stuff in very tiny doses. He noticed that the drug worked better that way. And after a short period Marcel also noticed that neither one of them could stand the stuff in his mouth anymore. It was as if the tiny doses gave them some kind of built-in resistance and repulsion to the drug.

As much fun as they were having, and as many customers as they had finally started pulling in, Marcel was worried nonetheless. Against his advice the rest of the group had been giving out freebies of the stuff, which had begun to eat into their inventory for people wanting to buy WP21. They were going to have to do something fast to get more of it.

The preliminary meetings of the Triennial General Conference had already begun. And they would need a whole lot more to meet the ever-increasing demand for the potion as more people came onto Evangeline T. Marshall University's campus. Those folk would be hungry for some entertainment, and this need would only intensify the closer they got to election day.

Marcel desperately needed money to buy off delegates and

purchase some votes for Sonny. They were far behind in the polls. So they were going to have to snatch votes away from Eddie Tate any way they could. And that was going to cost a whole lot of money. If they were going to make this work, they were going to have to figure out a way to manufacture this stuff themselves.

Time was not on their side. They had not been able to get enough of the drug in from Mozambique. Then, Chief had never sent them the full amount requested for the last shipments they had received. And as a result the new customer base Marcel had worked so hard to build was becoming frustrated, the men were uncomfortable with the side effects of the drug, and they were getting desperate to experience the benefits of this "magic potion" again. These men were worrying Marcel with their constant demands, and about to drive him crazy.

If that was not bad enough, Eddie Tate was gaining the support of more and more delegates every day. Marcel had learned right before coming to this meeting that ten more delegates had openly pledged their support to Tate. And they had also committed themselves to campaigning for Eddie to win over more undecided delegates. That was not good. Marcel had been working hard to convince those undecided delegates to pledge their votes to Sonny. But so far he'd been able to grab only a handful of folk in this group.

Marcel was sick of Eddie Tate and Theophilus Simmons. He had never liked them, and he had been working for over twenty years to take them down. But no matter what he did, and how good the plan, it never worked. It was as if there were angels shielding them, thwarting every single thing he thought to send their way. And that was exhausting.

People just didn't realize how much time and energy was used trying to do harm to another person. It was hard work. But Marcel reasoned that somebody had to do it—especially where Theophilus and Eddie were concerned. So if anybody was going to take those two down, it might as well be him. They had caused Marcel a whole lot of suffering, and he deserved to be the one to get the glory from putting Eddie and Theophilus in their place.

Marcel looked at his watch and hoped that his crew would show up soon. They had a lot of work to do, he was tired, and he wanted to get this meeting rolling. There was a late-night party in Bishop Conrad Brown's suite. He had promised Bishop Brown that he'd help get the party started with some WP21. He could make some money with the little bit of WP21 in the personal stash he kept on hand for moments just like this. And if the fine conference hos he'd connected with earlier showed up at the bishop's suite as promised, Marcel could count on half of the delegates in Bishop Brown's district casting votes for Sonny.

The very next day Sonny was sitting across from Marcel, wondering why Marcel looked so tired. He said, "You getting old, bro. Times past, you could hang out all night with some adventuresome hos, and then go through the next day with more zeal and energy than a brother who had caught a night-full of Zs."

Marcel drank his cup of coffee in three gulps. He was so tired he could barely move.

"Sonny, man," he said in between long yawns. "Who knew that Bishop Conrad Brown was a freak?"

"You lying, man," Sonny said with a chuckle.

"If I'm lyin', I'm flyin'," Marcel told him. "I gave Conrad a taste of WP21, and he ran through three hos just like that . . . ratta-tat-tat."

"So where were you when all of this was going on, Marcel? You have never been the kind of brother to steer off on Freaky Lane."

"And I'm still that way, Sonny. I'm a player and a ho'. But I ain't nobody's freak-a-leak. Man, I ended up spending the night in one of the spare bathrooms, in the tub, with a blanket, a pillow, and a fifth of Hennessey."

Sonny's eyes got big as he tried to form his mouth to ask the next question.

"No, Sonny, man," Marcel said, rubbing that tender spot between his eyebrows, "the bishop didn't have all of the women in his room together. We are, after all, at a church conference. He took more WP21 than he should have, and needed three women, back-to-back, to help him get back to normal."

Sonny was cracking up. He said, "You mean to tell me that old stuck-up, uptight, white-boy-talking Conrad Brown needed three women to work off WP21?"

Marcel nodded. He could hardly believe it himself, and he had been there.

"I don't understand why you didn't just get up and leave," Sonny was saying, interrupting his thoughts.

Marcel closed his eyes, sighed, and said, "I had to go to the bathroom—bad. And when I came out, stuff was happening."

"Then why didn't you act like you couldn't see them, and hurry out of there, Marcel?"

Sonny was having a hard time understanding why Marcel had gotten stuck like that. He knew he would have found a way to get out of that room if he had been in that situation.

"I did do that, Sonny, man. But the bishop kept calling me, telling me not to leave because he might need some more of that 'love potion.' Every time I tried to get out, he tried to get me over to where he was. So I pretended to have an upset stomach from a stomach virus, and made the bathroom my home for the night. It was the best I could do under the circumstances. The bishop had just promised up the delegates from his district, and I couldn't risk making him mad."

Sonny scratched at the back of his head. He was glad that he hadn't had to endure that. He would have never pegged Bishop Conrad Brown as the freak of the week.

He picked up the bag of WP21 and stared at it, as if it would give him a clue to making this all work on his behalf. This had been a genius of a plan when Rucker first put it on the table. But this thing was definitely not going as planned, and things were beginning to get out of hand.

The door of the suite opened and his least favorite negro in the world came strutting through the door grinning and wearing some big white aviator sunglasses. Sonny had always thought that he hated Theophilus Simmons more than anybody else in the world until he met Rico Sneed. But nothing Theophilus had done to make his life hard, including helping to get him demoted and sent to Fuquay-Varina, North Carolina, could make Sonny dislike the man more than he did Rico. And that was saying something, since Rico was technically on his side of the fence.

Sonny just could not stand Rico Sneed. He had disliked that skinny, big-tooth-grinning-over-nothing, Milk-Dud-shaped-head negro on sight. Sonny Washington had never met such a mediocre and plain negro who had such an overinflated opinion of himself. Rico was basically just the tech boy. But sometimes he acted as if he were large and in charge of this entire operation simply because he was the only one on the team with computer skills.

A tall, red, freckled, and bulky young man was following Rico with three small baggies filled with very pale powders in pink, yellow, and beige. Rico wasn't the only one these preachers weren't taking to. This new boy rubbed them the wrong way the moment he walked through the door.

Rucker Hemphill and Larsen Giles, who had just finished meeting, came out of one of the other rooms in the suite. Larsen took one look at Rico's friend and decided that he was too quiet and smug for his own good. He was the kind of man who lay in the cut planning dirt on a brother, just waiting for the perfect opportunity to go in for the kill.

That boy had walked up in this room as if he were paying the rent. Didn't he know better than to act like that in a room of prominent preachers and bishops? That was the problem—neither of these young men knew his proper place.

"Did I sleep with you last night?" Larsen Giles asked Rico.

"Huh?" Rico mumbled.

"You really are as dumb as you look," Larsen told him. "You and your friend here walked into a suite that I am paying for, eyeing my liquor, earning extra cash because of us, and you two have not spoken a word to any man in this room. Don't you have any kind of home training?"

Rico looked at Kordell, who stifled an urge to shrug his shoulders. Kordell didn't care what these preachers thought about him. But Rico cared because he'd been around them enough to know that a slip in what they called "home training" could cost him dearly.

He said, "My apologies, Bishop Larsen," and then walked over to the table with the Southern Comfort and the whiskey glasses.

"Bishop, if I may, I'd like to use some of your whiskey to show you all something."

Larsen nodded, wondering what Rico was going to show him with a glass of Southern Comfort. It wasn't as if watching a man drink up his liquor were a novelty to him.

Rico got three glasses and filled them with whiskey. Kordell handed him three baggies filled with different-colored powders. Rico put one tablespoon of the first powder in a glass, then a tablespoon of the second powder in the next glass, and did the same with the third powder and glass.

He said, "I know you all are having trouble with supply and demand. So I went and found two of my old track-and-field teammates from college, gave them some of the WP21, and asked them if they could reproduce this stuff. One of them was a chemistry major in college. He could make anything in the chem lab. The other…"

"Can we presume that this brother sitting here is the other one of them?" Marcel asked, clearly impatient with Rico.

"No, Rev. Brown. This is my friend, Kordell Bivens. My college friends live up in western North Carolina."

Rico had to work hard to hold his peace. The last time he had gone off on one of them he had found himself lying on the floor. These were some arrogant preachers, and they all got on his nerves.

Both Rico and Kordell were little boys when the last "business" had been established. But they knew that these men were greedy, messy, and careless, and had barely escaped arrest, prosecution, and some time in jail. Back then, and now, they didn't have enough hands-on action with their business. It was because they were spoiled and always looked to others to do all the work—clean or dirty.

This time, however, they were going to have to roll up their sleeves and earn this money. As far as Rico was concerned they needed more control over manufacturing WP21. They didn't need to rely on some old man over in Africa to control the supply needed to meet the growing demand for the drug.

Rucker picked up the glass with the pink powder in it and sniffed it. This stuff wasn't funky enough to be some decent WP21. He put that glass back down and picked up the one with the yellow powder. No smell at all, just a whiff of some very good liquor. No chance that stuff was WP21.

"What about the drink with the beige powder in it, Bishop?" Sonny Washington asked. He'd gotten a whiff and that stuff smelled so bad the whiskey couldn't even cut that nasty mess. Rucker picked up the glass and raised it to his face. His eyes watered, the stuff smelled so bad. He gulped it down and went and sat down and waited for something to happen. It didn't take long.

Rucker grinned and then asked, "You got a woman waiting for me to wear this stuff off?"

Kordell, who believed in always being prepared, started laughing. He walked to the door of the hotel suite and beckoned for a fine sister named LaShaye Boswell to come in. The tall, honey-colored sister with a short curly Afro went and stood by the man who had obviously swallowed that drink. She wrapped Bishop Hemphill's arms around her waist from the back and walked him out of the conference room to the back of his suite and closed the door.

"I guess that's the one we want," was all Bishop Giles could say, and put several blocks of cash on the table. He'd planned on giving it to Cleotis, until the fool had the audacity to put him on hold at a time like this. Election day was getting closer and closer, and they needed to do five times better than they were doing right now.

Larsen didn't know why they had thought they could do business with Cleotis Clayton on this level a second time. This was the same Cleotis who had stood back and let that Saphronia McComb James beat the living daylights out of Marcel twenty-three years ago. They must have been awfully dumb, greedy, and desperate to venture down that road again.

Rico picked up the two thick wads of bills. He wanted to count them so bad but knew better than to do so in front of these men, who would have considered such behavior offensive and in very bad taste. A mistake like that could cost him this business.

Kordell was practically sweating, he wanted his cut of the money so badly. Rico had been his boy for some time now, and always looked out for him. This wouldn't be the first time they had gotten into some dirt together. But it certainly was the first time that they had gotten paid for the dirt. To say that he and Rico had hit pay dirt was an understatement.

"How much can your contacts make for us? And can we have it at the official opening session of the Triennial Conference?"

Kordell mustered up his best poker face to hide his surprise. Based on all the hustle and bustle going on around Eva T., he could have sworn that the conference had already begun. But obviously that wasn't the case—which explained why all of those blocked rooms here at the Governor's Inn had not filled up with people.

"How much do you want, Bishop Giles?" Rico asked, trying to act as if he had all of this under control with his suppliers, Harold and Horace Dinkle. He hoped the brothers wouldn't ask for too much of his hard-earned money now that they were under the gun time-wise.

Those Dinkles were some crazy, smart, beer-guzzling, drug-making white boys who would hurt you bad if you messed with their money. They liked Rico. But the brothers made it clear to their only black friend from college that he, too, could be found lying in a ravine, praying that a wandering bear didn't find him before help came, if he tried to run some game on them.

Naturally, Rico had lied to those white boys about how much money he could get, just as he and Kordell called themselves running game on these preachers. They wanted that money. And they wanted to control this situation. It didn't occur to either Rico or Kordell that those two white boys had not issued an idle warning. They meant what they said, and could learn to live without their only black friend from college if they had to. Plus, those preachers had already made a secret pact to sacrifice Rico to the authorities if anything went wrong.

FIFTEEN

Cleotis, Big Dotsy, and Grady Grey had spent so much of their time with Bishop Hemphill and his boys they had almost forgotten that there were some real and decent preachers out there, and that a lot of them were at this conference. Sometimes the Marcel Browns and Sonny Washingtons of the world could make you become jaded and distrustful where preachers were concerned. So it was a like a breath of fresh air to run into young, saved, and sincere ministers like Obadiah Quincey and Denzelle Flowers.

Cleotis was sitting in Eva T.'s cafeteria sipping on a cup of hot coffee. How many times had his mother paid somebody off to let him enroll in Fisk University, Atlanta University, Virginia Union in Richmond, North Carolina Central University here in Durham, and North Carolina A & T in Greensboro, only to have to sit back and watch him flunk out of school over some foolishness?

He drank some more coffee. It was good—tasted like a cup of gourmet brew. This place made the best coffee, and he always made sure that he got a cup when he was on campus. Cleotis liked Eva T. Marshall University. It was a beautiful campus—trees, flowers, red brick walkways, gardens, ponds, those lovely buildings, and even lovelier coeds. It was like being in Heaven without the penalty he feared he'd have to face when he stood before the Lord for all the mess he'd been involved in throughout his life.

The whole week Cleotis had been in Durham and on this campus, he had walked around regretting that he had never appreciated college until now. Maybe if his mother had sent him here he'd have a degree and a different life. Being here had to be the best experience for these students. The dorms were nicer than many at historically black colleges. Each had large rooms with a private bathroom shared by only two residents. That was sweet. One of the major complaints coming from his cousins who went off to college was about those community bathrooms. Cleotis was a spoiled only child, and he couldn't imagine sharing the bathroom with a bunch of folk.

What many people didn't know about Cleotis Clayton was that all those years sitting up in church, wishing with all his heart that he could be anywhere other than Greater Hope Gospel United Church in Memphis, Tennessee, had made an impression on him in spite of himself. Cleotis had absorbed a lot during those years, and could quote Scripture with the best of them. In fact, remembering Scripture at a moment's notice had kept him safe in some of the scariest situations. And Cleotis had definitely had his fair share of scary situations.

When Denzelle Flowers walked into the cafeteria, the first person he saw was Cleotis Clayton. The two men had made only a brief acquaintance with each other here in this cafeteria. Denzelle hadn't said more to Cleotis than good morning, and that the best cup of coffee to be had in Durham could be found at the cafeteria on Eva T. Marshall University's campus. But something told him that he needed to talk to this brother this morning.

Denzelle walked right over to where Cleotis was sitting and sat down at his table. Cleotis was surprised. He had secretly wanted to talk to Denzelle Flowers. And the brother was right here, obviously wanting to talk to him, too.

Cleotis took a quick look at what the young brother was wearing. He always believed that a brother without flair and style was a brother who wouldn't be able to hold a decent conversation with him. He was impressed, and Denzelle passed his test with flying colors.

The preacher was "clean" in a pale orchid-colored Italian silk suit with a double-breasted jacket, white jacquard print silk shirt with a diamond pattern on the material, a gray-purple-and-orchid pocket handkerchief and some of the sharpest dove-gray gators he'd seen in a long time. He knew the young brother had purchased this suit in Chicago. Cleotis loved Chicago. And he always bought several sharp suits whenever he was in the Windy City.

As a matter of fact Rev. Flowers reminded Cleotis of this man in Chicago named Bernie Mac, who was a very talented and funny comedian. The only difference between the two men was that the comedian was a rich chocolate color, and Denzelle's skin was a very mellow caramel. The resemblance between the two men was so striking, they could have been kinfolk—high cheekbones, slanted eyes that could broaden and get big and wide when they got excited about something, and big grins that revealed good sets of white teeth.

Cleotis was sure that this brother had more than his fair share of women—which had to be kind of hard for a preacher trying to live right and be right. If there was one thing Cleotis Clayton was good at, it was sizing folk up. And he knew that this man was decent. Now, the good Rev. Flowers was definitely a playboy down to the bone. Because it was clear that this black man loved himself some black women. But he was a good man nonetheless—just needed to get married since he was a preacher. But Cleotis also figured that the young brother was hardheaded, enjoying chasing tail too much to submit to this truth.

Denzelle sat down at the table with a gray leather Bible in his hand, knowing that this brother, who had ex-con all over him, wouldn't ask him to move to another table. He hoped that the only thing the brother would sniff out on him was that he was a preacher. It might not sit too well with him that he was cop—and an FBI agent at that.

A cute cafeteria worker with a big, juicy behind bounced over to the table. She put a hot mug of coffee down, along with some delicious-looking chicken salad on toasted wheat bread, topped with some of the reddest and juiciest slices of thick tomatoes Cleotis had seen outside of his grandmother's farm in Mississippi. He looked up at the waitress and said, "I'll have one of those."

She nodded at Cleotis and then gave Rev. Flowers a warm "You need anything else, Daddy?" smile. All Denzelle did was wink, suck on that toothpick he'd just stuck in his mouth for style and effect, and then say, "Naw, baby...at least not right now."

The waitress got a slight twitch in her hips. She grinned some more and said, "Pastor, you so crazy."

Denzelle winked, took the toothpick out of his mouth, picked up his sandwich, and bit into it. Cleotis watched Rev. Flowers chomping down on that scrumptious sandwich, hoping the cute cafeteria lady with the brick-house body would hurry back with his food.

Denzelle finished the first half of his sandwich and sipped on some coffee. It was perfect. Baby had remembered to put some cinnamon in it. He was going to have to give her a little more than a tip later. She had been good to him all week, and had been giving him the lowdown on the preachers he'd been watching for his mentor, Eddie Tate, and his boss, Greg Williams, up in northern Virginia.

The woman put an identical sandwich down in front of Cleotis. He reached for his wallet but Denzelle shook his head and let him know that he had it covered. The woman smiled at Denzelle some more and then brushed her hip up against his shoulder. It took all of the strength Denzelle had in him not to reach out and pat her behind, which had to be as delectable as his sandwich.

Cleotis bit into the sandwich. Those tomatoes had to be homegrown. This was one of the best chicken salad sandwiches he'd eaten in a long time. He watched as Rev. Flowers finished his second half, and suddenly and out of the blue got the oddest feeling that he was sitting with a cop. He pretended to be into his sandwich and tried to observe the set of this preacher's eyes without being noticed too much. Cops had special eyes—as if they could see right through you, especially if you were lying to them.

This brother's eyes were kind of weird. Too kind for a cop but too sharp not to be one. Then it dawned on Cleotis that this brother was a preacher and a cop, no...

"FBI," Cleotis blurted out before he could catch himself.

"Huh," was all Denzelle could say. He hoped that his cover wasn't blown. He'd been being a cop all week, and pretending at being a preacher, even though when he was with the FBI he felt like a preacher pretending to be a cop.

"You are FBI, aren't you, Rev. Flowers? Dang, man, that's a ter-rifying combination. Work for the Lord *and* the feds. You are scary negro, brother-man."

Denzelle smiled. This time it was the cop smile—the one that sent chills through a brother-man who was up to no good. And under any other circumstances it would have sent chills through Cleotis. Only thing, he'd recently quit his illegal activity in this city, and was looking forward to going back home. So he didn't have anything to be worried about. Because as good a cop as he suspected this preacher was, he knew that whatever Rev. Flowers knew—and he suspected that the man knew plenty—he didn't have anything that could stick on Cleotis.

Denzelle smiled again. This time it was the smile of a preacher. The brother was beginning to give poor Cleotis the willies. He said, "Guilty as charged. Only thing, brother, is that I don't want this to get out. I don't have a lot on you right now. But if you blow my cover, I swear I'll get what I need and send you up for another stint in prison. Only this time you will not get anything that will make it possible for you to get clemency and get out. And you won't be going to a prison near your home. I like the federal prison system 'cause I can send you where I think you need to go."

Now the preacher was grinning like a preacher and sounding like a cop with eyes that held a combination of the Scriptures and the law. Cleotis was scared of this man, and wondered if anybody else had sense enough to be afraid of this brother. He hoped his boy Dotsy Hamilton was running late as usual. Because as soon as he got a whiff of this cop he was going to piss in his pants. And Grady Grey? Poor Grady wouldn't be able to keep any food in his system for the rest of the day. Folk didn't know that Grady Grey was a sensi-tive kind of brother. And his entire digestive tract went crazy when he encountered something like this.

This was a scary brother. And he was at this table to find out about the very operation that put the three of them at risk for a con-viction and some serious time.

"Tell me about WP21," Denzelle said evenly.

Cleotis choked on his sandwich. He thought, *Dang, this bro is good.*

Cleotis wasn't sure if he should spill his guts—even though he'd never been a snitch—or just play dumb. He opted for dumb, shrugged, and said, "What in the world is WP21?"

Denzelle appreciated this man's not selling out the folks he was involved with. But he didn't appreciate being played for a fool. He leaned into the table and stared into Cleotis's eyes. Cleotis started to sweat. This time the FBI agent, the one who would shoot you in the head without hesitation, was looking straight at him.

Denzelle said, "I'm gonna ask you one more time. And then if you don't answer me to my satisfaction, I'm putting a tail on you and your two boys from Durham, Dotsy Hamilton and Grady Grey. When we have something on you all, we'll beat what we want you to tell us out of you, simply because we can."

Cleotis pushed his sandwich away. All of a sudden he wasn't all that hungry. In fact, he was feeling kind of queasy. He pushed the coffee away. It would only upset his stomach more. Denzelle, on the other hand, was feeling as if he could use another sandwich. He gulped down the rest of his coffee and then drank up his glass of water.

Cleotis decided to stall for now until he could talk to Dotsy and Grady and get a better feel for this man. He decided to tell Denzelle Flowers just enough to keep the brother off of him until the three of them could figure out a plan, and then have enough information that they could get some immunity with if they needed it.

He said, "Pastor, all I know for the moment is that WP21 is a drug for the men preachers, especially the ones fifty and over, who want to make this week memorable."

Denzelle grinned and sucked on his tooth. He'd had a taste of the stuff and could only imagine what it would do for some of these old pimps parading around in clerical collars, being more trouble than they were worth, and continuing a tradition of womanizing that seriously undermined the spiritual growth of folks in the church. Denzelle sometimes worried about the fate of his beloved church if they didn't put a lid on this craziness.

There were people who wanted to turn their lives completely over to Christ. But they would never be able to take that leap of faith if some of these preachers kept doing stuff that was in complete opposition to the Word of God. Unfortunately, people like this would use a bad preacher as an excuse to run from Jesus, while they hoped in the innermost recesses of their hearts that a real preacher existed to point the way back to the Lord.

Cleotis Clayton was sitting across from him looking exactly like somebody who secretly wanted to connect with a good preacher. Of all of the people Denzelle would have expected to be searching for Jesus, it wasn't this brother. Maybe Bishop Hemphill, Bishop Giles, Sonny Washington, Ernest Brown, and Marcel Brown were not winning at their game. Maybe there was hope for the Gospel United Church after all.

"Cleotis," Denzelle began, "I'm FBI. I'm a preacher. And if all goes well at this Triennial Conference I'll be the pastor of a church here in my home state of North Carolina. I got this piece," Denzelle pulled his coat back to reveal a fancy charcoal leather shoulder holster weighed down by his gun.

"If I come back with enough information to help you, Reverend," Cleotis began, wondering if he was having a moment of temporary insanity, sitting here offering to help a cop, "will you make it possible for me to have a heart-to-heart talk with Murcheson James? Will you grant me immunity? Will you forget that my Durham boys, Grady Grey and Big Dotsy Hamilton, ever had anything to do with this? And will you let us keep all the money we've been making on the side with our own version of WP21?"

Denzelle started laughing and slapped the table. He said, "Are you telling me that the three of you figured out that formula? I've sent several batches to the FBI lab in Virginia, and they cannot duplicate that stuff."

"We haven't figured out a thing," Cleotis said, guarded, making a mental note to put a better watch on his big mouth. "We just made some money, okay. But uhhh, I could find out for sure if there is something out there being presented as the real deal, even though I suspect it's tainted."

"Tainted?" Denzelle queried. He'd had a taste of that stuff and it was awful. What could make what Cleotis had gotten ahold of worse than the stuff he had ingested?

"Yeah, preacher, tainted. Bishop Hemphill is as greedy and crooked as they come. I never thought I'd meet someone who was worse that the ungodly four—Bishop Larsen Giles, Rev. Marcel Brown, Rev. Sonny Washington, and the late Bishop Otis Caruthers. But as bad as they are, they ain't got jack on Rucker Hemphill."

"Okay," Denzelle said, thinking that Cleotis was right about Bishop Hemphill. "If you just happen to run up on some information, you can reach me here. And I suggest that you make sure to contact me. Don't get slick, and then find yourself locked up."

Denzelle pushed his FBI card with his mobile phone number on it across the table. Cleotis read it carefully and pushed it back. Denzelle put the card back in his breast pocket. This was serious if Cleotis had memorized his number because he didn't want to get caught with that card on him.

"If you and any of your friends need to talk to me, I'll make sure y'all are okay. So what you need to do right now is close down shop, so that I don't have to come and take what you already have."

Cleotis narrowed his eyes. Even though he was closing down his end of the business, there was still some good money to be made before he left Durham. Cleotis, Grady, and Dotsy, with the help of Twilight from the Sock It to Me Club in Warren County, had figured out the formula for WP21. Twilight's grandmother grew watermelons, and she also made natural medicines. It was Twilight's grandmother who had broken it down and made a couple of batches for them, as long as they sliced off some profits for her and her grandbaby. Nobody knew they had this because they had sold the potion on the down low and outside Durham County. They were making too much money to shut down shop now. They needed to sell a few more batches before closing down.

Denzelle could see straight through Cleotis. Yeah—he was going to lose a whole lot of money. But that was a drop in the bucket compared to losing your freedom, then having all kinds of fines and fees to pay that would eat up everything you had earned.

"So what you're about to tell me is that a suite in a federal prison of my choosing is better than what I'm trying to offer you and your colleagues."

Cleotis squirmed. Hadn't realized it was that serious. Just thought this was about some low-life preachers lapping up some of that nasty stuff to get their freak on.

"Look," Denzelle was saying. "I know Dotsy Hamilton. And I went to school with Grady Grey. They do not want to go to prison any more than you do. And while Dotsy is basically an okay brother, he'll still drop your butt to the bottom of the Atlantic Ocean, wearing some cement gators, if he thinks you had anything to do with him getting busted."

Cleotis sighed heavily. This cop/preacher was right. They'd have to give it up. He raised his hands in surrender and waited to find out what this deadly preacher was planning. It was a scary and yet strangely exhilarating feeling. He smiled at Denzelle Flowers, who grinned and held out his hand for some skin. Sometimes criminals made the best allies.

SIXTEEN

Theophilus and Essie, Eddie, Johnnie, Theophilus's sister Thayline, and her husband Willis packed into the modest-sized elevator at their hotel, the Governor's Inn in Research Triangle Park, North Carolina, right outside of Durham. It was a nice hotel, had decent food, and a good location for tonight's celebration.

They knew that they were in for a ferocious fight for that Episcopal seat, and had decided to "travel light" for this conference. The last time they had attended this conference they had had a much larger entourage. But this time the folk (Lee Allie, Mr. Pompey, Uncle Booker, Rose Neese, and Theophilus's parents) had decided to stay at home. They said they were too old to be bothered, would watch over the children, and would keep them lifted up in prayer.

They had come a long way since that Triennial General Conference back in 1963, when the only places they could have a big banquet was at church, at a historically black college, or at one of the Masonic halls. It was nice to celebrate this event at the Governor's Inn. And they hoped that being here would give them a respite from the cutthroat and intense church politics that permeated the campus meetings and the worship services held at Rev. Quincey's home church, Fayetteville Street Gospel United Church, not too far from Eva T. Marshall University.

Tonight's affair was the big fancy event held at every Triennial Conference. The tickets were pricey, and they hoped that the food would taste good. There was nothing worse than having to sit through a banquet with a bunch of nasty-tasting food spread out all over your table. And then you hoped the nearest McDonald's or Hardee's was still open when the banquet was finally over.

Thayline and Willis would have preferred to skip this old boring banquet and spend the evening eating at Mama Dip's Restaurant several miles down the way in Chapel Hill. But they had promised Theophilus, or Baybro, that they would stomach a bunch of hinctified negroes who didn't have a clue about what real life was all about.

Thayline, who had worked in food service for years, made a quick and thorough scan of the food tables as soon as they had given the mean-looking women at the front table their tickets and gone into the banquet room.

Good, she thought. *They are giving us a buffet. Maybe there is hope for this affair.*

Thayline walked up to one of the food tables to check out the servers and find out what was on the menu. She never ate off of any banquet table if the servers' uniforms were not crisp and clean, there was too much hand contact with the food, they talked and laughed too much over the dishes, they left the table messy, or they were slow and surly when you were trying to get something to eat.

Unfortunately, the generic church banquet hadn't changed much over the past ten or fifteen years. Usually, it was the same-old-same-old—baked chicken, string beans, some kind of potato, salad, rolls, chocolate cake, and potato pie. Sometimes they served you at your table. Sometimes they let you serve yourself at a mock buffet table. But it was still the same-old-same-old.

But tonight Thayline was pleasantly surprised by the spread laid out before her. It was a delight to behold. Fried chicken, Buffalo wings, huge shrimp, chopped barbecue, and baked chicken. There were three salads—spinach, seven-layer, and one of those old-fashioned lettuce-and-tomato salads with plenty of cucumbers, red onions, and boiled eggs. Plus, there were plenty of delectable side dishes including potato salad, deviled eggs, deep fried string beans coated with red pepper, fresh veggies and a homemade ranch dip, fried okra, cauliflower, zucchini, and squash, fresh fruit salad loaded down with red, juicy watermelon, and an assortment of homemade rolls. There was a delicious sparkling punch as well as fabulous desserts—red velvet cake squares, slices of German chocolate and lemon-coconut cake, huge chocolate chip and butterscotch cookies, and tiny squares of homemade fudge in white and rich milk chocolate.

While Thayline was walking around trying to find the caterer, Miss Hattie Lee Booth, who she heard had recently turned in her pole as a stripper at the Lucky Lady Club, her husband, Willis, was busy refilling his plate. This food was delicious and he was glad that they didn't have to sit at a boring banquet table, waiting for their section of the banquet hall to be served, and then have to wait even longer to eat because it was considered bad taste to start eating while there were folks still left to be served.

Johnnie Tate was so happy to see her girl Thayline. She remembered when the two of them used to cook and serve food in those ugly, hospital green service uniforms and black hairnets. Thayline used to fuss at her for hemming her uniform too short and taking it in on the sides so that it hugged all her curves.

The two of them laughed whenever they talked about Johnnie's sexy wardrobe back in the day, and how it got and kept Eddie's attention. The red chiffon chemise with the big dip in the back that Johnnie wore to that infamous service to vote for the new bishops in 1963 had been priceless. That dress was the defining moment for Eddie. He couldn't keep his hands and eyes off Johnnie in that outfit, and purposed in his heart that he would marry that girl and keep her supplied with an arsenal of sexy dresses. To this day there was no woman in their church who could compete with how good and sexy the first lady of Mount Zion Gospel United Church in Chicago looked in her clothes.

By the time Bishop James and Bishop Jennings had arrived at their table, they were all well into their second helpings of all of that good food. For once this was a decent banquet. At least it was decent thus far. Eddie waved at the bishops, jaw stuffed with those delicious fried string beans.

"Y'all, this food is so good." He chewed and swallowed, and put some more string beans in his mouth. "This is the best banquet we've had that I know of. Maybe we need to come to North Carolina more often, if we get to eat this good."

"Yeah," Theophilus added, wiping buffalo wing sauce off the corner of his mouth with a fancy white napkin. "Let's hope that the actual program is as good as this food."

"District One has really gone the extra mile to make this conference work," Percy Jennings told them.

"Yeah, and that is solely because the churches in the Triangle worked so hard on this conference," Percy's wife, Vivian Jennings, said. She had just arrived this morning and was looking like a million dollars in a white chiffon shirt with a big collar, silver silk slacks that were cropped at the ankle, and silver silk pumps. She really looked like Nancy Wilson with all that silver running through her beautifully cropped hair.

Percy used to be the presiding bishop for District One before he was elected to serve as the senior bishop for the entire denomination. It was a good district. And with few exceptions, like Sonny Washington, it had a good pool of preachers and pastors.

"Well," Theophilus began, "I, for one, am relieved that the First District didn't include that mess about announcing the top candidates for bishop at this conference. I hate going through that."

"Man, I hate that, too," Eddie said. "And they always pick the bishop who is so boring, and goes on and on and on about absolutely nothing, to make the announcements."

"I know," Susie James said, as she approached their table with a plate loaded down with good food. "I was just thinking about that very same thing. Y'all remember what happened at the preelection banquet at the last Triennial Conference in California?"

"How in the world could we forget that mess?" Murcheson asked his wife. "Bishop Willie Williams was presiding and he opted to let his favorite presiding elder, Rev. Juniper Dowd, handle the banquet."

"I know," Percy added, shaking his head. "They should have known it was going to be crazy dealing with a negro named 'Juniper.'"

"Yeah," Murcheson said. "Juniper 'hired' his mama to do the catering."

"Could she cook, Rev. James?" Essie asked. Even though Murcheson had been a bishop for many years and was now officially her husband's boy, she still called him "Rev. James."

"Yeah, surprisingly, she was a good cook—just stingy as heck. She doled out that food like we were being rationed. It was awful."

"Baby, tell them what they did when you asked for an extra chicken wing," Susie said.

"That stingy woman cussed me out," Murcheson told them. "But that wasn't the worst part of it. Juniper took it upon himself to announce the top candidates, and got the names wrong and just made a mess of the order of candidates from bottom to top."

"Well, I am so glad that we can bypass that tonight," Essie said. "And I hope that we can eat and get up out of here without too much drama. I would say without any drama but we are at a banquet for the Gospel United Church, and at a Triennial Conference."

Surprisingly, the evening was going smoothly. They were having a good time, and nothing crazy had jumped off. Sometimes craziness popped up as soon as they walked in the room. That had not happened—at least not yet. But, as Willis pointed out, the folk who always came in popping off drama had yet to put in an appearance.

This was turning out to be the most pleasant evening of the entire week. They had been spending long hours at the campaign booth. They worked the crowd in their assigned spot in the university's gymnasium until late in the evening. The booth was one of the nicest. Essie and Johnnie had spent a lot of time working with the rainbow color scheme.

The booth was decorated in an array of primary colors, with a rainbow arched across the top. Eddie's picture was prominent on the back wall of the booth, and they had canvas director's chairs circling the table in red, blue, purple, green, and yellow. Just the colors alone drew people over to them. And once they got there and got some of that good ice cream, along with a host of other goodies, folk left feeling good and encouraged to support the Eddie Tate campaign.

This had not been the case for the Sonny Washington campaign booth, which had been allocated a better and more visible spot than Eddie's booth. They knew this had been done intentionally. But what the Devil meant for evil, God had certainly worked out for their good.

Sonny's booth was bland—a plain setup with his campaign colors of blue and black. They didn't even have brochures—just some blue fliers. And they didn't give away anything, even though more men than women had come to the booth at odd hours of the day. About the only noticeable thing happening over in the Washington camp was that lockbox of cash they kept going into when folks came by the booth.

By the time most folk left that booth they were eager for something more substantive, and made their way to the back where the Tate booth was located. Folks came by Eddie's booth and stayed and talked and laughed and had a good time. They left with a bag of goodies, refreshed from the ice cream, and filled with joy. Everybody was buzzing that the Tate campaign booth was fun—not to mention that they had some good music, blasting gospel, old-school R & B, and a little bit of rap with clean lyrics for the youngsters.

Their campaign team was working tirelessly. Theophilus and Eddie had been up to the wee hours of the morning going from one district meeting to the next, connecting with the delegates and making sincere appeals for their support on the day of the election of bishops and new church officers for the next three years.

They had spent a lot of money giving financial aid to the delegates from districts in Africa and the Caribbean. Unfortunately, with the sole exception of Bishop Bobo Abeeku out of Ghana, all the overseas districts, including the ones in the Caribbean, were guilty of sending over a group of delegates on budgets so tight some of the pastors couldn't afford to catch a cab from the airport. The districts presided over by Bishops Hemphill, Caruthers, Jr., and Babatunde were the worst. And if that was not bad enough, these districts had plenty of money—most of it being directed to support the personal interests of the bishops.

So they were feeding folk and paying for a few hotel rooms, and they had even paid for a doctor's visit for one of the delegates who came from the airport coughing, sneezing, and running a high fever. And this didn't include the cost of all of those goodie bags filled with movie tickets, gift certificates to South Square and Northgate Malls, a van to take them to the malls, and snacks to nibble on.

It had been a long and grueling week. They were coming to the countdown to select two new Episcopal leaders. Despite the ups and downs, disputes and disagreements, and more drama than a soap opera, this Triennial Conference had been a good conference—one of the best in years. And they hoped that this banquet would end without any flare-ups, fights, or intrigue.

Just as the musicians selected and hired by Sonny Washington's church members made their way to the stage, Essie and Johnnie swung their heads around to witness the entrance of Sonny's entourage. Thayline's husband, Willis, who was usually content to sit back quietly nibbling and taking in the sights, blurted out loudly enough to be heard by every other nearby table, "Lawd Jesus, somebody has cleaned Hell out…'cause every devil in the lair is walking up in the banquet hall."

The folks at the next table leaned over and said, "Man, you ain't never lied on that one. I don't know if I've ever seen this much devilment ganged up and walking in a room together."

Leading the pack was the Episcopal candidate Sonny Washington, overdressed in a black tuxedo with a rich purple ruffled shirt, a silver-and-purple brocade bow tie, and matching cummerbund. He had on purple patent leather slip-on shoes with black leather bows on the tops.

"I thought you said that Sonny Washington was a womanizer," Thayline whispered to Essie.

"He is—big time," Essie whispered back, scared to talk too much for fear of missing something. She wondered why they were all dressed in formal attire when the banquet instructions clearly called for semiformal clothes.

"Well, he look gay to me," Thayline said.

"He a punk," Johnnie said, "but that negro ain't gay. He ain't even happy."

"Shhh!" all the men hissed. "Y'all gone make us miss the rest of the show."

Right behind Sonny was Marcel Brown, dressed in a pale purple tuxedo with a black ruffled shirt and black-and-silver brocade accessories. His newly done Jheri curl glistened in the strobe lights that somebody had just flipped on, obviously to enhance the "effect."

"I sho' hope that negro don't fling that hair in my direction," was all Johnnie said. She knew that all that curl activator in Marcel's already curly hair would do a terrible number on her pale peach silk halter dress. Johnnie had worried Essie to no end to get her to design and make this dress for her. It had taken over a month for the chiffon to get to Essie's boutique in St. Louis, and then an extra week for all the sequins spread out across the knee-length skirt of the dress to arrive.

"I hear you, girl," Essie said, looking protectively over her own pale pink, silk jersey knit dress that dipped low in the front, hugging every curve, and setting off those gold highlights in her hair, which was cut in a sleek and sophisticated bob. She knew that Sonny's wife, Glodean, was going to want to fight her over wearing what she considered to be her signature color at a big-time Gospel United Church affair. Essie wore this color on purpose because she knew it would make Glodean mad, and she wanted to let the girl know that she was not going to play by Glodean's myriad unspoken rules.

"Are you sure that they are not gay?" Thayline pressed. She couldn't believe that two men would come to this banquet wearing coordinated outfits and not be gay. "Because I can't help it. They look like they going together. You sure, you sure, they are not gay?"

"NO!" all the men at the table said in unison. Not one of them liked Sonny and Marcel—including Willis, who had had almost no contact with those two. But as ridiculous and "suspect" as those tuxedos appeared to the naked eye, those two were not gay. Crooks, liars, thieves, and hos? Most definitely. But not gay.

They would quickly discover that Marcel and Sonny's entrance was just the "appetizer" at the affair. As soon as Sonny had taken his seat at the head of the only square table in the room, with Marcel holding court right next to him, the rest of their committee walked in, acting as if this banquet had been held solely in their honor.

Ottah Babatunde brought new meaning to the term *showstopper* when he walked in practically resplendent in what Eddie Tate said had to be the baddest traditional Nigerian garb he'd ever seen. Bishop Babatunde was several inches past six feet, the color of ebony wood, and just so big and fine in that ivory-trimmed-with-gold outfit and matching hat and shoes that several preachers' wives searched their tables for something to fan themselves with.

Babatunde waved and smiled as if the folks in the room were his subjects, making mental notes of the women he knew would help him make good on his personal supply of WP21. It was almost too good to be true that he was in America looking this good, with a pocket full of pleasure, and practically a small village-full of luscious American women to choose from. Ottah, who didn't like open displays of emotion, felt like doing shouting laps around the banquet room at just the thought of how his evening promised to end.

"Are we in some kind of psychedelic drug nightmare? Or did that fake-African-King Negro just walk up in here like he owned the place?" Theophilus asked incredulously.

They had barely had time to digest Bishop Babatunde's brazen entrance when Bishop Rucker Lee Hemphill came in wearing a leopard skin draped over his black tuxedo, ivory shirt, and leopard-print bow tie and matching cummerbund. Essie's expert eyes traveled quickly to the bishop's shoes. She sighed in relief when all she saw were a pair of expensive patent leather slip-ons gracing Rucker Hemphill's feet. Because she just knew that crazy man would wear some leopard-print dress shoes.

"I thought animal skins like that were illegal," Susie James said.

"All depends when and where he got it," Murcheson told his wife. "Although I don't really think the folks Rucker bought that from were the kind of people who are overly concerned with the legalities and ethics of their enterprise."

"So Bishop Hemphill bought that leopard skin hot?" Essie asked. As far as she was concerned he looked ridiculous in a tuxedo with an animal skin draped over his shoulders like a woman's shawl. What in the world was he thinking to wear that to this affair, and in North Carolina at this time of the year? It was a miracle he hadn't passed out from heat stroke. But then the point was that he wasn't thinking— hadn't used half of a brain cell when he came up with this.

Eddie reached into his breast pocket and pulled out a twenty-dollar bill. He laid it on the table and said, "I bet that negro is going to pull two women tonight." He scanned the room for the women who appeared enamored of how good Bishop Hemphill looked in his African king suit. He found two.

The first one put the *g* in *gold digger*. Her eyes were so well trained to spot out authenticity when it came to luxury items—such as furs, gold, platinum, and diamonds—Eddie could have sworn she was working some kind of high-powered laser scope that required military clearance to use. Number two was just a straight up ho' with very expensive needs and taste.

Few of the "tomcatting" preachers at this conference would have been able to distinguish between the two women. And sadly, many of them would have gotten tangled up with contestant number one, thinking they were getting a good piece of expensive tail—rather than a pricey expense account with a few fringe benefits thrown in.

But Rev. Eddie Tate knew the difference, as did his assistant pastor, Denzelle Flowers. Early in his career Eddie had figured out how to spot out the good hos, and rule out the gold diggers, so he didn't waste money on a bad ho' who was a daggone good gold digger. While the good reverend had certainly sown some very wild oats, praise be to God, he had relinquished, repented of, and reformed from that worldly behavior many years ago.

Rev. Denzelle Flowers, on the other hand, had a ways to go toward total reform and repentance. That was one of the reasons Eddie had Denzelle tucked safely up under his wings. Baby boy needed protection, training, guidance, and prayer because he was too good a preacher to risk losing to the other side over some hot tail.

They were at war. Sometimes folks forgot that they were in a fierce battle with the forces of darkness, and that the Devil was dead serious about taking many folk, including the ones claiming to be God's own people, straight to Hell on a bullet train. This was the church, and from Eddie's vantage point they, the church, the preachers, were responsible for getting out on the battlefield for Jesus and fighting the Devil like the liar, thief, and murderer that the Word of God said he was.

Eddie was cool, streetwise, and a preacher who had once taken his calling way too lightly. But he didn't do that anymore. As cool as he knew he was, Eddie Tate counted as his greatest achievement in life, his ability to submit his life to Christ and be blessed with the anointing of the Holy Ghost.

Denzelle was a good man who was having trouble letting go of the flesh because he thought that he would miss out on something important in life if he did. And as Bishop James had told Eddie Tate when he was running from marrying Johnnie, the woman Eddie knew God had picked out to be his wife, the only thing he was missing out on was the first-class ticket to Hell the devil kept trying to give him.

They were at war all right. All anybody with half a brain had to do this evening was look around this room. It would become crystal-clear that all of this craziness was evidence that the Devil was busy tonight. Eddie wanted to laugh and cry at the same time. Some of this was comical and the rest was troubling. It practically broke his heart that this group of men could come up in this gathering of the saints with this mess. And not only were they going to get away with it, they were getting plenty of attention, some more votes, and more money, and pulling some women as an added bonus.

Eddie sighed so loudly and heavily, it gave Johnnie cause to stop laughing and go and tend to her man. She adored Eddie Tate and hated it when anything or anybody gave him a reason to give that sigh she knew so well. She slipped her slender, bejeweled hand into Eddie's huge hand and whispered words from the first chapter of Titus, verses six and seven.

"An elder must be well thought of for his good life. He must be faithful to his wife, and his children must be believers who are not wild or rebellious. An elder must live a blameless life because he is God's minister. He must not be arrogant or quick-tempered; he must not be a heavy drinker, violent, or greedy for money.

"You are that kind of elder, baby," Johnnie told her husband, and then kissed his hands, leaving soft peach lip prints on them.

Eddie smiled, resisted an urge to pat that wide butt, and kissed his wife's cheek. He must have been on some drugs to think that it made sense to run from this woman. She was fine, sexy, unconventional, smart, saved, and everything he'd ever wanted in a woman. He was a blessed man.

Denzelle Flowers watched the exchange between Rev. Tate and his wife from across the room, where he was standing with Obadiah Quincey. He felt a twinge in his heart—a longing for that kind of relationship. But where in the world would he find a woman who was worthy of being bone of his bone and flesh of his flesh? Denzelle had seen a lot of women to dabble with but had yet to come across that one.

He nudged Obadiah, who was standing there trying to ignore his wife Lena's antics. When Bishop Hemphill walked in with that leopard stole on his tuxedo, she made a paw with her hand and said, "Grrrrrrrr…Beeeshippp…" in a fake Eartha-Kitt-as-Catwoman voice.

All Denzelle could do was shake his head and laugh, saying, "Obie, that is your bone of your bone and flesh of your flesh."

Obadiah smiled and tried once more not to look at Lena, who was now thoroughly engrossed in part two of the "halftime show." It appeared that Rucker Hemphill's entrance wasn't enough. Never mind that he had on a leopard stole, it just wasn't enough. Because as soon as the bishop had taken his seat at their table, Ernest Brown rolled Bishop Larsen Giles into the room while Whitney Houston's "Saving All My Love for You" blasted out of the sound system.

Denzelle couldn't stand that song—especially when Whitney started belting out, "tonight is the night for feeling all right…we'll be making love the whole night through…" It was just ridiculous to him that a woman would get all excited over the thought of spending stolen time with another woman's husband. That was just plain stupid—not to mention dead wrong.

But what was beyond stupid was what Marcel Brown's dad was wearing. The buzz of voices came to a halt as soon as folks got an eyeful of Ernest's tuxedo. Whereas Rucker had on a leopard stole, Ernest Brown, never one to be outdone, not even by a bishop, was wearing a black silk tuxedo with a zebra cape, zebra-skin shoes, and a matching zebra fedora.

At the point when Bishop Percy Jennings was about to say, "I think I've seen it all," they all laid eyes on Bishop Larsen Giles. It was just as Theophilus would later describe to their folk who did not attend this banquet: "Never in this lifetime could I have wrapped my mind around the mere possibility of seeing what we all saw."

First, Larsen Giles was in a wheelchair, when just hours ago he'd been seen walking around the grounds of the hotel wearing a bishop-purple jogging suit and moving with considerable pep in his step. So folk thought it odd that the bishop was in a wheelchair—especially since no one had seen him get hurt, or heard about any recent health problems. Folk also thought it odd that he was being wheeled in by Rev. Ernest Brown instead of his wife, who they suddenly realized had not been seen since they had come to the conference.

It was practically church protocol for all the wheelchair folk with wives to be wheeled into anywhere by those wives. In fact, many of those wives would have been wheeling those men around with such haughtiness that folk would have thought it was a new status symbol among the crème de la crème in the denomination to wheel your man around a church conference in a wheelchair. And a few of the serious and determined social climbers in the ministerial ranks would have hoped for an occasion to wheel somebody through a Gospel United Church event.

No one knew why Bishop Giles was in a wheelchair but everyone was dying to find out. Some thought it curious that the bishop, who wore only the most expensive suits fashioned by a man who ran his shop out of the basement in his home, deep in the hood in Detroit, was dressed in only half a suit. The top was super-sharp—deep purple with lavender chalk stripes, lavender shirt, and deep purple tie with black and pale gray stripes in it.

This fifty percent of this outfit was the perfect "bishop's suit." But the remaining half of the outfit was problematic. While Larsen Giles was sporting silk on his torso, his bottom half was adorned with purple velour jogging-suit pants. Now, they were very expensive jogging pants but they were still jogging pants.

Murcheson got up to get some more deviled eggs, so he'd have an excuse to get a better look at Larsen in that wheelchair. When he came back, the others were sitting there waiting on the report. He popped a deviled egg in his mouth and said, "Y'all do know that Larsen is wearing fancy patent leather bedroom slippers."

The band started playing an upbeat and jazzy version of the gospel hymn "Blessed Assurance." It sounded good enough to get the attention off Bishop Giles—which is what Marcel had hoped for when he gave the band director a hundred-dollar bill to play this song. It worked for all of ten seconds. Once the folk got used to hearing the groove of the song, they immediately refocused their attention back on the bishop.

"Why is he in public like that?" Willis asked. "He is all covered up with that thick blanket like something is wrong with his legs."

"And he stiff, too," Thayline added, wondering why the man had such limited control over his joints, especially in the lower part of his body. She'd noticed that Bishop Giles's feet had remained in the same L-shaped, upward-facing position on those metal wheelchair foot rests for the entire time he'd been in the banquet area.

"Why are his hands and fingers so stiff?" Essie whispered to Theophilus, who shrugged. Right now he wasn't as interested in Larsen Giles as he was in what was happening in two corners of the room. Theophilus couldn't understand why Eddie's mentee, Denzelle Flowers, was so interested in that no-count boy who was supposed to be one of Bishop Giles's new assistants, Rico Sneed.

Theophilus was even more perplexed when he saw Denzelle sneak and check the shoulder holster inside his suit coat.

Thayline's husband, Willis, came up to and stood next to his wife's baby brother. He stared at that young preacher who worked under Eddie for a moment, and then said, "Baybro, what is that young buck doing walking around this hotel with an FBI-issued gun?"

"Man, how you know that from way over here?"

Willis just stared at Theophilus as he had when Theophilus was a skinny teenager and tried to jump bad with him for dating his sister. He rolled his eyes and said, "The way he handling that gun and the way he packing it is like somebody with training. Not some negro who trained himself or got some good directions from the so-called gun expert on his street. No, that brother is trained, and he learned that stuff up in northern Virginia. You hear what I'm sayin', Baybro?"

Theophilus nodded and then turned back toward Eddie, who also had questions about that Rico boy's presence at the conference. He'd heard that Sonny's crew had hired a computer hotshot from the area to help them. There was more to that boy being here than that.

Eddie came and stood next to his best friend. He said, "You think anybody else has picked up on that Denzelle is FBI?"

Theophilus shook his head and said, "Eddie, Willis, and Thayline will see stuff long before everybody else."

"That there boy is a good cop and even better preacher," Murcheson James said. "How many Gospel United Church preachers do you know of that are capable of having that kind of firepower up on them and not find a way to broadcast it at an affair like this one?"

They all nodded. Murcheson was on the money with that observation. A lot of the preachers they knew with a license to carry the smallest pistols had the biggest mouths in the denomination. They talked big junk, walked around big-time, told themselves they were big shots, and as a result always found themselves embroiled in some of the biggest messes going on at any time. The ones with the sense and authority to carry the greatest firepower were always very low-key. The last thing that group wanted was for folk to know just what they had on them.

When Ernest wheeled Bishop Giles near their table, Essie, Thayline, and Johnnie got up, intent on easing over to where they were to get a better view. But they stopped when they remembered that all of Sonny Washington's supporters were at the table, and that they needed to find a better way to get in Bishop Giles's business.

Johnnie plopped back down in her chair.

"Dang!" she exclaimed. "Why did Marcel's daddy roll that sucker over to the table with all of those 'original' black people from Bishop Hemphill's district? Shoot! I don't want to sit here watching them talk. I want to know what is wrong with Bishop Giles."

"I know what's wrong with the bishop," a very familiar and proper voice said, as two welcome sights approached their table.

Essie hopped up and ran to give both Saphronia McComb James and Precious Powers a big hug. She said, "Lawd knows we glad to see y'all big butts. This is the most messed up preelection banquet that I have ever been to. And it started off so right."

Saphronia grinned and hugged her friend and homegirl. They had come a long way from when they were young back in Charleston, Mississippi, and couldn't stand the air each other breathed. But that was then, and this was now. Essie Lane Simmons had always been cool people. Saphronia had been too silly and stuck up to see it. It had taken her other good friend, Precious Powers, to help set her straight. She was glad that Precious had done that. Otherwise she would have missed out on a tremendous blessing.

"Essie, I don't know why you thought this banquet was going to be right. And I don't care how well it started out," Saphronia said.

"See," she continued evenly, "if you are so busy staring at the mess—as in that mess over there"—Saphronia pointed to Larsen Giles sitting in that wheelchair as if he were ten seconds short of full rigor mortis setting in—"then you will miss the mess going on over there."

Saphronia directed their attention to Rico Sneed, Kordell Bivens, and a skinny white boy talking near the door, right before money changed hands between Rico and the white boy.

"They just passed some money over to that white boy, didn't they?" Thayline asked, tempted to go over there and get a closer look.

"Yes. They, as in Rico Sneed and his friend, Kordell Bivens, have been helping Sonny Washington, Marcel Brown, Larsen Giles, and Rucker Hemphill sell something right up under our noses. I don't know what it is but I know they aren't selling Bibles and prayer cloths."

"Are you telling me that they are dealing crack cocaine?" Essie asked incredulously. She knew that group was bad news. Essie had always hoped that they had some boundaries. But she knew that if a white boy, who was dressed like a stagehand for Aerosmith, came up in here with all of these black church folk, he was coming for a very good reason. And the best reason for a Mötley Crüe type of white boy to come up in here like that was cold hard cash.

"No, not that," Precious Powers told them. Back in 1963 she'd been instrumental in bringing Marcel Brown down to his knees and stopping some mess that would have torn the church to shreds. Marcel had been her lover, and he had also been engaged to Saphronia at the same time. Those two women had ganged up on that man and turned him inside out. He'd never been the same, and his ministry, or at least the sham of a ministry he was so enamored of, had crumbled at his feet. From that day on Marcel Brown hadn't been able to stand the sight of Precious Powers and Saphronia James, and they could not have cared less about what he could or could not stand.

"Then what?" Thayline demanded.

"They have some kind of male stuff," Saphronia told them. "I don't know all the specifics…"

"But what she does know," Precious added, "is that they have come up with this drug that enhances the you-know-what and is supposed to make it work better, and be a whole lot more than what it really is in a short period of time."

"They got some ho' pills?" Johnnie asked, causing Thayline to crack up. That was what she loved about Johnnie Tate—her straight-up, shoot-from-the hip way of putting things.

"Well, I don't really know if I would call them whoring pills," Saphronia said. "But what I do know is that this powder stuff is supposed to be the end-all for a man wanting to act like he is Marvin Gaye and 'get it on.'"

"So, how do they take it… not in their arms?" Essie asked, causing the other ladies, including the very proper Saphronia, to turn and look at her as if she had just gone crazy.

"You know you can be such a little country girl when you want to, Essie Simmons," Precious said. She had been born and raised in Detroit and always prided herself on having big-city ways.

"Forget you, Precious," Essie said. She didn't care one bit that she was from a small town like Charleston, Mississippi. Precious didn't know everything just because she was from *Dee-troit*.

"Okay, I can see how you would ask that question with this powder stuff," Precious conceded. She had gone too far but hadn't meant to be mean. It was refreshing that there were still folks walking around who had not become jaded with worldliness. That was one of the things she loved about Essie.

"Look," she went on, "they call this stuff WP21, or Watermelon Powder 21 because it's made from watermelons. And I've heard it's supposed to make a middle-aged man feel like he's twenty-one all over again."

"How does it work?" Essie asked.

"Saphronia and I have been nosing around and we only have a little bit of information. But from what we've been told, it works real good."

They started laughing. Precious and Saphronia were always collecting dirt on bad preachers. And they made it their business to keep tabs on Marcel Brown.

"Y'all know y'all wrong," Johnnie said, laughing.

Saphronia and Precious were cracking up. They knew they needed to leave Marcel and his cronies alone, but wouldn't.

"But on a serious note," Precious said, "that stuff is selling like hotcakes and making your enemies a whole lot of money—money they are going to use to buy themselves some votes."

Ernest Brown wheeled Bishop Giles to another table of potential voters. Some of the bossiest and most controlling lay delegates in the church were seated at this particular table. These were the folks who loved to write anonymous letters to their pastors, telling them how they needed to do their jobs. They were the ones who were always accusing their pastors of taking money that didn't belong to them, even when everybody in the congregation knew that pastors could not just up and take money without going through a series of checks and balances designed to protect the church's accounts.

And when all else failed, they were the folk who sat through a highly anointed and charged-up service as if they didn't have a pulse or a heartbeat. Then, when the service ended, these same dry folk had the nerve to get all up in the pastor's face complaining vehemently about the service and why he let *those people* shout and praise the Lord like that. And a few had enough nerve to tell the pastor that if one more person ran around the church, and then started speaking in tongues right before falling out, they were going to call the police and have every last one of those lunatics handcuffed and carted away in the police van.

It was clear that the table's head honchos were giving the bishop an earful of all the stuff that had gotten on their nerves during this conference week. Bishop Giles had never been one to approve of a vibrant church service, and he tried his best to avoid the churches in his district with high rates of folks getting saved, getting anointed with the Holy Ghost, and joining the church. So it was clear that Bishop Giles was enjoying the round of conversations at this table far more than he had while parked at the previous one.

Larsen was more animated than he had been since Ernest Brown had first wheeled him into the banquet room. He laughed and talked and tried to raise his hands to emphasize what he obviously believed were the good points in the conversation. At one point Ernest must have said something very funny because everyone seated in that area was laughing, slapping palms, shaking his shoulders, and hitting at the table.

Not one to be left out of the fun, Larsen forced himself to raise up an arm, and then proceeded to hit the arm of the wheelchair, right before he hit his knee. The blanket that had been wrapped carefully around Larsen's body started slipping down below his waist. He didn't notice or feel the blanket slipping down because his body was stiff and slightly numb from his abdomen down to his toes. His cronies had wrapped his body in that light blanket to protect his body, and to try to get him warmed up enough to charge up his circulation.

The bishop, eager to get his hands on more WP21, had decided to try a big dose of the newly made powder Rico Sneed had just paid that white boy with the long hair, Grateful Dead T-shirt, overpriced athletic shoes, and very expensive pickup truck for. That white boy, Harold Dinkle, and his younger brother, Horace, were good and efficient at making the drug. But there was a problem with giving these white boys province over the manufacturing of this drug.

First, they cared even less about the potential customers than the men in this room trying to use this drug to buy an Episcopal seat. And because Harold Dinkle only saw green when his eyes traveled across the rainbow of brown faces in the banquet room, he was going to make as much of his own cheap and synthetic brand of WP21 as possible.

Rico and Kordell were hardheaded and rash. Unbeknownst to the preachers they worked for, Cleotis had come to them with an offer to make the potion from Twilight's grandmother. It was a better drug, and she was offering a better deal. But Rico had gotten mad and thrown a temper tantrum when Twilight's grandmother chastised him about his ugly ways, and then called him out on a lie. In his customary manner Rico had talked trash to that old lady, and then stormed out of the house, making a point of slamming the door.

It had taken Cleotis, Dotsy, and Grady a whole lot of persuading to keep Twilight from smashing in Rico's face. But they all figured that it was best to leave this alone, and allow this door to close. Twilight's grandmother would have worked hard to make sure WP21 wasn't toxic. She'd even figured out a way to lower the amount of ingredients that caused folk to crave the powder. But now those greedy and trifling preachers, along with that rude sociopath, Rico Sneed, would come to regret the pact they had made with the Devil's little helpers, Harold and Horace Dinkle.

From the moment that Harold Dinkle figured out what made WP21 work, he and his brother had worked dead into the night to figure out which synthetic additives would increase the drug's addictive qualities. They knew this could cause an adverse reaction if the user ingested more than what was compatible with his age, weight, and height. But Harold and Horace didn't care about that type of danger one bit.

When that blanket slipped off Larsen's body, it was clear that he was having a bad reaction to something. And whatever it was had done him in. As soon as Eddie Tate saw that blanket slipping, he hurried over to where the bishop was holding court, with Theophilus, Johnnie, and Essie hot on his heels. That tent configuration of the blanket in the bishop's lap had piqued Johnnie's and Essie's interest when Larsen Giles was wheeled in. At first they thought that maybe it was some kind of health care machine he had sitting in his lap. But that thought was definitely a "grasping for straws" explanation. And they would quickly learn what was really jutting out on the bishop's lap.

The conversation that had been so lively and full of laughter just minutes ago was completely wiped out by a hush, followed by some "Lawd Jezuz"es, one or two "What in the world"s, and a very loud "Girl, move, so I can see that."

Essie and Johnnie got as close to the bishop's wheelchair as they could without being too obvious with their nosiness. They were, after all, in enemy territory. The last thing they needed was for the enemy camp to notice them creeping up, trying to get all in its business.

Denzelle and Obadiah had already made their way over to the wheelchair. Lena, whom Obadiah had given instructions to stay in her seat, had simply ignored her husband and gone right over to a spot where she could see and hear everything. When Lena had gotten herself an eyeful, she went and stood with Essie and Johnnie, who were about to burst with curiosity, since their fishing expedition hadn't yielded much.

"What is wrong with Bishop Giles, Lena?"

"He is real stiff, Miss Johnnie," Lena answered carefully. She wasn't exactly sure how to give them a more accurate description of the state that Bishop Giles was in.

"How stiff?" Essie asked.

"Well, Miss Essie," Lena began carefully in her slow and deliberate voice, "the entire bottom half of the bishop's body is real stiff, like something is wrong with him."

She started laughing and then stopped, as Essie and Johnnie were standing there just staring at her, clearly waiting on more information than this weak mess she was handing them.

"Okay," Lena continued, "his hands are stiff, his feet are stiff and swollen, his joints, especially his knees, are stiff and swollen. In fact, *everything* is stiff and swollen. It's like he is all stiff and swole up. And he looks like a mess, with everything all swole up and stiff. I don't know why he even came out like that. He is so stiff, they couldn't even put real pants on him. I don't even know how the bishop can pee, being all messed up like that."

"Baby girl," Johnnie said, "put this conversation in reverse. Did I hear you say that the bishop has some kind of affliction that would make it hard for him to wear pants and pee?"

"Yes, ma'am."

Johnnie grabbed Essie's arm.

"Come on. We are going over and seeing that. And I don't care who is over there in their so-called camp of supporters."

They hurried over to that table. And this time they went and stood where they could get a perfect cinematic view of Larsen Giles, who looked as if he was getting stiffer and stiffer all over his body. Essie thought he looked just as crazy, and also very frightened.

All of a sudden Bishop Giles's body jerked back and his mouth froze. Ernest stared down at his best friend, tears filling his eyes. He'd told Larsen not to take all that stuff. And now this fool had up and stroked out on him. He looked around for his son, who ran over to his side.

"Marcel, call an ambulance. We have to get Larsen to a hospital."

"Okay, Dad," Marcel said, now scared himself.

Marcel had never seen his father so afraid. He'd told them not to take that stuff, especially when that Rico and his friend, Kordell, had gone and found some mountain white boys to be their suppliers. He knew to be cautious when Rico told them their names. Harold and Horace Dinkle? Who in their right mind would trust two white boys who ate bear meat, named Harold and Horace Dinkle?

Marcel watched as the bishop's mouth went from stiff to slack. He hoped folks thought this was a stroke brought on by hard living, high blood pressure, and the stress of this conference. The last thing they needed was for one of their "clients" to start putting two and two together. If they were not able to continue to convince their waiting customers that this stuff was not only the baddest male drug around but the safest, they were not going to have the money needed to buy Sonny's Episcopal seat. Tonight alone they had folks lined up to get some of that batch Harold Dinkle had just brought down from western North Carolina.

Some of their flunkies ran over to follow Ernest and Marcel, who were rapidly wheeling Larsen Giles out of the room. A few were truly concerned. Many were curious. And some just wanted to look important—as if they were so close to Larsen Giles and the Browns they would be falling short of their responsibilities if they didn't hurry and accompany them to the waiting ambulance.

Eddie noticed that Denzelle had quietly slipped out, obviously following the Browns and the bishop. Denzelle took note of Larsen Giles's condition and then made a call on his mobile telephone.

"Theo, man. How long do you think the FBI has been in on whatever is going on behind the scenes at this conference?" asked Eddie.

"Since long before Denzelle went to Mozambique," was all Theophilus said.

SEVENTEEN

Eddie pulled at his tie. He was glad that they did not have to wear tuxedoes to these events anymore. He was a big man, six foot six and a good 262. Tuxedoes just weren't his thing.

It had been a long and exhausting evening. Leave it to Marcel Brown and "nem" to turn what could have been a great church party into a big funky mess. Eddie's folks were tired and fed up with the way these Triennial Conferences were run. They had decided to forgo their plans to talk about this evening, and go back to their rooms to get a good night's sleep. This was something, as ominous as it was, that needed to wait until tomorrow when they were fresh, rested, and ready to go to war.

He sat down on the side of the bed and pulled off his shoes.

"Man, my feet are killing me, baby."

"I would massage those dogs, if the funk wouldn't burn my fingers off first," Johnnie told him, laughing.

"You wrong, woman. You know you are so wrong. How you gone treat your man like that, when his feet are aching?"

"How you gone ask your woman to touch them stanky thangs in the name of love?"

Eddie got up off the bed and started stripping down to get in the shower. He held his hand out toward his wife.

"Want to join me?"

All Johnnie did was smile and peel down to Eddie's all-time favorite outfit—her birthday suit. She sucked on her sapphire tooth and licked her lips.

"You are a fast thing, Mrs. Tate," Eddie said, and then winked. He turned on the shower, made sure the water was at the perfect temperature, stepped in, and then pulled his wife close to his body.

Johnnie was not a short woman. But she had to stand on her tip-toes to reach her husband's mouth.

"Mmmmm," she murmured in sheer delight. They had been dog-tired when they got back to the room. Johnnie assumed that her hubby, who had been going strong since four-thirty that morning, would sit on the side of the bed and fall asleep before he got his shoes off good. But this boy was acting all frisky, and he didn't have any WP21. Now this was the way to end the evening.

Johnnie kissed Eddie's lips again. Just the touch of his lips on hers made Johnnie moan softly. That man had the best kisses in the Windy City. Before she met Eddie, Johnnie had had her fair share of men in her life. So she knew when a man knew how to put it on you and when he didn't. She always told Essie that you could look at a brother-man and tell whether or not he had any special "skills" worth paying any attention to.

In fact, one of Johnnie and Essie's favorite people-watching things to do when they were waiting on their husbands to emerge from one of those long and drawn-out conference meetings was a game called "Do you think he got skills?" They were having such a good time laughing and playing this game on the campus that Precious and Saphronia came over to find out what they were up to. And then they wouldn't leave until Essie and Johnnie promised to let them play, too. It turned out that Miss Saphronia McComb James was better than all of them at figuring out who was skillful and who was a dud.

The biggest surprise came when Saphronia told them that Rev. Denzelle Flowers had too many skills for his own good, and it was going to cause him problems if he didn't get on his knees more and cultivate a richer relationship with the Lord. And then she had them cracking up when she told them that Bishop Ottah Babatunde from Nigeria might have looked like an African king, running around the campus in all of that overpriced garb he liked to wear, but he was a measly peasant behind closed doors.

When they questioned her judgment because Babatunde was so big and fine, Saphronia made a bet that she could find a woman willing to confess whether she was right or wrong. They were mad at Saphronia when she managed to find a loose-legged heifer named Tangie Bonner who blabbed out all of Ottah's pitiful business. Johnnie had really hated handing over that hundred-dollar bill when they went shopping at one of those quaint boutiques in Raleigh's Cameron Village.

That day Saphronia spent three hundred dollars in that store and didn't have to pull a dime from her designer bag. Johnnie vowed that this would be the last time she tangled with Saphronia on a bet. Who knew that Miss Thang had all of those skills?

But the surprise came when Miss Saphronia told them that Bishop Abeeku from Ghana was the man in closed quarters. When they all looked at her with raised eyebrows because the bishop seemed so nerdy (even if he did have an African accent), all Saphronia did was roll her eyes and then tell them to check out the bishop's wife. It didn't take them long to note that Mrs. Abeeku, who was lush and beautiful, acted just as Susie James did with Bishop James.

And they knew just from the tiny bit Susie had let slip, that old country boy, who loved the feel of Mississippi soil running through his fingers, could put it on his wife. Susie once slipped and told them that Murcheson could clear up your skin better than anything that Clearasil could do. And Susie James had some of the most beautiful skin in the entire Gospel United Church.

Johnnie smiled to herself and practically purred when Eddie stood behind her, giving her the delightful experience of feeling the entire length of him pressed against her body. She blushed— something only Eddie had ever seen Johnnie do. He knew that his wife had been around the block. But when Johnnie decided to get saved and make Jesus Lord of her life, she became brand-new, washed clean, made whole, and purified from the inside to the outside. She was like the women in the Bible who had some very colorful pasts before it occurred to them that the Lord was what they'd been looking for all that time.

Eddie held Johnnie in his arms, his heart burning with love for this woman who was so totally his. He could feel her heart in his heart. It was the most miraculous experience and Eddie didn't think he'd ever grow used to this—that it would always be a wonder and breathtaking experience for him to feel Johnnie's heart beating just for him.

He kissed her neck. It was wet and soft, and he could still taste her perfume. She leaned closer to him and for a moment all Eddie could do was whisper, "Thank you, Lord," before he got busy making that hot water sizzle. It had been a long and very interesting day, and making love to his wife was just what he needed to bring it to a close.

Eddie and Johnnie were freezing when they came out of the shower. They had kept the heat going in there so long they found themselves having to take a cold shower for real. Shivering, they hopped in the bed and pulled up all the covers. Eddie pulled Johnnie into his arms and kissed her on the forehead. He said, "Girl, you keep that up and I'm gonna have to go and find some of whatever that stuff is Rucker Hemphill been running around the conference whispering about, and trying to convince folks to buy."

"Is that the same stuff that had Bishop Giles looking like this?" Johnnie asked. She sat up in bed and fixed her hands and legs as Bishop Giles had been positioned in the wheelchair.

Eddie started laughing and said, "You missing something."

Johnnie reached over to the nearby chair, grabbed one of the small decorative pillows, and placed it in the middle of her body to form the same kind of tent that Larsen Giles had had.

"You know you are so wrong," Eddie told her, cracking up with laughter. If that crazy girl didn't have Bishop Giles sitting up in the wheelchair down pat, he didn't know who did.

"Then why are you laughing?" Johnnie asked in between chuckles. "You know that Bishop Giles was looking just as crazy. And did he really believe that nobody would notice this?" She patted the pillow.

"I'm surprised it took as long as it did for somebody to see it," was all Eddie said. "Plus, I can't understand how Larsen Giles thought he wouldn't look weird. Why would Ernest wheel him in like that?

He is supposed to be the bishop's boy. Baby, you know good and well that I would not have wheeled Theophilus up into a banquet hall looking crazy like that."

Johnnie nodded. Neither Eddie nor Theophilus would have allowed that to happen. She didn't understand why no one in Larsen's camp had tried to dissuade him from showing up in public like that.

Eddie sat up and got the telephone off the nightstand.

"Who are you calling, baby? It's late."

"Denzelle Flowers. I want to know if there is any news on Bishop Giles's condition."

"Why not call Theophilus?"

Eddie blushed.

"Baby?" Johnnie said, laughing because like her, Eddie rarely blushed. "Is there a reason you can't call Theophilus?"

"Well...I kind of saw him heading back to his and Essie's suite with a very expensive bottle of champagne in the crook of his arm."

"Yep, you better call Denzelle. 'Cause if you call your ace boon coon, you will get cussed out."

Eddie nodded and said, "And it will be Essie and not Theophilus cutting up with me."

"You dang skippy it'll be Essie," Johnnie told him. "This conference has been the craziest and most stressful one we've ever attended with you guys. And I hate to tell you this but you and your ace have been slipping on the job just a taste, and not taking care of business behind closed doors."

Eddie hung up the phone and rolled Johnnie over on her back. He pulled a long, pale brown leg up around his hip.

"Slippin'? Me? I'll show you what is slippin', red bone."

"You are so nasty, Eddie Tate."

"You like it, too. Don't you, red bone?"

"Who you callin' a red bone, boy? You just as red as me."

"Yeah, I'm red and hot, like red hots. And you know how much you love yourself some red hot candy."

Eddie started kissing the nape of Johnnie's neck and pulled the other leg up on his hip.

"So, you like how I'm slippin' on the job now, baby?" he whispered in a voice that was so low and sexy, Johnnie could barely contain herself.

But she was not about to let the good pastor think he'd gotten the best of her just yet. She sucked on that sapphire tooth, grinned up at Eddie, and said, "I think you could do better."

"Better than this," Eddie whispered.

Johnnie blushed.

"Or better than that."

Johnnie blushed some more and didn't say another word.

"Can't get much better than this, can it, baby?" Eddie whispered and began to make up for what he knew had been a rough week. He even added some extra mileage for what he knew was the beginning of a few more rough days.

All Johnnie could say was, "You know you the man, baby."

"Yes, I am, baby," he replied. "And you better recognize."

EIGHTEEN

Denzelle stuffed a forkful of those delicious pancakes in his mouth. They had been eating hotel and campus food for over a week. And this meal at Rev. Quincey's old schoolmate Lamont Green's Aunt Queen Esther's house was just what the doctor ordered.

Rev. Tate had called him and asked if there was someplace they could meet away from everything and everybody. After giving it some serious thought, he and Obadiah settled on Miss Queen Esther's house. She was a loyal member of Obadiah's home church, Fayetteville Street Gospel United Church. Her family was good friends with Fayetteville Street's current senior pastor, Rev. Russell Flowers—Denzelle's uncle. And she was a praying woman who was real tight with Jesus. His uncle Russell always joked and called Miss Queen Esther Jesus' first cousin.

Most of the folk they wanted to avoid at the conference wouldn't be able to find them at Queen Esther's house, they wouldn't even know they were there, and they certainly wouldn't be able to find out what they were up to. It was a relief to be able to sit down together without having to deal with any of their adversaries, or worrying if any of their flunkies were nearby, working overtime to listen in on the conversation. All throughout the conference there had been some encounter with Marcel Brown, Ernest Brown, Sonny Washington, Rucker Hemphill, Ottah Babatunde, Larsen Giles, or that no-good Rico Sneed and his best friend, Kordell Bivens.

About the only one in that unholy alliance they didn't have to be bothered with was Ray Caruthers, who had been holed up in his room with a messed-up stomach since his feet touched American soil. What they didn't know was that Ray had been the first conference casualty of WP21. Bishop Caruthers had forgotten his promise to himself to leave that stuff alone, when he kept running into one fine and willing woman over and over again. Shortly after taking too many swigs of that nasty stuff, Caruthers was forced to spend most of his time in the bathroom once the substance made its way through his very sensitive digestive system.

Queen Esther was absolutely delighted when Rev. Flowers's nephew called her and asked if they could meet at her house. She had been at that infamous 1963 Triennial Conference in Richmond, Virginia. In fact Queen Esther, her best friend, Doreatha Parker, and their husbands had been in that first group of church folk who stormed that stage to find out if their pastors' names were in the infamous blue book Saphronia James's grandmother, the late Mother Leticia Harold, had given to Bishop James. That book had had the names of all the preachers and pastors who had been over to that funeral home ho' house having the time of their lives.

Only one preacher from their district had been listed in the blue book. Queen Esther remembered raising up her hands and praising the Lord when her pastor's name was nowhere to be found. The preacher listed in the book had just recently been reassigned to a new district, was in the process of moving, and had been going back and forth between his old church and new district until the bishop in the First District had found a suitable replacement.

But once that book showed up the bishop had to hurry up and fix that problem. The man's congregation couldn't stand him anyway. Plus, they were anxious for him to leave because he was a big phony who couldn't preach and mismanaged church funds. But even worse than that was his breath. That man's breath smelled like hog maws, chitlins, and whiskey. It was terrible. Saphronia McComb James said that his breath would burn your eyebrows clean off of your face if he breathed up on you real close, as he had done to her when she busted up in that ho' house twenty-three years ago.

Queen Esther put heapings of thick, crispy, fried-to-perfection pieces of hickory-smoked bacon on two layers of paper towels. She'd had it sliced by a butcher at the farmer's market in Raleigh. She broke off a piece of the bacon and bit into it.

"Hmmmm."

She loved fresh-sliced bacon, especially when it was real thick.

"Here," her husband Joseph said, as he handed her a glass of her famous homemade fresh-squeezed orange juice. "You can wash it down with a glass of juice."

"Queen," Thayline said, as she walked into the kitchen. "You need for me to whip up another batch of pancakes? They are gobbling them down fast, and will be calling back here for some more in a few minutes."

Queen Esther nodded and then said, "Yes, go ahead and do that."

She took the platter out of Thayline's hands and said, "Girl, I don't know how I would have gotten this all done without your help."

"You are so welcome," Thayline told her. She was glad that Queen Esther had allowed her to help out in the kitchen. Thayline had figured, correctly, that Queen allowed very few people the privilege of working in this kitchen.

Queen Esther started buttering up pancakes while Joseph put the bacon on one of her fancy platters and took it into the dining room.

"Queen," Thayline said. "What do you know about that Rico Sneed boy?"

Queen Esther frowned. She knew a lot about Rico Sneed. In fact, she knew way more than she cared to know about Julia Sneed and all of her bad-tailed kids. Those Sneed children were never able to get along with anybody in their old neighborhood, Cashmere Estates. If one of them did something mean to another child, Julia would not correct them, even though she would have plenty to say about or to the child her children had taken issue with. It got to the point where folk wouldn't allow their children to play with the Sneed children. Nobody appreciated Julia's giving them a piece of her mind because they wouldn't let one of those little Sneeds push and shove, snatch things from, and talk ugly to the other children in the neighborhood.

"Queen," Thayline said, hoping she had not gone too far when she asked about that Rico Sneed boy.

Queen Esther turned to Thayline and said, "I'm sorry. Just that your question reminded me of so many unpleasant things about Rico Sneed's family. That's what I dislike about folk like Rico and his people—you can't think about or talk about them without dredging up something bad."

"Maybe it's because they are so good at creating a trail of bad memories," Thayline told her.

Queen Esther smiled. "You and I think alike. I was wondering what it was about you that I liked so much, Thayline. Folks carry on about your brother. And don't get me wrong, I understand why. He's a remarkable man. But you are special to me."

Thayline's heart was deeply touched. She had always understood why folks went on so about her baby brother. But it was awfully nice when somebody was able to see the gem she knew herself to be.

"So what about that Rico Sneed, Queen? He's not right on so many levels. But nobody seems to pay much attention to him and all the dirt I've seen him doing since Willis and I came to Durham for this conference. Does he have any kind of connections to a church? Because Rico and that young man he hangs out with…"

"You mean Kordell Bivens?"

"Yes, Kordell Bivens. Do they go to church?"

"I don't know about that Kordell," Queen Esther told her. "But I do know that all of the Sneeds are members of Roxboro Chapel Gospel United Church in Roxboro, North Carolina. It's actually a good church filled with good people."

"Really?" Thayline asked, kind of skeptical about a church with people like that in it.

"Yes, there are some good people at Roxboro Chapel. But just like with any other church, there are always some folks who wouldn't know Jesus if He tossed them off of the Jericho wall. I know that the Sneeds go to church on a regular basis. But they don't act like people who listen to and take to heart what their pastor preaches. And honestly, I've never met a Sneed who acted as if they were saved and had a personal relationship with Christ."

"Yeah," Thayline agreed, "there's nothing about Rico to let you know that he even knows where a church is located, let alone has any interest in Jesus."

"You right about that, Thayline. But my answer to your question about Rico is that he is selfish, mean, heartless, and will do anything for a buck."

"And I'm surprised that Bishop Giles would want to fool with Rico Sneed," Thayline said. "He looks like a young man who will pilfer funds when he knows he can get away with it. You'd think Larsen Giles would know that, since he is greedy and prone to doing stuff like that himself. You know what they say, 'Like knows like.'"

"I don't think Rico was brought in by Larsen Giles. Somebody from North Carolina would have had to do that. And it would have to be somebody up to absolutely no good to figure out that Rico Sneed was their man," Queen Esther told her.

"Somebody like Rev. Sonny Washington?" Thayline queried. "He's from this area, right? And he would definitely be capable of being in cahoots with a jive-time little poot-butt like Rico Sneed."

All Queen Esther did was nod. That was nothing but the truth.

"But still, why would the ministers get hooked up with Rico? Surely Sonny Washington would know this."

"Thayline, Rico is good at putting together programs on the computer. He designed a program to keep track of everything and everybody. They don't have to have a book that folks can get their hands on. They can keep it on a floppy disk. And if need be, he can destroy that program to keep it out of the hands of the law because he knows that he has another one just like it hidden off somewhere else."

"How do you know so much about computers?"

"My husband, Joseph, started out working in maintenance at IBM. He went back to school and was moved up. We have an IBM back in the guest room and I've learned a lot about computers just from tinkering with that thing. So Rico is very valuable to them. But they better watch him and that Kordell Bivens because they are bad news, and will tear up anything they get their hands on."

"Queen," Joseph called out from the dining room. "You and

Thayline need to come in here with the rest of us. We are ready to get this meeting started."

"Joseph," Thayline called back, now thoroughly at home with her new extended family, "tell my Willis to come on back and help us bring this food up front."

Willis Bradford came back to help his wife and Queen Esther Green. Like Thayline and Queen Esther, he and Joseph had hit it off. It was nice to meet some church folk who were not in the lime-light of church life. He'd learned so much from Joseph, who had taken a liking to Willis from the moment he laid eyes on him.

Too often Willis, a stalwart and dependable black man, was overlooked when folks got excited about Eddie, Theophilus, and of course the bishops, Murcheson James and Percy Jennings. Folks loved to shout preachers up and down, but they could forget just how important those solid, salt-of-the-earth church men were to the black church.

Men like Willis Bradford were on the Steward Board, drove the church vans, did repairs on the church, and served as the armor-bearers for the pastor. People often claimed that the black church was primarily supported and held up by black women. But the black congregations that thrived and grew had a healthy supply of Willis Bradfords in the mix.

NINETEEN

When Queen Esther walked into her dining room, all she heard was forks and plates clicking everywhere. All she saw were some very satisfied-looking black folks with puffed-out jaws and arms waving forks over those plates. She loved cooking big breakfasts for folk. And she was delighted that these folks were enjoying her good food.

Theophilus stuffed one more forkful of pancakes in his mouth. He knew better but they were so good. He'd already eaten six but these pancakes were so light and fluffy, he just had to have more. Essie was in Heaven. The girl loved herself some pancakes.

"Man, these pancakes are good!" Eddie exclaimed and slurped up some coffee.

"Naw...it's the juice," Susie James said. "Queen, girl, what did you put in this orange juice? I've never had juice this fresh and sweet."

"Yeah," Joseph said, "my baby can squeeze up some oranges."

"Miss Queen Esther makes the best fresh-squeezed orange juice in Durham," Denzelle said, and gulped down an eight-ounce glass in a matter of seconds.

"So," Percy Jennings said in between bites of his own delicious food, "just what are we dealing with and how is that going to affect the election? I never considered that Rucker, Ernest, Marcel, Sonny, Ottah, and Larsen would team up as partners."

"Yeah, man," Murcheson said, "that is not a good thing. Those jokers are dangerous by themselves. But together? And they've managed to get along and work together without tearing each other apart? That's scary. And it means that they believe they have something going on that can make a whole lot of money."

"And buy a whole lot of votes," Percy added.

A telephone buzzed in the square black briefcase sitting next to Denzelle's feet.

"Is that a phone ringing in your briefcase, son?" Joseph asked Denzelle.

He had been wondering what that boy was up to for months now. Denzelle, who was a bit secretive by nature, had been even more undercover than he normally was. At first Joseph had thought that the boy was running back and forth between two women. But he had been disappearing up to the D.C. area for weeks on end. Denzelle was too smooth a player to be running back and forth between Durham and D.C. over some tail. He didn't have to go through all that kind of trouble. Then Joseph worried that the boy had gotten into some funky stuff. But the drug dealers he knew didn't carry portable phones in a standard and nondescript black leather briefcase.

Most of the frontline dealers folks knew about on the streets wanted folks to think they were some high rollers, that business was so good they had more people than they could handle on the payroll, and had done away with all the competition. The dealers at the top, the ones who were running things, knew better than to be that flamboyant.

But those other ones? If they had a portable phone, they sure wouldn't hide it in a briefcase. In fact, they would go somewhere where everybody in sight could watch them call and talk to everybody they knew. And if the briefcase was black it would have so much gold and trimming on it you'd need a pair of designer shades just to look at it.

So, the only other thing the good reverend could be was a cop. But he wasn't one of Durham's finest. He had FBI written all over him. Joseph didn't know how he had missed it. But then again he did. He hadn't met an FBI agent who wore anything but a conservative dark suit, white shirt, and somber-colored tie. He had never understood how enforcing the law required you to look like the man who drove the funeral home car.

There was nothing conservative or somber about Rev. Denzelle Flowers. That was one sharp brother, who made good use of color in many of his tailored suits. Like this morning, for instance. Denzelle was the cleanest brother in the room. He was wearing buff-colored silk-linen slacks, a buff-and-peach-and-gray-striped linen shirt, and charcoal-colored closed-toe sandals. And he topped it all off with a buff-colored straw Kangol cap.

Rev. Eddie Tate was usually the sharpest brother in the room. But Eddie didn't have it like Denzelle Flowers this morning. And that was saying a lot because Eddie was awfully sharp in a white linen leisure suit with navy pinstripes running through the pants and matching shirt, along with those navy closed-toe gatored sandals.

Denzelle had been on the back porch for a good ten minutes talking on that phone. Not everybody owned a portable telephone because they were expensive. And you certainly didn't stand around talking on one as if you were on your house phone. It was very hard for the rest of them to stay away from that back door, and not try to find out who in the world that boy was talking to.

Queen Esther was determined to find a way to listen in on that conversation. She thought about going to the bathroom and opening the window. But she wouldn't be able to hear a thing when she flushed the toilet to make it appear as if she were in there for the right reason. Then she was going to get some more food from the kitchen but everybody was stuffed. She thought about making some more coffee but there was still a half pot of the coffee she'd just recently made. So she eased over to the back door but stopped when she heard Joseph coming into the kitchen, and then heard Denzelle walking back toward the door.

"Queen…" Joseph began, but stopped when he saw Denzelle's face.

"Son? You okay?"

"That was Duke Hospital giving me the report on Bishop Larsen Giles."

"Why would Duke call you about Bishop Giles, Denzelle? You a preacher, not a doctor. Plus, you a young preacher—don't even have your own church. So why you instead of somebody like Murcheson or Percy?"

"Because he's an FBI agent working undercover on something that I'm not so sure I want to know about," Queen Esther said solemnly.

She wanted her Bible and wished she had been more diligent in studying the Scriptures. This was a time when she needed a word from the Lord to just come to her without her having to search the Bible for it. Folks just didn't know how important that was. Queen Esther made a silent promise to herself right then to start learning the Word cover to cover, by memory. She didn't want to be in this position ever again.

"How'd you know, Miss Queen Esther?" Denzelle asked, just as the Lord planted the answer in his heart.

Lamont Green kept telling him that his aunt had a special connection with the Lord, and always joked that he knew she could call God up and tell Him what she wanted because his aunt Queen Esther was probably the only person in Durham with God's private phone number.

"Baby," she began, "that big portable telephone for one thing, that ugly black briefcase for another. You're not a drug dealer. I know you think that briefcase is ugly, and wouldn't have it if it had not been issued to you. So the only thing you could be is a cop. But you are way too smooth and fancy to work for the local police. So the only other thing I could come up with was the FBI—especially after you started running your grown self up to the D.C. area and it wasn't to chase some tail."

Denzelle blushed and then started laughing. Miss Queen Esther had hit that nail square on the head.

"Now see there, Queen, why you all up in this boy's business. He a man and can go wherever he wants to and when he wants to. And he young. If he wants to chase some tail, then leave him be."

"Joseph, this good reverend right here is a preacher and don't have no business chasing illegal tail."

"Illegal?" Denzelle asked, wondering what was so illegal about chasing something unless you were trying to sneak and steal it from someone else.

"Yep, il-lee-gul. You married, Rev. Flowers?"

"You know I'm not married, Miss Queen Esther. Don't even have a steady girlfriend right now."

"So you know better than to go around here fornicating like it's going out of style—especially seeing that you a preacher and all," she told him. "I mean, I just have not found any Scriptures in the Bible that let you off the hook on that one. And the Lord just doesn't seem to care that you a young man in your prime with a high-powered nature. He said no and He meant it. And if He said no, He had a very good reason that will be a blessing to us if we let it."

A blessing? Denzelle couldn't imagine how blessed he'd feel if he purposefully walked around without the ability to get some good loving when he needed it. He searched for words but couldn't find any. How could he find a loophole that would let him off the hook? Denzelle knew there really wasn't one—not if he adhered to the standards set by the Book his day job as a pastor was based on. But being the smooth player that he was, Rev. Denzelle Flowers sure was going to try.

"Miss Queen Esther, I'm a man, a young man, and while I ascribe to a life in the spirit, I'm walking around on this Earth as a flesh-and-blood man."

Weak, Joseph thought to himself. *Pitiful and weak.* He braced himself for what was going to come out of his wife's mouth. He hoped her newest favorite statement about the Word being a double-edged sword didn't slice up the young reverend too bad. He liked Denzelle and would hate to see the boy's budding ministry suddenly crippled by one of Queen's "Thus sayeth the Lords".

"*In the beginning was the Word, and the Word was with God, and the Word was made flesh*," Queen Esther stated. "I don't recollect from reading the four Gospels that Jesus was playing mind games with Himself over living a spiritual life while being on Earth in the flesh. And you know, I don't think Jesus was ugly, puny, nerdy, goofy, or in general undesirable or unattractive to those little hoochie mamas running around Nazareth, Gilead, Jerusalem, and the rest of the

Bible-days hood trying to be cute. I'd say it was just the opposite. But since Jesus knew and was the Word, He was cool with God telling Him no."

Denzelle couldn't say a word. Folks always acted as if Jesus were so ethereal, so otherworldly, so Heaven-bound that there was nothing physically appealing about Him. But that just wasn't the case as far as he could tell. The brother was described as growing to be tall, He was strong enough to run away the money changers in the temple and not get His butt kicked, His disciples respected Him and some of them were some serious gangster types, the women loved Him, and you don't read anything about a Roman soldier taking Him down before the appointed time of His crucifixion.

And when that time came, they sent a whole squadron of armed guards to get Him. But they never rolled up on Him man-to-man. Those soldiers always had some backup when they dealt with Jesus. No, Jesus was a man to be reckoned with, even though He was the son of God, the Word made flesh.

"I thought so," was all Queen Esther told him before saying, "You need to come and fill us in on whatever transpired during that fancy-phone phone call. I know it has something to do with this conference. Why else would your bosses up at the FBI headquarters be calling you and getting all up in your church business? When has the FBI ever been interested in what black folk were doing at church outside of the civil rights movement?"

TWENTY

Took y'all long enough to come back and join the rest of us," Susie James said as she loosened the hook on her pants to get more comfortable. Like everybody else, she had been greedy and eaten way too much of Queen Esther Green's delicious food.

A few more folks had come by—Saphronia James and her husband, Bishop James's nephew, Precious Powers and her husband Tyrone, along with Obadiah and Lena Quincey, who had just been rehired as an anesthesia nurse over at Duke Hospital. It had been hard on the two of them with Lena commuting back and forth from North Carolina. But that was about to end because Theophilus had worked it out for Obadiah to get a church assignment in Alamance County, North Carolina, which wasn't too far from Durham. He had tried his best to get him to Chapel Hill but that church assignment fell through at the last minute.

"I had to take that call," Denzelle said, locking eyes with his best friend, Obadiah.

"And I had to follow him to find out what kind of call he was taking on the 'Batphone,'" Queen Esther said amid hearty laughter.

"Has anybody called Mrs. Giles to come and get the body?" Lena asked. "The hospital has been trying to get in contact with her all morning."

Obadiah looked at his wife. Sometimes, she gave him the willies. Lena always knew stuff before everybody else. He had known that Bishop Giles's condition was enough of a concern for the feds to dispatch folk to Duke Hospital. But he had thought the bishop was going to pull through whatever had caused him to be rushed to emergency in the first place.

"What...what you looking at me like that for, Obie? I keep telling you that when you in prayer and praying in tongues, the Lord reveals things to you. Obviously He thought it necessary for me to find out about this. I'm a nurse practitioner and know a whole lot about the body, medical conditions, and disease. It makes sense that God would want me to know—don't you agree?"

"Just nod your head in agreement with baby girl," Theophilus, who had been very quiet this morning, told his young associate pastor. "You are not going to win this one."

"Naw...you just need to concede and then let us find out what all the Lord has told Miss Lena," Murcheson added, making note that all the seasoned men in the room were in total agreement with him.

It was only the young bloods who were dumb enough to try and trump their woman when it was clear the Lord had revealed some pertinent information to her. He used to try that with Susie and all he got was hurt feelings, a convicted heart, and a serious chastisement from Heaven. Murcheson would never forget the day he was out working on the fresh and tender shoots of collard greens growing in his huge garden, and decided to take a break and question the Lord about that very matter.

He just knew the Lord was going to give him some brilliant and snappy revelation about how to check Susie when she came out of this bag. Murcheson got a brilliant and snappy revelation all right. In fact, he was stung when God put these words on his heart.

"She's your helpmeet, son. I made her that way to help you. What she tells you comes straight from Me. So you better come out of 'your bag' and listen to what I place on her heart for your benefit. Then you sit back and watch how blessed, protected, and wise you'll be."

"Lena, do you know what time Larsen Giles died?" Denzelle asked her, glad that somebody had been at the right place at the right time to get information he would have had to flash his badge left and right to the nth degree to obtain.

"He died an hour after he reached the hospital."

"Is that what the call was about?" Joseph asked Denzelle.

"Yeah...my superiors don't believe what happened to Larsen was due to a massive stroke and heart attack that occurred without provocation. They suspect foul play."

"Which is why you've been doing double duty all week," Percy Jennings announced. "One day you are a preacher, next day you are the feds' man of the year. It's time you keyed us in on what is happening. Last thing I want, or this denomination needs, is a swarm of federal agents rolling up on this conference, aiming guns at a bunch of mad, scared, and armed black church people. You know those folks will shoot back if they believe they are being attacked without cause."

"The medical examiner doesn't believe it was simply a massive stroke, either," Lena interjected. "They've sent some blood and tissue samples over to the toxicology lab. The death was caused by something in his system to set it off. I sneaked and talked to the examiner, and he told me that Bishop Giles was so full of some kind of toxin it is a miracle that man's heart didn't explode wide open. And he said he'd never seen a body so stiff so early in death. Told me it was not your typical rigor mortis."

"Lena, how long before they get the reports back from toxicology?" Eddie asked. He had gotten an eyeful of Larsen in that chair and wanted to know exactly what was wrong with old boy. He knew about WP21, but couldn't believe that stuff was capable of causing a fatality. Bishop Giles looked like somebody who had been to the neighborhood hoodoo lady to get some kind of mixture to make him better in the bedroom, and got something her blind and crazy aunt had concocted by accident.

"Usually takes four or five days but they are going to rush it through and get it back in three."

"That's too late," Theophilus told them. "Election day for the Episcopal seats is day after tomorrow. We need to know what's up before then."

"Yeah, Theo's right," Eddie added. "Tomorrow morning we go to the last set of delegates to garner support."

"Which districts?" Murcheson asked.

Theophilus and Eddie sighed at the same time.

"Mozambique, Ghana, Swaziland, and Nigeria," Eddie said, and sighed again. Last place he wanted to be in the morning was with a bunch of delegates who sold votes the way Mickey D's sold burgers.

"Ghana is one of our strongholds," Percy said.

"So you say," came from Susie. She couldn't put her finger on it, but something was up with Bishop Abeeku. He had a decent enough reputation but hard as she tried, Susie James didn't like that man.

Murcheson rolled his eyes, conveniently forgetting the pearls of wisdom he had recently imparted to Obadiah Quincey. He said, "My baby doesn't like Bobo. She is concerned that he's on the silent auction block and playing everybody."

"Why?" Essie asked, very curious. She had always thought she was all alone concerning her feelings about Bishop Abeeku. Didn't know what it was about him. On the surface he didn't do anything remotely close to the craziness pulled off by Bishop Babatunde. Now that was a crazy negro—scary, too. Still, something was up with the bishop.

"He ain't right. He good at hiding it but that little African ain't right," Susie said and curled up her lips.

"He is definitely not my cup of tea," Saphronia added.

"What has he ever done to you, baby?" her husband asked.

"Touched my behind when he knew nobody was looking."

"Mine, too," Precious said, frowning. She hadn't told anybody 'cause they were always shouting that little booty-feeling man up and down, and she didn't want to be the killjoy in the group. But she couldn't stand Bobo Abeeku.

"You didn't tell me that," Tyrone said, as he stood up, ready to go back to the hotel and wear that little African out.

"Sit down, Tyrone," Precious said. "I handled it."

"Just what did you do, Precious, baby?" Tyrone inquired. He hoped she hadn't used that stun gun he had bought her down in north St. Louis from one of his boys from high school. That thing was not readily available at the local hardware store or a Sears appliance and tool section. He had had to go through a lot to get it.

"I used the pepper spray you gave me. Not the stunner."

"Whew," was all Tyrone could say. Last thing he needed was somebody like Denzelle Flowers all up in his business over that thing.

"Whew?" Precious said with some attitude. "I know you didn't *whew* me, when that nasty little man felt my butt. You better be happy he has a hand and some other apparatuses still intact."

"Yeah, you ought to be happy she didn't cut that sneaky thang," Queen Esther said. "I've been telling Joseph about that man in those little bitty African suits and shoes ever since we had to pick him up from the airport.

"Now, you and you, and-you-and-you-and-you-and-you," Queen Esther went on as she pointed at Denzelle, Obadiah, Eddie, Theophilus, Murcheson James, and Percy Jennings. "You preachers need to pay more attention to those ugly vibes folks try to hide from view. Bishop Abeeku is slick. On the surface he seems okay but he's not. And my question is why? Why is he playing both ends against the middle? That's a question y'all need answered before you high-tail it off to get Rev. Tate here elected as a bishop."

"Bishop Abeeku is not a crook," Saphronia told them. "He hasn't stolen any money and he has not been a part of this fiasco we need to get back to. But what he has done is be a nasty little twit who needs the slop slapped out of him. And the reason Bobo can't be trusted is that he'll do whatever he has to do to get reassigned to Ghana. So don't consider him as an ally. He has served his purpose well in giving you all a head start on what's going on. But that is far as he can go, and don't forget it."

Nobody said a word. Saphronia McComb James never ceased to surprise them. She looked as if butter wouldn't melt in her mouth, and yet she could drop a much-needed 411 in a heartbeat.

Denzelle's portable telephone started ringing. He switched it on and was about to go back on the porch, then decided against it when he noticed that just about everybody in the room was prepared to get up and follow him, and then try to sneak in on his conversation.

"I see," Denzelle said after listening for a good thirty seconds. "I'll have to get back to you later in the afternoon. Will you send some backup? And will they let me know who they are?"

He paused a moment before saying, "Yes, you will definitely need to register and pay. And no, please don't send any white folk or any stuck-up black people in some white-people clothes."

There was a long pause and they all heard Denzelle sigh loudly. He rolled his eyes and switched the large phone to his other ear.

"Well then, give them some money and let them buy some decent church suits. Yes, some color and some gators would be more than appropriate."

Denzelle hung up. He could practically feel the questions twirling around in their heads.

"Bishop Giles's lab work came back."

"That was awfully fast, even for a rush order," Lena said. She'd had no idea that Denzelle had it like that. She had known he was FBI but hadn't thought he had any clout—just a gun and a badge. But Lena had been way off. Denzelle was not just a run-of-the-mill FBI agent, any more than he was a run-of-the-mill preacher.

"Not if you get it to the right lab and talk to the right people," Denzelle told her.

"So, how did he die?" Joseph asked. He had been trying to find out what all of this craziness was about from the moment Rev. Ernest Brown had wheeled that fool into the banquet room looking all stiff and crazy.

"Allergic reaction to a drug."

"A real drug, the kind prescribed by a doctor, or a *drug* drug," Essie Simmons asked.

"*Drug* drug, Miss Essie."

"Then isn't that an overdose?"

Denzelle thought about it for a moment and then said, "Technically it's that. But he was allergic to the drug and it killed him."

"What drug? Cocaine, weed, heroin, PCP? What?" Thayline asked. All of this back-and-forth was getting on her nerves.

"None of the above. It's a new drug."

"A new drug? That crack stuff that has been tearing up homes and neighborhoods at apocalyptic speed?" Lena asked. Her friend Trina Fountain always said that there was a special place in Hell for whoever had come up with a drug as deadly and horrific as crack cocaine.

"Nope," Denzelle answered. "This stuff originated in Africa—Mozambique to be more specific. And even worse, it has made its way across the Atlantic Ocean with the blessing and endorsement of one of our own bishops in the Gospel United Church, Rucker Lee Hemphill.

"I know you ladies are very put out with Bishop Abeeku—and I understand because he knows better. But we wouldn't have ever gotten our hands on this information without him. In fact, he has been our biggest help in the motherland, putting himself and a few of his pastors at risk when they bumped heads with Bishop Babatunde at one of the African conferences."

"You do know that Ottah Babatunde is a sociopath, right?" Eddie Tate asked his young protégé.

Most folks were either scared of Ottah, couldn't stand him, or just wished he'd go somewhere and quit taking up good oxygen. But what they hadn't comprehended was that Ottah was the most amoral man Eddie had run across in a very long time. He was also mean and willing to do whatever it took to get what he wanted—which made him a very dangerous man.

Eddie didn't know how Ottah flew low enough under the radar to pass the requirements for becoming a Gospel United Church preacher. Sure there were some corrupt and crazy negroes on this side of the Atlantic. But Ottah was in a category like folks who ran the South American drug cartels—dangerous and lethal. Even the most corrupt preacher in the denomination couldn't go down that low.

"Yeah, I know that Bishop Babatunde is crazy," Denzelle said, shaking his head. "I don't understand why the denomination keeps him. It's not right."

"But you still haven't told us any new details about the drug, son," Theophilus said. "You gave us a pretty good workup months ago. But this thing is much worse than we anticipated. A bishop in the Gospel United Church is dead. This is worse than anything we've encountered at a Triennial General Conference—even worse than the ho' house in Richmond."

"WP21, the drug," Denzelle responded, almost as if to himself.

He was having a hard time digesting that some watermelon was causing all of this trouble and grief.

"What?" Willis asked him chewing on a big, thick piece of bacon.

"Watermelon Powder 21. That's the drug Bishop Hemphill discovered on this farm owned by this little old man named Uncle Lee Lee, who is reported to be close to hundred years old. Although he doesn't look a day over seventy to me."

"Watermelon Powder 21," Murcheson repeated, still just in disbelief over all of this, even though he'd known about this stuff for months. He said, "You know that name is the countriest black people mess I've ever heard of. Who . . ." He stopped talking and just shook his head in disgust.

If this hadn't been so serious and deadly to their church community, he would have been doubled over with laughter. *Watermelon Powder 21.* And Murcheson thought he'd seen it all back in 1963 when those fools came up with the ho' house they planned on franchising across the denomination's districts like the booty version of McDonald's.

"I think Marcel Brown and Sonny Washington gave it that name when they went over there and Bishop Hemphill gave them some," Denzelle said evenly. "Word out by one of my informants is that one of them said that stuff made them feel like they were twenty-one all over again."

"But that doesn't explain the watermelon part," Joseph said.

"The drug is made from a special blend of watermelon powder, made up through some kind of special process made up by Uncle Lee Lee. He runs this watermelon farm. And I have to tell you, there is every kind of watermelon growing there that you could think of. He even had these exotic black watermelons. I have never tasted watermelons like the ones grown on that farm.

"But that powder is something else," Denzelle went on to say. "First it smells terrible and it tastes worse than it smells, if that is possible."

"Wait a minute, son," Joseph asked, a bit worried about one of the denomination's most valuable pastors-in-training. "You actually took this drug?"

Denzelle blushed because he was a bit embarrassed by what he knew he needed to share with the group. And the mixed company didn't help. When Denzelle had confided in Obadiah what all WP21 could and did do, Obadiah fell out on the floor in hysterical laughter, heedless of his friend's mortification over the drug's initial effect.

"I tasted a small amount of it."

"Like they do on the cop shows when they find kilos of drugs," Queen Esther asked, all excited. This was like being on *Miami Vice*.

"Yes, ma'am. Only the drug was so strong, that little cop-taste had an effect on me."

"Yeeesssss, lawd," Obadiah said from across the room, struggling not to laugh.

"Uhhh, just what did this drug do?" Susie James asked, full of curiosity. She'd never seen Denzelle, who was always full of swagger and bravado, this nervous and uncomfortable.

"It does things to the male anatomy," Denzelle said in a quiet voice.

"Big things!!!! Boom!!!" Obadiah shouted out.

"Obie, stop," Lena admonished in between chuckles. She knew exactly what had happened to Denzelle. In fact, she had made it her mission in life to get the inside scoop on all of this when he came back from Africa all upset over this WP21 stuff.

"I can't imagine what a full dose would do to a man," Denzelle began, now speaking in the most "preacherly" voice he could muster up, causing Obadiah to laugh harder. "But that little bit I was exposed to gave me enough stamina and *mileage* to take it all the way to the bridge, and then some."

"Oh my," Saphronia said, winking at Precious, as if to say, "Girl, we need to get some of that while we are in Durham."

Precious started grinning. Saphronia had a point. She glanced over at Tyrone and blew him a kiss.

Essie and Johnnie, who had been very quiet because they didn't want to miss a thing, sneaked a look at their men, and thought about the benefits of WP21.

Denzelle had not missed any of those silent "*Guuurrrrllll*, did you hear that" messages transpiring between these first ladies, future bishops' wives, and first-lady-to-be. But as comical as it was, they needed to hear the real deal on this drug.

"I hate to break up this party," he began drily, now sounding like an FBI agent, "but you all need to understand that this stuff is deadly and highly addictive. We have just lost one person at this conference as a direct result of using this drug. And I can tell you that when you come down from that high, you are sick. It feels like the worst flu virus you've ever had. You have diarrhea, nausea, and your joints are stiff and swollen, and it's a miserable feeling.

"The only thing that stops those symptoms is another small dose of the drug. You have to keep it in your system. And if you use it too long and too much, then stop, you lose some important things—like stamina, the ability to perform, and for some unfortunate men, you are not enhanced, but *de-hanced* if you know what I mean."

"Oh…no, we don't want our men taking nothing like that," Johnnie exclaimed, and then looked at Eddie as if to say, "Take that mess and I'll kill you."

Denzelle smiled. He knew just what to say to a roomful of black church women on the subject of their men. He continued.

"I met Uncle Lee Lee and members of his family. They are not bad people. They are not drug dealers. They didn't even make up this stuff to be used as a drug. And they certainly didn't come up with it just to ship it off to America.

"From what I've gathered, they wanted to use it in exchange for control over getting some luxury items at bargain-basement prices. It's the smuggling business that had some connections here in the States that first got the Bureau's attention. Now it's become something much bigger and deadlier—especially to black men."

"Plus, this Uncle Lee Lee probably figured out real quick just how much Rucker was going to cheat him and his family," Percy said solemnly.

"True, Bishop," Denzelle told him. "And remember, only a small amount of the pure and original drug made it to the States. As far as I know, Rucker and his boys tried everything to get it over here in a large quantity but couldn't make that work. Between Uncle Lee Lee and his great-great-nephew Chief getting mad at Rucker and his folk, and then getting the drug out of Mozambique and past customs in the US, they were not able to do what they planned."

"So, what in the world are they selling at this conference, since we know that the original plans blew up in their faces?"

"Bishop Tate," Denzelle began and then said, "I mean Reverend..."

"Naw son, gone and prophesy me into the episcopacy," Eddie said with a big grin.

"Okay, Bishop," Denzelle told him. "Look, you know that we, meaning the feds, let them bring in enough of that stuff to have a small inventory they could work with. My superiors wanted to follow the trail to the real drug dealers, who they knew would home in on this operation as soon as it left the conference. Fortunately for us, they ran out of their product so early in the game, they had to go to the local drug cartel to meet supply-and-demand issues."

"But now," Eddie said, "the folks they hired to make the drug made up something that was far worse than anything that affected you when you took that little 'cop taste' of WP21."

Denzelle sighed. He wished he had not shared that information. They were never going to let him live it down. He tried to ignore Eddie Tate, which was kind of hard amid the snickers going around the room. He said, "According to the toxicology report, Bishop Giles was not an anomaly. Others can be affected by that drug in the exact same way. So, I'm forewarning you all to expect some more casualties before this conference is over."

"Casualties would be a blessing over another straight-up fatality," Queen Esther said. "The preachers in charge of this operation don't know enough about that drug. And sadly, we can expect at least one more fatality. I hate to talk like that but it's the truth."

"Yeah," Denzelle said. "I hope that it isn't Bishop Hemphill. He uses the drug on a constant basis. I was watching him sign his name at the registration table, and I noticed that his fingers were very stiff and swollen. I know from the small portion of the drug that one of my local informants was able to buy, that the first level of adverse side effects is stiff and swollen extremities that can get very painful if left untreated.

"Bishop Babatunde takes the drug, too. But he will only do it on occasion and not in large doses—at least let's hope the doses are small enough to stop him from getting hurt from WP21. Rev. Sonny Washington uses it even less than Babatunde. And Rev. Marcel Brown along with Bishop Caruthers, takes even less than Washington."

"But they don't mind giving what they wouldn't dare take themselves to others."

"No, not at all, Miss Queen Esther. But that's how it is with people like that—especially people dealing drugs. And we"—Denzelle looked around the room with those big round eyes that never missed anything—"we have to work together to stop it. If that poison is let loose in Durham, it is going to tear our community to shreds. And I'm not having that—not in the city I grew up in."

TWENTY-ONE

Denzelle's mobile phone rang twice before he reached it. He walked off to take the call. He was frowning when he came back to join the others. Just minutes ago he had been ready to hop on the Bull City mascot and ride that bull all the way to justice's being served. But this phone call turned everything they had just discussed completely upside down.

He opened up the briefcase to reveal a double-barreled, sawed-off shotgun, a thirty-eight, which he promptly strapped to his ankle, and a forty-five, which he anchored down in the back of his slacks.

"Man, you better not trip and fall with all of that artillery packed up on you," Thayline's husband Willis said.

"Dang, man," Obadiah exclaimed, eyes lighting up like a little kid's at the sight of all of that hardware, "I didn't know you rolled like that!"

Eddie closed his eyes and rubbed the bridge of his nose. His associate pastor was John Shaft.

Saphronia knew that Gospel United preachers didn't shortchange when it came to protection—even the super-saved ones like Bishop James. But Rev. Flowers had taken it to an entirely different level. All of sudden she had an irresistible urge to sing the theme song from the movie *Shaft*.

"Who is the man who would risk his life for another man?" Saphronia sang in her off-key monotone voice.

"Shaft!" Precious added.

"Can you dig it?" Essie, Johnnie, and Thayline chimed in.

Denzelle didn't want to laugh. This was serious and these black people were in this living room singing the theme from *Shaft*. He tried to get everybody back on track. They had some work to do to get prepared for tomorrow's meeting. A bust was going down sometime close to the election for the bishops, and they needed to know the details.

"Look," he began in his most intimidating FBI voice, but was interrupted by the loud and very insistent knocking at the door.

Joseph looked at his wife and asked, "You know who that is?"

Queen Esther shook her head.

"I mean you have the entire Gospel United Church sitting right here. I can't imagine who else you've invited to the house," he said.

"Joseph!" Queen Esther admonished. "You are going to make these people feel unwelcome."

Joseph's eyes got wide. He didn't want his guests to think he didn't want them at his house—to the contrary. He was very happy to have these folks here. These people didn't take any mess off anybody entertaining foolishness—particularly if the fools were claiming to be church folk. They were determined to put their foot on the Devil's neck, right before they busted a cap in the behind of his minions. They were his kind of people, and certainly welcome in his home. He said, "Y'all, I am glad you are here. Just wanted to make sure my baby, Queen, did not feel sorry for some of those other black people over at the Governor's Inn, and told them that it was okay to come by here for some home-cooked food."

"Come on, Joseph, I wouldn't do that," Queen Esther protested.

"Okay…"

The pounding cut him off.

"Okay…okay," Joseph yelled, and hurried to answer the door. He looked out the panel on the side of the front door. Why were the undertaker man from Memphis, that Hamilton brother, and Lucille Grey's boy Grady standing on his porch looking mad and crazy, and as if they wanted to shoot somebody?

Grady Grey hoped Mr. Green would hurry up and open this door. He could see him peeking through the window panels on the side of his front door. He and Dotsy Hamilton really needed an audience with Denzelle Flowers before something ugly jumped off over this WP21 in the Bull City. They were not happy over what was going on down in their carefully carved-out territory in Durham.

Grady and Dotsy had each, in his own right, worked to monopolize certain commercial-friendly sections of the Bottom, a section of Durham's old-school black community that wasn't too far from North Carolina Central University. Grady's business consisted of the acquisition and sale of stolen home merchandise—mostly office supplies, furniture, and equipment. Business was booming with the increase of the use of home-based computers. And folks buying Grady's computers also needed the accessories that made all of this work—like printers, computer printing paper, a mouse, and so forth.

Dotsy Hamilton had formed a gentlemen's agreement with Grady several years ago to stay away from this area of the illegal commerce in Durham. After several unsuccessful business ventures, Dotsy found his niche in the regulation and enforcement side of larceny and other criminal activities. The consortium of crooks and thieves who attempted to conduct business in as orderly a manner as possible in this type of industry, hired Dotsy Hamilton to deal with the people who worked for them. It was Dotsy's job to handle "employees" who talked too much and bragged about what was going on to people in the neighborhood, had part-time employment as informants for the police department, pilfered funds when collecting money, or were bullies to civilians or innocent law-abiding citizens.

There was a code of business ethics and procedures that needed to be followed at this level of corporate activity. And when some knuckleheads got to smelling themselves and violated rules, trouble followed. The police hated it when criminals caused problems for decent folk. And decent folk, who always outnumbered the criminal element in a neighborhood, hated it as well. All it took was for one person too many to come to a block party or neighborhood gathering with complaints about those trifling thugs tearing up the community, and it was on.

Those black people would set up all kinds of neighborhood snoop activities, and then would bug and pester the cops, be all on television, and worry the mayor until the crooks had to leave that area and go and try to set up shop somewhere else. Even worse, they would stop patronizing your business, and then go and put the word out that you were bad, so that no one else would want to be bothered with you, either.

These were the people Dotsy had to handle. Some he simply talked to. Others he roughed up a bit. A few he had to chase with his car, shooting at them out of the car window to emphasize a point. And then there was that very small group of insubordinate employees he had to drag to a private location for a special meeting with their superiors. The people who hired Dotsy really had some very serious issues with insubordination and violation of company policies.

Prior to that inferior quality of WP21 infiltrating the community, Grady and Dotsy had been having a good run with their respective businesses. They were making plenty of money. And they were not seen as a menace to the communities they served. Folks liked them, and wouldn't turn them in when the cops came around needing to make an arrest just so folks on the other side of town could feel "safe."

But all of that goodwill and good business had started coming to a screeching halt when some rotten preachers and those two white boys came up in their territory selling WP21. Two old men in the neighborhood had died after taking the drug for two days straight. One middle-aged man had been rushed to Duke Medical Center in the middle of the night when he couldn't straighten out his body. His mistress and wife fought and cussed each other out all the way to the hospital. They just about drove the poor ambulance people crazy.

And one younger man had arrived at Lincoln Community Health Center wrapped in a huge comforter, walking crazy, hoping that they had something to relieve him of his obvious distress. His anxiety level went up even higher when the attending physician came at him with a needle three inches long to do something about his "medical problem."

Grady was mad, and when he met up with his new friend, Cleotis Clayton, decided that they were going to the source of all of their problems—church folk. Joseph opened the door and waved his hands for them to come in. He had been surprised to see Grady and Dotsy at his home. But as soon as he laid eyes on Cleotis Clayton, he knew this had something to do with the very thing they were dealing with.

Seeing Cleotis Clayton and the other two men, one with the freshly done curl, and the other with a flat-top fade, walking into the Greens' living room was like watching manna come down from Heaven to Murcheson, Percy, Theophilus, and Eddie. Never in a million years would they have expected Cleotis to come to them. They were the ones who were responsible for his last trip to jail.

Cleotis walked over to Saphronia and gave her a warm hug.

"Mrs. James, it is always a pleasure to see you. I hope you are doing well."

"Thank you, Cleotis," Saphronia told him, smiling, causing several eyebrows to rise. No one would have expected her to know, let alone be on warm and fuzzy speaking terms with a man like Cleotis Clayton.

Precious gave Cleotis a hug, too. She knew why he was such a big fan of Saphronia James. Cleotis had been at that ho' house in Richmond when Saphronia busted in and then commenced to whipping Marcel Brown's behind. Saphronia had been Cleotis's ace ever since, and he would hurt anybody who dared to even look at her wrong.

"You all know each other?" Susie James asked.

"Long story, Mrs. James," was all Saphronia said.

Essie's eyes narrowed. She was going to get Saphronia off to the side and find out more about this.

"Grady Grey," Denzelle said, and shook the hand of a man he'd been friends with in high school before they decided to operate from opposite sides of the law.

"My man, Rev. Flowers," Grady told him with a big grin spreading across his face. "Long time no see, negro. What's it been?"

"Four years," Denzelle said.

Grady opened up his man-purse, or a cool bag that looked like a plain pocketbook that was popular among the brothers who considered themselves true players, pulled out some curl activator, and sprayed his hair. He put the activator away and then pulled the back of his hair, which was hanging over his royal blue Members Only jacket, away from the collar for a few seconds, so that it wouldn't get too wet and greasy.

"Look," Grady said. "I asked my man C here to come over here with us, so that I could school you church people on what was happening in my business zone."

"What business zone you talking 'bout, Grady Grey?" Lena asked him before Obadiah thought to stop her from saying anything, all the while wondering how Grady, Dotsy, and this other man had known they were at the Greens' house.

"The one I've had for the last three years," he answered, and then turned to Denzelle and said, "Look, player, C, Dotsy, and me here need some immunity if you want to know the deal. Okay?"

"All depends on what you have for me, man," Denzelle told him.

He'd had to fight his superiors for the right to grant immunity for a potential suspect in this case. It had been a knock-down, drag-out, get-down-and-dirty brawl to get those white boys to let a brother excuse another brother who was clearly doing wrong in the eyes of the law. And Denzelle was not about to let some foolishness cause him to lose what he had fought so hard to get.

"How about if he tells you how the drug has left the Triennial Conference and made its way to the streets of Durham, caused two deaths, and seriously injured a brother, and who is behind it?" Cleotis said. "And how about if he tells you who helped to get the counterfeit version of WP21 into the conference, and then who made it."

"Daggone, Grady. You know all of that?"

Grady nodded, then said, "Denzelle, when have you known me not to know what's up when somebody was trying to encroach on my territory?"

"Okay, man," Denzelle conceded. "I will make sure you have full immunity."

"Look, Denzelle man, there are those two white boys who have been making a bootleg version of WP21."

"Uhhh, excuse me, Pastor," Cleotis said to Denzelle. "But before we get started, I'm gonna need some immunity from you, too."

"So you want to cash in on that immunity as well, huh?"

Denzelle looked at Dotsy Hamilton shifting nervously from left foot to right foot and back. He said, "I guess you want immunity as well."

"Yes," Saphronia and Precious said in unison. They didn't even know why Denzelle Flowers had to ask that stupid question of any of these men. You could just look at Cleotis Clayton in that brick-red silk suit with the short double-breasted coat, black shirt and matching tie, and brick-red gators, and know that he was the kind of brother-man who would be in need of "some immunity." And this Dotsy Hamilton character, with that yellow three-piece suit with forest-green pinstripes, practically screamed, "IMMUNITY PLEASE!"

Denzelle raised up his hands to agree to the immunity promise.

"Bishop Hemphill and Bishop Giles," Cleotis began, "who I know keeled over day before yesterday, tried everything to get that stuff in from Africa. And I can tell you that the original drug is off the chain. Only problem is that it is addictive and will kill you if you don't have this other ingredient that you take when you taking it."

Denzelle closed his eyes and whispered, "Thank You, Jesus."

It was always a blessing to have what you knew in your heart confirmed. He needed to learn to hear God's voice better. The Lord had told him that the reason those folks in Mozambique were okay was that they had something to offset the pure effects of the drug. Denzelle was beginning to fear that he was being overly imaginative when he hadn't been able to get any real confirmation on this suspicion about WP21. He had been praying to know whether or not he was right about this. And God had just answered his prayer.

"How'd you know that, preacher?"

"I just knew," Denzelle told Cleotis. "I just knew there was more to how that old man, Uncle Lee Lee was taking that stuff than what I could see. He was healthy, I mean..."

"I know what you saying," Cleotis answered. "I took a few trips to Mozambique to help with getting WP21 into the States. And I took some...whew-eee-whew..."

Cleotis stopped and looked sheepish. He had to remember they were in mixed company.

"That's all right, son," Queen Esther said. "We are all in the know about the extra-special 'powers' of Watermelon Powder 21."

Now, Johnnie and Essie were cracking up and slapping palms, saying, "I heard that," like Saphronia and Precious had been doing. They stopped when Eddie and Theophilus glanced over at them and frowned.

Johnnie sucked on her sapphire-and-gold tooth. She said, "You ain't been elected bishop yet, Eddie *Lee* Tate."

Eddie cut his eyes at his wife, who licked that tooth and wrote an invisible score in the air. She knew how much he hated folks knowing his middle name.

"Well," Cleotis continued, hoping that all Rev. Tate did was cut his eyes. That was one big, mean, and yellow black man. And he for one did not want to even witness an altercation with him.

"After having my fun, that stuff wore off, and I was so sick and stiff…" Cleotis blushed when he saw the women laughing. "Y'all stop. It was my fingers, okay!"

"Sorry," was all Saphronia said before falling out with laughter again, then straightened up when her husband gave her a "Behave" look. He was very quiet and preferred to stay in the background, doing all of those quiet and necessary tasks that were essential to making things work for his church and in his home.

Eddie wouldn't have made it if this Rev. James had not been so efficient with getting equipment, making sure they had supplies and lunch, and helping with the van that took people to and from the mall. A lot of people outside of Atlanta didn't know Rev. James. But he was a powerful and invaluable man of God to those who did. He was also very handsome and sweet, and absolutely adored Dr. Saphronia Anne McComb James and their two proper daughters.

"As I was trying to say," Cleotis went on, "after the mess wore off, I was messed up bad. But I noticed that Uncle Lee Lee and his people were fine. I had spent the night on their farm, and that next morning—"

"They were drinking this tea with breakfast," Denzelle said.

"Yep. And they didn't offer me any, either—which I thought strange because they are very nice and generous people. But they didn't give me a whiff of that tea."

"So they are not just taking that stuff and getting hooked and strung out," Denzelle was saying. "They are just fine. But when they got it over here, it was a different story."

"Plus, I bet this Uncle Lee Lee didn't trust Rucker as far as he could straighten out his fingers after the drug wore off," Eddie said.

"And gave the bishop just enough to make some money," Theophilus added. "But that man was not about to let Rucker take him for a ride and then take all of his money. I bet that old man is making a killing in his own town selling WP21."

"He is," Murcheson said. "That old man is African—Old World African to the tenth power. He was not about to give up all of his trade secrets to a New World negro like Rucker Hemphill. And especially one who was greedy and didn't have sense enough to hide it. I bet that fool's eyes lit up like a Christmas tree the first time he even got wind of that drug."

"So who is making the counterfeit drug and how did it get past the Triennial Conference to become a bona fide street drug?" Denzelle interjected, now in need of the information that would justify his request to grant them all immunity.

"Those two white boys, Harold and Horace Dinkle, from western North Carolina are the suppliers," Cleotis told them. "They are brothers, and they are working hard to mass-produce the drug. That Rico Sneed and his friend, Kordell Bivens, got ahold of a small batch of that stuff. They are the ones who actually gave it to the Dinkle brothers, to find out if they could reproduce it for them.

"But they are stupid and gave the instructions to the Dinkle brothers without even making a copy for themselves. Those white boys figured out the good part of the drug and then altered it, so that it would get black folk all strung out quick. And then they refused to give Rico and Kordell the formula back. Told them to let some professionals take care of this."

"Well, they ain't the best pros in the game when it comes to this stuff," Denzelle said. "I know all about Harold and Horace, and all that they've been into over the past few years. They have been busy trying to make a name for themselves on the drug cartel scene in the southeast.

"They started out with high-quality moonshine and weed farms. But they have been getting stronger and stronger ties to some lower-level mob people, and that is what has us worried. We know that if they get mob backing, they will have that drug all over our state. And we know those two white boys messed up that formula on purpose."

Denzelle frowned and hit the table.

"What's wrong, son?" Joseph inquired, concerned. Denzelle had been cool and in control most of the morning—had hardly ruffled a feather until now.

"I cannot charge Rico and Kordell."

"Why not?" Joseph asked. "Didn't they go to the Dimwits and gave them the formula?"

"The Dinkles," Denzelle said with a chuckle. "Rico and Kordell had only a tiny batch made from natural and legal ingredients. They gave some of it to a few of their boys, took some themselves, and then gave the rest of the ingredients to Harold and Horace. They never sold or solicited for anything and, whether we like it or not, have successfully circumvented the law."

Denzelle just shook his head. He had never liked Rico Sneed and Kordell Bivens. They were always walking around perpetrating as if they were some upstanding brothers. But they were nothing more than jive-tailed punks. And they were always in the mix with some mess. Strife, divisiveness, deceit, and chaos followed those two brothers all over the place. Wherever those two went, and whomever they encountered, there would come a time when they would do something to make those people mad enough to never want to see them again. They were like some serial killers—no stopping sense.

Obadiah always said that you could tell a lot about a brother if you took the time to watch him play some street basketball with a bunch of the fellas. If a negro talked trash and was mean and aggressive on court, you could bet some money he'd do the same thing off court. Denzelle had watched Rico play ball at the Y. He talked trash, cussed folk out, and pushed and elbowed other players as if his life depended on it.

A telephone rang but this time it didn't belong to Denzelle. Grady Grey pulled a mobile out of his man-bag and walked away from everybody. After a few minutes he came back with a grave expression on his face.

"Another one of y'all's bishops just died in the same way that Larsen Giles did."

"Do you remember the name of the bishop?" Murcheson asked with a heavy sigh.

"Bishop Josiah Samuels," Grady told him.

Percy Jennings just shook his head. He should have known that Josiah, who was a big ho' and too old to still be ho'ing around, would want some of that WP21. It troubled his soul that two of his bishops had died under some very awful circumstances, and were involved with activities that put their eternal souls in jeopardy. Folks needed to quit playing around and toying with Hell like that. It was as if these people thought that they would die and then discover that somebody had conveniently slipped "Get Out of Hell Free" cards in their caskets. He hoped that both men had repented and rededicated their lives to Christ before they took their last breaths.

The room was silent. Nobody knew what to say. What had started out as just some generic "boiling negro mess," as Queen Esther would say, was turning into something that was far more sinister than some preachers running off and acting the fool at a conference.

Murcheson James stood up and said, "We need to pray."

TWENTY-TWO

"Y ou'd think with a campus of this size, I'd be able to find a decent parking space," Theophilus grumbled as he drove down the main entrance road and off the campus, searched for parking on a side road, turned back around, and went right back the way he'd just come, fussing and sputtering the entire time.

"There are some spaces over there in the grass," Essie told him for the third time since they had come on campus.

If he hadn't been driving, Theophilus would have closed his eyes and grumbled, "Lord, give me strength." He didn't want to park in the grass.

"Theophilus, bear right to that parking space right next to the athletic building," Essie told him, glad that this space had become available so that she didn't have to beat her husband. She knew he was nervous and worried. But as she had told him before they left the hotel, and would certainly be more than willing to tell him again, this wasn't even their battle, it was the Lord's.

God had revealed it quite clearly to Essie, when she was up this morning praying, that He was working behind the scenes to set everything right. And that all of this had to unfold for them to finally understand how dangerous it was to the spiritual life of the church that they continued to allow so many corrupt preachers to have influence and presence in the denomination. This was a time of cleansing and purging—that was why it was so hard and painful. Being purified by fire was never an easy or pleasurable process— wasn't supposed to be.

Theophilus eased into the parking space, put the car in park, and unhooked his seat belt. He was close to fifty, and still a fine, muscular hunk of chocolate. In fact, some folk thought that the good Reverend Simmons had gotten better-looking with that silver sprinkled around the edges of his hair and mustache.

"Baby, wait," Essie said, and then reached into her purse for her bottle of oil. "We are not going up in that place without being covered in Jesus' name."

She poured a drop on her fingertip and touched the crown of her husband's head before she touched her own head. She said, "Father, we are going to a pre-election service. But you know that we are really walking up into the thick of a spiritual battle that has been going on for too many years. Cover us with the blood of Jesus. Dispatch our angels to prepare the way for us. Anoint us with the Holy Ghost, and shine a lamplight on our feet, so that we will walk through this center by Your guidance, grace, favor, and mercy.

"We cancel out, in Jesus' name, all assignments of the enemy against us, against Eddie Tate, against the campaign team, and against our bid for an Episcopal seat. We bind up the Devil and all of his minions in Jesus' name. And we ask that You give my baby here the word from You that You want him to speak this morning. Bless Your holy name, precious Lord, in Jesus' name. Give us victory in Christ Jesus, amen."

"Amen," Theophilus said, and took his wife's face in his hands. He kissed her lips and then kissed her again—deeply. That kiss reminded him of the time he'd kissed Essie the night they had dinner at Mable's Kitchen after leaving the Annual Conference when he pastored Greater Hope Gospel United Church in Memphis.

"I love you so much, Essie," he whispered in between kisses.

"I love you, too, Theophilus."

"Yes you do, woman," he said with a mannish grin that made her blush. Theophilus had been making his wife blush throughout their entire marriage, and it never failed to make him hot when she did that.

"Hmmm, baby, you think I need to get me some WP21 and tell them they are going to have to take a rain check on my sermon?"

"You don't need no WP21, Theophilus Simmons," Essie responded, and then rubbed her hand on his leg.

"Nahhhh," he said, and tweaked her ear. "I don't need that stuff. What you got, girl, works better than any watermelon powder could ever hope to do."

"You are so mannish and nasty, boy."

"You like it."

"I sho do...lawd knows I do."

"Come on, you fast little country girl. Let's find out where everybody else is and get this show on the road."

"You think anybody is going to get arrested today?" Essie asked him, eyes lighting up like one of the kids'.

"Nope. I think they are going to let them think a bust is going down today, and tomorrow they are coming in and going for the jugular. Still too much info out, and I know that Denzelle wants to see all of the players before he plays his hand. That boy didn't train under Eddie for nothing."

They walked in through the back entrance and found everybody standing there, robes hanging over their arms, waiting on them.

"What took you so long?" Thayline asked.

"Parking," Theophilus told her. "I can't believe that a school this big would not have a parking plan for their guests. Everywhere I looked, there was a sign that I needed a special parking sticker. You'd think that as much as we are paying Eva T. to host this event, they would have mailed out parking stickers to conference guests."

"What school did you attend, son?" Murcheson James asked him. He was an alumnus of both Rust College in Mississippi and Eva T. He wondered why Theophilus was so upset with the run-of-the-mill black college politics.

"Blackwell College."

"And did they do anything special for their guests with cars, even after receiving a hefty check for hosting a much-anticipated event?"

Theophilus didn't say a word, just started putting on his robe.

"Point made," was all Murcheson said. "Look, we need to get in the lineup. There are 123 preachers in this line, and I am going to use my bishop's stripes to get us closer to the front. I am not about to stand in line behind a bunch of slow-walking black people who will stop and chitchat with their friends along the way just to make sure that folks see them in this processional."

Eddie, Theophilus, and Percy followed Murcheson to the section of the gymnasium where the preachers were assembled to march in. Obadiah and Denzelle followed the rest of the folk to the regular seats, with their robes still hanging on their arms.

"Put your robes on," Eddie told them. "If we have to walk in that line with all of those negroes, you are walking in that line with all of those negroes."

"Man!" Obadiah groaned and started putting on his robe.

Denzelle checked his guns on both holsters under his arm and then put his robe on.

"You packing a lot of heat for a church service, Pastor," Eddie said.

"If you know what I knew, you'd have this much heat, too, Rev. Tate."

Eddie unzipped his robe and revealed some heat strapped to his shoulder. He said, "I do know a bit of what you know, son, and came prepared."

"What about Jesus and a Bible?" Queen Esther told them. She didn't have any problems with folks being strapped. But this was a bit much.

"Got that, too, Miss Queen Esther," Denzelle said, and pulled his Bible out of that black briefcase.

"Come on," Percy told them, "we need to get going, so we can get this show on the road."

There were so many preachers who had jockeyed their way into that coveted Triennial Conference pre-election day processional line, Percy had decided that it would be best if the choir simply took its places before the service started. They hurried over to where the other preachers were standing and waiting for the senior bishop, Percy Jennings, to take his place so they could get started.

As Percy and his entourage made their way to the front of the line, neither Eddie nor Theophilus missed the daggers shooting out of some folk's eyes.

"Aren't we supposed to be in church?" Eddie whispered.

"I know. So much hate. Where is the love?" Theophilus answered, shaking his head in disgust. When had they come to a point where the pomp and circumstance of being a preacher in a conference lineup, and religious posturing, had become more important than the Kingdom of God?

"Check it out," Denzelle whispered to Obadiah, as his eyes wandered appreciatively over one of the few new women preachers in the line. "Who is *that* and can I go and shake her daddy's hand?"

Obadiah took a quick look at Rev. Nadine Quarles. She was fine—tall, coffee-with-cream brown, thick brown shoulder-length hair, big full lips, and, based on the contours of her clerical robe, a nice round backside. The only problem with the good Rev. Quarles was that nasty attitude. It was so obvious it practically jumped out at him. The girl was arrogant and stuck up. He tapped his mentor on the shoulder, now curious about this heifer.

"Theophilus, how did she fly low enough under the radar to qualify for that collar she's wearing?"

"Son, that girl didn't fly under anything, unless you consider doing the backstroke a new form of flying."

"Who with?" Denzelle asked, disappointed but wanting to know just the same.

"Ernest Brown—when she first applied to get in the program. She is from District Nine and went through Ernest to get into the training program."

"But I thought Bishop Jerome Falls was a decent guy. Why would he let anyone Ernest Brown recommended get admitted into the denomination's ministerial training program? And what was her reason for becoming a minister anyway?"

"She told Bishop Falls that she had been called after breaking off with her fiancé," Percy Jennings said.

"Uhhh, Bishop Jennings," Obadiah said, "do you really believe that is a reason to join the ministry?"

"Nope, and frankly neither did Jerome. But the Ninth District has been coming under more and more scrutiny to get women into the ranks. I believe Nadine is one of their first candidates, and she has let that go to her head. I don't care how many discrimination lawsuits were being filed against me, I would not have let that Jezebel join the ranks. That is trouble, nothing but trouble."

Denzelle had to agree. Since they had been standing in that line, Nadine had tucked four notes down in the sleeve of her robe. It saddened him to see that. There were some good sisters out there who would make excellent ministers and pastors. And this woman was making an already difficult process for women called into the ministry excruciating.

He looked around the huge gymnasium to see if he could spot some more women ministers. The ones he wished had been in this line were sitting in the audience with their friends, their families, their fiancés, their husbands and children, and members of the churches they were assigned to as associate or senior pastors. Good, saved, anointed, kind, sweet, pretty, dynamic, and Holy Ghost–filled women. He looked back at Nadine and then upward to whisper, "Help us, Father."

The musicians tuned up and started playing a smooth and bluesy version of "At the Cross." The rest of the ministers hurried and got into place and they began the processional. A great big woman, wearing a straight, black satin brocade dress with a huge flap collar trimmed in pink lace and a ruffled hem, stepped up to the microphone. She patted the top of her Jheri curl wig several times, hoping that would ease her itchy scalp. She stood through several runs of the song's introduction, waiting for the choir to open up in song.

"I bet that woman can really sing," Thayline leaned over and whispered to Willis.

"What makes you say that?" he asked, wondering how his wife could tell all of that just by looking at somebody.

"Well, she is the soloist at one of the main Triennial Conference sessions, she is big, she has on that outfit, and she has gigantic teeth with a huge gap."

"Baby, you are a big, tall woman and you can't sing a lick," Willis said.

"Well, what about the gap and the teeth and this session?"

"I'll concede to that until it's time for her to open her mouth," he said, still not convinced that woman could sing. Although that dress was making him wonder if she could hold a line of notes just a little bit. It was definitely a church soloist dress.

The choir started in on "At the cross, at the cross, where I first saw the light,/And the burdens of my heart rolled away,/It was there by faith, I received my sight,/And now I am happy all the day."

There were so many people in line the choir had to sing the verse three more times after already having sung it four times. The choir director decided it was taking these preachers too long to get in and sit down. At this rate it would take an hour for the processional alone. So the choir director signaled to the musicians to speed it up so they could get this part of the service done with.

The musicians kicked up the beat several notches, causing the preachers in the processional to walk faster and with some bounce in their steps. The music was sounding awfully good, and the folks in the audience started singing and rocking with the musicians. This went on for close to fifteen minutes, until the last preacher had taken a seat.

There was only one woman in that huge sea of preachers, and this after several heated sessions earlier in the week addressing the sexism that permeated the ministerial ranks. Denzelle thought it a crying shame that these men would not let more women march in this processional. And he thought it a travesty that the one female minister accorded this privilege was a fish-house woman like Rev. Nadine Quarles.

The soloist grabbed the microphone, took a deep breath, and started to sing. The choir was so good folks were up clapping, and a few came out in the aisle to do the holy dance. But that all came to a complete stop when the soloist sang louder and completely out of sync with the choir and musicians, just so she could profile and show off before the bishops and other prominent preachers in the audience.

A few folks frowned and hit at their ears, just certain that they hadn't heard what they had heard. The woman would have done well to blend in with the choir. Because even though she had the outward appearance of a good church singer—the black dress with that collar, the big teeth, the gap in her upper front teeth, the big singer's breasts that looked as if they could help propel sound from her mouth, and the hair—Miss Lady couldn't sing a lick.

She looked as if she would have one of those rich and heavy contralto voices, only to reveal a frail and weak voice that had poor tone quality and was terribly flat.

"Blessed assurance, Jesus is mine...oh what a foretaste of glory divine...heir of salvation," she sang out loudly, heedless of the frowns on the faces of the other choir members.

"Aren't they trying to sing 'At the Cross'?" Willis said to Thayline.

"I guess," Thayline whispered back.

"Then why is that thang singing 'Blessed Assurance' like she thinks she is on *Star Search*?" he said.

"More like a reunion for *The Gong Show*," Thayline whispered.

"Man, this is terrible," Eddie, who was sitting next to Theophilus on the raised podium, whispered. "Is she serious?"

"As a heart attack," Theophilus whispered back. "But the main question I have is how that thang got up there to sing with anybody's choir, let alone a solo in the first place. Surely, *somebody* knew *it* couldn't sing."

"She is Bishop Rucker Hemphill's wife's sister's oldest baby girl," Murcheson told them.

"And nobody told her no when she hopped up demanding to sing the lead at this conference?" Eddie asked. "'Cause I know that is just what she did because there is a presiding bishop in her family."

"What do you think?" Murcheson answered him, wondering why folks let being seen at a major church conference override their common sense. There was no way he would have let anybody he knew who sounded like that sing a solo in his backyard, let alone at the Triennial General Conference. Didn't they think that somebody would get to talking about the girl and her "musical abilities"?

Plus, Murcheson couldn't understand how Rucker Hemphill was able to talk those folks into letting that ugly woman with the horrible voice sing. And he didn't care if the knucklehead was a bishop. Everybody wasn't in awe or afraid of a bishop. Some folks would have told the bishop exactly where to put that request. This conference just kept getting worse. And he feared that this wasn't even the worst moment of the day.

The choir director, who was going to strangle that woman if she sang one more note, looked over at the musicians and signaled for them to bring the song to a close. The choir was so embarrassed. Their church, pastored by one of the few good pastors in the Ninth District, had the best mass choir in the entire district. The only reason that girl, who was out of the Tenth District, had been allowed to sing with them was that Bishop Hemphill had purchased the new robes they were wearing.

The choir sat down, mad that the hot and fired-up number they had practiced for weeks had been messed up. Their original soloist would have turned this gymnasium out and had folks running and shouting all over the place. The only thing that chick had done was make people feel like running out of the building screaming.

Rev. Nadine Quarles walked up to the podium to welcome everyone to this session of the Triennial Conference. She was actually foolish enough to believe that no one knew she was going with Rev. Ernest Brown, and had used that relationship to get into this spot of visibility. Nadine was ambitious, sneaky, unscrupulous, a ho', and not even remotely interested in getting saved. In fact, she had only read her Bible to pass her ministerial training classes and obtain her ministerial license.

It was a travesty that the one woman on the podium at the Triennial Conference wasn't about anything righteous. There were some dynamic and anointed women ministers sitting in the audience—women who loved the Lord and had been called to serve Him by ministering to the flocks of the Gospel United Church. It was discouraging to have to sit by and watch a collared floozy accorded the privileges and accolades that came with giving the welcome address to their denomination's most important gathering. But as one woman minister had told a few of her disgruntled sister-colleagues, they had not been called to serve these men. They had been given this calling to work for the Lord. She said, "Let that fish-house hussy have her moment. Because it is the only moment she'll ever have. Even an old player like Marcel Brown's daddy knows better than to let her do any more than she is doing right now."

Nadine raised her hands for the congregation to stand. She opened the Bible and turned to the Scripture she had picked out, even though Rev. Theophilus Simmons, the preacher for this session, had given her one that complimented what was in his sermon.

"Good morning, Christian friends," Nadine began, heedless of the expressions on the folk's faces. This was the second shock to their systems in less than twenty minutes' time. First there was the singer from Hell, and now this woman in a very expensive clerical robe was given charge to speak before them, and she was so tongue-tied she sounded as if her tongue were stuck to the roof of her mouth.

"Essie," Johnnie said, not caring who heard her, "how does that thang think she is going to deliver a sermon talking like this: 'Dood mownin' Chwistun fwends.'"

"What?" Saphronia asked, clearly annoyed at the woman's horrific speaking patterns. Saphronia was a clinical speech pathologist and had done some groundbreaking work at the Morehouse School of Medicine with stroke victims who had to learn to speak all over again. And if there was one thing Saphronia could not stand, it was a black person who couldn't talk right—especially one who had the nerve to get up in front of a bunch of folk and speak in a public forum.

Johnnie sighed. She really loved Saphronia and liked her a lot, too. But sometimes that girl could be a little bit stuck up.

"Girl, what that heifer is trying to say is 'Good morning, Christian friends.'"

Saphronia looked up and said, "Jesus, give me strength."

"Whet uz tuwn..."

"Did that girl just say, 'Let us turn'?" Theophilus leaned over and whispered to Eddie, who nodded and said, "Umm...hmmm."

Theophilus had had enough. Here he was, the guest speaker for the last session before the election of bishops, and he felt like preaching about as much as he wanted to go around this campus picking up trash with his bare hands. He got up and tapped Nadine on the shoulder. Enough was enough.

"Sit down, Rev. Quarles."

"But," she said, amazing him with her ability to speak clearly when talking one-on-one.

"But nothing," he said. "You have no business up here giving the welcome and…"

Theophilus just happened to see the Scripture reading on the large Bible on the podium. He'd given her 1 Corinthians 5:9–11, *"I have written you in my letter not to associate with sexually immoral people—not at all meaning the people of this world who are immoral, or the greedy and swindlers, or idolaters. In that case you would have to leave this world. But now I am writing you that you must not associate with anyone who calls himself a brother but is sexually immoral or greedy, an idolater or a slanderer, a drunkard or a swindler. With such a man do not even eat."*

Instead, this trollop was getting ready to read from Psalm 1. Not that he had any problems with the first chapter in the Book of Psalms. To the contrary—Theophilus loved that chapter. But it had nothing to do with what he wanted and needed to say this morning. This woman had no right to deny his or anyone's Scripture request prior to preaching a sermon, no matter how powerful the person she was sleeping with.

"You go and sit your non-talking self down there," Theophilus ordered, pointing to the first row of seats, where Ernest Brown was sitting next to his son, Marcel.

But he had underestimated Rev. Nadine Quarles. The girl hadn't gotten this far being scared of folks. She bristled up at Theophilus, whom she'd never liked, and said loud enough to be heard by everybody, "I am part of this distinguished platform." She hissed through that tied tongue. "And you have no right to make me sit down."

Theophilus Simmons was a good preacher. But he had a mean streak underneath that smooth exterior, and didn't take any mess off of these preachers—especially one he didn't think belonged in the ranks. As far as Theophilus was concerned, Nadine Quarles barely had a right to be in this building.

It wasn't because Quarles was a woman, or a new preacher. It was because she wasn't qualified and it showed. She wasn't well trained and it showed. She didn't have any respect for this church and it showed. She reveled in being on that podium more than she valued being able to talk right and it showed. And Nadine Quarles was a dumb broad who needed to go get a clue, and it showed.

"Sit your dumb, non-talking, no-preaching butt-up-on-your-shoulders behind down there before I initiate action to strip you of your license to preach and ordination papers," Theophilus ordered, and pointed to the floor again.

Nadine was so mad she was having trouble breathing. Nobody had ever spoken to her like that, even though she was long overdue for a dressing-down. Nadine Quarles was the kind of woman who got away with bad behavior, and had always been able to get away with bad behavior. She expected to get her way and had learned to make that expectation a tangible reality on many an occasion—that is, until now.

She sneered at Theophilus and walked off, not even realizing how bad she looked to the people sitting in the audience. Most of them did not appreciate the way Rev. Nadine Quarles had carried on with Rev. Simmons, who was a favorite of many of the people in the audience.

A man sitting in the middle of the gymnasium could not believe the nerve of this woman. And he couldn't believe that those preachers had had to wait until she messed up big-time to get her straight. He stood up and said, "Would you pa-leeze sit your non-talking self down," loud enough to be heard throughout the gymnasium.

Rev. Quarles almost forgot herself and gave that man the finger. She stormed off the stage en route to the first row to sit next to Ernest Brown, but had to go all the way back to row seven to find a seat.

Nadine was furious over how this had turned out. This morning she had been on cloud nine. And now she had been ordered back here like a lay delegate, and that was totally unacceptable. As soon as she finished pushing past folk to get to the only seat in the middle of the row she snatched a pen out of her bag, wrote Ernest a nasty note, and gave it to an usher to put in his hand.

The usher gave Rev. Ernest Brown the note. He read it, frowned, crumpled it up, and threw it on the floor under his chair. He waved the usher away and focused his attention back on the podium. As far as Ernest was concerned, Nadine had messed up. He really didn't understand why that girl didn't know she was dumb and out of her league.

It took a minute for Nadine to figure out that Ernest wasn't going to lift a finger to help her. She was pissed. Ernest Brown wasn't the easiest man to get along with. In fact, the two of them fought like cats and dogs. And just this morning Ernest had told her that their fighting was the perfect ingredient for "good and hot makeup sex." And that proved true only on the occasions when Ernest took some WP21 in a glass of Crown Royal.

In fact, if her memory served her right, the last time she and Ernest had had a fight, he had cussed her out while they were having dinner at the Darryl's Restaurant on the 15-501 Boulevard here in Durham. Nadine thought about that fight, a sly grin spreading across her face, as she remembered what she had told Ernest loud enough to be overheard by everybody seated nearby.

"Don't let that WP21 fool you into thinking you mack daddy, preacher. 'Cause I don't need you enough to put up with being disrespected like this."

Ernest had turned his mouth down. He'd said, "You are dismissed. And let's see if that attitude can give you what WP21 and I have been giving you all week."

At that point Nadine wiped away the tears that started streaming down her face. She had leaned down and got all the way up in Ernest's face and said, "Neither you nor your WP21 can compete with the five battery-operated trinkets I brought to this conference with me, just for moments such as these."

Theophilus turned back to the choir and said, "Choir, I have a sermon to preach. Now, that first song didn't work because that girl couldn't sing."

"Dang, Essie," Johnnie said, "your man is on a roll, girl."

Johnnie pointed toward the stage where the soloist was sitting.

"Look. Old girl is not happy."

"Johnnie," Essie replied, "she can't possibly be as unhappy as that thang sitting back there."

Essie turned around and pointed to the area where Nadine Quarles was sitting, rolling her eyes at the back of Ernest Brown's head. She was mad that Ernest didn't even think enough of her to get mad back.

"Come on, choir," Theophilus was saying, "help a preacher out."

The choir director was happy for another chance to showcase the talents of his choir and musicians. He hopped up out of his seat and raised his palms upward to signal to the choir to stand. The choir stood slowly as the musicians moved into place. The same soloist hopped up and was on her way to the microphone to destroy another good song.

Theophilus groaned and said, "Do you have another soloist, Mr. Choir Director?"

The choir director smiled and pointed at one of the altos to go to the microphone. As the lady made her way up front, Bishop Rucker Hemphill stood and faced the choir director, as if to remind him that they were wearing fancy red robes with gold trimming and tassels because of him. But the choir didn't give a hoot about Bishop Hemphill and those fancy robes. They were not about to torture these people with another bad song. The choir director unzipped his robe, dropped it on the floor, and kicked it out of his way. The choir followed suit and got out of those robes. The folks in the audience clapped and cheered, calling out, "Praise the Lord."

The musicians started playing "Come Thou Fount of Every Blessing," followed by the choir singing it in the style of a classical piece. They sang one entire verse in this musical vernacular, which showcased the orchestra accompanying the choir—piano, keyboards, upright bass, cello, French horn, trumpet, flute, alto and tenor saxophones, two violins, bass guitar, electric lead guitar, drums, and a harp thanks to the music department at the university.

After singing two verses in the classical style, the choir and orchestra got quiet for five seconds before the drummer and bassist began to play a funky rhythm that reminded a whole bunch of folk, including the platform guests, of Bootsy Collins, George Clinton, and Parliament and Funkadelic. The only thing missing was Bootsy stepping up to the mike with some enormous white star-shaped glasses, saying, "Ahh…baby…bubba…" in that smooth and curiously low falsetto voice of his.

The musicians played long enough for folks to stand up and start jamming with the music. Soon the choir started back singing the same song in this new P-Funk beat. The harmony was tight, the words were clear, and they were on fire for the Lord, which made it all that more delightful to listen to.

Soon the soloist came in with that rich contralto voice, ad-libbing around that beat and her fellow choir members. When the song got good to her, she did a smooth step to the front of the podium, waved for the choir to stop singing, and turned the gymnasium out with her version of the song. Then she signaled to the musicians to stop playing and did a few riffs a cappella.

When folks were all out in the aisle, singing with her and having a good time in the Lord, she nodded at the musicians to resume playing. Then the choir director, who was enjoying this performance himself, brought the choir back in, starting with the tenors and working his way up to the first sopranos.

But that wasn't enough. This time the choir director had the soloist stop singing, and once more silenced the musicians so the choir could showcase what it could do with the song. Then, when folks thought this song couldn't get any hotter, he stopped the choir from singing, brought the musicians back in, and brought the choir back in with each voice part singing as if they were singing a round.

Once the round of the song was on point, he brought the soloist back in and they sang this several times before being brought to an abrupt stop, causing the people in the audience to give them a standing ovation amid a flurry of "Amen"s, "Thank You, Jesuses," and "Praise the Lords." Now that was a song a preacher could preach to!

TWENTY-THREE

The audience was on its feet for a good five minutes, clapping, shouting, and praising the Lord. It didn't matter that a brief portion of the song matched the secular song "Make My Funk the P-Funk." The orchestra, the choir, and the soloist were all on fire with the Holy Ghost and delivered what God had given them to this conference gathering. Black gospel choirs were experts at taking secular, get-down, and even rump-shaking music and putting a new spin on it—one that qualified the music for church—and then charging up the service by touching the hearts and souls of the folk in all the right ways.

Theophilus walked over to the soloist and gave her a big hug. He said, "Now, that's what I'm talking about. Miss Lady, you keep on singing like that for the Lord."

"Amen"s, reverberated around the entire gymnasium.

"Mr. Choir Director."

"Yes sir, Bishop," the choir director said.

Theophilus laughed and said, "Now son, I have to thank you for the esteemed compliment. But one of our next bishops is my ace boon coon, Rev. Eddie Tate, sitting right here next to two of the best bishops in the Gospel United Church, Murcheson James and Percy Jennings."

A bunch of folks wearing TATE FOR BISHOP T-shirts in his rainbow colors jumped up yelling, "Tate, Tate, Tate, Tate!"

Eddie stood up and waved with that big grin of his spreading across his face. His enemies glared up at the stage and exchanged a few "over my dead body" looks, which were not missed by the folks in the Tate campaign camp.

Obadiah leaned over and whispered to Denzelle, "Looks like there gonna be a lot of dead folk at the conference come tomorrow afternoon."

Denzelle reached out and slapped Obadiah's palm and said, "I heard that, man."

"Can these negroes let us get to the election before they start buying up all the purple clerical robes in sight?" Sonny whispered to Marcel with a sneer covering his face. He was so sick of them. They had been a pain in the butt for most of Sonny's career as a preacher—always around getting on his nerves and making it hard for him to do anything in any way that he wanted to do it.

"...And you know something, choir," Theophilus was saying, "y'all looking pretty good in those jeans and Carolina Blue T-shirts. I like them better than those robes you just kicked to the curb."

"Ohhhh...no. My man didn't go *there*?" Obadiah said to Denzelle.

"I know. Rev pretty much said that he didn't like those fancy robes Bishop Hemphill spent all of that money on."

Both Obadiah and Denzelle made a point of looking down the row of platform guests to where Rucker Hemphill was sitting. They started laughing when they saw his face all twisted up in anger, and then stopped when Bishop Percy Jennings turned back toward them and whispered, "Y'all behave," right before a chuckle escaped his lips.

Murcheson closed his eyes to choke back his laugh. This was the wildest Triennial Conference he'd ever been to. And he hadn't thought that *anything* could have topped what had happened in Richmond back in 1963. But somehow, some way, these church folk had managed to do what he'd once believed was the impossible.

In 1963 the rogues in the denomination had started, in a funeral home, a brothel they planned on taking from conference to conference—almost like a franchise, or McDonald's. Thank the good Lord, this enterprise had fallen flat on its face. But now the very folk who had started all that mess back then were right back with some new and improved mayhem.

Drugs—and not just some high-quality weed pre-rolled to make it seem the dealers were really doing you a favor. Rather, these folks had decided that they needed to come up with something that would cause every self-appointed ladies' man attending the conference to make a beeline to their door. Just based on what Murcheson had learned, WP21 promised some often-desired results—enhancement of things that were better left the way God had made them, and a level of longevity that was never meant to be for a normal and reasonably minded man.

Bishop James recognized that the so-called masterminds behind this insanity had never planned on taking the drug past the boundaries of this denomination. Like the Richmond brothel, this was supposed to have been an in-house deal, designed to make a few corrupt preachers a whole lot of money at the expense of church folk gone astray. But drug dealing was not something that could be contained, especially when it was clear that the drug was capable of making tons of money. And it was these tons of money that had made those running this enterprise become so greedy they had placed themselves, their church, and their community in jeopardy.

The synthetic version of WP21 did everything the real drug promised to do. Only problem is that without the pure and natural ingredients, this drug promised to be more addictive and deadly than crack cocaine. And the scariest part was that it had been introduced into their community by the very men who had been called to bless and protect it. But what was absolutely terrifying was that now the new dealers didn't care if every single black man in this gymnasium was rolled out on a stretcher, stiff and on his way out of this earthly life due to a massive stroke and heart attack. All they wanted was their money, up front and in cash—lots and lots and lots of cash.

Murcheson had been so deep in thought over this troubling matter, he hadn't realized that they had rolled through most of the service, and Theophilus was standing at the podium ready to preach.

"Gospel United Church," Theophilus began, "I greet you in the matchless name of our Lord and Savior Jesus Christ. I come before you humbly and determined to bring you God's Word. Just like the Apostle Paul, I do not come before you with fancy words and fancy

ideas. Rather, I bring the sweet simplicity of the Gospel of Jesus
Christ. It is a message that doesn't need fancy fixings. It is just fine
on its own.

"And what I love about the Gospel is that it can look so foolish to
those who pride themselves on being the purveyors of intellectual-
ism that is devoid of the wisdom of the ages. Because the Lord saw
fit to make this life-giving message seem absolutely foolish to those
who believe that they know it all. But Church, if you set aside the
world's knowledge for just a minute, you will come to bask in this
'foolishness' and have the wisdom that is full of revelation knowledge from Heaven.

"This kind of knowledge will teach you what true joy is, and then
show you how to get it and keep it. You'll absorb the reality of 1 Corinthians 13 and come to understand that love is truly the greatest
and most powerful force in the universe. Folk think that if you love
your neighbor as yourself, if you forgive seventy times seven, and if
you commit to praying for those who despitefully use you, that you
are a punk—weak, a pushover, and of no use to anyone.

"Actually, Church, walking under the fruit of the spirit called
love makes you stronger than anything you can imagine. Jesus was
love, and He was full of power. In fact, He was so full of that power
that it says in John 18:4–6, *Jesus therefore, knowing all things that
would come upon Him, went forward and said to them, "Whom are you
seeking?" They answered Him, "Jesus of Nazareth." Jesus said to them, "I
am He." And Judas, who betrayed Him, also stood with them. Now when
He said to them, "I am He," they drew back and fell to the ground.'*

"Imagine that," Theophilus told them, a smile lighting up his
face. "Jesus was so bad, all He had to say was 'I am He,' and folks
had to draw back and fall to the ground. Good people of the Gospel
United Church, the Lord is calling us to love Him so much that we
just can't help ourselves and have to do His will, we have to study
His Word, we have to let go and let God have His way in our lives.
That is the only way that we as a church will make it.

"And before I finish, I have one more thing to share with you.
Church, be a righteous and holy people. Starting today, let go of
everything that tries to be a wedge between you and the Lord. Let's

go by the scripture in 1 Corinthians 5:9–11, and stop putting up with the kind of folk the Lord told us to stay away from."

Percy Jennings took note of who started to squirm when Theophilus said that. The list was way too long for his comfort—Rucker Hemphill, Ottah Babatunde, Marcel Brown, Sonny Washington, Nadine Quarles, Ernest Brown, and several more. He hoped that these people could find a way to take this message to heart.

"Today, decide to put an end to our tolerance of such people in the Gospel United Church. It's time for a change, and that change begins with you and with me. I can preach this message all day long. But you must decide that you've had enough, and that you want this great denomination to be what our founding father, Rev. Z. T. Meeting, prayed and worked so hard for it to be. We can do it, Church.

"Decide now to stop the evil spreading through our beloved church like cancer. And take it one step further by showing up tomorrow, determined to vote for preachers who you know will be the right kind of bishops. Find out who is who. Talk to folk. Be ready to commit to electing righteous men. Help us, Church, to turn this thing around, because enough is enough. God bless you, Church, in the name of Jesus."

Theophilus went and sat down next to Eddie Tate. He hadn't preached a sermon that odd and different since God had worked him over the very first time he delivered the Word at Essie's old church, Mount Nebo, in Charleston, Mississippi. He had wanted to cut up and preach the roof off of this building. But God had said no.

"Bro, that was one of your best sermons, and you never even raised your voice."

"I hope so, Eddie. It wasn't remotely close to what I had written down."

"Good," Eddie told him. "Lets me know that you listen when God calls. That is far more important than any fancy sermon you could give."

Theophilus nodded and then looked at Essie to gauge her reaction. She smiled and gave him a thumbs-up. He released a sigh of relief, looked up, and whispered, "Thank You, Lord."

"You've done your part, son," Murcheson told him. "Now it's up to these people to be obedient and do what the good Lord has called them to do for this church."

Percy Jennings had gotten up to open the doors of the church for conference attendees, and the ushers were lining up for the last collection of this service. Theophilus gulped down a cold glass of water, glad that this service was over but still concerned as to what would happen next. There was still that legal matter with WP21, and the election of bishops.

By the time he and Essie got back to the hotel, they learned that Bishop Willie Williams had been rushed to the hospital because he couldn't straighten out anything on his body. Thankfully, he hadn't had a stroke. But he would not be able to leave Duke University Medical Center for another week. When they got back to campus for the evening service there were undercover cops everywhere.

Theophilus had to hold back the tears when he saw all of those FBI agents. Here they were, preachers, the black church, the backbone of the black community, and one of the biggest drug busts in Durham, North Carolina, was about to go down right in the midst of one of the most respected and powerful black denominations in the country. Just thinking about the legal problems brewing on the horizon was enough to give *him* a stroke. For a moment he wondered if Eddie needed to drop out of the bishops' race but quickly dismissed that thought when he heard the Lord whispering *"Peace, be still"* to his heart.

TWENTY-FOUR

S ir," Denzelle said, barely able to contain his joy that his superior had been able to come down and work on this case with him after all.

"Yes, Agent Flowers?" Gregory Williams said. He had had to hide his laughter when Denzelle laid eyes on him at the airport, forgot himself, and exclaimed, "Thank You, Jesus."

"Do we have to go into the election day service with our guns out and making outright arrests? You know, most of the folks are law-abiding church people. And a good number of them are the saints."

"Saints, Flowers?" Agent Williams asked.

They were getting ready to make a drug bust that would make it possible for them to get their hands on information about the third-largest drug cartel in the US. And this boy was worried about a cohort of religious people called saints? Those "saints" should have been virtuous enough to stop this thing from getting so out of hand that two of their religious leaders had died, and a third was on the critical list at Duke Hospital.

Greg knew he was wrong. But couldn't stop laughing every time he thought about that old preacher lying up in that hospital bed with his toes and fingers curled up stiff, knees bent into hard angles, elbows locked, and that other part on *display*. It was the other part that put the icing on the cake. Greg, the head of this operation, had almost lost his professional demeanor and asked that old man to give him a description of the foxy thang who'd made him want to take that much WP21.

"Yeah sir, saints...holy rollers...sanctified people...you know," Denzelle was telling him, breaking through his reverie about that old man at Duke Hospital.

"Oh," Greg said. It had been a long time since he'd been in a black church. He wasn't a big churchgoer. But when he did attend services, it was at the prestigious and beautifully constructed Washington Cathedral, where the services were predictable. No one would ever have to worry about some church woman falling out on them, people blocking your view of the pulpit because they had on enormous hats, folks running around the church as if they were on fire, and shouting that lasted ten minutes past the sermonic hymn. Yes, that was his kind of church when he attended a service—neat, precise, orderly, timely, and rather white with regard to the demographic composition of the congregants.

It was the church of some American presidents. Kind of made Greg wonder what would happen if the country ever got big and bad enough to get a brother elected as president of the United States. One thing for sure, even though Mr. President would go there for official types of services, there was a good chance he would want to worship somewhere on the other side of town where he could raise his hands and say a few "Yes, Lord"s when the members of the Congress and the Senate were acting as if all of their mamas had dropped them on their heads.

"Uhh...sir...uhh...I don't mean any harm or disrespect," Denzelle began, "but do you go to church?"

"Yes, Flowers, I do attend church services."

"Then where is your church home?"

"Huh?"

"Your...church home? You know—the church where you hold your membership."

"Oh...yeah...that. I attend the Washington Cathedral," Greg told him, wondering why black folks from traditional Southern communities believed that having a "church home" was as important as having a Social Security number.

Denzelle just looked at his superior officer with his mouth hanging open before saying, "Sir, you go to that fancy church in D.C.

that they make the president go to for those special services they sometimes make us watch on TV?"

"They don't make the president go to the church," Greg told him.

"Yes, they do. Well, let me put it this way, if I were the president of the United States, they would have to make me go. 'Cause that is the only way I'd sit through that. I want some meat and potatoes when I go to church. I want to be set on fire with the Holy Ghost. I want to go where I can stand up and praise the Lord. Because my God is an awesome God and He is worthy of my praise!"

Greg didn't know what to say. His colleagues in D.C. had told him that Flowers was as much a preacher as he was an FBI agent, and could have a Jesus fit on you at a moment's notice. He finally said, "Flowers, do you honestly believe that your church is where it's happening where God is concerned?"

"Yes sir, when my church is doing what the Lord has called it to do, it is definitely where something wonderful is happening in the Kingdom of God. We love the Lord so much that we don't mind praising Him, singing with fire and the Holy Ghost, shouting, and getting slain in the spirit. And we love the Word, we love to pray, and we love to have the Word given to us in such a way that we leave so on fire for the Lord that we want somebody else to have what we have—salvation and the Holy Ghost.

"Plus, I don't want my God to be a God of my intellect, sir. I'm reborn of the Spirit. And I don't care if I look foolish, or country, or peculiar when I think of His goodness, of all He's done in my life, and how He has brought me through, and then get so happy I might be inclined to run all over the church.

"I am not trying to be rude or ugly to you and your church, sir, but the few times I saw one of those services, something was missing for me. I mean everything was done right, the choir could obviously read music very well, and it was clear that the man preaching had gone to one of those fancy, smart white-boy divinity schools and earned several degrees.

"I listened to that sermon and knew that man had done a lot of research on the scripture he used, read some of the text in Hebrew, and had done a bunch of extra reading on the subject that came from the scripture. But laaawwwdddd if that sermon wasn't as dry as those bones Ezekiel was talking 'bout in the Old Testament. Ooooohhhh… weee!!! I mean old boy was working it and he was so dull I was about to fall prostrate on the floor and holler out, 'Take me, Jesus! Just forget about the Rapture and come and take me NOW!!!'

"And get this, sir, I wasn't even there. So I know what it must have been like for the poor people in that congregation—especially the ones who were in the front row. You know they couldn't let on that the sermon was boring because that preacher and all of those highly musically trained choir members would have seen them doing it."

Agent Gregory Williams was hollering with laughter for the second time today. He was beginning to love being in Durham, North Carolina, which seemed to be light-years from the world he had moved in farther north in D.C. And his D.C. wasn't even the real D.C.—the Chocolate City D.C. Agent Williams's D.C. was the capital D.C. and the Georgetown D.C.

"So are you going to find a better way to go in and get the folks you're after, sir, without having to get people like my grandmother so mad, she and her girls take you down with prayer and speaking in tongues?"

Greg smiled as he put two high-powered rifles and three boxes of ammo on the card table. He had rented out this one-bedroom apartment not too far from one of the rougher projects. Folks had told him that it was rough over here and he had laughed. How rough could it be in a sleepy, midsize Southern city like Durham, North Carolina? But Greg had had to eat crow over that one.

Durham was a very pretty city with a host of amenities, as well as all kinds of quaint and charming places. The people were congenial. And for the most part it was a relatively safe city when compared to larger, more congested, and more urban types of places. But there were some hot spots in this bustling Southern town that were off the chain. And this particular area of the city was a hotbed of all kinds of activities that kept him gainfully employed.

"You crazy, man. You know that, right?" Greg said to Denzelle, who smiled and said, "Naw, what's crazy is moving into this place."

"Looks like something out of a movie, don't it, Flowers?" Agent Williams said.

"A horror movie," was all Denzelle said as he checked the scope on his gun. He was from Durham, an FBI agent, and he still didn't like coming to this spot. He said, "Sir, how are we going to do this?"

"Right down here, where we are."

Denzelle was confused. He wasn't quite sure what Agent Williams meant. Greg caught that and said, "Two of the Dinkles' flunkies are coming here."

"Boss, how did you manage that? Rico Sneed and Kordell Bivens are some punks. They are too scared to come here," Denzelle said.

"Yeah, that they are. But they are more scared of those Dinkles than they are of coming here. See, Rico, with his *dumb* self, skimmed $2,500 off the top of those white boys' money and got caught."

"Dang, boss. How dumb can a man get?"

"Pretty dumb, Denzelle. Honestly, I don't know how Rico went that far with those Dinkles. I don't think Kordell and Rico knew just who the Dinkles were. They actually believed that Harold and his brother Horace were some crazy, good-time, beer-guzzling mountain boys who liked making some extra tax-free money on the side. Never occurred to them that these two brothers were setting up an entire operation on this side of town, and had cut a deal to be the main suppliers with some people most folk don't even know exist."

"I see."

A fist pounded on the heavy door that had been built in an earlier time when folks actually cared about having a real front door.

"Do I need to go in the back?" Denzelle asked. "You know they think I'm just a preacher."

"Well, it's high time they found out otherwise. I need Rico and Kordell to get to the Dinkles. And they will be real upset when they see you. They'll be scared not to talk when they stare down the barrel of an FBI agent's gun, who is a preacher in the very denomination they have been trying to dupe with this WP21."

They pounded on the door again, only this time it was harder and louder. Denzelle opened the door with the gun in his hand, trying not to bust out laughing at a very stunned Rico Sneed. He moved aside, and Rico and Kordell brushed by him as if they were super-bad. But Denzelle knew they were scared when Rico's eyes started darting around, trying to look into the apartment to see who else was there, and Kordell kept licking his lips, trying not to look around as Rico was doing.

Denzelle waved them all the way into the apartment. When Rico figured out that that the Dinkles were not there, he figured it was safe enough to "get bad."

He puffed up some hot air in his cheeks, and growled out, "What you doing here, preacher?"

Hmm, Denzelle thought, *maybe the negro has at least one ball*. He said, "My man, Rico Sneed. I was just about to ask you the very same thing."

Kordell, on the other hand, wasn't trying to get bad with this preacher. He had not missed the two guns on each shoulder holster Denzelle was wearing. Kordell couldn't believe Denzelle Flowers moved in the world like this—Bible in one hand, piece in the other. He thought, *Bishop Hemphill sure did a piss-poor job giving us the skinny on the enemy camp. This preacher is walking around this room like he is John Shaft.*

He took a harder look at the good Rev. Flowers, and wanted to slap himself. That boy was a fed. Kordell had believed that their current circumstances couldn't get any worse. But right now, looking at this federal agent let him know that things could get much worse.

Rico was Kordell's boy, but he had messed up big-time. Rico could do some stupid stuff. But he'd never done anything that would put them in danger. He had made a horrible mistake when he messed with the Dinkle brothers. Kordell had never been all that gung ho about doing business with those white boys because they struck him as being kind of crazy. Plus, he was very uncomfortable with white boys who had top-of-the-line combat gear but had never served in the armed forces.

And if that was not bad enough, the reason they were in some deep funky stuff with the Dinkles was that Rico had gotten beside himself over a piece of tail. Kordell almost hurt Rico himself when he discovered that the fool had skimmed $2,500 off the top of the Dinkles' money so that he could impress a woman.

Rico had met the woman in Atlanta, gone bonkers over her, and then proceeded to run his credit cards past their limits trying to make this woman think he was a high roller. Then, if that was not bad enough, Rico was still pretending to be seriously involved with his Durham woman. He couldn't just up and quit that girl because he believed he had found something better. That girl worked at IBM, and had just put in an order for Rico to get his hands on a top-of-the-line computer system and printer at a bargain-basement price. Plus, she had gotten him a system on loan until the one he was buying was ready to be shipped to his house.

This was not the time for Rico to get so excited over that new tail that he made this girl mad enough to pull the plug on everything. The new woman, who mistakenly believed that her worth was much higher than it was, was getting impatient to be recognized as Rico's woman in public. She complained that her quality of life was being diminished because she couldn't tell the world that Rico Sneed was her man.

Kordell had just rolled his eyes in disgust when he heard that silly woman tell Rico, "I mean it's like this. My friends and family and coworkers are all watching me, and seeing me glow and smile and looking my absolute best. They want to know what is going on with me. It's a shame that I am this happy, looking this good, and I can't even tell anyone that it is all because of you, my king."

What had made Kordell almost hurl his dinner across the room was figuring out how deeply in debt "my king" was as he tried to make the new woman happy, because he had to wait until the new computer came before he broke up with the old woman. That $2,500 had been spent on plane tickets to Durham, hotel stays, candlelight dinners at expensive restaurants, and a shopping spree at Crabtree Valley Mall in Raleigh.

Not only was Rico in debt, they were in danger of being seriously injured or even killed by two very crazy and disgruntled white boys with mob connections they hadn't even known existed at that level with folks in North Carolina. And now they had just stepped up in a deeper mess, listening to Dotsy Hamilton and Grady Grey.

Those two slick players had tricked them into believing that by coming to this scary apartment they would find a safe and secure resource to help them get back that money. Instead they were standing face-to-face with some brothers who were now flashing FBI badges. If Kordell hadn't been so in love with things of the world, he might have asked that gun-toting preacher if he could tell him what he needed to do to get saved.

"Dotsy and Grady didn't say anything about meeting with a preacher and a cop," Rico said, his bottom lip jutting out and nostrils flaring as they did when he wasn't happy about the way things were going. He couldn't believe that they had been set up like this.

"Dotsy and Grady had better not have said anything, either," Denzelle told him.

"Who are you to give directions to Dotsy Hamilton and Grady Grey?" Rico snapped in that loud and nasty voice that always helped to put him on the outs with folks.

Denzelle laid his FBI badge on the table. He walked over to where Rico was standing and got up in his face. He said, "Who I am is no concern of yours. But looka here, playah. You really need to be worried about that $2,500 you owe those crazy white boys, who are on their way down here from the mountains to collect on your debt."

Rico heaved air out of his mouth as if he was getting angrier by the second. But Denzelle knew that was nothing but hot air needing a release. Rico could heave and ho all he wanted to but Denzelle knew that fool was terrified. He should have been scared, too. The Dinkles were dangerous men, and they had some very scary connections. The two things a black man did not need to do to Harold and Horace Dinkle was to take their money and then put them at risk for being investigated by the feds.

"That's why—" Rico started, then stopped when he saw Kordell shaking his head. It was true that they had come here thinking they were going to get in on some kind of deal to earn that $2,500 back with a few extra bucks on the side. But these two men were not the kind of contacts who were interested in providing that kind of opportunity.

"You need to be more like your friend here," Greg Williams said, after being content to remain silent and get a handle on these two jokers. He didn't know how they had been stupid enough to think that they could get in bed with the Dinkles and not get screwed.

"Who the hell are you?" Rico bellowed, ignoring the sharp poke Kordell had just given him.

"Your worst nightmare and best chance out of this mess," Greg answered him, as he laid $1,500 on the table between the four men.

Just a few hours ago he had met with Grady Grey and Dotsy Hamilton. They were crooks. They were not killers, they were not drug dealers, they didn't bother innocent and law-abiding citizens, and they were not enemies of the state. But those two brothers were definitely on the wrong side of the law, and didn't seem inclined to cross over to the right of crime anytime soon. Yet in spite of those obvious shortcomings, Greg Williams liked them. Now, he wouldn't hesitate to arrest Grady and Dotsy. But he still liked those two brothers.

That is more than he could ever say about Rico Sneed and Kordell Bivens. Greg Williams couldn't stand them. They managed to remain safely behind the line on the right side of the law, even though they were covetous, liars, greedy, and filled with lust. But even worse, they bothered innocent people because they were too scared, too dumb, and too jive to go after the kinds of folk that the Grady Greys and Dotsy Hamiltons dealt with on a regular basis.

"What's that for?" Kordell asked carefully. He was afraid of this brother, who looked as if he could blow you away with a gun in one hand while holding a big, fat turkey club sandwich in the other.

"You," Greg told him in a cold and hard voice. He was not playing with these jokers and wanted information that would help him nail this case. He was up for promotion, and this case was the one that would get him over the hump. Greg Williams was tired of answering to those white boys, and wanted to move up the ranks to reduce the number of white folk he had to do the FBI-agent shuffle for.

"We need $2,500," Rico interjected, trying to sound tough, even though he was worried, and with good reason. Harold Dinkle had told him that he would shoot his black ear off his head if he didn't bring him his money—and that was just for starters.

"What you need is some daggone sense," Denzelle said. He was tired of fooling around with Rico Sneed, Kordell Bivens, and the rest of those idiots who had caused this problem in the first place. If he'd had his druthers he'd have just beaten the information out of them and threatened to kill them if they were stupid enough to tell anybody. Not that he'd actually kill Kordell and Rico. But he sure would do enough to make them think he'd kill them.

"Forget you, man," Rico said. "I've had enough of you and will..."

Denzelle whipped his Magnum, and not his standard-issue weapon, out of the shoulder holster. He stuck the gun up Rico's nose.

"Will what, Rico? What you gone do? Huh...huh?" he snapped in a cold and deadly voice.

The barrel of that gun was cold. Rico took in shallow breaths through his mouth. He was scared to breathe through his nose— might inadvertently cause that gun to go off.

Denzelle started laughing, took the gun down, and checked to make sure the safety was still on. He said, "You are such a punk, Rico."

Rico was relieved to have that gun out of his nose. But he was pissed that Denzelle had played him like that and called him a punk. He stepped up on Denzelle and pushed him, heedless of Kordell's calling his name and telling him to stop.

Denzelle didn't move. He held his place and hoped that Rico would not push him again. But Rico was stupid and not one to stop when he was ahead. Denzelle remembered his mother once saying that Rico Sneed was like one of those serial killers you read about— wouldn't stop until somebody stopped him.

Rico pushed Denzelle again, harder, and then grabbed a pistol off the table and pointed it at Denzelle.

"Put the gun down, Rico," Greg Williams said calmly, without even making a move to his own gun. He knew that this Rico was posturing because Denzelle had called him a punk. But he didn't want this fool to start thinking he was in the Wild West and try to shoot somebody, and then get his ignorant self killed for real.

"Shut up," Rico ordered, "and give me the rest of my money."

Agent Gregory Williams got real quiet. He couldn't believe that this fool had tried to go gangster on them. Not only was Rico no longer getting the rest of his so-called money, now he wasn't going to get that $1,500. And he was going to tell them what they wanted to know, if he didn't want to have some sociopath named Goldie, Machete, or Sliver as his cell mate.

Denzelle didn't blink. He whispered a prayer and before anybody knew it was holding a gun with a silencer on it that seemed to come out of nowhere. Kordell was real scared because he knew that FBI agents were not supposed to carry guns with silencers. He had really underestimated the good Rev. Flowers. Who knew that Denzelle was a weapons freak, who got excited at just the thought of firing a gun? Rev. Flowers didn't need any WP21—a gun in his hand could do the job for him any day.

Rico, who couldn't shoot his way out of a wet paper bag, aimed the gun at Denzelle and then fell to the floor screaming, the leather on the middle of his left shoe hanging open and oozing blood.

"Help me, lawd. My toes are shot off."

Now he calls on the Lord, Greg Williams thought to himself, and then said, "Shut up, punk. Denzelle didn't shoot your toes off."

"Uhhh…yes he did," Kordell told him, getting sick to his stomach when he saw the second and third toes from Rico's left foot lying twelve inches away from his body in a pool of blood.

Greg looked at the toes and started laughing. "Daggone it, Flowers. I didn't know you could shoot like that." He gave Denzelle five and then inspected Rico's foot. "Man! That's a pretty shot. Looks like you took those toes off with a scalpel."

"Ahhhhhh!!!! My foot. Laaaawwwdddd, I'm dying…Jesus…"

"Shut up!" Denzelle snapped and tapped Rico on the head with his gun.

"You just tried to kill me."

"You pulled a gun on a federal agent in the middle of an investigation for drug dealing, and you are a suspect," Denzelle told him.

"Be thankful that I didn't pump your raggedy behind full of holes. 'Cause trust me—that really would have made my day."

Rico shut up and lay flat on the floor as if he was losing consciousness.

Greg nudged that shot-up foot with his shoe and laughed when Rico started screaming like a woman.

"I want you, and this fool standing here crying like he is some little girl, to tell me everything you know about the Dinkles."

Kordell wiped at his eyes with both hands, and tried to "man up." He was glad that he had kept it together enough not to mess in his pants.

"What about the money I owe them?" Rico sniffled. "They gone kill me."

"No they're not. You tell me what I want to know and you'll never have to worry about those jokers again," Greg said.

"What's the catch?"

Greg wasn't sure what the catch was at this point but Denzelle did.

"I want you to tithe all of what you and *How the Grinch Stole Christmas!* made from selling WP21, back to my Uncle Russell's church, Fayetteville Street Gospel United Church," Denzelle said. "And I want that money tomorrow in cash. Or this deal is off."

"But it is supposed to be only ten percent," Kordell said, pissed that Denzelle had called him the Grinch. He knew people whispered behind his back that he had a mouth like the Dr. Seuss Grinch.

"Ten percent is only the bare minimum cover charge. You can give all of that money back, or you can go talk to the Dinkle brothers on your own."

Greg was cracking up, watching Kordell mentally counting up all of that money he had to put back into his community.

"Okay," Kordell spat out. "But you know that's messed up, Denzelle, man."

"What's messed up is you being made into some fertilizer for one of Harold Dinkle's weed gardens. Now that's messed up. Look at it this way, bro-man. You and your friend Toe Jam here can really put Malachi 3:10–11 to work in your lives."

Kordell looked dumbfounded. It was clear that he didn't know what that scripture said.

"Let me help you out," Denzelle said. "This is the scripture read on every Sunday morning during offering, and it says, *'Bring all the tithes into the storehouse, that there may be food in My house, and try Me now in this,' says the Lord of hosts, 'If I will not open for you the windows of heaven and pour out for you such blessing that there will not be room enough to receive it. And I will rebuke the devourer for your sakes, so that he will not destroy the fruit of your ground...'"*

Gregory Williams studied Rico's two toes lying on the floor. They almost looked fake—like some rubber toes someone had made, and then thrown on the floor to get a rise out of somebody.

"Deal, Rico?" Denzelle asked him.

Rico reached out his hand and whispered, "Deal," before he fainted, and left it in Kordell's hands to tell Denzelle and Greg everything about the operation. Once they had the information they needed, Greg doctored up the scene of the crime to make it look as if Rico had accidentally shot his own self by the time the ambulance arrived.

TWENTY-FIVE

Twenty-three years ago they had all gathered outside the gymnasium at Virginia Union University to go in and set things right at the Triennial Conference. On that day in Richmond, Virginia, this group had not even been sure they would have a church once they left that building. Theophilus had had to face what he believed at the time to be the scariest moment in his career. He had been given the task of exposing corruption, at the risk of losing all that he had worked so hard to build as a minister. But Theophilus had not been consecrated to serve just the Gospel United Church—he had been called to serve the Lord and build His church. This denomination was merely the vehicle that God used to work through Theophilus on behalf of building the Kingdom of God on Earth. And God couldn't work with a mess.

More than two decades later, he and Eddie Tate had become bold for Christ in a way they could never have imagined back then. What a journey it had been, and what a joy to have traveled this road with the lamplight of the Lord at their feet. Theophilus always said that folks didn't know what they were missing, trying to live without Jesus as Lord of their lives.

He and Eddie looked at their two protégés, Obadiah Quincey and Denzelle Flowers. Those two reminded them so much of what they had been like back in the day when they were young and full of themselves. Good young preachers, with the promise of being top-notch pastors. Now he knew what it must have felt like to Murcheson and Percy to take Eddie and himself under their wings.

Eddie was hollering with laughter listening to Denzelle relay the events of the previous night. Several arrests had been made but they had spared the folk who had helped them get WP21 off of the street. Rico Sneed was mending nicely, even though the trauma team at Duke University Medical Center had not been able to reattach his toes. Rico would have to go through the rest of his life with three toes on one foot. He'd never be able to wear a slip-on gator or an open-toed sandal ever again. Eddie figured correctly that there would be some very bad blood between Denzelle and this Rico for many years to come. But that was all right—Denzelle was a big boy and could handle it.

"Show me the part when that joker got shot one more time, man," Eddie said, bringing a frown from his wife, who said, "Bishop, you ought to be ashamed of yourself," before breaking down in laughter herself.

"Okay, Rev. Tate," Denzelle said, more than happy to oblige his request. He snorted out his nostrils like Rico, and then pretended he had been shot and started hollering and calling out "Laaawwwwd-ddd," and then broke down in a fit of laughter.

"See, that is why Toe Jam doesn't like your behind," Obadiah said, and then started laughing. He knew that he shouldn't feel that way. But of all the stupid people in Durham who deserved this, it really was Rico Sneed.

Obadiah knew the Lord knew he felt that way. He glanced upward and said, "Sorry, Jesus, please forgive me that weakness."

"You okay, Obie?" Lena asked him.

"Yeah, sweetie. Just had to do a bit of repenting."

Lena kissed him on the cheek and patted his hand. Obadiah was a preacher and pastor down to the bone. It was her calling to keep him covered and protected with prayer.

Denzelle smiled at his two best friends, and then felt a twinge of sadness tugging at his heart. He wondered if he would ever find a treasure of the same quality as Lena, or Miss Johnnie and Miss Essie.

Essie hadn't missed the sadness that had swept across Denzelle's face. She came over to him and said, "All in God's perfect timing.

He needs you for a few things that you wouldn't be able to do with a wife or fiancée."

Tears welled up in Denzelle's eyes. He whispered, "Thank you," as he felt God's peace and joy pouring all over his heart. Most folk didn't know how much it could hurt when a man couldn't find his true wife. And this was just as true for a player like Denzelle. In fact, it was probably truer for him, since his being a skilled player made all of the good sisters (those with wife credentials) very cautious about getting involved with Denzelle.

"So, now that we old heads missed all of the best stuff," Rev. James said, obviously disappointed that he hadn't been at the shoot-out, "we need to know what we are doing when we roll up in there on those folks. There are still some very ugly loose ends that need to be dealt with. And while WP21 is now permanently off the street, it is still alive and well at this conference. From what Greg Williams has been telling me, there is enough of that stuff floating around the conference to put every man here in the hospital."

"We need to get on inside and to our seats," Percy told them, "because the voting will begin in forty-five minutes."

They all hurried in, found their section, and took their seats. This session was light-years ahead of the previous ones, when they had had a full church service, some campaign messages (mini-sermons from the candidates with lots of money to sling around), and an hour-long discussion about how to fill out a ballot that was designed to be read and understood by someone with a fifth-grade education.

This year they had gone a step beyond where they'd been for the last Triennial Conference, which had been held in St. Louis, Missouri. As the senior bishop, Percy had eliminated the processional and announcement of all bishops and their districts. He contended that everybody in the building had a program with all of that information at his or her fingertips. All campaign booths had to be taken down. And actual voting booths were set up around the entire gymnasium, much as they would have been for a presidential election.

Percy had hired an independent company outside of the denomination to operate the booths, check in and ID the delegates, monitor the ballots being placed in a lockbox, and tally up the results. Some folks complained about having a team of white boys in blue, gray, and brown suits, white shirts, striped ties, and those shoes with the one-inch soles keeping score on who would become the next bishops at a black church conference. But Percy ignored them because he knew those white boys were efficient, they prided themselves on their accuracy, and they couldn't care less who won this election as long as they got paid when they gave Percy Jennings the final results.

Percy, along with Murcheson, who had been elected to serve as the next senior bishop by the entire denomination, took his seat on the raised platform. They glanced around to make sure that all the voting booths were in place. When the head of the accounting firm sent a note that the accountants were ready, Percy walked up to the podium. He raised his hands and everybody stood up.

"Good morning, Christian friends. I greet you in the name of our Lord and Savior Jesus Christ. We have come here this morning to conclude our business at this Triennial Conference by electing new bishops…"

All of a sudden Marcel Brown busted through the back door, dressed as if he were getting ready to audition for Whodini's newest music video on Black Entertainment Television. He was wearing a chocolate suit with baggy pants with pleats in the front and a short double-breasted coat, along with a light pink shirt and matching tie. Just looking at him made Percy feel like going to get some turntables and a few 33½ albums to scratch while somebody spit out some church rhymes.

When Marcel knew that all eyes were on him, he smiled and then pimp-walked to the section where his father and their cronies were seated. Eddie Tate rolled his eyes and mumbled, "Jesus, Father, God…help us."

Theophilus wondered if that jacket was uncomfortable, because it was cut tight and high. Plus, Marcel knew he was way past the age of someone who should wear a suit like that. But he was in good shape, and actually wore the suit well. The women who loved preachers like Marcel got overly excited and immediately started plotting as to how they were going to get their room keys into Rev. Brown's hands.

Once more Percy Jennings tried to open this session so that they could vote in the new bishops, consecrate them that evening, and go home. Percy was sick of this conference and all that had been going on. He was about to pray when Greg Williams walked in wearing the sharpest so-called standard FBI suit Percy had ever laid eyes on. It was a lightweight navy cashmere-and-silk blend, cut as if it had been sewn on his body, dove-gray shirt, and dove-gray silk tie with navy and light blue dots on it. And even more impressive were Greg's shoes. Lace-up navy Stacy Adamses that were a far cry from those thick-soled white-boy shoes folks were used to seeing on an agent's feet.

Marcel, Sonny, and Rucker Hemphill looked very uncomfortable and not at all happy to see Gregory Williams, who had been trying to contact them unsuccessfully for the last two days. Marcel began to wish that he had not let Grady Grey sell him this suit for two hundred dollars. This suit had conveniently "fallen" off a truck carrying a shipload of expensive and very hip menswear coming out of New York. Two hundred dollars was a steal for a suit he knew would have easily sold for a grand at retail prices.

Greg petitioned Bishop Jennings as respectfully as possible. He hated to come up in here like this. He now understood that most of these folks were decent and genuine church folk. It was unfortunate that a few bad apples made the whole cart appear rotten. Greg just didn't feel comfortable flashing that badge in here, when he hadn't set foot in a black church event in years. Plus, his grandmother, who had been a devoted member of St. Peter Gospel United Church in his hometown of Oakland, California, had stayed on him to go to the church of his family until the day she died. Looking around, he saw a whole lot of women who reminded him of his Nanapooh.

This had been a difficult case because there had been so many twists and turns, and a huge hodgepodge of people involved with the enterprise. There had actually been two separate operations with one set of folk working with both. Rico Sneed, who was recovering nicely, and figuring out how to walk with two toes missing on his left foot, had been brought in on the ground level to design a computer program to log the sales, customers, and movement of the drug. He had then brought in his best friend just to help out and earn some money as if it were a part-time job at Wendy's.

When the church-based crooks realized that they were short of the amount of WP21 needed for their growing customer base, Rico took his silly self off and hooked up with the Dinkle brothers. The Dinkles, who had been in the drug business for seven years, couldn't believe their good fortune when former classmate Rico Sneed brought that stuff to them. They, along with the folks they were now being protected from, decided that Durham could use one more highly addictive substance—especially now that they had doctored it up and increased the addictive and lethal qualities of what had once been a very naturally manufactured substance.

That was enough on its own. It didn't even include the hardcore church element of dealers. Rucker Hemphill wasn't worth a pile of poop. And Ottah Babatunde was just plain mean and hateful. Greg was a top FBI agent, and even he was intimidated by this Bishop Babatunde. It had been a long time since he met a man as danger-ous, evil, and scary as Ottah was. The only decent criminal among them had been Cleotis Clayton, who had bailed out and left town as soon as he gave Denzelle the information needed to get them to this point on election day.

The main arrests had been made. But there was no way they were going to sit back and let Rucker Hemphill and Ottah Babatunde waltz out of Durham just like that. Two of the church's bishops were dead and one was in the hospital still trying to straighten himself out—literally.

Greg looked up at the podium, praying that the bishop would oblige his silent request and come to the edge of the platform. He had never been much of a praying man but the last thing he wanted to be forced to do was flash that badge and take over this meeting. Denzelle had filled him in on who was who, and Greg agreed with his subordinate agent's assertion that Rev. Eddie Tate needed to be elected bishop today as soon as possible. And here he was slowing everything down, fooling with those clowns sitting over to his left looking as if they should have been running the pimp palace.

Percy was as eager to get this show on the road as the next guy. But it couldn't be done until the business that had brought Agent Williams to his doorstep had been taken care of. Arrests being made at a Triennial Conference. As bad as the 1963 Triennial Conference brothel fiasco had been, it had never gone this far.

"Bishop," Greg said, "we need to do this now."

Percy nodded and waved for everybody to sit down. Most of the folks were confused. They had come to vote in new bishops, and now the bishop was slowing things down. It was so difficult to come to a Triennial Conference and elect the new bishops in a timely manner.

It had taken Rucker Hemphill a few minutes to place that brother. But as soon as he did, the bishop decided that it was time to take a bathroom break at the airport. He eased up and tried to make his way through those tight seats without bringing too much attention to himself.

Ottah Babatunde was African royalty. He didn't slink out for anybody—especially some American infidels whose ancestors had been too dumb to avoid getting caught by some white men. Just the thought made him want to spit and curse everybody in this room—not cuss out—curse.

The last time Theophilus and Eddie, along with their band of cohorts, had seen this kind of action at a church event, they had been right up in the thick of it. In fact, they had been solely responsible for getting information, finding the bad guys, and fighting it out until they won. This time they were all comfortably seated, kind of wishing for some popcorn, while they watched the show.

Denzelle Flowers was the only one in the group who couldn't remain seated while this played out. As soon as he saw Bishop Babatunde reach up under that fancy purple Nigerian robe, Denzelle reached inside his coat and hurried over to that side of the room. Several other FBI agents, sitting in the audience in church clothes, got up, too, when two of Babatunde's henchmen got up to help their bishop.

Johnnie wasn't so sure they needed to be sitting here. If these fools started shooting, there was nowhere to go. These chairs were way too small and shallow to offer any decent kind of protection. That Ottah Babatunde looked as if he would pump a few rounds into the crowd if he had to—and would enjoy doing it, too.

Denzelle was moving into place, and keeping an eye on Babatunde's right-hand man. Just when it looked as if things were going to get ugly, the door opened again, and there was Bishop Abeeku, dressed in a pale purple Ghanaian robe and matching hat, with an entourage of six people following him. *His* right-hand man was carrying a large satchel that was handcuffed to his left wrist. The man's right hand was resting securely inside his suit coat as they made their way to the platform where Percy Jennings was standing.

"Beeship...Beeeessshhippp," Abeeku hollered out. "I calm."

"Did that joker just say *calm* for *come*?" Johnnie leaned over and whispered to Essie, who started laughing and then stopped when she saw Theophilus frowning at her. He could be such a goody two-shoes sometimes.

"I am here to offer theeese great denomination a donation to help with our overseas meeshons."

"What?" Lena said to Obadiah. "Isn't he the head of the overseas missions programs?"

Obadiah nodded in amazement.

Abeeku pulled out a key and unlocked the handcuffs on the assistant's wrist and put the bag on the edge of the stage.

"I swear I think I've gotten lost in a rap video," Lena said.

"Now, Beeesshhiipp Jeeennnings," Bishop Abeeku was saying. "I am bringing theeese to you because I have problems with one of our candidates and I am going to ask all of the African delegates to refrain from voting for Rev. Eddie Tate out of Chicago, Illinois."

"NO!!!!" rang out around the gymnasium, as folks stood up and started getting ready to get rowdy. Who did those two overdressed negroes think they were, coming up in here starting some mess like this?

"Don't start nothing, Bishop, won't be nothing!" one of the younger preachers in Eddie's district hollered out, and stood up to take off his coat. Back in the day he used to fight everything in sight, and hadn't had an altercation in five years since getting saved and called into the ministry. To have a legitimate reason to jump up and fight was like being given some manna from Heaven.

"Yeah!" his best friend, former partner in crime, and current partner in the ministry said. "It's about to get ugly up in this place."

Bishop Abeeku was undaunted. He said, "Beeeshhhiipp, there is seventy-five thousand dollars of tax-free money in that bag. And I am giving it to theeese great church if you wheel only heed my advice and not vote for Eddie Tate."

At that point, those two young preachers from Chicago started walking toward the front but stopped and started back to their seats when one of them sniffed the air and whispered, "Cops."

Greg Williams believed that as much as he had tried to avoid doing this, it was high time he flashed that badge and got this meeting back under control. He said, "If I were you, Bishop, I'd put that money away."

Abeeku didn't say a word. He retrieved his bag, reattached it to his man's arm, and made an attempt to leave. He knew better than to push this envelope with the feds staring down his throat.

Greg, who loved to let folks get themselves all tangled up in their own webs of deceit, flashed his badge and nodded to some of the agents in the back.

"FBI, Bishop. I don't know what you all call it across the water but over here it's a bribe, it's against the law, and it is definitely not tax-free, if it becomes some preacher's 'church bonus.'"

Two agents came and escorted the bishop out, making sure to unhook all of that cash he had brought to work against Eddie Tate.

"Why did that negro offer to pray for our campaign committee when we first came to this conference like he was all in our corner, and then turn around and knife me in the back like that?" Eddie asked.

"Yeah," Theophilus answered. "And think about the trips Murcheson and Percy made over to Ghana, and all of that information he gave us to help us out, and he was a mole working against us all the time. If it wasn't so bad, I'd have to go and give that punk some skin for being so slick."

"I know, man," Eddie said. "Who in the world would have believed that Bobo Abeeku was a mole? Dang, that joker is good."

Bishop Babatunde figured correctly that if they snatched Bobo like that for some petty cash, they were really going to stick it to him. He eased over to a side door and tried to make an escape but was stopped by the agent on the other side of the door. The young man, who had just recently finished his training, gladly walked this big, mean man back through the gymnasium doors.

Greg had to issue the arrest but he didn't want to do it all cold and FBI-like in front of all of these church folk. He beckoned for the two bishops to come to the edge of the platform.

"Bishops, I have to make these arrests but I feel this uneasiness in my heart over doing it by the book. Do you have any suggestions that might work for this setting? Last thing I want to do is insult the folks who came here to elect new bishops to run this church."

Murcheson and Percy looked at each other and thought about what Greg Williams was saying. It seemed to them that a lot more was going on in this brother's heart than what he'd said. When Percy had met Greg, he'd gotten the impression that the man was long overdue for an overhaul in his soul. He almost started shouting and praising God right there. In the midst of all of this mayhem, something had gone right enough to convict this man's heart.

"Son, let me handle it," Murcheson told him. "You just wait right here and I'll give you the heads-up on what to do."

Greg nodded and then radioed his directives to all the agents except Denzelle Flowers. He didn't want Denzelle in the limelight with this bust. The fewer people figuring out how instrumental Agent/Reverend Flowers had been in all of this, the better.

Murcheson James stood before the congregation with joy flooding his heart. He should have been upset but he wasn't. Some men he had long hoped would be purged from the ranks of bishop were on their way out, the Lord had put a floodlight on Bishop Abeeku and exposed the darkness lurking in his heart, and a man who he suspected had many questions about Jesus was on his way to becoming saved and sanctified and filled with the Holy Ghost.

He whispered a prayer, asking the Lord for a Scripture to give to these folk. God blessed him with the words of Psalm 5:8–12 and Murcheson spoke these words to the people:

Lead me, O Lord, in Your righteousness because of my enemies;
Make Your way straight before my face. For there is no faithfulness
in their mouth;
Their inward part is destruction;
Their throat is an open tomb;
They flatter with their tongue. Pronounce them guilty, O God! Let
them fall by their own counsels;
Cast them out in the multitude of their transgressions, for they have
rebelled against You. But let all those rejoice who put their trust
in You;
Let them ever shout for joy, because You defend them;
Let those also who love Your name be joyful in You. For You, O
Lord, will bless the righteous;
With favor You will surround him as with a shield.

"How many of you good church folk love the Lord?" Murcheson asked.

Just about everybody in the room raised his or her hand. Percy took note that Ernest Brown, Marcel Brown, and Sonny Washington were just sitting there looking at them as if they were all crazy.

"How many of you are crazy about Jesus and sold out to Him?" Murcheson continued.

A good number of people jumped up and shouted out "Blessed be the name of the Lord!"

"How many of you want us to let the Lord lead us this day in what we do about our bishops and the election of new bishops?"

The people jumped up and waved their hands.

"Then bear with me as we set some things right. Now, I know that you all have some kind of knowledge about WP21."

Chuckles went all around the gymnasium, with a few of the men slapping palms and nodding their heads.

"Ummm...hmmm, thought so," Murcheson said with a smile

tugging at the corner of his mouth. "Now, tell me this," he went on, "how many of you got yourself a little taste of that stuff while at this conference?"

Nobody raised his hand, but there were some under-the-seat palm-slaps going on around the room—and a few of them were coming from some women who had learned about it during a very hot and frisky romp with their men.

"Well, let me ask you just one more question. How many of you know that this stuff is an illegal drug, that it is more addictive than crack cocaine, that two of our bishops have died during this conference, and that a third bishop is in intensive care at Duke University Medical Center right now?"

The gymnasium was still and silent.

"Church, right now the FBI is going to cuff the men behind this." Murcheson nodded to Greg to dispatch his agents to get the folks they had warrants for. Marcel Brown and Sonny Washington didn't even think enough of their cohorts to hide their joy when the agents cuffed Rucker Hemphill and Ray Caruthers, and left them seated. Ray tried to jump bad but backed down when the agent touched the handle of his gun. Rucker was now so sick he didn't seem to care about anything. Two agents had to practically carry him out of the building.

"I know this doesn't look right at a church gathering," Murcheson was saying. "But we can no longer continue to let evil breed and fester in the Gospel United Church. Neither can we sit by and let folks who are wicked and just plain wrong remain in positions of power and influence."

Ernest, who was in shock that he was being cuffed and taken away, snatched his arm away from the agent's grasp and turned back around to yell, "I'll see you in Hell for this, Murcheson."

"Ernest, I am saved, sanctified, and full of the Holy Ghost. And unlike you, I believe every word in the Bible. I fear the Lord, I seek Him with all of my heart, mind, and soul. And I do my best to obey the Lord. So you might see somebody you know in Hell but it sho' won't be me."

The agent started cracking up, and dragged Ernest out kicking and cussing as if he had never ever set foot in a church.

Murcheson and Percy both felt tremendous weights being lifted off of their shoulders because their beloved church was being delivered from a powerful and deadly stronghold. They hoped others felt the same way, too.

Eddie Tate, glad that for once those jokers had been checked, stood up and shouted out, "Praise the Lord!!!!! Let's get our praise on! God is good!"

All of a sudden the musicians, who had been in the audience waiting for the voting to begin, ran up to the instruments, warmed up a few seconds, and started playing the shouting song. The pianist's fingers practically flew across that piano as he belted out "Dum dum...dum-dum-dum-dum...dum-dum-dum-dum" in the middle of some dancing, shouting, and crying church people.

Those people danced, shouted, and raised up their hands and cried out shouts of thanksgiving. They had been so sick of the men who had been dragged out of the building, and were glad that their church leaders had finally gotten some sense and kicked them out of the building.

Some of the FBI agents regretted that they had to leave the building with these men. They would have much rather been in that gymnasium with those shouting, dancing, and praising church folk.

Greg Williams was still in the building. His heart was so full, the tears streamed down his face. He put the safety on his gun and put it back in the shoulder holster. He walked up to where Percy and Murcheson were standing and said, "Before I put the finishing touches on this job, I want to give my life over to Christ."

Percy smiled through the tears welling up in eyes. It had hurt him so badly to see all of this happening in his church. Murcheson always said, "You know the Devil loves to go to church. He'll go to the clubs and taverns when he's bored and doesn't have anything to do. But his favorite place to go is to church."

Now God was blessing them. In the midst of all of the craziness the Devil had tried to inflict on their church, the Lord had seen fit to help them win a soul to Christ. He said, "Rev. Flowers, come down here and walk this brother through his confession of faith and salvation. I think it will mean so much more to him if he takes this walk with you by his side."

Denzelle hurried down to the platform. He said, "In Romans 10:9–10 it says, *'That if you confess with your mouth, "Jesus is Lord," and believe in your heart that God raised him from the dead, you will be saved. For it is with your heart that you believe and are justified, and it is with your mouth that you confess and are saved.'*"

Greg said, "I confess with my mouth that Jesus is Lord, and I believe with all of my heart that God raised Him from the dead."

"You are saved," Denzelle told him then laid his hands on Gregory's head. He prayed.

"Father in Heaven, I thank You for blessing Gregory Williams with the ability to come to You and to seek salvation. I ask that You bless him in this new life with You. Because when we are saved we become brand-new creatures in Christ. Lord, bless this man, who is now Your child, with the Holy Ghost in Jesus' name, amen."

Greg shook Denzelle's hand and left to join his team of agents so that they could wrap this up and go back up to D.C. He pulled out his mobile telephone and dialed his mother's number.

"Mom, I'm saved."

Greg couldn't help but laugh when she dropped the telephone and started shouting, heedless of the fact that he was on the other end holding on to a telephone with very expensive rates.

TWENTY-SIX

Percy Jennings turned toward his new boss, Murcheson James, and said, "Now what do we do?"

At first Murcheson shrugged, and then got prayerful for a moment before answering. He said, "Let's turn this sucker out."

Percy reached out for some skin and they both walked up to the podium. Murcheson said, "Church, we have had a morning to remember."

"Amen"s circulated around the gymnasium.

"So let's go all the way and make this Triennial Conference the most memorable one of the twentieth century by changing up how we are going to vote for our new bishops. First, we now have more than two openings due to the turn of events and the untimely deaths of Bishops Giles and Samuels."

Bishop James stood still in the midst of the absolute silence that enveloped the room. Nobody knew how to respond to that because there were so many folks who seriously wondered if Bishop Larsen Giles and Bishop Josiah Samuels were saved and therefore able to "be called home." Home for these folks meant that you were at rest with the Lord. And as much as they wished they thought differently, they just didn't know if "home" was the bishops' final destination.

It was a terrifying and sobering thought. Here they were sitting up in one of the most important church gatherings that their church would have over the next three years, and they had to question if two of their top leaders had died and gone to Heaven, or suddenly kicked the bucket and found themselves busting Hell wide open. As much as the Bible clearly stated that this could happen to those who turned their back on the Lord, few Christians wanted to grapple with that reality.

Murcheson knew that everybody was thinking that because he was thinking the exact same thing. He was at a loss for words until he felt the Lord tugging at his heart to speak the truth.

"Saints, the truth is that based on the way these two bishops lived out the last years of their lives, we don't know if they were right with God and able to be confident that they would see the pearly gates open up to them, and then hear those incredibly beautiful words, 'Well done, thou good and faithful servant.'

"And you know something, if you are sitting out there right now, and worried what you'll hear when you die, you need to come on down to edge of this platform and give your lives over to Christ. If you've been saved and have reconnected to the world of sin, come down and rededicate your lives to Christ. And if there are some things pulling at you, trying to get you away from the Lord, come on down and repent and get right with Jesus.

"This is not the time to play games. We have two men who held the highest office possible in our great church, and not a one of us can claim that they went to Heaven upon their deaths. If there was anything to learn from that great tragedy, it is to get right ourselves and make sure we stay within the safety of His arms.

"So come on down and we'll take a few minutes for each of you to spend time with the Lord at what has now become the altar at His feet."

Just about everybody got as close to that platform as possible. Some people whispered their prayers. Some folks cried out to the Lord with hands raised high in the air. A few were off to the side, lying prostrate on the floor. All were in deep prayer and repenting of their sins and seeking to be on the right side of God.

Theophilus held Essie's hand, tears streaming down his cheeks, as he thanked God for loving him so much, He would make a way for him to come down and confess and repent of his sins. Essie was asking for the Lord to be her everything and thanking Him for this moment to become one with Him.

Eddie and Johnnie held on to each other tightly, telling the Lord and each other that they were sold out for Jesus and wanted everything about their lives to be for His glory. Eddie told God that he didn't care if he ever became a bishop. Because as long as the Lord let him serve Him, he'd be just fine.

Johnnie told the Lord, "Here I am, send me."

Denzelle, Obadiah, and Lena knelt together in a circle, holding hands and dedicating their lives to serving the Lord. They thanked God for all that He had done for them, and shouted their thanksgiving that He had touched their hearts with the revelation that they were truly saved. Denzelle asked for God's forgiveness of his sins of the flesh, and begged for His help and guidance in that area of his life.

There wasn't a dry eye in the place. And when the prayer was over, folks started shouting and praising God, without one note of music being played. Then somebody started singing, "My faith looks up to Thee / Thou Lamb of Calvary, Savior divine! / Now hear me while I pray / Take all my guilt away / O let me from this day be wholly Thine!"

The entire congregation sang that verse twice before people went back to their seats praising God, joy flooding their hearts. The Holy Ghost was up in the gymnasium so strong until people who wanted to hide from Jesus had to get up and get out of that room fast. Marcel, Sonny, and a few others tried to make a beeline for the men's room.

When those devils left the room, Murcheson decided that it was the perfect time to introduce the next level of information the Lord had placed on his heart. He said, "Church, we can vote for three new bishops today. And we also have extra seats available for the districts in Ghana, Mozambique, and Nigeria. I am recommending that you write in these names for those extra seats. Rev. Theophilus Simmons, Senior Pastor of Freedom Temple Gospel United Church in St. Louis, Missouri, for one of the stateside districts. Of course, there is Rev. Eddie Tate out in Chicago. And I will leave it up to you to decide on the third person.

"For the African districts, I am recommending, Rev. Cecil Witherspoon for Nigeria. Reverend Witherspoon's mother is a native Nigerian, his father is a well-respected African-American businessman in Nigeria, who runs several enterprises with Rev. Witherspoon's mother's brothers. He was born and raised in Nigeria, holds dual citizenship in the US and Nigeria, and will be a tremendous blessing to that district."

What Murcheson didn't add was that Cecil's father and uncles were tough and couldn't be bullied or frightened by Babatunde's henchmen. If Ottah was crazy enough to roll up on those black folk, he would get his butt kicked for sure. Plus, two of Cecil's uncles had high positions in the Nigerian government, and Ottah Babatunde couldn't pull that royalty mess on them.

"For Ghana, I recommend Rev. Walter Peoples, whose father Rev. Wilber Peoples served as a diplomat for the US government. Rev. Peoples was born and raised in Ghana, his wife is a native Ghanaian, and all of her people are members of the Gospel United Church.

"Lastly, I ask that you strongly consider the Rev. Dr. Hezekiah Ambrose, Senior Pastor of Southeast D.C. Gospel United Church, to serve in Mozambique. Rev. Ambrose built that church up from twenty-three members to a thriving church of 3,500 members. Plus, Rev. Ambrose's dissertation was titled 'Christian Faith and Healing in Traditional Agrarian Communities in Mozambique.' He spent many years there, has great connections, and is loved and respected by most of the pastors and ministers in Mozambique."

Percy was still smiling at the surprised looks on the faces of the ministers to whom Murcheson had just issued God's calling for them to become members of the episcopacy. Unbeknownst to most folk, being a bishop was a calling, just like being a minister or a pastor. Many good preachers were called but it was hard to get them past all of what he always called "Pharisee mess," or the politics of the position that had nothing to do with the calling or the Lord. They had lost a lot of good pastors truly called to serve in this capacity. But today the windows of Heaven had opened up to pour out a blessing on them with this election, and he hoped the people would follow the direction of the Lord.

The speed with which those delegates voted for their new bishops was unprecedented. Percy, who had done everything possible to lessen the time, was amazed himself. Now, three hours later, the accounting firm was standing on the platform with the final results. The white accountant put the envelope in Percy Jennings's hands.

Percy was so nervous. He prayed, and then proceeded to open the envelope. He read the names of the new bishops with tears streaming down his cheeks. He'd seen some wonderful things in this church. But it had been a long time since he had seen it like this. He said, "Would Bishops Tate, Simmons, Witherspoon, Ambrose, and Peoples please come up to the platform?"

Folks jumped up yelling and screaming and shouting out "Hallelujah" as loudly as they could. Eddie planted a big fat kiss on Johnnie's mouth. Theophilus picked up Essie and swung her around. He had not even thought about being a bishop before now. And here he was elected without one campaign speech—it was enough to make his cool self run all over this building.

Then came that moment when you felt the enemy was always there to try to steal the joy of the saints. But Percy was not going to let that happen because the Devil was a liar. And he knew that this last Episcopal seat had been purchased at a high price.

"Somebody go and get Bishop Washington and tell him to come forth."

The room was so quiet that Murcheson James felt kind of sorry for Sonny Washington as he walked up holding his wife Glodean Benson Washington's hand. About the only thing that folks liked about seeing Sonny Washington get elected was being able to watch his wife do her famous walk in that hot pink brocade pantsuit she was wearing.

"Where does that heifer find all of those pretty clothes in pink?" Saphronia whispered to Precious. The two of them had been sitting with the rest of their folk, feeling as if they had been on a roller-coaster ride. There had been more excitement in the room than when Saphronia had sneaked into that brothel her ex-fiancé, Marcel Brown, had helped to run in Richmond.

All Precious did was shrug. She said, "I wonder how much pink Pepto-Bismol Sonny Washington has taken over the course of the years because he is sick of all of that pink."

"That boy don't get sick of that pank," an old preacher who used to go with Glodean back in the day whispered to his friend. "That there gal can put some pank on me any day…laaawwwd ha' mercy." He started hyperventilating just thinking about that girl. What did those little stuck-up heifers know about "pank." They needed to go somewhere and just shut their mouths.

The new bishops stood on the platform in amazement. They had been going to Triennial Conferences most of their lives and had witnessed many runs for Episcopal seats. But they'd never seen or experienced anything like this. Even Sonny Washington, who knew he had not earned this position, was in awe of what had just happened. The thought that church folk would vote right when given the chance was overwhelming and kind of scary. It let Bishop Washington know that these people were not stupid, they were watching them and paying attention to what was going on, and when given the chance they would err on the side of righteousness. Sonny had big plans for what he wanted to do as a bishop. But he wasn't so sure that he would be able to do much, as long as the men standing on this stage with him were members of the episcopacy.

The other new bishops knew that God had put them in those positions. And they knew that even though Sonny Washington had bought his seat, God had still allowed for him to slip through the ranks. And since they all trusted the Lord, they knew everything would be all right. They shook hands, glad to come into the ranks of the episcopacy with some real men who truly loved the Lord standing by their sides. And it didn't hurt that these were some of the toughest and baddest brothers in the denomination. It felt good to win like this and in such a big way.

Murcheson was grinning from ear to ear. This new class of bishops had the kind of men who should have always been elected to the sacred episcopacy. He looked up and said, "Thank You, Lord," before telling the congregation, "Please stand for the new bishops of the Gospel United Church!"

Folks jumped up yelling and laughing. They could barely believe that right had won. What a wonderful God they served. And to think, they truly got beauty for their ashes and double for their trouble. What a blessed thing it was to see the Word of God in action. What a good God they served!

EPILOGUE

The new bishops, now affectionately called "the class of '86," draped their purple silk robes over their arms. They had been very solemn during the consecration ceremony. Now they could enjoy being bishops before the very hard work of running Episcopal districts hit them square in the face.

Theophilus grinned as if he were nine years old and had just won the title for a Little League baseball tournament.

"Negro, why are you grinning so?" Eddie asked him. "You didn't even want to run for this office."

"Me neither," Bishop Ambrose said. "The last thing on my mind was being a bishop. Because I knew that I would have hurt somebody if I had to run that race. Shoot, running for bishop in a black denomination is about as bad as running for president of the United States of America."

"I heard that," Bishop Witherspoon said in his rich and beautiful Nigerian accent. He was a good-looking man, made even better-looking by the light of the Lord glowing in his eyes.

Essie studied Bishop Witherspoon for a moment and thought that he was going to make a wonderful bishop for the Nigerian district. Those people had been under a cloud of bondage for so long, they were going to be simply awed at how God had answered the prayers she just knew they had been sending up to Heaven under Ottah Babatunde's regime. It was a shame that there were bishops who could get in a position of power that rivaled anything any despot could hold.

"Well, we are definitely bishops," Theophilus said, laughing. He put his arm around Essie and said, "What's my name, girl?"

"Bishop Simmons," she said in a sassy voice that held so many promises in it.

"Ohhhh...yeah...that's how you say, 'Bishop,'" Theophilus said.

"Well, you know," Essie told him, "anything for *my* bishop."

"Yesss...laawwwd," Theophilus said.

"Y'all need to stop that, Bishop," Obadiah told them, smiling all over himself. He could barely believe it. He and Lena were still rejoicing over what had happened in their church, and it made him determined to be the best pastor he could be.

"This is such a powerful testimony," Denzelle Flowers told them. "From now on, these preachers out here doing all of that dirt for personal gain will think twice about what they're doing."

"Naahhh...they won't do that."

"Why do you say that, Bishop Tate?" Denzelle asked his boss and mentor.

"Because folks like that are in so much bondage to sin, they lose all sight of right and wrong. The Devil is their pimp and they will do his bidding come hell or high water. The testimony is that the people of God can discern this and walk right over the Devil's head. That is the blessing."

"You ain't telling nothing but the truth, Bishop," Murcheson James told them, as Percy Jennings nodded his head in complete agreement.

"Well," Percy said, "what do we do now?"

"I think I'm up for a little celebration," Theophilus answered, as he grabbed Essie's hand and hurried off as if he had to put out a fire.

"He is so mannish," Susie James told them.

"And on point," Eddie said, winking at Johnnie.

"Okay...before y'all keep going off on this tangent," Murcheson said, "let's meet for dinner at the Angus Barn in, say, four or five hours. That should give some folks enough time to *celebrate* and then come and eat."

"Solid," Eddie said, and then added, "Do you think it feels this good to be president of the United States?"

"Ummm...hmmm," Johnnie said. "And I'll bet it'll feel even better if you a brother who is president of the United States."

"You think that will ever happen?" Obadiah asked in earnest.

"In our lifetime," Lena said, knowing deep in her heart that the Lord had just dropped a prophetic word on her.

"You think Prez will run off like Bishop Simmons to go to a special post-election 'celebration'?" Denzelle was saying, laughing.

"Fo sho'...cause he a bro..." Obadiah said amid laughter.

"What a day that will be," was all that Susie James could say.

"What a day this has been," Murcheson said.

"What a good God we serve," Percy added.

"Amen, amen, and amen," was all anybody could say to that gospel truth.

READING GROUP GUIDE

1.) God and Mammon. The Word clearly states that you can't serve both. But we know that there were some folk in *More Church Folk* who really tried to make that work. Who were they? How did they try to work this craziness? And how did righteousness prevail in spite of their efforts?

2.) What preachers were truly called to serve in the Gospel United Church? Who had been called and then lost their way? Who do you think were never called? And why do you think some folk enter the ministry knowing good and well that they have never been called? Is there a way to stop this from happening?

3.) Why was WP21, or Watermelon Powder 21, a problem and, even worse, a threat to the well-being of the Gospel United Church?

4.) At first glance, it appears as if the battle between the good and bad preachers is simply about power, dominance, and control. But if you scratch beneath the surface, there is a more ominous battle raging in the church. What is it? And how did they (meaning the good guys) fight it? Plus, do you think that they were successful when they waged war against the bad guys?

5.) Why did Theophilus Simmons, Eddie Tate, Murcheson James, and Percy Jennings need the help of Denzelle Flowers and Obadiah Quincey?

6.) Do you think they could have made things work without the two younger pastors?

7.)   Why did Marcel Brown, Sonny Washington, Larsen Giles, and Ernest Brown need Rico Sneed and Kordell Bivens?

8.)   In *Church Folk*, the women played a key role in the battle between the good and bad preachers. But it seemed as if more men were needed to fight the battle in *More Church Folk*. Why do you think that was so?

9.)   Why did Theophilus Simmons and Eddie Tate have to be forced out of their comfort zones?

10.) Who were your favorite characters?

11.) Who were your least favorite characters?

12.) When you think about these questions, what scriptures come to mind, and how do they apply to what the good preachers were faced with?

13.) What scriptures come to mind when you think about what the bad preachers were doing?